Finding Annie

life imperfect book one

Finding Annie

life imperfect book one

a novel by

katherine turner

First edition: April 2020

Editing by Madeline Jones
Editing and Proofreading by Olivia Castetter
Cover design by Murphy Rae
Cover photography by Jonatán Becerra, Carlos "Grury" Santos, and Johann Siemens

Library of Congress Control Number:2019920737
Library of Congress Cataloging-in-Publication Data available upon request.

ISBN 978-1-7344230-0-6 (ebook)
ISBN 978-1-7344230-1-3 (paperback)
ISBN 978-1-7344230-2-0 (hardcover)

Josha Publishing, Independent Publisher
www.joshapublishing.com
Haymarket, VA

Printed in the United States of America

for joe, who has seen all of me and loves me harder for it

i love you, always

preface

"Every secret of a writer's soul, every experience of his life, every quality of his mind is written large in his works."
-Virginia Woolf

Some of my earliest childhood memories involve being utterly lost in a book, sometimes until the sun rising the next morning startled me into realizing I'd never slept. The kind of lost that when someone called my name, it took a few moments to place the person and figure out where I was because it wasn't what I'd just been experiencing through the words typed onto the pages I held. The kind of lost that meant whatever I'd been reading about had the ability to impact me for hours after I'd set the book aside to continue my day. The kind of lost that meant I felt a real sense of grief after I'd read the last word; a grief that could linger for weeks.

I read just about anything I could get my hands on: encyclopedias, memoirs, travel journals, dictionaries, self-help tomes, historical accounts, pamphlets. But my real love was fiction.

Great fiction.

And I don't mean the classics when I say great fiction, though they undoubtedly are. I have always been most drawn to stories that have realistically flawed, gloriously imperfect characters. People who make serious mistakes and survive the most unlikely circumstances that have been pulled straight out of real life; the kind of real life most people are lucky enough to have never experienced. People who triumph over their greatest oppressors—including themselves.

Maybe *especially* themselves.

And while I enjoy any story that fits this bill, the genre I have the biggest weak spot for is romance.

I've thought a lot throughout writing this book about why I have such a deep love for a genre that is often not taken seriously. I felt that it was somehow a pronouncement on my worthiness as a writer. What I've come to realize is that my affinity for romance was born out of my childhood.

My formative years were spent in a series of abusive and neglectful environments. For years, I was passed back and forth between my biological parents like a toy they'd both lost interest in but weren't quite ready to toss out yet. I was sexually abused, and then silenced. I was physically assaulted and left alone to deal with it. I witnessed substance abuse daily and begged on the streets for money I'd have to hide from my alcoholic mother in order to feed my younger sister and myself. Love was sorely lacking during those years, scarce and sometimes conditional. But a young child *needs* love in order to develop, to grow, to become any sort of compassionate being.

Later, once I'd been lucky enough to be placed in a wonderful foster home, I had trouble accepting the love that was then freely given because, as any person from a childhood like mine will understand, I simply didn't know how. It was a painful and difficult dichotomy to both crave and refuse to accept love from others who had no agenda other than to care about me; one that also made me a challenging person to love.

It's no wonder, then, that I've always been drawn to tales of love. But not just romantic love; familial love, platonic love. A person needs it all, unconditionally, and books are where I found it, for many years. Even my own writing since I was young focused on love—having it, giving it, receiving it, losing it, pining for it.

For many years, I tried to shut off my writing side after a painful experience with sharing a story I'd written with a teacher that left me feeling less normal than ever and like I had no business aspiring to be a writer one day. I followed a different career path that would provide stability and financial security and keep me too busy to think about the what-ifs.

But, as I've learned since then, a true passion is impossible to ignore for long. With the overwhelming support of my family and friends, I picked up my pen again and stopped trying to quiet the voice inside. And what I'm doing today is really no different from that story I wrote and shared with my teacher when I was ten.

I'm writing the stories that I want to read, that I know others like me want to read, because we want to see ourselves in the books we pick up. I'm writing stories about people who struggle with the life-long impacts of physical and emotional abuse and sexual assault.

People who battle anxiety disorders and PTSD from childhood trauma.

People like me.

Instead of hiding them as if they don't exist, I'm exposing those raw and gritty and sometimes infuriating imperfections that are simultaneously what make us strong and beautiful. I'm shedding light on the sometimes nonsensical path we take when we are healing from wounds you cannot see, revealing the devastating soul-shattering that is sometimes required in order to fully put ourselves back together in this imperfect life in which we are all players. I'm demonstrating the incredible healing power of love by crafting stories that *other* people stay up way past their bedtimes to finish, as they discover the true strength of the human spirit.

I'm not telling a story of easy fixes or a story where the characters suddenly realize their mistake and then ride off into the sunset never to make another mistake again and live happily ever after. If that's what you're looking for, you've come to the wrong place. If instead you are looking for a tale of realistic life experiences, wanting to feel true despair and regret, cry and rail against the characters, and then discover hope alongside them, then welcome. This book is only the beginning of the tale for the characters, who will continue to err and learn from their mistakes over the course of the series, but if you're ready to start that journey with them, I invite you to turn the page.

They are waiting for you.

How to Love a Woman Who Has Been to Hell and Back

(excerpt)

"The woman who has been to hell and back is not easy to love.

The weak need not attempt, for it will take more strength than you even know you possess; more patience, more resilience, more tenacity, more resolve. It requires a relentless love, one that is determined and not easily defeated.

For the woman who has been to hell and back will push you away. She will test you in her desire to know what you are made of, whether you have what it takes to weather her storm. Because she is unpredictable, at times a hurricane, a force of nature that rides on the fury of her suffering, other times a gentle rain; calm, still, quiet.

She is a contradiction, a pendulum that will forever swing between fear of suffocation and fear of abandonment, and even she will not know how to find the balance between the two. Because today, although she will never tell you, she will feel insecure. She will want you to stay close, to tuck her hair behind her ear and kiss her on the forehead and hold her in the strength of your arms. But tomorrow she will crave her independence, her space, her solitude.

For while you have slept, she has been awake, unable to slow her thoughts, watching clocks and chasing time, trying to make the broken pieces fit, to make sense of it all, of where she fits, of how she fits. She fights her demons and slays her dragons, afraid if she goes to sleep they will gain the upper hand, afraid if she goes to sleep she will no longer be in control. Tomorrow she will be tired, and your presence will smother her, she will need only herself.

When she reaches out to you, love her.

When she pushes you away, ***love her harder***."

\- Kathy Parker

prologue

rob

My steps slowed as I walked into the classroom, already craving a cigarette and wondering if I should have just listened to Charlie and bailed. At least I actually liked books, as long as the teacher wasn't a dick. No way in hell I'd stay for any of the stupid classes, but if I went to at least one, my foster parents might get off my ass. Not that they really cared, it's just that they were pissed they'd have to go to court if I kept skipping and threatened to throw me out on the street. A few more years, then I'd be eighteen and out of there anyway.

There were a few more minutes before class started, so I surveyed the other students, looking for a new conquest and my eyes stopped on a girl in the front row, responding shyly to greetings from other students. Her mess of dark curls, her soft chestnut-colored eyes, and her curviness kept my attention. Everything about her was softer, more natural than the other girls in school. She didn't even dress like them; she wore a long-sleeved t-shirt, jeans, and tennis shoes. Perfectly ordinary clothing. Conservative, even. Definitely not my type.

But there was something about her.

I sauntered over to her desk to invite her to a party that night, knowing before I even took my first step in her direction that she would say yes, just like every other girl in school would. High school girls were all the same; they found rule-breakers irresistible and I was nothing if not a rule-breaker.

When I got to her desk, I intentionally stopped so my dick would be eye-level for her when she turned.

"Hey gorgeous."

I waited for a response, but she didn't even acknowledge that she heard me. While I waited, I looked her over more slowly, wondering briefly why the hell she was wearing long sleeves in late August. But it wasn't the strangest thing about her, and I immediately dismissed the thought, focusing instead on her ample rack as I waited.

But even that wasn't enough to keep me from getting pissed that she was snubbing me, so I bent over and slapped her desk at the same time I shouted into her ear.

"Hey!"

When her head jerked up and our eyes met for a fraction of an instant, all I saw was a fear akin to terror. I'd never unintentionally elicited that kind of a response in someone, let alone a girl I was trying to pick up, and it threw me off balance. I opened my mouth to say something that would teach her a lesson for ignoring me, but nothing came out, the words sticking in my throat. After a moment, I turned and left the classroom.

But after I left, I couldn't stop thinking about the way she'd looked at me. I'd never felt guilty for anything I'd done before, and I'd done some really screwed up things with Charlie, but I felt like an asshole for scaring that strange girl. And the more I thought about it, the more I wondered why she was so easy to scare anyway. Until out of nowhere, my curiosity morphed into a need that crushed my chest. So, after a sleepless night filled with haunting images of her eyes, I went back to class the next day. I even arrived early so I could grab a seat next to her, the first time in my life I'd willingly sat in the front row.

"Hey, I'm sorry about yesterday. I'm Rob."

She stared at her lap as she replied quietly. "I'm Annie."

"Perhaps it is our imperfections that make us so perfect for one another."

-Jane Austen, *Emma*

chapter one

annie

I sat in the driveway for a moment before exiting my car, trying unsuccessfully to will away the unease growing in the pit of my stomach. Not that there was a damn thing I could do about it; I'd already dropped Mom at the airport, and I couldn't let her down after everything she'd done for me. Like it or not, I was living in that house for the next year.

The house was originally a farmhouse, like most of the older homes in that part of the state, though the original clapboard had been replaced by white vinyl siding and the front porch shortened when part of it was enclosed to create a sunroom. Looking around, I could tell that Mom hadn't changed much of the landscaping since I'd moved out; everything looked pretty much the same. Just quite a bit wilder, apparent even in early March. The property was really too much for Mom to keep up with by herself, but she was as stubborn as they come about having someone help her; being a single mother had created an incurable independence streak in her.

Oh well. It would take some effort once everything started growing in, but I would get the landscaping cleaned up for her before she returned so she'd have one less thing to worry about.

Grabbing the two suitcases I'd brought with me, I headed inside with trepidation. A short thirty minutes later found me unpacked and standing in the middle of Mom's bedroom in confusion. I hadn't had an idle minute in the last twelve years and had no idea what the hell I was supposed to do with myself now.

What did I use to do when I had free time under this roof?

Intentionally skipping past the mythology section, I perused the bookshelves in the living room until I grabbed one of Mom's favorite vacation novels. I couldn't help smiling softly as I smoothed my thumb across the cover in reverance and inhaled the musty scent seeping from the aged and yellowing pages. It was one of a collection of vintage historical romances we'd picked up at a stuffy old bookstore in a charming hole-in-the-wall village somewhere in the English countryside the year I turned fifteen. Mom and I had devoured them all from cover to cover before we'd even come back to the US that summer.

Forty minutes. I'd been sitting there for forty minutes and hadn't finished a single damn page yet.

It took only a fraction of a second to register that my leg was bouncing violently, my heart was racing, and I felt like something was crushing my chest. Anxiety. I was familiar enough with it to recognize it creeping up on me, as it inevitably did at some point or another every time I came home.

Which was precisely why I rarely came home and never stayed long when I did. It was going to be a long year. I was already regretting letting Mom talk me into it, something that never would have happened if she hadn't caught me in a moment of weakness, calling just as I was leaving my doctor's office.

Ever since I'd left Stockwood the day after graduating from high school, I'd dedicated myself to getting a good education, to being successful at a career that was both lucrative and stable. There wasn't a time in my life that I didn't dream of being everything my biological parents hadn't been. Failure just wasn't an option. Naturally, dedication of that caliber had come at the price of having no time for hobbies and very little for friendships. That insatiable drive to fill every waking hour led me to my chosen career as a financial statement auditor. Turnover in the industry was extremely high since that type of lifestyle didn't suit most people for long; they wanted to have a life. But I needed the security of having my job, my house, of knowing that I was competent and far from my past, so the lack of personal life wasn't much of a sacrifice. I'd realized years before that happiness just wasn't in the cards for some people and accepted that I was among them. But I'd been unprepared for my anxiety to get as bad as it had. I knew it was starting to impact my health in life-threatening ways. Enter Mom's brilliant idea for me to house-sit while she traveled around Europe and Asia with my Aunt Jeanine.

In-2-3-4, Out-2-3-4.

I repeated a few times, each round presenting more of a challenge for stretching my breaths that long. Maybe running would help.

On the way out after setting down the book and lacing up my running shoes, I paused at the front door, debating whether I should lock it or not. On the one hand, where I had been living the past eight years, in a suburb of DC, I wouldn't dream of leaving the door unlocked. But on the other hand, we'd never locked the door of my childhood home.

Well, I was supposed to be letting go.

Setting the key onto the table inside the front door with shaking fingers, I stepped out. The click as the door closed sent my heartrate into overdrive.

As I stood there trying to will my muscles to obey and carry me away from the house, I heard my mom's voice in my head.

"Oh, for god's sake, Annie, just go. Nothing is going to happen! Stop overthinking it and just GO!"

A sharp, tremulous inhale, two quick steps off the porch, and I was running. Within a few moments, the repetitive motion of pumping my arms, my legs continually reaching forward, the rhythmic thumping of my feet as they hit the asphalt lulled my breathing and heart rate into a steady tempo. Just as I'd expected.

After I'd passed the one-mile mark, I turned off the softly curving country road onto a dirt running path carved through the tall wild grass on the property of a deserted farm that had been town property for decades.

Running on treadmills and flat streets certainly didn't use the same muscles as running over soft earth and rolling hills, and I tired quickly. At least there was no one around to see my embarrassing performance; I was on the cross-country course for my old high school. I doubted they even used it anymore.

I'd never run cross-country myself—I'd passionately hated running all my life. I still did, really, but I couldn't deny its ability to calm my anxiety, which I'd discovered during my freshman year of college. But I used to love walking the course, visiting a beautiful willow along the back side of the property. As I crested the last hill and neared the dilapidated part-garage-part-barn structure that held rusty farm equipment at least twice my age, my vision clouded with anxiety. I veered sharply to the right off the established course and ran across the field between two rows of dead cornstalks.

Maybe next time.

Once back on the road, my heart rate slowed and the adrenaline faded, leaving me acutely aware of the exhaustion that remained. Every step felt as if I had concrete in my shoes and I longed to rest. But I'd set out to run five miles; I'd be damned if I quit any sooner. Ignoring my aching muscles, I picked up my pace until I was in a full sprint for the last half-mile.

Once I reached the five-mile mark at the fence along the back side of Mrs. Renner's property, I stopped, gulping in air as I rested my hands on my head and paced until my breathing normalized.

When I was growing up, I walked to the cross-country course to visit the willow tree whenever I was angry or upset. Mrs. Renner somehow always knew I was passing and would call out to me, asking me to help her with something. Weeding, winding her hose, shoveling her walkway, watering her plants, getting something down from a high cabinet; you name it, I probably did it for her at some point. And the more distraught I was, the longer the list of tasks with which she needed assistance. Even when I really just wanted to be alone, though, I'd been raised with better manners than to refuse someone's request for help—especially when that someone was my elder—so I always agreed.

After a while, she'd ask if I wanted to talk about it, somehow timing it so I'd blurt out everything on my mind in the fuming stream-of-consciousness way at which teenagers are experts. No matter how irrational I was, she'd just nod with a thoughtful expression until I was finished. Then she'd make eye contact with me and wait expectantly for me to talk some more, occasionally asking a seemingly innocent question or two. Eventually, I'd calm down, her nonjudgmental, patient, grandmotherly presence apparently all I'd needed.

Guilt stole my breath; I hadn't seen her in so many years. After what happened, I'd never gone back to the cross-country course, never seen her again. I'd been afraid that she would see into me in that uncanny way she could always see what was on my mind, and I couldn't face the inevitable disgust and disappointment that would accompany discovery of what I'd done. Still, I regretted that I'd never even said goodbye.

Turning, I walked quickly back toward her house and up to her porch before I had a chance to talk myself out of it. In the short moment between my knuckles rapping on the wood and the door swinging open, I realized I was smiling.

My thoughts were interrupted by the door swinging open to reveal *not* Mrs. Renner, but instead an attractive man in his mid-20s. Late 20s? He had short, dark brown hair, and the eyes above his neatly trimmed facial hair reminded me of warm caramel. He seemed so familiar.

My head cocked to the side as I studied his features, trying to place him.

"May I help you?" the man asked, his voice tinged with amusement.

My eyes darted up to his for the briefest of moments before I looked away. But not so quickly that I missed the fact that his danced with humor.

Or that I liked his smile.

I hadn't realized I was staring while I was trying to figure out who he was until he spoke. Flustered, I felt something on my neck and remembered that I'd just been running and had sweat dripping down the side of my face and neck. My skin instantly heated with embarrassment.

Oh, god, I was disgusting, what the hell was I thinking?

The man waited patiently for me to find my voice and respond, his friendly gaze now appraising me with warmth and curiosity.

"Um, I'm sorry. I was hoping to see an old friend, but she must have moved. Sorry to bother you," I said, flushing further as I turned on my heel and began rushing down the walkway toward the street, mentally crossing my fingers that my legs wouldn't give out. If only I could have magically disappeared and pretended the interaction had never occurred.

"Are you looking for Scarlet Renner?" he called after me.

"Yes. Do you know where she moved to?"

"She didn't move."

Guilt and sadness hit me so hard my legs wobbled, necessitating that I reach out to grasp the railing for support as I fought a rising wave of nausea. For a terrible moment, I was no more able to move another step than I was able to stop the tears that were already falling.

"She'll be home after a while. Miss, are you okay?"

My breath rushed out with a shaky laugh of relief. "I thought... I just thought... it doesn't matter. I'll come back another time."

"Who should I tell her came by?"

"Annie."

"Annie who?"

"Just Annie. And tell her to save her chores for me."

I couldn't help the snort-laugh that escaped as I said that last part, knowing she'd be amused when she heard it. The mysterious man's expression was a mask of confusion, like he wasn't sure if he'd heard me correctly. But my relief that she was alive overshadowed any embarrassment, so I just called out, "Thanks!"

Pausing for a moment when I was halfway down her walkway, my face tipped up toward the sky. I drew in a deep breath and held it as I drank in the sunshine, basking in its promise for the future.

chapter two

rob

I **sighed as** I navigated my pickup truck into my driveway and shifted into park. Mrs. Crabill was a crabby old lady who had changed her mind every few days about how she wanted me to design her side tables; two small tables had never taken me so fucking long to make. But at least the woman seemed to know she was a pain in the ass, always paying me a lot more than I charged. Even if that weren't the case, I'd have kept her as a customer. She was one of the chattiest people in the state; I'd guess about a third of my customers were thanks to referrals from her. So, annoying as she was, it was worth every minute I had to deal with her—I'd soon have enough to buy a proper workshop complete with a storefront for my woodworking business, which was about the only thing I really gave a shit about.

As I stepped down out of my truck, a woman on the porch next door drew my attention. Shutting my door, I turned to see who it was and the air in my lungs rushed out.

No fucking way.

But there was no doubt about it—I'd know that face anywhere. The face I'd seen every time I'd closed my eyes for the last fifteen years.

She looked a bit different than the last time I'd seen her over a decade earlier. She was now thin—too thin—and pale. But it was unmistakably her. There was something else that was different, though I couldn't quite put my finger on it from where I was.

What the hell was she doing outside Mrs. Renner's house?

Annie knocked and a moment later, Mrs. Renner's grandson, Lucas, opened the door and they gave each other a once-over. The sudden rush of burning jealousy was familiar, even after all those years. I tried in vain to make out their conversation, but I was too far away. When she got upset as he was speaking, more feelings I'd thought long buried came crashing back like a tidal wave: protectiveness, possessiveness, and rage. I balled my fists in restraint; it was all I could do to keep from walking over there and telling Lucas to go fuck himself.

But that wasn't my fucking job anymore.

She'd made that perfectly clear twelve years before, when she broke up with me without warning, explanation, or even a fucking goodbye. Just disappeared from my life. I spent years agonizing over every moment leading up to our break-up, trying to figure out what I'd done wrong. What I could have done better. Searching for any reason I could have given her to stay. And maybe if I'd known why she left, I could have come up with something.

For some time after Annie left, my brother, Charlie, and I fought over her even more than we had before she'd left. He'd never liked her, and always told me that she was the same as everyone else and would kick me to the curb one day once she was tired of me. I'd never believed him. I'd just *known* that Annie was different. But in the end, I was wrong since she *did* leave me. Even still, I couldn't tolerate him calling her names or saying anything disparaging about her, so we ended up in a fistfight whenever he did. In the end, we'd agreed to just never talk about her again. Even if he was an asshole, he was still my brother, after all, and the only family I had in the world. I'd thought Annie would change that, that *she* would be my family, too, but I'd obviously been wrong about her.

I'd thought I was angry before I met Annie, but, fuck, it was nothing like the rage I had after she left me. It was too big, too consuming for me to control it. Until I was forced unwillingly to confront that it was leading me down a path I didn't really want to be on; the same path I'd already left once. For *her*.

After meeting Annie, I had goals for the first time in my life; I suddenly wanted something better for myself, for *her*. So, partying and breaking the law with Charlie became a thing of the past. I started going to classes and doing my homework, spending my free time with Annie instead of looking for trouble with Charlie. I made the honor-roll and, thanks to Annie, I believed there was a world of opportunity out there for me.

I never understood why, but she had unending faith in me. She was like that—she could see the good in people and believed in them even when they didn't believe in themselves, her instinct to give everyone the benefit of the doubt. And she could always find the silver lining in any cloud life presented.

When she left me, though, everything changed. I had all this rage inside. I didn't know what to do with it without her there to help me, so I went back to what I'd known before her, what I was doing until the day I met her and she flipped my life upside down. I trashed the idea of going to college and started hanging out with Charlie again. Fighting? Check. Destruction of property? Check. Drugs? Theft? Unprotected sex? Check, check, and check. If it was self-destructive, I did it for the next year or so after she was gone. Until I got so drunk one night that I could barely walk. Stumbling down the road from the cross-country course, I was in Mrs. Renner's side yard en route to steal her garden gnomes when I fell, passing out before I managed to get back up again.

I couldn't help chuckling as I thought back to what had happened the next day; Mrs. Renner was undeniably a force to be reckoned with, something I'd never given her credit for prior to that morning. I'd met her before, of course, but Annie was the one who had a special relationship with her. Me? I never trusted anyone except Annie and Charlie, so I had been polite for Annie's sake when we were together, but that was it. I wouldn't have even done that, but Annie's enthusiasm for the old woman had been infectious. And I would have done just about anything Annie asked me to.

Well, when I came to and cracked my eyes open, all I could discern was a dark figure enshrouded in blinding light. For a moment, I sincerely thought I'd finally done it: partied too hard and was meeting the maker I'd never believed in.

Until that figure laughed with a dry, creaky voice, and said, "I think the pain you're going to feel today is lecture enough, so I'll bite my tongue, but I do need some help pulling weeds out back. It's going to be hot today, so we should go ahead and get started."

I realized the figure was Mrs. Renner, sitting in a lawn chair close by, and the blinding light was the sun directly behind her.

I groaned. "Well, fuck that, lady, I'm not doing your fucking yard work."

"Hm, Annie never told me you were an asshole. I guess she was wrong about you." She shrugged, got up and walked toward the back of her house.

I had no sense of time passing as I lay there, reflecting on what I'd become and how I'd gotten there. As always, thinking about Annie made my chest hurt, tightening to the point it was hard to breathe.

Laying there with my eyes closed, I could see her face, her smile, hear her telling me that I could be anything I wanted. That, in a way, I had an advantage over others who hadn't had such a terrible childhood because I didn't have to waste time figuring out what rock bottom felt like before doing something with myself.

Fuck, I was glad Annie was gone right then and couldn't see what I'd turned into. A wave of shame washed over me, intensifying the hangover-induced nausea I was already battling. Even if she had broken my heart, she'd first taught me how to be a decent human being.

Staggering to my feet, the pain from the bright sunshine blinding, I made my way slowly to Mrs. Renner's backyard, where she was setting out some gardening tools.

"You see these here? They have little white flowers on them, but these are weeds. We need to get all those pulled out of here, but be careful not to disturb the roots on the other plants, you hear?"

I nodded and did my best to pay attention through the throbbing in my temples as she continued to show me what needed to go.

We worked mostly in silence, the only sound the scraping of the trowels in the dry earth or the soft swish of the weeds as they landed on the compost pile.

"You know," Mrs. Renner said about an hour later, her voice laced with sympathy, "I miss her, too."

A glance over my shoulder revealed that she meant it. That, somehow, she understood the pain I was feeling. And it occurred to me for the first time that Annie hadn't just left *me*.

After that, I started going to Mrs. Renner's periodically to help her around the house, and Annie was a frequent topic of conversation. I was surprised by how much talking about her helped to dull the constant pain in my chest to a more manageable ache. Eventually, I started talking to Mrs. Renner about other things, too.

Mrs. Renner was the one who helped me find a healthier outlet for my anger. She was the one who believed in me and encouraged me when I was struggling to find the confidence to start my own business. She was the one who helped me get through those days when I missed Annie to such an extreme that I couldn't even find the will to get out of bed. Like real family, she'd seen me at my worst and stuck by me anyway.

My focus returned to the present, and to Lucas, who was now studying Annie with a mixture of confusion, curiosity, and interest while she smiled—beamed, really. She closed her eyes and turned her face to the sky, and it looked as much like she was providing the world with light as like she was soaking up the sunshine herself. Her whole face was lit up, her long, dark curls tumbling from her ponytail and blowing gently in the breeze, some of them caught in the sweat on her neck; she was radiant. I felt the ache for her spread through my chest. My hand moved instinctively over my heart and rubbed as if it could ease the pain that grew there.

She turned after a few seconds and started walking away without looking back. Lucas was still watching her from his grandmother's doorway.

As I fought against knee-jerk possessiveness, my eyes shifted back to Annie of their own volition. Like they always had.

Like they always would, it seemed.

I'd heard, like everyone in our small town, that Miriam was going to travel across Europe and Asia for a year, and I'd wondered who would take care of her house. Considering how quickly she had left without a backward glance, it never occurred to me that person would be Annie, and I couldn't figure out how I felt about it as I watched her figure shrink into the distance until she turned down her mom's street and out of sight altogether.

With a heavy sigh, I turned to find Lucas watching me with a quizzical expression.

Well, fuck.

"Hey, Rob," he called out as he started down his grandmother's porch stairs.

"Lucas," I called back with a nod of acknowledgement. "How's business?"

"Great! I can't believe how much we get from such a small town. I'm glad I listened to Grams when she suggested I open the brewery here. Of course, it helps to be related to her since she knows everyone in town."

I snorted. "Town? Try county. At least. I'm pretty sure I haven't talked to someone who hasn't at least met her since I moved here. Your grams is something else."

"That she is." He laughed. "I told her I'd pay for the delivery and setup of her new washer and dryer and the next thing I know, Nick and I are unloading the damn things from his truck and now I've got to set them up. I don't know what the hell happened."

I snorted; I knew exactly what he meant.

"You grew up around here, right?" he asked after a moment.

"Yep."

"Do you know who that woman was? She only said her name was Annie and to tell Grams to save her chores for her."

"I do."

"Who is she?" Lucas asked as he came to a stop in front of me. "How does she know Grams? I've been here for a few years now, and I've never seen her before."

Fuck. I didn't want to talk about her. I hadn't even uttered her name aloud in years. Swallowing to alleviate the sudden dryness in my throat, I dragged my sweaty palms discreetly over my jeans before reaching out to shake Lucas's hand in greeting.

"Annie Turner. She and your grams were close until Annie moved away."

"Any relation to the Miriam Turner Grams is friends with?"

"Her daughter."

"I guess that means she must be here to stay while Miriam is overseas. Hm."

He stared thoughtfully in the direction of Miriam's house. I had a feeling I knew *exactly* what he was thinking about and forcibly unclenched my fists.

She wasn't mine anymore.

chapter three

annie

I **glanced at** the clock—1:07 AM. The creaking had woken me hours before, and I couldn't quiet my mind enough to fall back asleep. In fact, I felt even more anxious about being alone in my mom's house than I did in the city.

How the hell did I ever sleep here? This house makes so much damn noise!

My bare feet thumped mutedly on the old wood planks as I padded to the kitchen, filled the tea kettle, and ignited a burner on the stove. The kitchen was lined with windows along the exterior wall, allowing for a naturally bright area during the day. In the middle of the night, though? Eerie as hell with all the inky darkness on the other side of the glass. No way to see what—or who—might be out there. And Mom had never put blinds or curtains in the kitchen, so there was no way to cover the windows. With a shiver, I decided to hunt down something to read from the living room while I waited for the water to boil.

Two soft clicks as I twisted the switch rod turned the lamp by the sofa to the low-light setting. I couldn't believe the old thing still worked; it was already ancient when I met Mom decades before.

Built-in floor-to-ceiling bookshelves positively overflowing with books comprised two of the walls in the living room, always my favorite room in the house. Travel, history, gardening, self-help, finance, mystery, historical fiction, literary classics, and more. I browsed through the titles, not searching for anything in particular, but rather hoping for something to catch my eye. Historical romance hadn't held my attention earlier in the day, so I passed by those and continued browsing.

Old photo albums were stacked on a shelf near the ceiling, and one of them had an unfamiliar spine with my name on it. I fetched a small stepladder from the hall closet, the same ladder I used throughout my childhood to reach the many sundry items my small stature made impossible to access without some means of vertical assistance, and reached up for the old, dusty album. It required the use of both hands to keep from dropping it as I shimmied it from the shelf with my fingertips—the damn thing was huge and must have weighed at least ten pounds.

Setting the album on the coffee table with a loud *thunk* as the tea kettle began its high-pitched song, I replaced the step ladder in the hall closet on my way back to the kitchen. After turning off the stove, I headed to the pantry to find a tea bag but froze as I swung open the pantry door.

My eyes fell closed involuntarily, and I took as deep a breath as I could manage, savoring the familiar nostalgic aroma of herbs, spices, and tea. I was instantly eight years old again, scared and confused, but doing my best to hide it for the sake of my little sister, Lori. I didn't understand what was happening or why we were in that big, old house with a strange old woman who told us to call her Miriam. The lady who'd taken us from school earlier that day had only said we were never going back home, would never see our parents again.

Miriam smiled warmly at my sister and then turned that same warmth toward me. No one had ever smiled at me like that before and it made me uncomfortable. I didn't know what she wanted.

"I'm going to share a secret with you two. Follow me."

She led us from the living room, through the dining room, into the kitchen, and finally over to a door, where she turned to wink at us. With the same warm smile, she slowly pulled open the door.

For a moment, I couldn't comprehend what I was experiencing as I stood rooted in the doorway, trying to process the amazing smells and what I was seeing. I'd never seen or even heard of a closet for food before, let alone seen enough food to fill one, other than at a grocery store.

Until right then.

Miriam was talking to us, but I couldn't focus enough to listen; I was entranced, alternately looking and sniffing, trying to figure out where the heavenly, exotic smells were coming from.

After a glance at me and another warm smile, Miriam started opening containers. One by one she twisted off the lids, wafted the jars in front of her nose, and sniffed the contents before offering for Lori and me to do the same. After each, she said the same thing.

"No, this can't be it. Let's try the next one."

We went through every spice container, every jar of dried herbs from her garden, every tin of tea in the same way, until there was only one left.

The very last item to sniff was in an antique tin that had Sleepytime Tea embossed on the side. The tin was green, with bits of rust along the rolled edges, and a friendly-looking bear wearing a stocking cap on the lid. I didn't understand it, but the scene on that tin resonated with something inside me; just gazing at it provided me with a small measure of comfort.

Miriam opened the tin, sniffed, and then smiled triumphantly, her eyes dancing.

"Aha! I found it! This is the one. I knew it was in here somewhere!"

She offered the tin to me, and I inhaled deeply through my nose. It smelled like comfort and security and happiness.

"I like that one."

"Wonderful! Now, this is my extra special tea. I always keep some in this pantry. When I'm feeling sad, I make a cup of it, and it helps me to feel a little bit better. Shall we all have a cup?"

"Are you sad today, Miss Miriam?"

"I confess that I am a little bit sad today."

"Me, too! I'm sad because I miss my mommy and daddy. Why are you sad?"

"Well, sweetie, I miss my mommy and daddy, too. They live far away, so I haven't seen them in a very long time."

I didn't like that the nice lady was sad, and I wanted to give her a hug to make her feel better. But hugs also made me uncomfortable, so I wrapped my arms around myself instead.

"I'm sorry, Miss Miriam. Maybe we can both see our mommies and daddies again soon."

"I think that sounds lovely, Annie! In the meantime, how about some tea?"

Settled into the corner of the sofa with my cup of Sleepytime on the coffee table to steep and cool enough to sip, I pulled the album onto my lap. After using my palm to swipe off the copious dust from the heavy brown leather cover, I flipped it open, sending even more dust billowing into the air.

On top was a manila folder, yellowed with age and overflowing with papers that I hadn't noticed within when the album was closed, which would explain the album's unexpected weightiness. Carefully, I lifted the flap. My lungs froze as I found myself face-to-face with people I never expected to see again.

Why the hell had I never seen these before? How long had Mom had them?

The picture on the left was of my biological mother and looked just as I remembered her. She wore the same smile she had every time she promised to stop drinking, get herself cleaned up, and get a job so she could finally put food on the table and properly take care of my sister and me. And, God, I was always so excited, believing in her every single time she uttered those words. Just as I was always devastated when she inevitably broke every single promise.

The very first time was a warm afternoon when I'd just arrived back to our trailer from school to find her asleep. I didn't want to wake her up just to get me some water, so I grabbed the glass on the table next to her and took a big gulp, discovering in milliseconds that some clear liquids were *not* water. I was seven. My whole body shuddered at the memory.

My eyes moved over to the next picture, this one of my father.

"Daddy, I'm scared."

"Of what?"

I shifted, embarrassed and scared and uncomfortable. But it was my daddy, and he would keep me safe.

"Trevor."

"Your cousin? Why?"

"He... he..." I started crying.

Trevor had warned me that he would hurt me if I told anyone. But, no, Daddy wouldn't let him.

"He made me sit on his lap and watch naked people on tv. And he... he... touched me... down there, between my legs."

"Annie! Don't say things like that!"

"D-Daddy, it's true."

"Stop lying!"

Lying? I never lied to Daddy, ever. Why did he think I was lying?

"Daddy, I'm not lying, I promise. He said he would hurt me if I told you, Daddy. I'm scared."

"Annie! None of that is true! Do you hear me?! You can't ever say that to anyone, ever again, do you understand me?"

Daddy didn't believe me? I was crying so hard that I couldn't talk. I'd thought Daddy would keep Trevor away from me, but instead, he thought I was lying.

"Annie! Answer me! Do you understand that you never, ever, say that again to anyone? No one Annie!"

Daddy was yelling, which meant he was mad. I had to calm down and listen or he would spank me. Swallowing my next sob, I nodded my head in agreement.

"Okay, Daddy."

I scrubbed both my hands roughly over my face to clear the moisture there, then gathered handfuls of hair and tugged until the sting on my scalp was strong enough to pull me back into the present.

I knew I should have closed the album at that point. I knew I should have tried to read a book instead. Or turned on the television. Or taken a shower.

Anything except what I did next.

But I couldn't help myself; my body simply wouldn't obey. I gingerly lifted the photos with my fingertips and began reading what was typed onto the page underneath.

> SOCIAL ASSESSMENT
> Annie and Lori Ashland appear to reflect the effects of their parents' life experiences. While the relative stability of their very early years contributes to their ability to perform well in academic work, the more recent inconsistency in residence and unavailability of their parents for affection and protection can be seen in their anxious and withdrawn behaviors. Annie, in particular, is a child who has been subjected to personal violations, including multiple instances of sexual abuse and physical assault, from which a parent should be expected to protect their child. Similarly, although not always present during these times, the children's belief that their father was coming back to get them has affected their sense of trust and security in relationships with caregivers. Even peer relationships were

> affected by the changes in the availability of food and the inability to maintain personal hygiene habits. Consequently, in understanding that children of similar background who feel a sense of helplessness, lack of trust in their environment and are exposed to sexually explicit behaviors, a treatment plan for Annie and Lori should include a resolution of issues in their environment, as well as individual therapy that would focus on the issues unique to themselves.

My breath was coming in short, violent, painful bursts and the edges of my vision were darkening rapidly.

I should have stopped, right fucking there.

But, again, I couldn't. I was compelled to flip through the remaining pages. The Emergency Removal Order from the day my sister and I became wards of the state. Initial and subsequent foster care plans. Various court documentation from over the years until we were adopted. I continued to sift through the mass of paperwork and saw the dates my biological parents stopped contacting social services to notify them of their whereabouts, the date their rights were officially and irrevocably terminated. The adoption order from when Miriam adopted us.

But the next document stopped me in my tracks: the outcome of the hearing to prosecute the last man who molested me before I entered foster care. I was holding the page between my fingers, though I couldn't focus my vision to see the words. But I didn't need to—I remembered it all.

I remembered every. Last. Fucking. Detail.

It had taken years, *so many years*, of sickeningly horrifying nightmares to finally free myself enough to keep those memories at bay, to keep them locked up in a box deep inside where they couldn't haunt me anymore, where I wouldn't have to relive them every single time I closed my eyes. And because I couldn't just shut the album and walk away like the intelligent person I was supposed to be, I'd just ripped the lock off that box with a crowbar and flung open the lid.

Knocking over a basket of yarn, I frantically made my way to the bedroom and threw on some clothes and running shoes before locking the front door behind me and breaking into a sprint down the street.

And after a while, when I was wheezing with the effort to get enough oxygen, it seemed I had succeeded enough to keep the vivid images at bay, all my attention focused on trying to catch my breath. I relaxed my pace just enough to allow me to breathe sufficiently to continue, though barely.

But where the hell was I?

In my desperation to escape, I hadn't even noticed that I was alone in the blackness of night, and I was disoriented as I tried to make sense of my surroundings and figure out where I was.

As I stopped and looked around, the only sound that of my labored breathing, my eyes adjusted, and I realized I was on the cross-country course.

Shit. Of all places.

I was hyperaware of every insect sound, the faint flashing of lights from planes passing high in the sky, the vibrations that made their way up my legs after each strike of my foot on the hard earth. Everything in my body screamed for me to sprint as fast as I could away from that place, but I determinedly forced myself to maintain a moderate jog, making sure I could more or less see where my feet were going to land.

At the last second to make the decision, I opted for expediency and veered to the left as I gulped in a deep breath; cutting behind the old garage would get me back to the road much faster. Time slowed as I approached the building—only a few more steps and I'd be clear of it.

Almost there, Annie, almost th—

I was rounding the back corner of the building when I tripped over something and flew forward, my right foot twisting unnaturally. As my face plummeted toward the ground, my heart stopped beating as it flooded with dread; a distinctly male voice had just grunted in surprise.

chapter four

rob

A **sound of** pain and shock escaped my lungs as I tried to process what had just happened. After a few seconds, I realized someone had tripped over me and landed pretty hard.

"Hey, are you okay?" I grunted as I pushed up to my feet. "Let me help you up."

"No! Stay away from me!"

My feet immediately carried me back from the screaming woman, but something tugged at the recesses of my mind. That voice was familiar.

"Get away from me! Somebody help me!"

"Annie?"

There was rustling on the ground like she was scrambling around as she continued screaming for help. Fucking clouds; they were blocking the moon, preventing me from being able to see anything. But there was no mistaking that voice, even filled with terror.

"Annie!" I shouted, unreasonably annoyed that she was calling for help as if *I* would ever do anything to her. "It's Rob Weller. Quit fucking screaming, I'm not gonna hurt you!"

The sudden silence was almost eerie as the moon finally peeked out from behind the clouds, allowing me to make out the mixture of confusion and panic on her face. She was clearly hyperventilating, and I was concerned she might actually pass out at any moment.

"R-Rob?"

"Yes."

"You're lying. Rob doesn't have a beard."

"Oh, for fuck's sake, Annie, yes, I do."

"Oh god, are you alone?!"

"What? I mean, yes, but why?"

"Why are you out here in the middle of the night?"

"I come out here to think when I can't sleep. Why the hell are *you* out here in the middle of the night?"

Silence, except for the sound of her rapid, shallow breathing. I stood there for a moment, unsure what I should do or say until I remembered that she had fallen and probably needed help getting up.

"Here, I'll help you," I said as I extended a hand in her direction.

"No!" The sound of a few quick, shallow breaths, then, "I mean, I can do it myself."

Folding my arms over my chest in irritation, I watched as she tried and failed several times to get to her feet, a strangled cry of pain accompanying each failure. It seemed as if she'd sprained her ankle and wasn't able to stand on it. Finally, I couldn't take it anymore.

"Jesus Christ, Annie, just let me fucking help you. You're only making it worse."

She stared at me unseeing for a moment, her eyes brimming with tears. After quickly taking and releasing a deep breath, her shoulders slumped.

"Okay, I need help," she admitted, her voice watery as she turned away from me.

Seeing her upset and fighting tears did something unwelcome and that damn ache that had taken residence in my chest when I saw her on Mrs. Renner's porch worsened. I searched for something to say but came up empty; it would have been easier if I'd known what the problem was.

Besides, it's not my fucking job anymore.

But I still couldn't help wondering what had brought her out there in the middle of the night in the first place. She'd never been comfortable in the dark, so I figured something serious, but fuck if I was going to ask her.

As I moved behind her, reaching under her armpits to help her stand, my heart found an irregular rhythm and my stomach bottomed out, like I was in a freefall instead of standing with my feet planted on solid ground.

Twelve years.

It had been twelve long years since the last time I'd touched her, the last time I'd had her in my arms. As hard as I'd tried for years to forget it, I remembered that day as vividly as if the intervening years had been merely hours.

AP Literature was our last class of the day in the spring of our senior year, and that particular day had been beautiful—sunny and unseasonably warm—so Mr. Allenrich decided to hold class outside. We were all supposed to be reading *The Grapes of Wrath*, but most of the other kids were chatting and enjoying the sunshine instead.

Grabbing her hand, I silently pulled Annie away from the rest of the class to find some quiet; she wasn't interested in gossiping with everyone else, preferring quiet and solitude, and I didn't give a shit what anyone except her had to say, anyway. Mr. Allenrich wasn't paying attention, so I led us around the corner of the building until we were alone with each other and the woods that flanked the school's property.

The sun was warm, and I shrugged off my jacket, laying it out for Annie to sit on. After pulling my book out, I settled down on my back next to my jacket, using my backpack as a pillow, and held my arm out as I waited for her to get comfortable.

"I don't know, Rob, someone might come around the corner," she said indecisively, her eyes darting around nervously.

"No one is paying any attention to where we are. They're too wrapped up in themselves. Come on."

She hesitated. "No hanky-panky, got it?"

I laughed. "No hanky-panky. Got it." I laughed some more. "Hanky-panky? Really?"

She shrugged. "My mom's older, you know that. Her expressions rub off on me."

"I think it's adorable that my girlfriend is secretly an old lady. Now lay the fuck down, you're wasting our time together."

She smiled, blushing like she so often did, pulled out her book and settled on her side, her head on my chest, and her book propped up in front of her. I couldn't keep from sliding my hand under the back of her sweater until I was touching the bare skin above the waistline of her jeans.

"Hey! I said no hanky-panky!" she protested as she tried to scoot away from me.

I clamped my hand down onto her waist to prevent her from going anywhere.

"I'm not. Calm down, love. I wanted to feel your skin, that's all. I won't try anything. I just need to touch you."

"Better not," she replied, resting her head back down and starting to read.

I'd been truthful. I wouldn't try anything out there, but fuck if I could keep myself from touching her soft skin; it was a compulsion. The calm I experienced when I could feel her warm flesh under my hands… I was an addict. My eyes closed as I skimmed my fingertips back and forth along her lower back and side, my breathing deep and even, as it only ever was when I was with her.

"Are you cold, love?" I asked softly when I felt her shiver and goosebumps spread across her skin.

"No," she breathed out. "Aren't you going to read?"

"I'll do it later."

What I didn't say was that I would need both hands to read and there wasn't a chance in hell I was going to stop what I was doing.

After several minutes, when I realized she hadn't turned a page in a while, I opened my eyes and tilted my chin down. Annie was asleep, her book closed on her hand. As carefully as I could manage, I reached up and removed it, setting it down next to me. My heart skipped as her hand spread out across my chest in her sleep, and I covered it with mine to keep it there.

My eyes may have closed again, but I was nowhere close to sleep. I felt awake, alive, my body humming with energy. I'd never thought I could love so deeply, but the last couple of years with Annie had taught me that anything was possible. And somehow, some fucking way that defied all reason, she loved me back.

When the bell rang to signal the end of the school day, I gently woke Annie, though I wanted to do anything but. As she yawned and stretched into me, I felt much like the Grinch must have at the end of the story when his heart grew so big it broke the box that was holding it; my chest positively ached with the love I felt for her.

Annie planted her chin on my chest and looked up at me, her eyes searching mine for a minute or two before her lips tipped up into an irrepressible grin as her cheeks pinked and her eyes grew bright and luminous. Whatever she was thinking about, she could keep right on thinking about it—she looked like a goddess.

My goddess.

"As much as I want to stay here like this, love, I don't wanna get you in trouble. It would just give your mom yet another reason not to like me, and then we'd really never see each other."

"I know, I'm going," she replied, leaning up to give me a peck on the lips after glancing around to make sure we were still alone. It wasn't enough, so I wrapped my arm around her back, holding her to me for a deeper kiss.

"I fucking love you, you know."

She flushed a deep red as she sat up and reached into her backpack. I continued smoothing my hand back and forth across her back, closing my eyes again so I could focus on the way her skin felt under my hand without any distractions.

"I'd much rather stay, but I seriously have to go now, or I'm going to miss my bus. I love you more."

I snorted softly. "Not a chance, love. Now get out of here."

After another quick kiss, I watched her walk away, wondering idly what I'd done to deserve her. Once she was out of sight around the corner of the building, I let my lids close again and laid my head back down, trying to hold on to all the feelings she'd stirred up in me.

"Hey fuckhead, what the fuck are you doing? I have shit to do other than waiting on your fuckin' ass. I almost left. You're lucky I came looking for you, or your ass would be fucking walking."

I laughed, not at all perturbed as I opened my eyes to look up into my older brother's pissed-off glare.

"Nice to see you, too, Charlie. Why, yes, I had a great day today, thanks for asking."

"What the fuck are you doing, anyway?" he asked as he bent over and snatched something off the ground from near my foot, glancing at it before smirking and stuffing it into his pocket.

"What's that?"

"My question first, fucker."

I shrugged as I closed my eyes again, aware that I couldn't keep from smiling as I pictured Annie sleeping on my chest. Just as I was aware how much it would annoy the hell out of Charlie. Everything about Annie pissed him off, but I didn't give a shit.

"Thinking about Annie."

"Fucking Christ, Rob, she's turned you into a fucking pussy."

"Don't fucking start, Charlie."

"Man, who the fuck *are* you? I'm not fucking good enough for you now?"

I laughed. "Dude, calm down. You know that's not what I mean."

"Whatever, asshole. You'll be singing a different fuckin' tune when you finally realize what I've been telling you for years: that she's just a stupid slut like everyone else, and she'll leave your ass when she gets bored with you. Then what?"

"Don't talk about her like that unless you want me to break your fucking nose again," I warned. "You're lucky I'm in such a good mood, or I'd have done it already. Besides, it doesn't fucking matter what you think—you just don't get it. I know she would never leave me—she loves me, too."

I was filled to capacity with a happiness and contentment I didn't even know was possible before I met Annie, and I took a deep breath, refusing to let Charlie spoil it, committing everything about that afternoon to memory.

Well, I'd succeeded in doing just that, even though for years after that day I'd wanted desperately to forget. And I definitely didn't want to be thinking about it at *that* moment, with her unexpectedly in my arms again.

As I lifted her, my heart beating angrily against my chest cavity, I tried to hide that *I* was now the one with erratic breathing. And, Christ, it suddenly felt like it was the middle of a hot August day in the deep south rather than the frigid late winter night it actually was.

"Can you put weight on it at all?"

She gingerly shifted some of her weight from her left foot onto her right before yelping in pain and jerking her injured foot into the air. "Not really."

"Okay, I can carry y—"

"No. I can wait here while you get your car."

I snorted derisively. "You've lost your fucking mind if you think I'm going to leave you here alone in the middle of the night. Now, what's gonna happen is I'm going to carry you to my house to get my truck, and then I'll drive you to Miriam's from there."

"How do you know I'm staying at Mom's house?"

"Seriously? Everyone in the damn county knew your mom was going overseas and would have someone living in her house while she was gone. No one knew who that someone would be, but considering you showed up when she left..." I shrugged in lieu of finishing the sentence—it was obvious.

She nodded, quiet. When she didn't say anything else, I squatted down in front of her and told her to grab ahold of me. I waited, but she didn't move.

"Look, Annie, I know a piggyback ride might not be ideal, but beggars can't be fucking choosers. Now grab my damn shoulders before I change my mind and decide I'd rather leave your ass here to freeze after all."

Like she fucking left me.

After another moment, she finally leaned forward, wrapping her arms around the tops of my shoulders. I hooked my arms under her knees as I stood up, trying to ignore the fact that a whole lot of Annie would be touching me if it weren't for my heavy jacket, and instead focus on remembering why I should be pissed off.

"Ready?" I bit out after adjusting her into a more comfortable position.

"Yes."

I started toward the road, turning left once we got there. Trying to sort out how Annie's presence made me feel as I walked was a useless endeavor; I couldn't think straight with her weight on my back, her legs under my hands, her arms wrapped around my shoulders. Instead, I kept having flashbacks of us together before she left me, intensifying that ache in my chest to the point it was getting hard to breathe.

"Wait, you live here?" Annie asked suddenly on a sharp inhale.

"Yep."

"When did you come back?"

"Never left."

"You never left? But you wanted out of this town. You always said you felt trapped here and wanted to live in a city, somewhere bigger."

"Things change. Hell, you of all people should know that. One minute you loved me and wanted to spend the rest of your life with me, and the next you just fucking disappeared without so much as a goodbye and never came back."

As if she hadn't heard more than the first two words I'd said, she replied, "How could that have changed? Hell, Rob, we were about to graduate and head to college the last time we talked about it."

I didn't want to even think about what made things change, and I sure as shit didn't want to talk about it, especially with *her*.

A litany of reasons why she had no fucking right to even ask me that question was on the tip of my tongue when I remembered what Mrs. Renner had said to me all those years ago that had helped me tame the rage: "You know about Annie's childhood. She's no stranger to abandonment. That girl would never just leave without a damn good reason. No, something happened. Something terrible enough that she was more afraid of that than of leaving. It's not fair of us to judge her for leaving without knowing why, no matter how much it might hurt that she's gone."

My anger toward Annie faded. "You left me," I sighed.

"I don't understand. How did that keep you here? I figured you would have had even less reason to stay."

Why did she sound so panicky?

"Annie, it's fine. Really. I didn't say that to be an asshole, it's just the truth. I was really fucking hung up on you back then, so when you left me the way you did, I struggled for a while. But I eventually got over it and moved on. You used to tell me there's a silver lining to every cloud, you just have to look hard enough, remember? Well, I guess you could say that I found one, and that's what kept me here."

A few minutes later, Annie's breathing choppy in my ear, I turned onto my street and walked past Mrs. Renner's house.

"No," she breathed out. "You didn't..." She swallowed. "Did you buy it?"

"Yep. I need to go inside to get my keys if you'd like to look around."

Why the fuck did I say that? I didn't want her in my house; not like this. Please, for the love of God, say no.

"No, thank you. If you'll just put me down by the truck, I'll wait for you out here."

Stifling my sigh of relief, I opened the passenger door of my truck and turned so she could slide off my back onto the seat. Once she was settled, I shut her door and headed inside the house. As soon as the front door closed behind me, I leaned back against it, taking and releasing a few deep breaths as tears burned the backs of my eyes. Being over her was complete bullshit, and having her near me was harder than I had ever thought it could be. Nothing like I'd imagined—dreamed about, even—for years; not even fucking close.

One more deep breath as I grabbed the keys from the entryway table, and I was out the door to take her home; just a few more minutes and I could pretend none of the night had happened.

Annie turned away from me as I climbed into my truck and I took a moment to study her profile in the moonlight before backing out. She looked unhappy. Just so damn sad. My whole body ached for her, hurt with the force of my desire to erase whatever was causing her pain. Without thinking, I reached out to pull her into my arms and tell her that whatever it was, we'd figure it out, like I used to do. But just before I touched her, I froze, reminding myself yet again that it wasn't my job anymore.

After twelve years, why was it so fucking hard for me to remember that?

"Give me your key so I can unlock the door, then I'll come back and get you," I said, holding out my palm after pulling into her mom's driveway.

Instead of giving me the key, though, after a pause, she laughed. It started as a chuckle that rapidly evolved into hysterical laughter as tears streaked down her cheeks.

"What's so funny?" I barked out, irritated; I just wanted to get her out of my truck and get back to trying to forget her.

"I... I uh... I lost my key," she said between fits of laughter.

I realized suddenly that she wasn't really laughing; she was having a breakdown. And that's when I figured out the mysterious difference I couldn't quite put my finger on when I saw her talking to Lucas: her spirit was broken.

What the hell had happened to her?

"You can stay at my house," I said, trying to swallow the unwelcome emotion that threatened to swell my throat closed. "I have a guest room. I'll help you look for your key in the morning."

She nodded but continued to laugh as I slowly backed out. Instead of turning right at the corner, however, I took a left for a long, roundabout route back to my house to give her time to work through whatever was happening and calm down.

By the time I pulled into my driveway about a half-hour later, the laughter had subsided, and she was just staring through the window with an expression so full of pain and sadness that it stole my breath.

"Do you live alone? I mean, I don't mean it that way... I just... is anyone here?"

"Yes, I live alone, Annie. I'm not married. Or seeing anyone," I replied slowly and quietly, staring at my hands on the steering wheel as my heartrate kicked up.

"What? Oh, um, okay, but is anyone here?"

"No, no one's here."

I looked at her quizzically, but she quickly turned away to look back out the window before nodding slowly and letting out a breath she must have been holding. When she spoke, I almost didn't even hear her.

"May I have a few minutes alone before we go in?"

"Take as long as you need. I'll get the guest room ready for you."

I stepped out of the truck, hearing the click of the locks engaging as I forced myself to walk away from her, willing one foot in front of the other until I'd reached the front door. I was doing what she asked, so why did it feel like I was doing the *wrong* thing?

There wasn't in fact anything to ready in the guest room, but I thought she might want to clean up, so I grabbed a towel from the linen closet and sweatpants and a t-shirt from my bedroom and left them on the bed for her. Steadfastly ignoring the images of Annie in my house and wearing my clothes that paraded through my mind, I headed to the kitchen to start the tea kettle and pull out an ice pack before walking back out to the truck.

I heard the doors unlock as I approached, but waited before reaching for the door handle. I needed a moment to steel myself in preparation for touching her again.

"Ready?" I asked as I swung the truck door open.

I carried her cradled in my arms this time, trying desperately not to sniff her hair like a fucking creep as I crushed her into my chest more tightly than strictly necessary. After settling her into a chair at the kitchen table and pulling one over for myself, I removed her right shoe and sock as she hissed in pain. Her ankle was swollen and already bruising, but I didn't see anything I thought warranted a trip to the hospital.

"Definitely a sprain. This will help," I said as I began securing the icepack around her ankle, taking care to be as gentle as I could. Just as I set her foot down on a stool, the kettle began to whistle.

"Tea?"

"Um, sure. No caffeine. Please."

Rising, I pulled two mugs out of the cabinet. "Not a problem. I only have one kind."

After putting a tea bag in each mug and covering them with hot water, I turned, only to be gutted by the scene in front of me. Annie was slumped over, her arms wrapped tightly around her waist, her eyes, red and swollen from crying and ringed with dark circles, were closed. She looked like a deflated balloon. A very pale, very unhappy one. In short, she looked like shit.

Was she okay? Maybe she was sick. That would explain a lot if she was. Fuck, what was wrong?

I cleared my throat loudly as the ache in my chest intensified. "I made you a cup of tea, but I understand if you just want to go to bed. You must be tired."

"Tea first. I'll go to bed after the tea," she said without opening her eyes.

The two mugs clattered loudly when my shaky hands set them down and I fell into the chair across from her, watching for her reaction. I knew the moment the steam from her cup made it to her nostrils because her eyes shot open as she jerked herself upright.

"Is this—"

"Sleepytime. Your favorite," I said softly as I held her gaze.

Her eyes brimmed anew with fresh tears just before she turned sharply away from me. She was upset again. What had I been thinking?

She may have been sitting in my kitchen, but it wasn't by choice, and it didn't change the fact that she'd walked out on me twelve years before. She wasn't back to stay. And she hadn't come back for *me*.

After a few minutes of awkward silence, I cleared my throat again.

"I'll let you relax with your tea. I need a shower anyway. I'll come out and help you to the guest room when I'm done."

I stood so abruptly that my chair skidded a few feet and fell over. I opened my mouth to say something, belatedly realizing I had no words to fix it. So, I clamped my jaw shut, righted the chair, then turned and strode quickly to my bedroom.

Jesus, it was so much harder than I had ever imagined it would be. My life had been calm and ordered for years, and now Annie had suddenly and violently flipped everything upside down.

Again.

I took my time showering and getting dressed, not looking forward to the painful awkwardness that waited in my kitchen. I had no idea what I even wanted. Part of me wanted to ask her why she left me, demand to know why she had destroyed me without so much as a goodbye. But a different part of me just wanted to say the past was the past and do whatever it took to convince her to stay. Yet another part of me didn't want to know anything and just wanted to go back to the way things were up until that morning when I'd seen her standing on Mrs. Renner's porch.

Annie hadn't moved except to lean her head against the back of the chair and close her eyes. She didn't even flinch when I cleared my throat; she'd fallen asleep. She obviously needed the rest, but I couldn't let her sleep like that, so I removed the ice pack and gently wrapped her ankle with an ace bandage. When I was satisfied with my work, I picked her up as carefully as I could with my entire body trembling at the prospect of holding her again.

This time without a heavy jacket between us.

Feeling her relaxed in my arms and seeing her head full of unruly curls resting against my chest as I carried her through my house brought back such a torrent of memories and emotion that my legs threatened to buckle under me. I still loved her as much as I ever had and missed her so goddamn much.

She shifted in my arms, her eyes fluttering open a fraction before closing again.

"Rob? Is that you?" she murmured sleepily, barely audible.

"Yes, it's me, love."

"Oh, not Charlie," she murmured before sighing.

My footsteps stopped abruptly as if her words had been an invisible wall in front of me. Charlie?

chapter five

annie

I was in a dark and unfamiliar room, and someone was shaking me roughly by the shoulders.

"NO! NO!" I screamed, flinging my arms out without discretion, hoping to fend off my assailant.

"Annie! Wake up for Christ's sake!"

Recognition of the voice as Rob's settled over me as I opened my eyes in the dim light spilling through the open bedroom door from the hall to find it was him shaking my shoulders. I was drenched in fresh sweat, panting and reeling from the flashback he'd interrupted.

"It's okay, love, it's just a dream," Rob said, his voice deep, thick, and soft as his hands smoothed soothingly up and down my arms. "Just breathe."

I concentrated on decelerating my breathing and my heart rate, and as I did, I stopped sweating, the tears slowed, and my shaking subsided to trembling.

"Do you want to talk? Which one was it?"

"My parents trying to commit suicide in front of me. And no, I don't. Sorry I woke you."

"Don't fucking apologize to me for having a nightmare. You know better."

His eyes bored into mine for several minutes until he cleared his throat and averted his gaze.

"I, uh, I don't know what you do nowadays when you have them, but if you want me to stay in here until you fall back asleep... I don't mind."

When we were teenagers, I would call Rob after a nightmare, and he would talk to me until I'd calmed down and could fall asleep. If it was a particularly nasty one, he would sneak over, climb in my window, and hold me until I fell asleep. For the nights those options weren't possible, he'd bought me a giant stuffed hippo so I would have something to snuggle with; he even slept with it for a week before giving it to me so it would smell like him.

My feelings were at war with each other; I wanted nothing more than what he offered, but there were so many more reasons to decline. For starters, I'd inconvenienced him enough already. And I didn't want to send the wrong message. Or seem desperate. Even if I felt like I really was.

Rob stood abruptly as he spoke, his tone gruff as he stared at the floor. "Okay, um, my room is right next door if you need anything."

The next time I woke, the room was flooded with sunshine. Yawning, I opened my eyes and took a moment to look around. The small room was simple and cozy, painted a soft periwinkle and the bedding a delicate floral pattern in cream and varying shades of blue. In the corner was a sitting chair, upholstered in navy and cream stripes with brass nail heads along the edges, and the single table lamp had a matching shade. White lace curtains filtered and softened the bright light coming through the windows. There was a small, beautiful dresser on the opposite wall and a matching nightstand next to me, both a pale tan and littered with dark knots in the wood.

"Why is that considered to be shitty wood?" I asked Rob as he dug through wood scraps at the local lumber yard.

The long, rough-sawn planks he'd been referring to were the most interesting pieces I'd seen as we'd made our way past all the prime wood with sky-high prices to match until we'd reached the area designated as the scrapyard. If that was the shitty wood, I wasn't sure why he'd insisted I come with him; I knew nothing about woodworking or wood.

He glanced up from where he'd begun carefully inspecting each piece and separating them into two piles. His face was earnest, his eyes alight with excitement, and I couldn't help smiling. I'd had my doubts, but I knew right then that getting him a gift card to the lumber yard had been the perfect birthday gift.

"See all the knots?"

"Yeah, they're beautiful."

"Just like you."

I deadpanned, biting my cheeks to keep from laughing. "So I look like a brown lump?"

He snorted as he straightened up and looked back and forth between me and the knotted plank of wood. "With long curly hair."

I rolled my eyes and succumbed to the giggles I'd been holding in as his deep laughter filled the air around us. After a moment, he shook his head, gave me a peck on the cheek and squatted back down.

"Anyway. The knots are next to impossible to work with. They have a different density than the surrounding wood, they can have gaps between the edges and the edges of the area around—like here, see?—and they react differently to temperature and moisture changes. It's a pain in the fucking ass. And it can also get expensive because you end up with a lot more waste, so most people don't want this stuff."

"Oh," I said, eying the planks dubiously.

Visually, I would have chosen them out of all the other wood we'd seen, and I'd thought Rob was doing the same, but I must have been wrong. He turned, placing the plank he'd been using to demonstrate carefully to the side with several others like it.

"So, I guess that's the pile you're *not* keeping?"

"Why would you think that?" he asked, not looking up from his inspection of the next plank he'd pulled out.

"Well, you just said it's way more difficult to work with and that no one wants it."

He glanced up, smirking as he set the plank in his hands into his actual discard pile. "No, I said *most* people don't want it. But I'm not most people."

"But aren't you just making things harder for yourself?"

"That surprises you?" he laughed.

"Well, I guess not," I laughed back. "But why? When you have your pick of whatever you want, why would you choose something that's harder?"

He shrugged, turning back to the wood and looking for the next plank to inspect. "Harder doesn't mean it isn't worth it. It takes me more work, sure, and it might piss me the fuck off while I'm working on it. But like you said, it's beautiful. And in the end, what I've made is even better because of the extra effort."

My gaze shifted from the furniture I knew Rob must have made to the ceiling as the events from the night before replayed through my mind. I still couldn't figure Rob out. One minute it seemed like he still cared about me, and the next like he was pissed off and hated me. Though I was sure the night had ended on the latter, especially after I basically went batshit crazy when I realized I didn't have my key. Not to mention waking him up when I had a nightmare.

It was inarguably the worst night I'd had in years. In fact, the last time I'd had an actual breakdown like the night before had been right after I started college, the event that precipitated my friendship with Haley.

My eyes burned with fresh emotion as I allowed them to wander around the room once more, daydreaming of the life Rob and I might have had together if events had played out differently. But I willed myself to hold the tears in check and cut my daydream short when my chest started caving in on itself; there was no use in dwelling on what-ifs. The only thing to do with the past was figure out what could be learned from it, and then move forward without *ever* looking back.

After a few deep breaths, I decided I was as ready as I was ever going to be to face him, though my heart vehemently disagreed as it beat an uneven cadence. Sighing, I pushed myself up and swung my legs over the edge of the bed, noticing that I was still in the clothes I'd gotten sweaty in the night before. Twice.

Gross.

But at least Rob hadn't undressed me when I was sleeping. Not only would that have been embarrassing, but if he was anything like the Rob I'd known years before, I'd have woken up to him demanding responses to questions I couldn't possibly answer.

Another quick glance around the room revealed a towel and pile of clothes Rob must have left for me at the foot of the bed. I decided if I could stand, I'd take a quick shower.

Breath held and fingers crossed, I slid off the edge of the mattress and gingerly attempted to weight my legs evenly. *Shit, that hurt!* So, walking normally was out, but maybe I could hobble around if I barely used that foot. Looking down to check the degree of swelling, I saw that my ankle was wrapped in an ace bandage; Rob must have done it after I'd fallen asleep.

Closing my eyes conjured his mess of unruly hair bent over me as he tenderly wrapped the ice pack around my ankle. He certainly looked different than he had the last time I'd seen him. He'd always been tall, but he was noticeably larger now, broader, more muscular. He also never kept facial hair, but he now sported a full beard. I'd never liked beards, or any facial hair for that matter, but it did seem to suit him and his surly personality. I had also seen tattoos poking out of the wrists and neck of his long-sleeved shirt, so he must have gotten a lot more since high school. Even his hands were different. They'd always been scarred and his knuckles a bit knobby from fighting and punching things, but the scars were far more numerous. And several were too large and smooth; something had cut him. The skin on his hands was tanned and leathery, his palms and fingers calloused and rough, his fingertips stained a dark brown.

Other things, however, were exactly the same. Like his deep, gravelly, grumpy voice, and the smell of his mixture of spicy, leathery cologne and Rob that had always been so intoxicating. Though he also smelled faintly of sawdust and something else I couldn't quite identify. And his touch still set my skin on fire. His dark brown eyes still drew me in until I felt that I was lost and drowning in them.

His sharp, tremulous intake of breath whenever our skin made contact the night before still lingered in my ears. Or maybe I'd imagined how affected he was because a part of me wanted him to feel the same way I did? Really, it didn't matter. I could never be with him again, that's why I had left in the first place, and nothing had changed. Nothing would *ever* change, no matter how much I might've wanted it to because there was simply no way to undo the past. So, with a sigh of resignation, I limped my way into the en suite bathroom to get cleaned up.

By the time I hobbled into the kitchen after showering, swimming comically in Rob's clothing, it was practically lunchtime. I really couldn't remember the last time the sun had risen before me; I'd have sworn it to be impossible. Now that I was clean, I felt somewhat refreshed, though I also felt a pang of guilt for having wasted so much of the day in bed. Not that I had anything to do, but still. As I slowly made my way into the kitchen, a sudden stab of disappointment at finding it empty made me realize just how much I longed to see Rob again. Meandering slowly, taking in my surroundings as I passed through each room, I set off to look for him.

I used to dream about what the house would look like inside with some TLC, telling Rob that one day I'd buy the old place and fix it up, but he'd done it instead. It was another old farmhouse, with a large front porch, a sunroom, and a vast living room with a wood-burning fireplace that I'd fantasized about converting into a library with built-in shelves like the ones in my mom's house.

The house sat on a few acres, with vegetable beds and fruit trees in the backyard, which was about an acre in size. The remainder of the property was wooded and shared a rear property line with the land that contained the old cross-country course. And of course, it was close to my mom and Mrs. Renner, which had been the icing on the cake for me back then when I'd wanted nothing more than to settle down in the only place that had ever felt like home. I'd always loved the house, from the first time I'd seen it. But when Rob and I were together? I would imagine exactly what I wanted to do with it and could see us living in it together.

I couldn't believe he bought it.

And it looked like he'd done pretty much everything I used to talk about doing. I had dreamed of an olive and cream color palette; he had chosen blue and cream. That was the only difference I could find. It was the right decision, though; the colors suited the personality of the house. I smiled and stopped myself from thinking about why he would have bought the house I'd always loved and decorated it the way I told him I would.

When I didn't find him inside, I peered out the back door. But he wasn't there, either. Maybe things had been too awkward for him? But that was fine. Actually, it was better. I made my way back through the house, searching for a jacket. As I passed through the kitchen, I noticed a note on the fridge that I'd somehow missed earlier.

Annie –
I had to run out for a bit. There's a fresh pot of coffee by the sink, tea in the cabinet above the stove, and fresh fruit in the refrigerator. Keep your foot elevated until I get back.
-Rob

I stood there for a moment as I stared at his note, transfixed by his familiar handwriting. What I really wanted was to get a cup of coffee, sit down, and wait for him to return, so I could take him in, really look at him, smell him, hear his voice—*without* the distraction of a mental breakdown. But what was the point? Besides, I'd already imposed on him enough. I was sure he was eager to get rid of me.

I decided to take advantage of being next door to Mrs. Renner and walk over to see her. Maybe she would even drive me up to look for my keys.

My mind made up, I slowly made my way back to gather up my clothes. After tossing them into an old grocery bag I found under the sink, I located a pad of paper and a pen to scribble a note.

Rob –
Thank you for your kindness and hospitality—you really didn't have to go to so much trouble, and I'm sorry to have inconvenienced you. Please excuse my behavior last night; it was late, and I was exhausted. Also, thank you for the clean clothes. I'll wash them and return to you soon.
-Annie

Voices floated around from the back of Mrs. Renner's house as I approached. I made my way toward them, taking care not to twist my ankle on any uneven ground in her yard when I suddenly recognized one of the voices as Rob's and froze. When had they become friends?

"I just can't make sense of it. What the hell could that have meant?" Rob said angrily.

"Everything makes sense in the right context, honey," Mrs. Renner replied. "If it doesn't, you just don't have all the information you need. Don't start jumping to conclusions."

"How can I not? There's no mistaking what she said. I was awake all fucking night trying to come up with a single scenario where it would make sense, and there's none. Not one! If she... if she was... I can't even make myself fucking say it, but you know what I'm getting at, then everything I thought, everything I know—fuck, everything I *am* is a goddamn lie!"

"Get a grip, Rob. Your life is not a lie. You're a good man. And nothing that might have happened in the past changes that. Besides, there's no way she was ever unfaithful to you, so don't even think it."

"If that were true, why would she be dreaming about Charlie? I thought they hated each other, but what if..."

Rob's voice faded and was drowned out by the rushing of blood in my ears as I flipped around and limped away as quickly as I could.

It was all my doing.

But that's why I'd left instead of telling him—to spare him the pain. But he was in pain anyway; his voice was laced with it. Even so, the truth would be so much worse.

He could never find out.

My ankle worsened with each step closer to the cross-country course and slowed my progress down the road. I slipped and almost fell as I tried to move off the narrow shoulder into the slope of a ditch to give space to the car I heard approaching from behind, miraculously regaining my footing and my balance just in time.

"Annie, wasn't it?"

Stumbling with surprise at being spoken to, I glanced over to see the man from Mrs. Renner's house watching me with curiosity and a friendly smile after he'd inched up next to me in his car. My feet stopped moving as he held me trapped in his gaze; the turmoil from what I'd just overheard was settling, my heart rate slowing, the nausea in the pit of my stomach receding. My normal unease in the presence of men was noticeably absent.

"That's right. Unfortunately, I was so rude I didn't get your name yesterday," I said sheepishly, embarrassed by my lack of good manners; my mom would be appalled.

"I'm Lucas Renner."

"Renner? So, you're related to Mrs. Renner?"

"Yeah. She's my grams." He smiled warmly, affectionately even, as he paused for a moment to look over my bizarre attire. "Can I take you somewhere? I was on my way over to have lunch with Grams when I saw someone limping down the road, and, well, what kind of person would I be if I didn't at least offer to help?"

"Thank you. I appreciate the offer, but I wouldn't want to hold you up."

"It's no trouble. Really, you'd be doing me a favor, because otherwise I'd spend all day worrying about whether you got where you needed to go, and then blaming myself for not helping you if you didn't. So, you see, it's really helping *me* more than *you*."

He winked playfully as he finished speaking and then flashed me a cheesy grin. I couldn't stop the laughter that spilled out as I rolled my eyes, wondering if he'd used that line before and whether it had worked or not.

I took a moment to study him through the open car window. His eyes twinkled with laughter, and he seemed friendly. Down-to-earth. Genuine.

Most importantly, I didn't sense he was hiding something like I did with a lot of people. He didn't intimidate me and make me uncomfortable like every other man I'd ever met except Rob; surely that counted for something. And he was Mrs. Renner's family, after all. No way on earth anyone related to that woman was anything but good.

Lucas's smile broadened as I studied him, as if he could tell that I was going to agree before *I* even did.

Oh, what the hell, I really needed the help. I could barely walk.

Sighing in mock annoyance, I failed to hold back an answering grin as I grabbed his passenger door handle and tried to ignore the blush I felt creeping up my neck.

"Okay."

chapter six

annie

For about a week, I packed and unpacked a minimum of once a day, in a constant tug-of-war with myself over staying. I desperately wanted to escape the unwelcome memories and the resurgence of debilitating nightmares. But if I were to flee? I'd be allowing the past to control me. And, ultimately, I was determined to prove that *I* was the one in control.

So, instead of leaving, I combed Mom's bookshelves for mental health volumes and researched new ideas for ridding myself of the nightmares and taming my anxiety. Many of the suggestions and recommendations I came across were familiar, things I'd tried that hadn't worked for me, but there were a few fresh ideas. One author discussed the importance of simplicity and regularity in daily life. That sounded like something I could manage, so I created a quiet routine for myself.

I would rise early and enjoy a cup of coffee as I watched the sunrise from the front porch. If the sunrise was obscured by the weather, I sat on the porch anyway, watching and listening to that instead. After that, once my ankle had healed, I'd run, taking the same route every day; having my feet travel the same path allowed me to mentally disconnect in a form of moving meditation. Next, I'd spend a few hours working outside: shoveling snow, pruning bushes, planting flowers and vegetables, pulling weeds, cutting grass—whatever needed to be done, which shifted with the weather as well as the transition of seasons.

Whenever I got hungry, I'd head in and make lunch after showering. Most days, I'd spend the next few hours reading. On Tuesday and Thursday afternoons, though, I ventured out, volunteering at the local public library, ending my shifts with a children's reading hour. Those two hours were the highlight of my week. I'd discovered my own love of reading as a young child, and sharing that enthusiasm for the written word and the magical escape it could provide both excited and satisfied me in a way my career never had.

After my library shift or a few extra hours of reading, I'd make dinner and go for a walk until just before dusk, at which point I'd head back to the house and watch the sunset from the porch. As soon as the sun was down and darkness began settling around me, I locked myself safely inside with a cup of Sleepytime tea and a good book until I was drowsy enough to fall asleep.

As I established my routine, Lucas started dropping by unannounced a few times per week. Before that, he'd called every few days to ask if I would meet him for lunch or a cup of coffee or drinks. For some inexplicable reason, though I refused to pick up when Rob called, I answered every one of Lucas's calls, even though I knew before I'd said hello that I would turn him down. It was after a few weeks of this back and forth that he appeared on my porch for the first time, two cups of coffee in hand. And that damn cheesy grin of his that I'd already realized I had a weakness for.

Some people would find my routine lonely. Lucas certainly did, though that made sense for someone who ran a business that thrived on crowds of people. But after living in the frenetic bustle and constant rush of the city for so many years, the slower pace was exactly what I needed to begin to reset myself, and the time alone was rejuvenating in a way.

The nightmares began to subside again after several weeks. I was still having them, but more sporadically. And the yard work was giving me muscle definition I hadn't had since I'd left for college.

But I hadn't been to see Mrs. Renner yet. Despite the guilt that weighed on me, I was too afraid to go. Afraid of what she might ask me after the conversation I'd overheard between her and Rob.

Afraid of running into Rob at her house.

Lucas asked me a few times why I hadn't gone back to see her like I'd said I would, but I just shook my head; it wasn't something I could discuss with him. Over time, he learned there were certain topics I just couldn't talk about, and once he stopped asking about them, we fell into an easy friendship.

Instead of pressing me to open up to him, he was content to talk to me instead, telling me about growing up in the Midwest with his dad. It was clear that he missed his life out there, that he'd been happy before his mother was diagnosed with terminal cancer when he was a young teen. He had no siblings, so after she died, it'd just been him and his dad. What little family he had left lived on the East coast and his father couldn't afford to travel on his mechanic's salary, so Lucas didn't really know any of his extended family except his grandmother, especially after his mother passed away.

My heart ached for the young boy who had lost his mother, remembering how hard it had been to lose mine and she wasn't even close to the model of a caring parent that Lucas's mother had apparently been. Even so, I enjoyed listening to him talk about a childhood that was so carefree, simpler and happier than I could have even dreamed about as a child. I'd drink my tea with him on the porch instead of locked inside the house by myself on those evenings he was there, resting my head on his shoulder with my eyes closed, imagining that I was there with him as he talked. Slowly, I'd feel some of my ever-present tension melt away until the soft, rich timbre of his voice, the warmth of his shoulder under my cheek, and the security of his arm wrapped around my shoulders lulled me to sleep.

I felt like I was doing something wrong as I slowly climbed the few steps up to Mrs. Renner's porch. Lucas had offered to come with me, but I'd felt that I needed to do it alone. However, I was doubting my judgement as I approached her front door. I reached up to knock, but stopped with my hand a matter of inches from the thick wooden door.

I heard voices.

My entire body froze and I struggled to make out the words over the tumultuous pounding of my heart. I hadn't seen Rob's truck in his driveway, but what if he was there?

The crunch of gravel from somewhere behind me caused my heart to skip as I spun around. Walking up the street were two men in dusty overalls and work boots, one of them carrying a toolbox. As they got closer, I could make out bits of their conversation; a tractor had broken down and they were headed up to fix it.

I exhaled sharply in relief and turned back to the door, using a full body shake to expel some of the remaining tension, and then firmly knocked before I could change my mind. While I waited, I inspected my hands, realizing I should have cut my fingernails before I left; they were getting too long. Maybe I should run back home and return another time, maybe in—

"Annie!" Mrs. Renner interrupted my thoughts.

Too late to turn back now.

"H-hi, Mrs. Renner," I stuttered, my voice shaking. I could feel my face reddening with embarrassment, and I wished briefly that I hadn't come.

"Come in, come in. It's so wonderful to see you, honey! Let's make a cup of tea, shall we? And while we're waiting, I could use some help pulling out my cookie tins from above the stove. I was getting ready to climb up myself, but I'm not as steady on a ladder as I used to be..."

I stepped inside, shutting the door behind me and following her as she headed to the kitchen, listening to her continue on about the various small tasks with which I could help her. As we neared the kitchen, I closed my eyes as I felt an easing inside, the nostalgic comfort of the familiar sound of her voice and smell of her house—a mix between fresh flowers and peppermint—melting my anxiety at facing her after so many years.

I smiled, glad I'd finally come to see her.

chapter seven

annie

I'd promised Lucas that I would support him by going to his brewery, Stockwood Brewery—or SB—for the debut of their latest beer. If I hadn't promised, I'd have found some excuse to miss it; I was nervous beyond comprehension.

I'd always loathed crowds. And I was concerned about running into Rob in this one. It would also be my first time out of the house with Lucas—hell, it would be my first time out of the house for any reason aside from my quiet routine and grocery shopping.

The deep inhale and slow exhale I forced as I stepped out of the shower were useless. I really wished I hadn't let Lucas charm me into agreeing to go with that damn grin and boyish playfulness. I'd known when he was sweet-talking me that he was doing so, just as I'd known that agreeing to go was a terrible idea. And yet, his enthusiastic badgering had worn me down until I'd promised to be there.

The middle of June meant it was hot as hell and even more humid outside. I studied the sundress I'd bought earlier in the week. It was navy blue and cream gingham, with wide straps and an empire waist, complete with a red sash that tied around the high waist and a matching red hair ribbon, all very Norman Rockwell-esque. I'd been drawn to the dress like a moth to a flame, as Mom would say, even though it didn't remotely resemble the kind of clothing I typically wore. But it reminded me of the dress I'd worn on my first real date with Rob. My first date ever. And the first time in my life that I'd ever felt pretty.

But if I couldn't wear it without thinking about Rob, I needed to wear something else.

I debated for another few minutes, but it was pointless since I didn't have anything else appropriate to wear to an event at a brewery, other than jeans and a t-shirt. And I really *did* want to make an effort for Lucas, to demonstrate for him that I cared about and supported him. So, I stepped into the dress and began working on the column of buttons in the back, dismayed when I realized there were a few that I couldn't reach no matter how I contorted myself and twisted my arms.

I had planned to braid my hair to get it off my neck in the heat, the heaviness like a blanket that stuck to my skin in the summer, but it looked like it would need to stay down to hide the open buttons.

Sighing in resignation and steadfastly ignoring the anxiety that was already twisting my stomach into knots and crushing my chest, I shoved the hair ribbon into a pocket in my dress—along with my license, a credit card, and my house key—and started down to the brewery on foot.

The music was loud enough that I heard it well before I arrived. Lucas had mentioned they would have a live band, but I hadn't recognized the name. Which wasn't surprising since I was out of touch with just about everything that didn't relate directly to my job. The band sounded decent as I approached, though I had mixed feelings listening to the country song they were playing; it was almost comforting, like coming home after a long trip.

Almost.

"Where are we going?" I asked Rob from his passenger seat as we sped down the highway.

"It wouldn't be a surprise if I told you, now would it?"

"Come on! You know I hate surprises."

"I do, but I'm determined to change that. Trust me. You're gonna love this one."

"Can you give me a hint?"

"Nope."

"Are we going into the city?" I asked, suddenly anxious. "Rob, I don't want to do that, I'm sorry, I know you miss it, but I can't, there's—"

"Seriously?!" he cut me off angrily. "What the fuck, Annie? I know how you feel—I would *never* take you there unless you wanted to go."

"I know, I'm sorry, it's just, we're driving that way, I thought—"

"I get that, but give me some fucking credit." He sighed deeply, and when he spoke next, the anger and frustration were subdued. "Look, I know a lot of people in your life have let you down. But I'm not one of them."

It was hard to speak over the lump in my throat caused by the guilt I felt from having made the assumption I did.

"I'm sorry. I'm trying. This is all new to me."

He lifted my hand to his lips and kissed the back of it softly as we exited the highway into a gridlock of cars.

"Well, I hope wherever you're taking me doesn't have a reservation," I muttered. "We're going to be stuck in this traffic for a while."

His eyes were positively dancing when he glanced at me, a small smile breaking free despite his not-so-subtle efforts to conceal it.

"What the hell are you up to?" I asked, the first inkling of real excitement filling my chest as I looked around for a clue.

He remained silent, shaking his head at me as we crept forward. Up ahead, I could see a billboard, though I couldn't quite make it out until we'd moved a few more feet down the road.

"Wait, is that... are we... no freaking way! We're going to a Train concert?!?"

Rob winked at me, a rare broad grin stretched across his face.

"Oh my god, Rob!"

His deep laughter filled the car. "I told you that you'd love it."

"But... but... I thought you *hated* country music?"

"Love, I can like anything as long as I'm with you."

I was yanked back to the present when a car slowed as it approached from behind. Adrenaline instantly spiked my bloodstream, my heartrate skyrocketing in response.

"Annie, wasn't it?" a voice called playfully. A familiar voice. Lucas's voice.

I should have guessed.

A sharp exhale of relief accompanied my smile and soft laugh as Lucas pulled alongside where I was walking on the sidewalk. When I looked over at him, he was grinning, seemingly pleased with himself, and I shook my head in mock exasperation.

"What are you doing? Don't you need to be inside making sure everything runs smoothly?"

"That's what I pay other people to do, of course," he replied with a wink. "Actually, if you can believe it, we ran out of trash bags. Trash bags! And someone needed to run out to get some more. I was afraid you'd back out of coming, so I swung by your house on the way back so I could drag you here kicking and screaming if I had to. But instead, I was pleasantly surprised to find that you had already left."

"Hey, that's not fair! I may be a hermit, as you say, but I promised you I would come."

"To be fair," he said in a mocking tone, "you have also been promising for months that we can hang out somewhere other than your house, but..."

I laughed. "Fine. You've got a point." I shook my head at him, though I couldn't even pretend that I wasn't enjoying our flirty banter. "Well, tonight's your lucky night because I'm supporting you *and* we can hang out, if you can get away long enough."

"I can certainly get away long enough for you," he replied smoothly, winking at me.

A car horn honked, and I realized that Lucas was holding up traffic—a lot of it. In a town as small as Stockwood, even the main road consisted of a single lane in each direction. Rolling my eyes, I stepped back from the curb.

"Go ahead and park, you nutjob, you're holding up traffic. I'll catch up with you later."

"Sweetheart, you think I'm going to give you a chance to change your mind and slip away? Uh-uh, no way. Get in."

I rolled my eyes again for effect, his playfulness rubbing off on me as it always did, but my heart had stuttered when he'd called me "sweetheart". My whole body felt even warmer than the weather warranted, and I knew my face was flushed as I opened his door and climbed in. My stomach flipped as I sat, and I couldn't keep from smiling back at him, relishing the novel and unexpected thrill from his palm resting possessively on my arm, his lips brushing lightly against my skin when he leaned over to kiss my cheek.

The whole town had turned out for the event, and everyone was tipsy. Well, some were flat-out falling-down drunk, but everyone was having a good time. Luckily, everyone was so engrossed in the music, dancing, and—of course—the beer, that I was able to sit quietly and simply observe without anyone engaging me in conversation.

The skin along the back of my neck prickled with awareness as I got the distinct feeling that I was being watched. An instant later, Lucas's voice wafted into my ear, barely audible over the music, and I jumped.

"Hey, sorry about ditching you the second we parked," he said.

"No need. I understand. What I *don't* understand is how you found me in this crowd! I thought the whole town was here, but it might actually be the whole county."

His laugh was light and carefree as he glanced around us before returning his warm gaze to me. "I can't divulge all my secrets, now, can I? And I don't think we've had this many people here at once since the grand opening—maybe not even then. Which tells me two things. One, we should have live music more often. And two, we should change up our beer line up more frequently. The new beer is selling like crazy."

"Crazy, huh? Nice choice of words, scoundrel; you omitted the fact that you named your new beer Crazy Annie."

I attempted to give him a withering glare, but it was impossible when his eyes were dancing with boyish laughter and he was giving me that ridiculous cheesy grin, obviously pleased with himself.

What was it about that grin that was so charming and irresistible?

"I wanted it to be a surprise. Do you like it?"

"Actually, yes. I mean, you know I don't really like beer, but it's not bad. Trying to remember what you've taught me, I guess I would say, complex, but not too heavy. Unexpectedly smooth."

"Hm... reminds me of someone I know..."

His eyes were locked on mine as they spilled over with laughter. And that damn grin that made it impossible not to smile back at him.

"Ha. Ha. Very funny."

Using the laminated info sheet I'd snagged shortly after arriving, I fanned myself in an attempt to provide a modicum of relief from the weather as I shook my head at his antics.

"Oh, that reminds me, I need a favor. I can't believe I forgot to ask! I couldn't reach a few of the buttons on my dress. That's the only reason my hair is still down in this nasty humidity, so I could hide the open buttons. Would you mind getting them for me?"

Lucas's laughter was full and vibrant and bouyant as he shook his head at me. "You know, you could have just led with your request."

"What fun would that have been?" I teased, his playfulness infectious.

Lucas stepped back around behind me and gently swept my now frizzy curls to one side, his fingertips whispering along the tops of my shoulders as he did so and my whole body shivered, despite the sweltering heat. His hands stilled in response to my shiver, then began fastening the buttons, but ever so slowly. After he had pushed the last button through its accompanying buttonhole, his hands smoothed across my back and clasped my shoulders, his lips lightly brushing my ear as he spoke into it slowly.

"All done. But I'm sorry you're going to pull your hair up. It's sexy the way it is."

My breath deserted me as hormones and anxiety surged through my bloodstream. I felt like I was suffocating. I liked Lucas, a whole lot more than friendship warranted if I was being honest, but I wasn't prepared for our relationship to change; anything more would come with expectations I already knew I could never live up to.

"Um, I need some air, actually. It's too hot in here with all these people. Maybe I should just go? Yeah, that's what I should do. Congratulations, Lucas. Really. The beer is fantastic. And thank you. For your help with the buttons, I mean. But I should go. Um... bye? Or... or see you later? I mean, not tonight, but... or not, I mean you don't have to come if you don't want to, I just meant..."

I was mortified by my rambling and wished for something, *anything*, to happen to distract from the disastrously embarrassing situation I'd created. But nothing was forthcoming, so I stopped mid-sentence before anything else unintelligible could escape my mouth and started pushing my way through the crowd toward the exit.

If I could just get out of the throng of people, I'd be able to breathe. I'd be okay. I could go home and hide in shame.

I thought I heard Lucas's voice floating above the noise of the crowd and the music, but knew it must have been a figment of my imagination. There's no way he would follow me after *that* exchange. And regardless, I had to get out of there. A hand latched onto my arm from behind, providing the nudge needed to take me to full-blown panic.

"NO!" I screamed as I pulled away with without even looking to see who the hand belonged to, shoving through the crowd in desperation to reach the other side.

At last, I broke through to the street, my momentum carrying me forward a few steps until I was pitched precariously over the edge of the curb. Stopping just millimeters shy of tumbling over face-first into the road, I hunched over, holding myself up with my hands on my knees. I cycled through my counting exercises in an attempt to catch my breath, but still couldn't manage to get enough oxygen. My vision narrowed as the shaking in my legs worsened, threatening to topple me headfirst into the street.

Suddenly, Lucas was there, squatting in the street in front of me as his eyes, brimming with concern and confusion, searched my face.

"Annie? Are you okay? What just happened?"

I was frozen, unable to speak, but also unable to look away. His patient, caring gaze was my anchor, tethering me to solid ground through the roiling emotional tempest within. Miraculously, the black edges on my vision began to recede, my breathing began to slow. Something about him had the power to settle my anxiety just by virtue of being near me. Finally, I nodded.

Lucas reached out, encircled my wrists with his hands, and stood, tugging gently until I was upright.

"Come on, sweetheart, I'll take you home."

Why hadn't he walked away from my particular brand of crazy yet?

"No, it's okay, really. I can walk. You should stay here."

He released my wrists and grabbed one hand with his, lacing our fingers together before I had a chance to stop him, and started leading me toward his car.

"I can spare enough time to take you home."

"Lucas—really. I don't want to interfere any more than I already have. And I really think I could use the walk."

"We'll walk, then."

He flipped around, pulling me with him, and started in the direction of my mom's house. The twenty-minute walk was punctuated with silence. I knew he had questions, but I wasn't prepared to answer them, and he, thankfully, must have sensed that, because he didn't ask.

I pulled my hand out of his to fish around clumsily in my pocket to find my key and unlock the front door, immediately stepping inside and heaving a deep sigh of relief that he remained on the porch instead of following me in and probing for information.

"Are you all right?" he asked, his eyes boring into mine.

I forced a smile, figuring reassurance was what he was really after.

"Of course, I'm fine. The heat just went to my head, that's all. I'll take a cool shower, read for a bit, and then go to bed."

Lucas didn't speak or move as he studied me contemplatively, looking less than satisfied with my response. I felt like he was looking through me and into my soul, and seeing things I didn't want him to, but I couldn't look away. After several uncomfortable moments, he sighed in resignation, placing a hand on the doorframe and leaning closer to me.

"I really don't want to, but I have to go. If there was any way I could get out of returning to SB right now, I would, but..." He sighed again as his gaze intensified. "Can I come back once we're closed up?"

My chest caved in on itself, and I opened my mouth to tell him no, that it was too much, that it would change things between us, and that change was something I couldn't handle. But nothing came out.

"You don't have to wait up for me. I just want to make sure you're all right. Please?"

Too cowardly to take any more of the deepening emotion I saw in his eyes, I looked away. I wanted to say yes, but I couldn't—it was a step too far from friendship. But what if I said no and he decided to walk away?

The pressure in my chest worsened. I had to risk changing our friendship because the thought of not having him in my life anymore was even scarier.

He closed his fingers around the key I held out shakily, his hand lingering to hold onto mine until I finally looked up to find his eyes burning with intensity as they studied me.

Clearing my throat, as my head began to spin, I pulled my hand back and cast my eyes downward.

"Um, good night, I guess. For now."

"Call me if you need anything, sweetheart, anything at all, and I'll come right away. Okay? I mean it. Otherwise, I'll see you in a few hours."

Lucas returned when I was in the throes of a nightmare, screaming in my sleep. After waking me and holding me as I shook and cried, he mercifully didn't ask a single question. As soon as I'd been able to speak, I'd tried to convince him that I was fine, that he should go home.

Instead, Lucas quietly ignored my entreaty. He'd brought me a glass of water and gently instructed me to drink it while he showered.

When we were both done, he climbed into my bed, pulling me into his arms and kissing the back of my head as my objections died on my tongue. And then he spent the night for the first time since I'd met him.

I insisted that he shouldn't return the following night as well, but I might as well have saved my breath for all the good it did; he showed up and stayed the night anyway.

Two nights turned into three, and then five, until he was staying with me almost every night. Even once the nightmares began to taper off in frequency, he took advantage of being able to let himself in, not once so much as offering to return my key, just coming and going as he pleased, despite my protestations. And then, one night, he asked me what I'd known was coming sooner or later.

"Annie, I know something happened to you. I don't know what, but something, and all the worst scenarios play through my mind. I really care about you, sweetheart, and it's hard for me not knowing what happened or how to help. You know you can trust me, don't you?"

I looked out the window, thinking about how balanced I'd felt in the weeks leading up to that conversation, not having to talk or even think about my past or my nightmares. I was afraid if I told him—if he knew—I'd lose him and that blessed balance. Lucas was possibly the least judgmental person I'd ever met, aside from his grandmother, but I wasn't fool enough to think that meant he'd stay once he knew. Someone from such a loving, stable background wouldn't understand the things in my past. Let alone want anything to do with my never-ending emotional rollercoaster. And even if he could look past that, my genetics carried a predilection toward addiction and a history of mental health issues. At a minimum. No one in their right mind would want to pass those genes on to their children, if I could even have children. And I knew that Lucas wanted them one day.

Of course, that wasn't even all of it. There were the other things, things that could never be undone, things that would forever hold me captive under a shroud of filth. I knew it as definitively as I knew the sun would come up the next day: he'd bail like any decent, rational person would.

"I... I understand why you want to know, but I'm not comfortable... I can't... maybe one day, but..."

He answered me with a sad smile, nodding in resigned acceptance of my refusal to explain.

chapter eight

rob

The six months after Annie came barging back into town and spent the night at my house had been hard. Fuck that, more than hard. Knowing that Lucas was with her almost every day while she had refused to answer any of *my* calls or come to the door even once when *I* had tried to see her. Lucas and I were friends as much as I was friends with anyone, so I had to listen to him talk about her whenever I saw him. Pretending that I didn't feel anything for her. Pretending that I didn't want to rip his arms off and then beat him unconscious with them for spending time with her. Talking to her. Touching her. Thinking for even a heartbeat that *my* Annie was *his*. I watched him fall for her, unable to do a single fucking thing to stop it.

To reduce the symphony of jealousy and rage that consumed me to a level I could manage, I worked feverishly, growing my woodworking business more quickly and lucratively than ever before. And when I wasn't working, I was spending extra quality time with my heavy bag. Which meant I was in the best shape of my life. Not that it mattered; the one fucking person I cared about noticing wouldn't even answer my goddamn phone calls.

She may not have wanted anything to do with me, but I got to see her anyway. Annie had started visiting Mrs. Renner twice a week like clockwork; once I'd figured that out, I'd rearranged my schedule so I could watch her come and go from my front porch. She didn't know—she had never noticed me—but I was there. Getting that glimpse of her two times per week may have been tearing out what was left of my heart and my sanity, but I couldn't stop myself from doing it any more than I could stop breathing.

And then, without fail, I'd go over to Mrs. Renner's after Annie had left to find out if Annie had said anything about me, about the reason she had left in the first place. And, every time, Mrs. Renner would look at me, her eyes sympathetic as she shook her head from side to side and said, "No, honey, she didn't."

But I'd soon get my chance to talk to her myself. I couldn't take another fucking day of not knowing. Annie would *have* to tell me why she'd left. I desperately needed to understand why she wouldn't even talk to me. And, damn it, I needed to know why the fuck she was dreaming about Charlie! That night had been on repeat in my head since it happened, and I was going to lose my damn mind if I didn't find out the truth.

With that thought, yet another replay began only to be interrupted a moment later by a loud banging on the front door that could only mean one thing.

As I neared the front door, the thought crossed my mind that I could drag him along with me for moral support as payback for being a pain in my ass. But I didn't really want to do that if my worst fears about Annie were confirmed.

"You're going to break my fucking door, jackass. Why do you always do that shit?"

"Well, hello to you, too, little brother. How about a welcome back, it's been too long, how've you been?"

He stumbled past me as he entered, the stench of alcohol assaulting my nostrils at the same time I noticed his bloodshot eyes.

"Christ, Charlie, you're shitfaced. And you're fucking high again."

"What you don't know won't hurt you, little brother."

"Look, *brother*, you know I don't want you here when you're using. I've told you that before."

"Come on, man, I don't have anywhere else to go. Don't be such a hard-ass."

"I swear to God, you better be fucking sober by tomorrow morning, or you need to leave. I'm serious. I don't want that shit around here."

"So fucking bossy, little bro. Don't worry your puny ass about a thing, I'm fine. I just need a place to crash for a while, and I missed your ugly face."

We'd been moving through the house, and as Charlie finished speaking, he sprawled out on my sofa.

"Wanna go out and have some fun for old times' sake? I think some of those preppy assholes we used to fuck with are having a party out by the river. We can go kick the shit out of them for the hell of it. We'll hit a bar first, though. You're always more fun when you've had a few. You're such a fucking pussy since you quit partying, though, you'd probably be shitfaced after one fucking drink. I've also got some of those pills you used to like, you remem—"

"Seriously, asshole?" I took a slow, deep breath, as I glared at him, debating taking a swing at him. His lack of respect for me wanting to stay clean pissed me the fuck off, and I was already on the edge without dealing with *his* shit, too. I knew from experience that a brawl would take the edge off. Hell, not that many years before, I'd have already hit him without even thinking twice about it.

"Look, I'm going out. I'll be back later. Take a shower—you smell like shit. And for the millionth fucking time, get your goddamn shoes off my furniture."

chapter nine

annie

"**Sweetheart, you look** incredible," Lucas murmured as his gaze flickered between my eyes and my lips.

Blushing, self-conscious, I leaned into his chest. "Thank you."

He held me close, his heartbeat under my cheek calming and grounding me as I breathed deeply and enjoyed the inexplicable peace I always felt when I was in his arms. My hair tickled my shoulder as he brushed it back from my face and bent to kiss the sensitive spot under my ear. I shivered involuntarily in response as warmth spread through my veins.

Another deep inhale of Lucas's now-familiar scent helped to tame the butterflies that took flight when his lips touched just below my ear.

"Can we just stay in tonight?" I asked hopefully.

His laughter filled the room as he pulled back and kissed my forehead before flashing that charming, boyish grin I had such a weakness for.

"I swear you would be a hermit if I let you. I hear stories from the locals about how social you were in high school, and it makes me wonder if they've confused you with someone else. Getting you to leave the house with me is such a chore!"

That's because they don't really know me.

"Is that a yes, then?" I asked hopefully.

"NO! It's your birthday, sweetheart, and I wanna take you out."

"Sounds like this is more for you than for me," I teased.

"Now you're getting it." He winked playfully and kissed me again, more deeply this time. "Let's go before I cave and let us be hermits. I don't want to miss our reservation, and we have to stop by SB on the way."

"I can wait here for you," I suggested as Lucas parked outside the brewery.

"Why? So you can escape? Uh-uh, no way. Out of the car, you're coming in with me. Unless you're embarrassed to be seen in public with me?" Lucas raised his eyebrow dramatically, mischief in his eyes.

"What are you up to?"

"Why do you think I'm up to something?" he laughed, grinning.

"I can't quite put my finger on it, but you seem like you're up to no good."

"Well, I guess you'll just have to wait to find out. But first, come in with me. You can hang out at the bar with Nick while you wait."

I groaned. "Nick? You know he asks me out every single time I see him, right?"

Lucas laughed. "I do. But I also happen to know that he's just a flirt. You *have* noticed that he asks out every woman who steps foot into the brewery, haven't you?"

"Maybe I should say yes this time to get you back for dragging me out tonight."

"Hm, try it and see what happens," Lucas replied, not a trace of concern in his voice. "I might go full caveman and come running in, brandishing a club and everything, and then toss you over my shoulder and run off with you."

I laughed at the image he'd painted. I'd never once seen Lucas lose his temper or raise his voice with anyone, or in any way exhibit even one iota of jealousy or violence. He had the temperament of a saint.

"I think I'd pay to see that."

He winked again, the twinkle in his eyes betraying that he was hiding something. The skin on my face suddenly felt too tight and I had trouble with my next inhale.

"Lucas... I don't... I don't really like surprises. You know that, right?"

"What? Who doesn't like surprises?"

He shook his head as he laughed, making it apparent he didn't really believe me. But I'd told him that before, hadn't I? Or maybe I hadn't... I rarely talked about myself with him.

As we passed through the door into the brewery, I glanced up to find Lucas's eyes on mine, and what was unmistakably doubt and anxiety flickered across his features.

I opened my mouth to ask him what was going on when there was a thunderous roar of voices shouting "SURPRISE!"

"Leave my sister alone," I shouted, sounding much braver than I felt.

Being picked on was common in the trailer park where my sister and I lived with our mom, but it was my responsibility to take care of my sister, so I had to stand up for her. My eyes darted around the group, at least twelve or fifteen kids, mostly bigger and older than me.

"What are you going to do about it, fatty?"

I froze. There was nothing I *could* do about it. Not really. There was no one else on my side. As I stood there, unsure what to say, one of the older boys shoved my sister again as he muttered about how she looked like she belonged in a concentration camp and I snapped into action. No matter what happened to me, I had to protect my little sister.

I charged toward the boy, yelling for Lori to run home amidst the chorus of shouts for a fight, but before I made it to him, another kid had shoved me from behind, sending me face-first into the gravel. I rolled over and had just enough time to see the sky disappear from view as the crowd of kids descended, using me as the outlet for their own unfortunate circumstances as they hit and kicked me until I lost consciousness.

My movements, my breath, my heartbeat. Everything stalled as I sluggishly processed what was happening. The chorus of happy birthdays surrounding me sounded muffled as if from afar at the same time it was deafening. At least half the town had squeezed inside the brewery, and every single person surged toward me at that moment, the press of their attention suffocating. Until my back slammed into something firm, I hadn't even realized that I was backstepping the way I'd come. Flipping around, I realized I'd backed into Lucas, whose features immediately darkened in concern as he bent close to my ear.

"I'm sorry, sweetheart, I thought you would like it..."

His normally playful demeanor was instead crestfallen and deflated, driving home just how good and normal he was. He only wanted to make my birthday special—I needed to fix what I'd just done to him. He didn't deserve to be upset because I *wasn't* normal.

Being in a large crowd staring at me expectantly ranked pretty high up on the list of the last places on earth I ever wanted to be, but I forced as much cheerfulness as I could summon under the circumstances into my voice when I replied, working to mask my panic and discomfort in the way I had been so adept at doing before my return to Stockwood.

"Sorry for what? This is amazingly thoughtful. No one has ever done something like this for me, so I wasn't expecting it. It took me by surprise, that's all."

I painted the most convincing smile I could manage onto my face, keenly aware of the sickening guilt I felt for not being more genuinely grateful, more normal for him. Turning before my mask slipped, I began making my way around the room. All the people there had come out to wish me a happy birthday, and it was my responsibility to personally thank each of them, regardless of how I felt about being there.

chapter ten

rob

Maybe I should have listened to Charlie after all. At least having a few drinks in me would have made it easier to watch the disaster that unfolded right before my eyes. Annie was making her way from person to person, dutifully thanking each one for coming, just as I could have told anyone she would. She was hiding how she felt, but she didn't want to be there. I could see it plain as day in her eyes, even if everyone else was oblivious—not that *that* was anything new. No one had ever really seen her, truly understood her.

No one.

Except *me*.

I almost felt bad for her, but sympathy was drowned out by my growing wrath as I watched. She'd nearly run right back out the front door when she'd realized what was happening. I'd watched it myself, fighting my instinct to jump up and follow her. To comfort her. To be a protective barrier between her and all those fucking people who didn't really care, not like I did. All those people who were making her uncomfortable.

But then she didn't leave. Instead, she stayed. For *him*. For Lucas. She hadn't stayed for *me* all those years ago when I'd done nothing but love her so hard that I didn't know how to exist without her. But she was staying somewhere she desperately didn't want to be for a man who would never understand her the way I did or love her the way I did.

My hand mashed into the left side of my chest, trying desperately to ease the pain.

"Hey, Nick."

"Hey man, how's it going?"

"I'll take a tall of whatever the strongest shit is you've got."

"IPA okay?"

"Sure, doesn't matter. And go ahead and pour me two."

Nick eyed me for a moment, his mouth open like he was on the verge of saying something. My guess was that he was going to mention the fact that I'd never had more than one beer before. But he must have realized I wasn't in the mood and nodded instead.

The glasses barely touched the counter in front of me before I grabbed the first one, tipping it up and downing it in one go. It was disgusting. I'd never liked IPAs, but it didn't really matter. I wasn't drinking for enjoyment.

Annie had talked to every single fucking person there except me. How did I know that? Because I hadn't been able to tear my eyes away from her, watching her every move as I guzzled glass after glass of beer. I wasn't feeling any pain anymore, just fucking rage. As I watched, my hands balled and my jaw clenched so tightly I wouldn't have been surprised if a few teeth ended up cracked. Annie turned her head, anxiously scanning the crowd. For a brief moment, the ache returned as I longed to go to her.

Fucking Lucas, how did he not know she didn't like crowds? That she hated surprises? How did he know so fucking little about her? He didn't fucking deserve her.

Her eyes settled on Lucas and the tension melted from her features as he made his way quickly through the crowd in her direction. Bending over until his face was near her ear, his hands found her hips and rested there.

She nodded as he talked to her and then started laughing. She looked happy. But she *couldn't* be. She was smiling, and seemed glad he was there, but no way that clueless asshole could really make her happy. Every second I watched them together inflamed my anger until I was near the breaking point as I watched them kiss.

Her hand clasped tightly in his, Lucas turned, and led them toward the exit.

I downed the rest of my beer, slamming the glass down on the bar as I stood from the barstool I'd been in since I'd arrived. My feet hit the floor, and I stumbled sideways; I was more drunk than I'd realized.

Stumbling a few more times, I forced my way through the crowd, ignoring the protests of the people I shoved out of my way.

"Hey! You can't leave. You haven't thanked *me* for coming yet!" I shouted, my speech irritatingly slurred courtesy of the alcohol.

Annie and Lucas both stopped and turned. As they did, the blood drained from Annie's face, her eyes widening in... What? Fear? The reaction was unexpected, and it gave me pause as I briefly reconsidered accosting her. But then Lucas spoke, and all rational thought scattered.

"Rob? What's going on? Is everything okay?"

"You're so fucking perfect. Perfect fucking Lucas. Is that why you want him, Annie? Because he's not a fuck-up like me?"

"I'm not sure what's going on, man, but just calm down."

"Is that why you left me, huh?" I continued, ignoring Lucas altogether. "No one here was good enough for you? *I* wasn't good enough for you? What about Charlie? Was *he* good enough for you?!"

Air neither entered nor exited my lungs as I awaited her response, silently begging her to deny it, to say anything to indicate I was wrong. Time crept by as her silence became deafening. Each second clawed out another chunk of my heart, the pain more excruciating than anything I'd ever experienced. In a matter of heartbeats, I had my answer, the one I had begged the universe to not allow to be true.

"That's it, isn't it? I guessed it—you left because of him. That's who you always wanted, but you got stuck with me instead, so you left?"

"What the hell, Rob? Leave her the hell alone!"

Lucas's voice barely registered in the periphery of my consciousness.

"Am I right, Annie? You ruined my fucking life, and I never knew why. But I do now, don't I? Did you ever really care about me? Or was I just your way of trying to get to Charlie?" I paused for the span of a single harsh breath. "Fucking answer me, Annie! You owe me that goddamn much!"

I kept shouting even as some of Lucas's employees started forcing me away from her. I shoved hard, breaking free of them.

"Get the fuck off me! I'm leaving anyway, now that I know she's the slut Charlie always tried to tell me she was."

My traitorous eyes were still fixed on her where she hadn't moved, though I knew she must have been able to hear me. She just stood there, her chest rising and falling rapidly as tears tracked down her face. Why the fuck did she look haunted, like she was seeing a ghost?

I closed my eyes, swaying on my feet as I scrubbed my hand over my face. When I opened them, nothing had changed, but I was too drunk to think through the possible implications of her unexpected reaction to my accusations. Besides, being drunk and heartbroken was probably the only reason I thought she looked that way.

Wishful fucking thinking.

Lucas was talking to her, too quietly for me to hear him, and using his hands to tug at her, trying to turn her around, but she still wasn't moving at all, not even blinking. Only her chest moved, heaving up and down as if she was having trouble breathing. I glanced in Lucas's direction when he looked up, recognizing what I saw in his face: barely contained rage.

I glared back, daring him to do something. I was in the mood to fight. After a few moments, however, he turned back to Annie, who still hadn't moved. I almost lost the battle I waged to keep from checking on her, making sure she was okay. My concern for her, worry over the cause of the haunted look on her face, wanted to take over. But I managed to stumble past them, the pain in my chest growing as I did so until it eclipsed the anger.

Which emotion held the most prominent position quickly reversed back to a more normal state with each step closer to my house.

My house. How fucking hilarious.

The house I had bought because *she* loved it. The house I had decorated the way *she* always wanted to. The house I had been saving for *her* for all those years, hoping she'd come back one day. I'd had no idea how wrong I'd been about her.

Fuck it, I'd sell the lot after bulldozing the fucking house.

By the time I reached my property, I was so filled with hostility that I could scarcely breathe. I knew I had to do something to get it out. Something to distract from what I'd just found out, something to keep me numb. No, my heavy bag was nowhere near enough to do the trick. Thank fuck I had Charlie—he'd know what to do to get it out of my system.

I couldn't believe it. Charlie was gone. The one fucking time I actually wanted to do something destructive, he was fucking gone.

I hadn't kept alcohol in the house since I'd bought the damn thing, so that meant I'd need to find a bar. As I turned to make my way back to the front door, there was a loud banging from that direction.

"I thought you'd gone out for the night, asshole! I'm ready now, let's go start some shit somewhere," I called as I swung the door open, only to be immediately shoved backward by Lucas, his face contorted in anger.

"You need to start talking *now*. I don't know what the fuck is going on, and someone's going to tell me."

A growl ripped up my throat as I lunged at him, sending us both flying down the porch stairs. As we scrambled to our feet, I charged him again. He fought defensively, but both of us still ended up taking hits to the face, chest, and gut. I was much bigger, much stronger, and way fucking angrier than Lucas, but he fought better than I ever would have guessed he could, and I was utterly shitfaced. After a while, he gained the advantage and pinned me to the ground with my face in the dirt.

"This is the first time I've ever seen you pissed. How the fuck do you know how to fight, asshole?" I ground out.

"What the hell, Rob?" he shouted. "You said you knew who she was. That's it! But you accused her of ruining your life. That's a lot more than just knowing who she is. What the hell is your history with her, huh?"

I bucked backward, trying to get free, but I didn't really stand a chance with that much alcohol coursing through my veins and eventually gave up my struggle.

"Why the fuck do *you* care? She wants *you*. Our history doesn't fucking matter."

"You verbally attacked her, Rob. You called her a slut, for God's sake! And she was so... so... I don't know, but *something* that she passed out!"

"Is she okay?"

"She's fine now, but this is what I'm talking about. What's the deal with you guys?"

"Why don't you go ask your fucking girlfriend?" I spat out.

My moment of concern over Annie's wellbeing had disappeared the instant Lucas had started talking again, a reminder that she had chosen him.

"Why are you being such a dick? Look, forget it, just leave her the hell alone. Stay away from her."

His weight lifted, and from my position prone on the ground, I could see his feet as he moved away.

"Fuck you, Lucas!"

I'd shouted, but he didn't reply as he walked away, leaving me on the cold ground. Alone.

chapter eleven

annie

After a long bath, I sat on the porch to wait for Lucas. Two hours later, it was evident to me that I'd lost him, too. He was either gone already, or he would be if I told him about my past the way he'd asked before his sudden departure. I remained where I was, unable to summon enough will to move inside, hugging my knees to my chest and staring into the darkness that had fallen.

I was shocked when Lucas walked onto the porch sometime later, stopping to stare at me in silence, his expression inscrutable. After a few moments, he continued across the porch and opened the front door, passing inside without waiting for me. Scrambling after him, I locked the front door behind me out of habit.

Lucas didn't slow until he reached the hutch in the dining room, and with a deep sigh, poured himself a healthy shot of bourbon. My arms provided little comfort wrapped around me where I stood off to the side and watched. He swirled the glass, the amber liquid that matched his eyes shifting around as he stared at it before suddenly tossing the contents into his mouth and refilling his glass. His eyes were stormy when he turned and considered me for a moment as he slowly swallowed. My vision tunneled and my breathing shallowed under his extended scrutiny.

"I think we should talk," he said without emotion, finally breaking the silence between us as he handed me my own glass of bourbon.

I'd never really liked bourbon, or doing shots of anything, for that matter, but I opened my mouth and tipped the glass back, pouring every drop of the liquid down my throat as I fought my reflexive response to spit it out. I couldn't stop the cough that followed, though, as I handed the empty glass back to Lucas and walked to the living room. When he brought me another, I downed that one, too, already noticing the warmth flooding my body from the first one, bringing with it a welcome numbness. Really, I would have downed as many of those glasses as I needed, as many as he wanted to bring to me, to stave off the conversation looming over my head.

But he simply held my glass after I handed it back to him the second time, and I understood that the time had come. I'd been standing in front of a chair in the living room and I sat, wanting to feel smaller, to shrink away as much as I could before the inevitable happened. Lucas remained standing as he cleared his throat and I braced myself for whatever he was about to say.

"This is new territory for me," he began. "I've never really been in a relationship before you. Not something serious, anyway. I've never been a jealous person. And except when my mother died, I've never really gotten angry about anything. Those things just aren't who I am. But something's going on between you and Rob, and I'm completely in the dark. And I'm pissed off about it." He took and released a deep breath before continuing. "I've respected your desire for privacy, for secrecy. I've never pushed you about any of the many things you never want to talk about. But I need to know what the deal is with you and Rob."

I should have known better than to lift my head as he finished speaking; his eyes, filled with pain and confusion, captured mine and held them with a determined intensity.

I couldn't tell him, though. He'd hate me. He'd be disgusted.

"Annie," his voice cracked on my name as his eyes became glassy. He took a deep breath, then continued. "I love you. I never wanted to, but it's too late. I love you. But I can't continue down this road with you if you're keeping me in the dark. I *need* to understand. Rob is—*was*—my friend, but we beat the shit out of each other tonight. Because of you. I think I deserve to know why."

I started begging shamelessly, barely cognizant of the wetness expanding across my cheeks. I'd known it was coming, but now that it had arrived, I couldn't accept the end of our relationship.

"Please, don't make me do this, please don't."

"You have to, Annie. I can't do this blindly anymore, it's not fair. I mean... hell, Annie. I practically live here with you, but, really, I barely know anything about you from before we met. I'm begging you. Trust me enough to tell me. Tell me why you have horrible nightmares. Tell me why you won't talk about your past. Tell me why you hyperventilated tonight when Rob confronted you. Just tell me *something*! I mean, I keep imagining the worst possible scenarios. Has Rob hurt you? Is that what's going on? Instead of fighting with him, should I have called the police? Annie, please. I love you. But you have to tell me what the hell is going on. I'm begging you, sweetheart. Trust me."

I wanted so badly to believe him, but there was no way he would stay once he knew. But he was also already on his way out, and I was positively desperate to keep that from happening, so I had to take the risk.

"He's right." My voice was scarcely a whisper, but it was all I could manage.

"What? He's right? Right about what?"

"About me."

"What? You're not making sense. *What* was he right about?"

I swallowed, my saliva thickening in my throat and gluing my tongue to the roof of my mouth. My body was trying to suffocate me, but this time I didn't mind—any distraction was welcome.

"R-Rob and I dated... in high school. I broke up with him our senior year because... because of..." The deep breath I tried to take in refused to enter my lungs. Closing my eyes, I pretended my audience was the furniture, the wall—anything that couldn't talk back. Anything but Lucas. "Because of Charlie."

"Rob's asshole brother?"

"Yes," I squeaked out, but the living room walls were closing in on me, crushing my chest as they moved, keeping me from breathing. It was all too much; I had to get out. Leaping to my feet, I pushed past Lucas to the front door, but was slowed by fumbling with the lock; my hands shook so violently I couldn't get it open.

Lucas was there beside me in an instant, leaning on the door and gently stilling my hands.

"Annie. Sweetheart," he said softly, soothingly. "I'm trying to understand, that's all. So, you're saying that you and Charlie were together?"

I nodded almost imperceptibly.

"Okay. So, you dated Charlie, had sex with Charlie, something, whatever, doesn't matter. Aside from them being brothers, why is that such a big deal?"

My jaw clamped shut; that was territory I was incapable of entering.

"Unless..." his voice trailed off as he looked thoughtfully into space, and I knew he was putting together the pieces. "Unless you were dating Rob when it happened?"

I couldn't reply, but my chin fell lower in shame. Soon Lucas would understand, and he, too, would be disgusted. Though nothing he felt could ever touch my own self-loathing and regret at what had transpired.

"You slept with Charlie while you were dating Rob?" Lucas asked, incredulous.

In reality, it couldn't have been more than a second, two at most, before nausea overwhelmed me, but it felt more like years that I was standing before Lucas in judgment, the shock and distaste in his voice poisoning the air around us.

Lucas was gone when I was finally able to leave the bathroom. I felt... empty, numb. It was familiar, but no longer welcome. I'd gotten used to not feeling so alone, so isolated. Used to not needing to shut off all of my emotions.

I started for the kitchen, the realization that I'd barely had a cup of tea alone in months bringing me to a halt.

Tea was for comfort. I'd brought the situation on myself and deserved everything I felt.

Turning, I shuffled slowly through the house, turning off lights as I went. As each light was extinguished, plunging the house deeper into darkness, the anguish inside grew, pulling me back to my dark and lonely reality, the one I'd pretended for a time to have escaped. The blackness that surrounded me was familiar and provided a wretched comfort as it began to envelop me once more. My hands shook—large, jerky movements—as I reached for the last light, the only thing remaining to keep me from being swallowed whole by the darkness. Knowledge that I deserved it was of little consolation as my fingers twisted the switch rod.

Click.

chapter twelve

annie

Lucas looked like hell standing on my porch, dark circles ringing his eyes, bruises on his face. From his fight with Rob? How had I missed them the night before?

His exhaustion was palpable but did nothing to take the edge off the severity of his gaze.

"People are who they are," Lucas began. "They never really change—not the important things, anyway. And honesty, faithfulness, those are important things."

He took a deep breath and released it slowly, his stormy eyes never wavering from mine.

"So, I've been up all night trying to reconcile Annie the cheater with the Annie that I know, and I can't. I can't imagine you ever doing something like that. But I also realize there's obviously a lot I don't know about you because I had no idea until yesterday that you and Rob had any kind of history."

He paused, inhaling deeply again as he rubbed the back of his neck with his hand, shifting his gaze down toward his feet. I wanted to interject, to stop him from continuing, from doing the inevitable, but I couldn't seem to make my body obey my mind.

"Look, I realize that I might have been unfair to you last night because I was taken by surprise that there was history between you guys that no one wanted to tell me about. And I'm sorry for jumping to conclusions that I really had no right to make because I was pissed about that. You have never tried to hide the fact that there are things you don't want to talk about, it's not like you were pretending that I knew everything or making things up. I've never before had a reason to doubt you."

He swallowed and shook his head before raising it and again capturing my eyes. I should have looked away, but it was too late, the pain in Lucas's eyes held me captive.

"What I'm getting at is this: I'm sorry for walking out last night. I shouldn't have done that. But I *do* need you to explain what happened with Rob and Charlie."

His eyes were begging me to talk to him. But I couldn't, I'd never spoken to anyone about it before, I'd sworn to myself that I never would.

"Please, anything else. I can do anything else, but... not this. I just... I can't."

"You have to. You *have* to trust me. That's what you do when you love someone. You take a chance, and you trust them. You... you do love me, too, don't you?" he asked shakily, his eyes betraying his vulnerability.

Love? Oh, god.

"Lucas... I can't."

"Is there something going on between you and Rob right now?"

I shook my head.

"Has anything happened between you guys since I've known you?"

"No," I whispered back.

"Have you lied to me about anything?"

"No."

"Then I'm not going to hold anything against you. But you have to talk to me. I need honesty and openness. Or I can't stay in this relationship."

I wanted to believe him; I really did. I knew right then that I loved him, somehow. I'd never thought it would be possible to love someone after Rob, but I did.

But I *couldn't* do what he was asking. I opened my mouth to try to explain, in some way, that what he wanted was more than I was capable of giving to him, to beg him to stay if I had to, but no sound came out.

He sighed, his eyes falling, his shoulders sagging.

"I haven't slept, and you look like you haven't either. I'm going to go home and rest. You should do the same. Then I need to think about whether or not I can be okay with knowing there are things you're hiding from me."

Lucas seemed undecided, almost like he was waiting for something, like he'd said those words without having really meant them. I got the sense he'd expected them to loosen my tongue. And I felt that I was failing him, that I was letting him down when I remained frozen, but I didn't have a choice. After the span of a few breaths, he got into his car and pulled away.

chapter thirteen

rob

"**What the fuck** happened to *you*, little bro?" Charlie laughed. "You fall off the wagon and get the shit kicked out of you? Sorry I missed it. Looks like you had one hell of a good night."

I groaned as Charlie continued laughing, kicking at my legs just lightly enough not to cause any real damage. My head throbbed, making it immeasurably more difficult to fight through the fog shrouding my brain to figure out why the fuck I was lying in my front yard.

As hard as I tried, I just couldn't remember, at least not while my temples were in a vice. As I moved to push up to my hands and knees, pain shot up through my hand and I promptly fell back down. A quick glance revealed that my knuckles were painted with dried blood, and I realized I must have been in a fight as pain signals from the rest of my body began to register rapid fire. I felt like I'd been hit by a fucking train.

"I don't remember. I can't fucking think straight right now. And I think I broke fucking everything in my hand. Help me up, man."

He extended a hand and pulled me to my feet, his laughter exacerbating the pounding in my head.

As I got my feet under me, I scanned the yard, looking for a clue to what had happened the night before. As I turned, I noticed Lucas walking out of his grandmother's house and something tugged at the recesses of my mind. He glanced in my direction and froze, his face masked in hatred.

I stared back, confused until I noticed the bruises on his face. Actually, he looked like shit, like...

Oh, fuck.

The night before started to come back: confronting Annie, her confirmation of my worst fears, fighting with Lucas. All of it.

Regret teased the surface, but blind anger quickly took over.

"Wanna go again, asshole?" I shouted belligerently.

Lucas's eyes flashed, and I thought for a moment that he might take me up on the offer when I was distracted by Charlie's raucous laughter.

"That's the asshole who kicked your ass, you pussy? I didn't think that fucker had it in him. Way to go, Lucas! I'm proud of you!" He laughed as he turned and started up the porch steps. "So, what happened? He fuck your girl or something?"

I could feel the desire for violence flare at his words. "Something like that."

"You're such a fucking pussy, man. You always get your panties in a twist over some tits and ass. Remember how whipped you were over that one slut, Annie? Then she left your ass, just like I fucking told you she would."

"Shut the fuck up!"

I started to lunge toward him, but the pounding in my head threw off my balance and he easily side-stepped me.

"Take it easy, little bro—you wouldn't stand a fucking chance right now. And I have no problem beating your ass to teach you a lesson if you fucking hit me."

"Fuck you, Charlie. I can take your ass any day."

I knew that was mostly untrue. I'd said it to bait him because I wanted to hit someone. But he just laughed again as he walked inside.

"Come on, little bro. I've got a hangover cure for you."

Tamping down and steadfastly ignoring any reservations about doing shit I'd promised myself I was done with, I followed him inside.

chapter fourteen

annie

My eyes darted around nervously as I rang the doorbell. Three weeks after my birthday party, I'd finally reached the point where I could no longer handle being alone with my thoughts; I needed someone to talk to. But my options were limited, or I never would have been standing where I was, risking seeing Rob. I glanced behind me at Mrs. Renner's driveway for assurance that her car was the only one there. At least I wouldn't have to worry about running into Lucas.

"Annie?"

My stomach bottomed out as my heart slammed against my ribs in a bid to escape.

"L-Lucas... I'm sorry—I wanted—I'll go. I'll come back, I'm sorry. I didn't realize you...sorry."

I flipped around, ready to flee, but Lucas grabbed my hand before I had a chance, his grip firm as he gently pulled me back around to face him.

"It's fine," he said softly. "I was leaving anyway. I have to get back to the brewery. I just ran up here to help her with some planting before the freeze we're supposed to get tonight."

Before I had a chance to think and stop myself, I blurted out, "I thought Rob helped her with yard work."

"He did, but he hasn't been around since..." his voice trailed off as he looked at me, his eyes full of emotion I wasn't prepared to deal with, so I had to look away. "Anyway, he hasn't been around, so I'm helping her. But I'm leaving, you can go in. I know she'll be happy to see you."

More guilt settled onto the pile of shitty things I felt. I would have known she needed help if I'd been there myself, but I hadn't seen her since my birthday either. In fact, the only reason I'd stepped outside my mom's house since Lucas had left me standing on the porch the morning after my birthday had been to buy a few groceries, and I'd barely done that. I couldn't keep much down and had more or less given up trying, so my need for food had been minimal.

When I realized my hand was still in Lucas's, his thumb smoothing across the back of it, I yanked it back, keenly aware of the coldness settling over me at the loss of contact. Without looking up, I stepped around him and walked inside, turning to close the front door, his words wafting in just as the door clicked into place.

"I've missed you, sweetheart."

I stood for a moment with my hand on the door, hearing him call me sweetheart nearly enough to make me go running after him. Nearly. But instead, I continued inside.

"I was wondering when you'd show up again." Mrs. Renner's tone was almost reprimanding, but not quite.

"I'm sorry. I shouldn't have stayed away."

"At least this time it was only a few weeks instead of years," she replied with a wink. "Come on, let's have a cup of tea."

She sat at the kitchen table while I made us a cup of tea, her eyes following me as I moved around gathering the mugs and teabags. After I'd filled the kettle and turned the stove on, I couldn't stand the silence anymore.

"Why aren't you mad at me?" I blurted out.

"Why would I be mad at you, honey?"

"About Lucas."

She laughed. "He's a grown man. He doesn't need his grandmother to defend him. Besides, who says it shouldn't be the other way around? That I shouldn't be mad at *him*?"

"He didn't do anything wrong. Everything is my fault, not his."

"No one is ever blameless, Annie. It takes two people to have a relationship."

Silence settled after her words while I mulled them over, trying to figure out where Lucas could have possibly had any blame in what happened between us. When the kettle whistled, I got up and poured the water over our tea bags. After setting our mugs on the table, I sat back down across from Mrs. Renner, mindlessly watching the steam rise from my cup.

"Annie," she said a few minutes later, so softly I barely heard her. "Why didn't you tell me?"

My eyes flew up to find her watching me with so much pain and sadness on her face that she *must* have known. But, how could she? I felt like a deer in headlights under her stare, unable to move or look away.

"Tell you what?" I asked as my heart pounded in my chest.

"What happened."

"What?"

She sighed. "With Charlie."

"What happened with Ch-Charlie?"

As hard as I tried to sound nonchalant, I knew my voice was shaking and I could hardly speak Charlie's name.

Mrs. Renner's voice was uncharacteristically gentle when she continued. "I always knew that something had happened to you when you up and disappeared from everyone. When you came back earlier this year, and Rob heard you talking about Charlie in your sleep, I had a hunch. But then Lucas came over here a few days after your birthday, needing someone to talk to about what had happened between you guys. He told me what you said to him. That's when I figured it out."

My face burned with shame and self-disgust as I swallowed hard, not even trying to fight the tears as I stared into nothingness, my heart fluttering wildly.

"You don't know the whole story. You just said yourself that no one is ever blameless."

"Tell me, then. Annie, honey, I've known you for most of your life, and I care about you like you're my own flesh and blood. I'm not going anywhere. I've never once judged you, and I'm not about to start now, so out with it already."

"I let him," the words rushed out.

"Okay. Why?"

"Why doesn't matter—I didn't stop it."

"It *does* matter. Tell me why. You wanted it?"

I shoved up angrily from the table. "How can you ask me something like that?! You know more than anyone else how I felt about him!"

"Then why didn't you stop him?"

"I don't know!"

"Yes, you do. Why didn't you stop him, Annie?"

"I... I couldn't, all right! I was so scared. All I could think about was that I didn't want him to hurt me. All those times Dwayne had touched me, if I kept still, he wouldn't hurt me, and it would be over faster. I begged him to stop, but... The more I struggled, the more he was hurting me, so I stopped and just let him do what he wanted with me."

My arms would have come out of their sockets if I wrapped them any more tightly around myself, but it was nowhere near tightly enough to hold in the shame and pain that overflowed from deep within my soul.

"Annie, honey. That's rape."

"No. I let him do it. I didn't fight him."

"Listen to me, young lady. You did nothing wrong. You are not in any way responsible. That man raped you. Do you understand me? You didn't just let him do it. You said no, you did what you could, Annie. If you had struggled more than you did, he might have..."

Mrs. Renner didn't finish her thought, but she didn't have to. We sat without talking for a long time, the only sound my sobs as she rubbed my back soothingly, guiding me to sit back down in my chair.

Long after my tear ducts had emptied themselves and everything below my waist had lost feeling from lack of movement, I finally asked what I was afraid of finding out, the only thing I had left to hold on to, to give me any comfort from the ordeal.

"Does he know?" I asked, sick at the prospect.

"No."

I nodded in relief. Rob could never find out.

"What about Lucas?"

"No, honey, he doesn't know either."

After several minutes of the only sounds our breathing and the clicking from the heat pumping throughout the old house, Mrs. Renner spoke again.

"Why are you with Lucas?"

"I'm not."

"But you were. Why? Why not Rob?"

"He made me happy. It was simple, I didn't have to think about all the... bad. And he accepted that, was okay with me having flaws and not wanting to talk about them, and he cared about me anyway."

"You love him, honey?"

I paused before responding. "Y-yes... I do... but..."

"But he's not Rob," Mrs. Renner whispered, finishing my words for me.

Nodding in confirmation, I said, "They're so different. Rob... he could always see into my soul with a glance. I never had to try to explain why I was the way I was, he just *knew*. But there was also never anywhere to hide, to get away from his intensity. The weight of his expectations, his need for me was crushing. When I came back to town, I had never expected to see him again. And we could never have a future together anyway because of what happened with his brother."

I swallowed, drowning in guilt for comparing the two men I cared about, but I felt like I owed an explanation to Mrs. Renner.

"Lucas is so different. He calmed me from the first time I met him. That's never happened before, you know? Rather than feeling like my issues were understood, I felt like they just... didn't matter. But in a good way, almost like I've escaped it all when we're together. He didn't make me dredge things up and discuss them, he just accepted that I had issues and didn't want to talk—Rob never would have accepted that. He always forced me to tell him everything; he didn't *care* that I didn't want to talk about them. With Lucas, it was like taking a vacation. I could just pack it all away and leave it when I was with him. At least until what happened at the party."

"Packing it away and leaving it alone isn't escaping, honey, it's just hiding. You'll never escape until you've confronted it all and learned to live with it. I'm not saying you should be with either of them, but Rob's way—while more painful—might be better for you in the long run."

"It doesn't matter. Rob can never find out. No matter what happened in the past, Charlie is the only family he has. I can't take that away from him."

"You wouldn't be taking anything away from him by telling him. Charlie's the one who did that when he raped you. The only thing you're taking away from Rob is his right to make his own decisions."

"No! I can't do it. Telling him would crush him. I can't do that to him, I can't hurt him like that. He's been hurt so much in his life already, let down by so many people already. Knowing about Charlie? God, it would destroy him. And it wouldn't even accomplish anything anyway. Rob's jealous, he's possessive. He'd never want me after knowing his brother had me first."

"You know, you're pretty stupid sometimes for someone who's supposed to be so smart, young lady."

She didn't know Rob like I did. She couldn't possibly understand what I did. A wave of exhaustion washed over me, and I thought I might keel over if someone breathed too hard in my direction. I knew I should go back home, but I desperately didn't want to be so utterly alone again. Not yet.

"May I lay down for a while?"

"Of course, honey, you can stay as long as you like. The guest room's all made up, you can rest in there."

"Thank you."

I rose and shuffled to the guest room unsteadily, my legs not very cooperative in performing their duties in transporting me. Once I climbed under the covers and rested my head on the pillow, I drifted off quickly into a mercifully dreamless sleep.

Lucas's hushed voice on the other side of the door sometime later in the day woke me.

"I won't bother her, I promise, Grams."

"Leave her be, grandson. You can see her when she wakes up. But I don't want you here if you're going to argue with her. She's been through enough already."

"No, Grams, I don't wanna argue with her. I, uh, I heard you guys talking earlier. I left, but I turned around before I got too far. I wanted to talk to her. When I came through the door, you guys were shouting at each other, though, so you didn't hear me.

"How much did you hear?"

"I heard her telling you what happened with Charlie and I left after you explained to her that it was rape. I wanted to stay, to tell her how sorry I was... but I felt guilty for eavesdropping, so I left again."

"She's going to be upset that you heard."

"I'm glad I did. I couldn't imagine Annie being the kind of person who would cheat on someone, who would be interested in someone like Charlie. But I also couldn't understand why she would say Rob was right to call her a slut and then tell me that she'd slept with him if that wasn't the case. But I get it now."

"I'm guessing you know that Annie was dating Rob when it happened and—"

"You don't have to tell me that she loved him, I know that already," Lucas interrupted angrily.

"No, not that. But she was a virgin."

"What?"

"Don't you know anything at all about Annie's past?"

"No, she's not comfortable talking about it. I would never try to force her to do something that upsets her."

"Grandson! I'm ashamed of you! When she said you didn't make her talk about things, I didn't realize she meant that you didn't know a damn thing about her! What did you do? Spend all your time talking about yourself? Look, it's not my place to tell you this stuff, you need to talk to her about it, but before Miriam, she was exposed to a lot of neglect and abuse, including sexual abuse."

I cringed, knowing that Lucas would be disgusted, and he didn't even know the details of what had happened. I could feel the dirt crawling across my skin, sticking to it, the kind of filth that couldn't be washed away with soap and water.

I would know, because I'd tried.

"Oh, god, Grams, I had no idea. I need to see her."

"Don't wake her up, young man. I mean it."

chapter fifteen

annie

After I heard Mrs. Renner and Lucas talking about me, I knew Lucas would want nothing to do with me, not once everything had a chance to sink in and he realized how damaged and tainted I really was. So, when he quietly stepped into the guest room, I pretended I was still asleep, giving a moment of thanks that my back was toward the door. His feet shuffled mutedly across the rug a few steps, then stopped, followed by silence for several minutes. When he finally began to speak, his voice was soft and thick with emotion.

"Annie, sweetheart, I am so sorry about what happened to you. I didn't know, but I should have had more faith in you. I wish I knew what I could do to help, but I don't. All I know is that I love you, and I miss you. And I promise to do better if you let me."

He wouldn't feel the same way once the shock and pity had an opportunity to wear off. He'd always know that I didn't fight back.

I didn't speak, silently listening as he continued to talk, apologizing over and over and telling me how much he'd missed me, how much he loved me. Instead of interrupting to tell him he'd done nothing wrong, that it was *my* fault, I let him say everything he wanted to get off his chest before asking to be left alone. He was reluctant to leave, so I forced myself to get up and go back to my mom's house. Really, I shouldn't have even gone to Mrs. Renner's in the first place; she didn't need the extra burden at her age.

Mrs. Renner succeeded in talking me into seeing a therapist. Slowly, painfully, I began to see that what had transpired with Charlie was, as Mrs. Renner had told me, rape. That I really didn't have responsibility for what had happened, that I really couldn't have done anything more to stop it. What I had seen as my complicity when I'd stopped fighting was really my body taking over for self-preservation. It was nothing I should have been ashamed for, though it would take a long time to rid myself of the years of shame and self-disgust I'd amassed as a result.

I resumed my volunteer schedule at the library and even started a program for providing books and reading services to the elderly members of the community. The idea had formed after Mrs. Renner asked me to drop some books off with a shut-in friend of hers when she hadn't felt well enough to make her regular weekly visit.

And though I expected it, waited for it to happen, Lucas never had a change of heart. He came by most mornings before he went to the brewery for the day. I wouldn't have let him in, but he sat on the porch and waited, and it was too cold to leave him out there. I didn't understand why he never used the key he still had, but I was grateful. It meant he was coming in on *my* terms and I appreciated the little bit of control that gave me.

He didn't try to make me talk, though I knew he wanted me to; instead, he told me about the happenings at the brewery the day before and his plans for the rest of the day. When he ran out of work-related topics of conversation, he talked about the future, things he wanted to show me or experience with me. Most of it didn't sound like activities I'd ever had an interest in before, but the fact that he wanted to share things he was passionate about with *me* crumbled my resolve to remain aloof from him and brought me closer to believing he might actually stay.

chapter sixteen

annie

It was several days before Thanksgiving, and there was already a lot to be done. The only two real friends I had, Carol and Haley, were coming to visit for the first time since I'd begun house-sitting for Mom. I held out hope that my sister, Lori, would show up at some point, but I wasn't counting on it. Dependability was not one of her strengths.

With Lucas's help, I had organized an open house so anyone in need in the community would have somewhere to enjoy a hot meal and friendship on Thanksgiving. The idea had been born out of my reading hour at the library when one of the children had requested I read a book about Thanksgiving. As was my custom when I received a special request, I asked why she had chosen that book. She'd responded that she wanted to see all the food she might get to eat at her own Thanksgiving one day since her family barely could afford food on a daily basis. Her words had broken my heart, reminding me of my life before I'd met Mom, when I'd known true hunger.

My first iteration of the Community Thanksgiving concept had been to hold it at my mom's house, but there was so much community support for the idea that Lucas had offered to use the brewery to host it since it could accommodate significantly more people.

With the volume of food we were going to need, we had to start cooking days in advance. Luckily, the local catering business was supplying all the chafers, plates, bowls, and utensils for the event and the local bakery was donating fifteen pies and cakes as well as ten trays of cookies. Even so, I had spent the whole day running around from store to store, trying to gather everything needed to prepare the meal and dropping items off with various community members who had volunteered to cook as well. Support for the event had been staggering; every grocery store in the county volunteered to donate turkeys or stuffing mix or green beans and yams—you name it. It was heartwarming to see the community so interested in helping, but it made for one hell of a tiring day.

Lucas had intended to split the running around with me to alleviate the burden, but someone at the brewery had called out sick, and he hadn't been able to find anyone else to fill in. After eating dinner and cleaning the kitchen, I built a fire and settled down with a book on the sofa, so exhausted that I dozed off before I'd even made it through a full page.

Sometime later, groggy with sleep, I realized my reading light was off.

Wasn't it on when I fell asleep?

I opened my eyes, but the room was shrouded in darkness. The sun had set, and the fire had burned down to embers. Movement in the next room seized my attention, and my heart stuttered painfully as I realized someone was moving around in the dark.

The figure quietly approached, and, just as in my nightmares, I was paralyzed with fear, unable to move or even make a sound. As the intruder passed in front of the fireplace, there was just enough light for me to discern who it was as Lucas reached in to place a fresh log on the coals. An involuntary animalistic sound of relief escaped my throat as I began to shake uncontrollably.

"Annie? I thought you were sleeping. What's wrong?" Lucas asked in alarm.

My body still in the throes of the subsiding fear-driven adrenaline, I struggled to catch my breath and just shook my head, practically falling into his arms when he sat beside me.

"What happened? Are you hurt? What's going on?"

"I... I woke up, and I thought... I didn't know you were here. I fell asleep, and I didn't know who..." I was unable to finish, hysteria threatening to take over.

"Shh, it's okay. It's just me, no one's here. You're safe."

Once I'd stopped crying and shaking, I remained wrapped in his arms with my head on his chest, allowing the feeling of safety his heartbeat cultivated lull me into a state of calm.

"I don't think I'll ever tire of seeing the firelight play across your face," he said softly. He paused, swallowing loudly. "You know, I can't even remember what my life was like before you, before that day you knocked on Grams' door. The past eight months have been the best eight months of my life. I love you so much, sweetheart."

"I love you, too."

I couldn't believe how easy that was to say. And it was one-hundred percent true, though it was the first time I'd told him.

"You have no idea how happy that makes me."

I turned to find him studying my face in earnest, his eyes confirming the truth of his words. His face drew closer until his lips were pressing into mine, soft and warm and perfect, and my blood warmed as it raced through my veins. Lucas rested his forehead against mine as he paused, his breathing labored. Then he kissed me again. Still soft, but more insistent this time, his hands moving to cradle my face and hold me gently in place. My heart rate shot through the roof as desire and anxiety bloomed in tandem.

I was only dimly aware that we had shifted. I was lying back on the sofa and Lucas had lowered himself over me by the time I fully registered what was happening. Suddenly, the air around me was stiflingly hot—suffocating, really—and I struggled to breathe. As I opened my mouth to tell him I needed space, he whispered against my ear, his voice filled with emotion.

"I love you."

His words gave me pause, but when he rested his weight on top of me, I felt his erection pressing into me. Before I realized what was happening, I'd shoved him away, sending him toppling to the floor.

"Oh, my god, I'm sorry, I'm so sorry, I didn't mean to, I swear, I'm—"

"Annie," he interrupted me gently as he got to his feet, his voice sad. "Don't apologize. I understand. I mean, I don't, I can't possibly understand, what an insensitive thing for me to say, but I'm trying to. I don't want to push you. I..." He trailed off, as his eyes stared into the distance for a moment before refocusing on me.

Guilt delivered a swift and heavy blow, squeezing my heart in a vice. He'd been so patient already; I owed it to him to try. Besides, I was so sick of being controlled by what happened to me.

Maybe this would help me to finally get past Charlie. Right? I swallowed dryly as I tried to untangle my jumbled and contradictory emotions.

"H-help me... help me get him out of my head."

After a short hesitation during which Lucas seemed undecided, he climbed back onto the sofa with me, pulling me into his arms and holding me for several moments before his hands framed my face.

"Are you sure?" he asked gently, his eyes searching mine.

I nodded, though I didn't feel any of the certainty I was attempting to project. Lucas closed the distance between us and kissed me softly, patiently, coaxing my desire to the forefront once more. His hands skimmed my sides as we shifted until he was stretched over me again, but this time I was prepared and was able to fight the urge to push him away when he rested his weight on top of me.

It's Lucas, he won't hurt me.

I believed what I told myself, but it was hard to remember as his erection grew, his breathing choppy as his hips rocked into me. The only thing I could think about, the only thing I could remember was Charlie, panting and grinding into me while I was pinned down by my neck.

"Lucas, I can't—"

"It's okay, sweetheart, I won't hurt you. I would never hurt you. I love you."

I knew what he said was true and tried to use that knowledge to swallow my mounting panic as his lips moved down my neck. But the cocktail of fear and desire in my blood battled each other, making my mind even harder to control.

I want this. I need to get Charlie out of my head, and this is how. I really do want this.

The words became my mantra, but with every repetition, they rang less true. Yet, at the same time, my blood continued to heat, desire continued to flow freely through my body, which didn't make any sense at all.

Lucas kissed me with a deepening urgency, and I wanted him to continue, but I also wanted to scream at him to stop. I thought for a moment he had somehow read my mind when he pulled away, but then his shirt was coming off, followed by the rest of his clothing. I turned away from him, focused on willing away the tension and fear, the embarrassment that his nakedness created.

As he leaned over to remove my clothes, slowly peeling them off as he trailed his fingers along my skin, my whole body went from flaming to numb; suddenly, I felt nothing.

And then I was naked, wishing it could all just be over with.

"You're so beautiful."

His whispered words were full of love, full of reverence, but I only felt embarrassed, dirty, and wished for a way to extricate myself from the situation I'd agreed to in the first place. But I didn't find one that wouldn't involve hurting Lucas. Besides, a normal woman should *want* to have sex with her boyfriend.

And I did. But I also didn't.

My eyes squeezed shut when I saw him pull a condom from his wallet and begin tearing the wrapper. And I tried desperately to imagine myself somewhere, *anywhere* else. However, that backfired, conjuring images of Charlie, so I forced them open again and stared blindly in the direction of the ceiling, reminding myself over and over and over again that I really did want to be doing what I was.

Didn't I?

Lucas lowered himself between my legs, his unsteady fingers gentle as they guided my knees apart. Once his weight was resting on me, he cradled my face with his hands. After brushing his lips against my cheek, which sparked a confusing rush of love and hormones, his lips found mine again as he started slowly pushing himself in.

At first, the pressure was akin to slight discomfort, but that quickly grew until it had passed the threshold into pain territory. I inhaled sharply at the unpleasant and painful intrusion and Lucas, who I could only assume had mistaken my small gasp of surprise for one of pleasure, rocked his hips forward until he could go no further.

I had been reasonably sure that nothing consensual could ever compare to the horror of what had happened with Charlie, but the pain was inarguably reminiscent of that experience. Though I tried to hold it in, a small cry escaped.

Lucas froze, his breath choppy across my face and his hands trembling against my cheeks.

"Did I hurt you?" he asked, despondent.

"I'm okay," I managed to get out around the effort I was making to hold back my tears, and it must have been enough; he showered my face with lingering, chaste kisses as his hips slowly began to move.

I wanted to be happy I was sharing such intimacy with him. And I was, but I also wasn't. I wanted to feel liberated that I was having sex for the first time since Charlie raped me. And I did, but I also didn't. I wanted to be able to communicate how I felt. But I couldn't. I wanted us to be connected enough for him to understand that I was so conflicted without having to say it aloud.

But we weren't.

chapter seventeen

annie

The sunlight beginning to brighten the sky outside the window coaxed me into a sleepy state of wakefulness. My eyes still closed, I thought back to the events of the night before. Sex had hurt. A lot. But it was also over. I had finally done it for the first time since Charlie. My face burned with embarrassment and shame, but even so, I could make out a glimmer of hope, however small, that I hadn't been able to find the night before. As difficult and unpleasant an experience as it had been, I'd made it through, and I just needed to focus on that.

Lucas shifted in his sleep, his arm tightening around my waist. In less time than it took to blink, I remembered that he had never dressed, and I tensed, uncomfortable with his nakedness so close to me. I, of course, had gotten up after he'd fallen asleep and donned pajamas. I'd really wanted to be alone to try to process what I'd done, but I hadn't wanted his feelings hurt if he woke up and I'd snuck away. So instead, I'd climbed back onto the sofa with him, bringing a blanket to cover us.

God, when was the last time I'd slept on a sofa? It must have been in high school...

And it had been—Rob and I had fallen asleep during a movie.

Rob.

I'd thought back then that he was my happy-ever-after. I'd never believed in them until him. We'd been two perfectly-fitted puzzle pieces, two damaged souls completing each other. A lump formed in my throat as guilt clawed its way deeper. Rob was always supposed to be the only man to ever see me, to ever touch me. And I'd betrayed him, betrayed everything we'd ever had, by having sex with Lucas.

After brushing my teeth, I found Lucas busy in the kitchen. He was lost in thought and didn't notice me approaching, so I watched him from the doorway as he moved around, absentmindedly gathering things. After setting out a mug and putting a tea bag in it, he laid out the cookbooks I'd pulled out to start the cooking for Thanksgiving and began perusing the papers on which I'd recorded the dishes I was responsible for cooking and the timing for each.

As I studied him, I worked to sort out the tangle of emotions that threatened to suffocate me. The only thing I was sure of was that I really *did* love him. As if he could hear my thoughts, his head turned sharply in my direction, his eyes immediately locking onto mine.

"Hey, I didn't hear you come in. Peppermint okay?" he asked, his voice full of hope, his gaze intense.

Lucas had spent enough time with me that he knew I drank peppermint tea when I was feeling upbeat, so I could only assume that he was trying to gauge how I felt after the night before. I wasn't even sure, but there was no reason to make him worry.

"Peppermint sounds perfect."

Relief flickered in his eyes an instant before his broad, boyish smile lit up his face.

"But, would you mind waiting to pour it?" I added. "I'd like to take a quick shower first."

His hand reached out before I'd even finished speaking and twisted the knob to turn the burner off. "Sure."

"Actually, what are you doing? I thought you were going to be at the brewery all day today? Don't you need to leave in a few minutes?"

He leaned his hip against the counter and smirked, mischief in his eyes. "I have decided to play hooky and spend the day with my girlfriend."

"Girlfriend, huh?

"Yes, girlfriend. *My* girlfriend. I know I've shied away from using labels, but it's what you are."

I blushed as a grin tugged at my lips. "Are you sure? I'd love to have you here all day, but not if you need to be at SB."

"I want to spend the day with you, so that's what I'm going to do. Anything that absolutely has to be taken care of has been delegated, and everything else can wait until after the holiday."

"Okay. As long as you're—wait! Did you say after the holiday?"

He padded over to me, his whole face lit up with his irresistible grin, and squeezed my arms affectionately as he kissed my cheek.

"That's right."

"Do you really mean that? I get you for three full days?" I asked with genuine excitement.

Since I'd met him, he'd literally never gone a whole day without going into the brewery for at least a few hours. More than ever, I realized, I wanted to spend some uninterrupted time with him, to explore and sort out the new dimension to our relationship and my feelings for him. And having him near would keep the other thoughts—the unwelcome ones—at bay.

"No, not exactly."

"Oh."

"Unfortunately, it's not three full days. It's actually *four* full days," he said with a smirk. "Other than for the event, I'm not stepping foot back on SB property until Saturday unless the building is burning down."

"You jackass!" I shouted, but I was laughing, too.

"I need to start trusting others to do their jobs. I'm aware I tend to micromanage everything, so I'm letting Nick handle everything for the next few days. He's excited about the opportunity to prove that he can handle the additional management responsibility. And if he does well, which I expect he will, he gets a promotion and a raise, so he has incentive to keep things running smoothly while I take some overdue time off with my *girlfriend*."

Lucas kissed my cheek again before continuing. "Now, go take your shower so you can make sure I don't ruin any of this food!" As he spoke, he sauntered back over to the cookbooks, whistling.

"That's what your grandmother is going to do," I laughed. "I'm supposed to get all the prep work done, then pick her up and bring her over here around lunchtime to supervise the actual cooking. If it was all left to me, it would likely be completely inedible."

"Yeah, probably," he teased with a wink. "I'll go over with you, I need to look at her sink anyway. She called yesterday and said her disposal isn't working, *again*. I swear that thing breaks at least once a month. I wish she would just buy a new one. Anyway, I haven't had a chance to stop by to take a look yet."

"Sounds good. I'll be out in a few minutes."

He looked up at me with a smile that was light and boyish and infectiously joyful.

He's so happy...

I could feel the remnants of my dark mood fall away, and as they did, I felt closer to him than ever before. The night before hadn't been a mistake after all. It would have been awkward and uncomfortable no matter what.

As we held each other's gazes in silence for a few moments, Lucas's expression began to shift. The playfulness faded to be replaced by something more intense: he was looking at me like he had the night before. My heart fluttered in response as I felt the heat of my blush spread up my neck and across my cheeks.

Turning, I walked quickly into the bathroom. It may not have been a mistake, but I was nowhere near ready to repeat the experience.

chapter eighteen

rob

Years of sobriety had dulled my memory of what it was like to be fucked up all the time, but I'd become reacquainted; Charlie and I had been high or drunk more often than not for... weeks? Months? Hell, I didn't really know how long. Time was impossible to discern through the fog of intoxication I'd lost myself in.

"Ow, Charlie, you're hurting me!"

The whiny, high-pitched voice tinged with fear was enough to force my eyes open to search in the direction it had originated, which wasn't far—Charlie was only a few feet away, pinning down some blonde chick I didn't recognize by her neck.

"Jesus Christ, what the hell, Charlie? You're fucking someone right in front of me? At least go to a different fucking room, man."

"Charlie—I'm serious—I can't breathe!" the blonde choked out, panicked.

Charlie ignored both of us, grunting harder with each successive thrust.

"Come on, knock that shit off. She said she can't breathe."

"She likes it, trust me, bro."

"Just fucking let her go, man."

I didn't give a shit what he said, she didn't seem like she liked it. And I wasn't so far gone that I could sit idly by and let him hurt a woman. I'd force him off her first, if it came to that.

"Apparently, bro, I gotta' teach you how to fuck," he said without even slowing. "Chicks love this shit, they get off on it. Doesn't matter what they say—they do. Even your precious little Annie—"

I slammed into him before my actions registered, both of us tumbling to the floor. Flipping around with surprising agility considering my intoxicated state, I pinned him down in much the same way he'd just been holding down the blonde, who scrambled quickly to her feet and fled.

"What the fuck did you just say?" I asked slowly, sure I must have imagined the words I'd heard.

"Get off me, bro," he wheezed out around the hand I had on his throat. "Yeah, I fucked her, who gives a shit?"

"*I* give a shit! She was my girlfriend!"

"So what, dude? She's not your girlfriend anymore, and she was just a lay, anyway. Really, you should be thanking me. I did you a fucking favor, man."

"How is fucking my girlfriend doing me a favor?!"

"Jesus, bro, chill out and get the fuck off me before I get pissed. I knew she'd do it if she had a chance, so I gave her one. I'd have told you if she'd stuck around, so you'd know what a slut she was, but she split like I told you she would, so I didn't have to. I guess you were a boring lay and she didn't want to go back to boring after I showed her a good time."

Showed her a good time?

"Who the fuck knows? Either way, I did you a favor, getting rid of that dead weight for you."

Somehow, the rational side of my brain was winning out over the drug and alcohol-fogged jealous side and I knew it couldn't have happened the way he described.

Very slowly, very deliberately, draining all emotion from my voice, I asked, "What exactly do you mean by you 'showed her a good time'?"

"She acted like she didn't want it at first, but I knew she did, so I gave it to her anyway, just like blondie here until you lost your shit."

The edges of my vision had turned to black and were closing in, and I could hear nothing over the pounding of my blood in my ears, even though I saw his lips moving as he continued to speak. I'd spent most of my life angry and violent, but I'd never, *never* felt anything akin to what I experienced in that moment. I suddenly understood what it meant to murder in a blind rage, how easy it would be, knowing I was on the precipice of joining that population.

With superhuman effort, I peeled my fingers off Charlie's neck, one by one, and forced myself to move off him.

I can't kill my own brother. I can't kill my own brother.

I repeated the words to myself over and over as I pushed up to my feet, the loathing, the disgust, the pure unadulterated hatred I felt toward him growing with every breath.

"Get. Out."

"Dude, chill—"

"Now! Get out before I fucking kill you!"

He got to his feet, pulled on his pants, and walked slowly over to me, not stopping until we were toe-to-toe and I had to tip my head up to look at him. I knew it was supposed to intimidate me, but it didn't.

"Are you fucking serious, bro?" he asked quietly, a threat implicit in his voice and stance.

My arm moved back and darted forward, my fist connecting with his face. But the sensation of bone crunching under my hand only whet my appetite for more.

"You raped her!" I fisted my hair and pulled with both hands, desperate to keep myself from attacking him; I knew that once I started, I'd be unable to stop. "If you ever come near either of us again, I swear to God I will kill you."

Charlie struggled back to his feet clumsily, one hand on his bleeding nose. It was suddenly so clear that I should have realized back then what he was capable of. I followed him to the front door and watched as he stepped over the threshold onto the porch, then turned.

"We're blood. I can't believe you're letting some bitch come between us."

That was the last straw for my self-control, and I lunged. He was bigger, a better fighter, but I was enraged; more than I'd ever been in my life. Once I had him pinned down again, this time in the front yard, my wrath took the reins and I hit him repeatedly. In the recesses of my mind, I registered when he stopped fighting back, stopped moving entirely, but I wanted to make sure he never woke up.

There was movement in my peripheral, and I froze when my eyes darted up to find Annie watching me from Mrs. Renner's driveway. Her lips moved, but I heard nothing over the rushing of my blood and pounding of my heart. My hands remained limp at my sides as I stared at her, as unable to tear my gaze away as I'd been unable to stop hitting Charlie only a moment before—until I unexpectedly flew sideways to the ground.

"He's not worth it, Rob. He's not worth it," Lucas panted out from the ground beside me.

"You don't know what he did to her! He deserves to fucking die!"

"I know enough. I didn't say he doesn't deserve it, I said he isn't worth it. Think about what watching this is doing to Annie."

A wave of grief and guilt for what she'd been through crashed over me and hot tears spilled over out of nowhere. None of it would have happened to her if it hadn't been for me, if I hadn't been a part of her life. For more than a decade, I'd thought she had ruined my life, when the reality was that *I* had utterly demolished hers in unfathomable ways.

Lucas had made his way back to her side and was trying to pull her away, but she was tethered to my gaze. What was passing between us was so intense that I didn't realize Charlie had come to until he'd stood and spit a glob of blood onto the ground in front of me.

"You're making a huge fucking mistake, little bro. And for what? A worthless little whore from your past?"

I turned back to Annie. For her, I could let it go, so she wouldn't have to watch the violence.

"Stop calling me bro, you piece of shit. No brother of mine would do something like this—you're nothing to me. Now get the fuck off my property."

chapter nineteen

annie

Graduation was just around the corner. Even more than being somewhere unfamiliar with all new faces, I was terrified of losing Rob. I'd be leaving within days of graduation and we were going to different schools. I was sure he would find a way more beautiful, way less broken and needy girl.

Though we'd been dating for a couple of years, I was still a virgin. But I felt so safe, so enveloped in love and understanding and acceptance lying in Rob's arms during our outdoor advanced literature class that day, listening to his heart beating steadily, that I'd decided I was finally ready. We kissed often and made out whenever Rob could coax me into it, though I always freaked out when I thought things might take the next step. But I knew in my heart that Rob would never hurt me, and I trusted him to help me through it.

I wanted to surprise him, so I left a note by his feet at the end of class that told him to meet me at the old garage at the cross-country course at ten that night. My mom thought I was spending the night at my friend Katie's house, and the knowledge that I'd lied to her weighed so heavily on me that I almost chickened out of the whole thing.

Almost.

The full moon that night was bright, except when passing clouds plunged everything into darkness. The chilly spring air was crisp and fresh, and I'd tossed a sweatshirt over my favorite jeans to guard against the slight chill, opting for black so I wouldn't draw attention from anyone passing on the road as I made my way to our rendezvous.

I knew the route to the course well enough to walk it with my eyes closed, but walking there after dark was different and eerie. I moved quickly, my breath coming in short bursts as I looked over my shoulder every few minutes, sure I was being followed. There was a reason I never went out in the dark alone, but I kept reminding myself it would be worth it.

As I approached the garage, I could just make out that someone was standing outside it, and a wave of relief washed over me. I took a few deep breaths as I drew closer. Rob could always tell when something was bothering me, and I didn't want him to worry.

When I got within a few feet, I flipped my hood down, steadfastly ignoring the nerves and excitement that turned my stomach and forcing some bravado and playfulness into my voice.

"Hey there, hot stuff. I can't believe you beat me here. I'm even early! But I'm glad you're here already. Sorry for being cryptic in my note—I was afraid you wouldn't agree. But it's too late now, so you'll have to get over it. I told my mom that I'm spending the night with Katie. We have all night together."

I was barely an arm's length away when he turned.

"All night, huh?"

My heart skipped and sputtered as it tried to beat again, making speaking practically impossible.

"Charlie? Where's Rob?" I choked out.

Charlie gave me the creeps. He'd look at me with derision when Rob couldn't see and make lewd gestures. I'd never told Rob because I didn't want to make things worse; I knew they already fought about me all the time. It had started shortly after I met Rob, when he stopped partying and getting into trouble with Charlie. But he was the only real family Rob had left and he'd never actually done anything to me.

"Rob?" he sneered. "Oh, my mistake, I was sure you left that note for me. And I didn't want my poor brother to know what a slut of a girlfriend he has."

Every hair on my body stood on end, my skin prickled, and time seemed to slow down; my body instinctively knew that danger was imminent.

"No, that's not true, Charlie. I'm sorry if you thought... I'm just going to go."

I had been backing up as I spoke, but he'd kept in step with me. Turning, I tried to run but was yanked backward by my hair so roughly it felt as if the skin had been ripped off my head as I fell onto my back. The scream that started up my throat ended abruptly as I landed, and the wind was knocked out of me. My feet kicked wildly as I scrambled to get my feet under me, but his foot slammed into my face, keeping me down.

"Charlie," I gasped through the fear, the tears, the pain, again scrambling to get my footing. "Charlie, please, *please* don't hurt me, please!"

"Keep begging, bitch." The back of his hand cracked across my face as the last word left his mouth. As I fell again, he climbed on top of me, his weight pinning me down. "I know your type. You act like you're better than everyone else, but you're not. And my brother seems to think you're some goddamned saint, but that's about to change."

I tried to scream, but his hand was squeezing my throat so hard I couldn't even breathe. I clawed at my neck, trying to loosen his grip enough to draw in some oxygen, but it was all a useless endeavor. I didn't stand a chance against his much larger and stronger form.

Charlie reached down with his free hand, unbuckled his pants and pulled his erection free. After stroking himself a few times as he watched me with a smile on his face, he shifted to use that same hand to unbutton my pants and tug them down to just past my knees.

Next, he shoved my shirt up around my neck and yanked down my bra, leaning forward to rub his penis against my breasts. Laughing cruelly, he bent over and bit down hard on an exposed area of my neck, using his teeth to rip the skin open.

I was losing steam, the lack of oxygen taking its toll, but I was acutely aware of the tickly sensation of blood dripping down the side of my neck. I shifted, trying to move my neck away from him, but he responded by biting and squeezing harder as he pumped his hips against me and grunted.

Through the overwhelming panic, all I could think was that I didn't want to die. With that thought, as I flirted with unconsciousness, my body went completely limp.

Charlie loosened his grip on my neck and released my skin from his teeth. He still hit me, pulled my hair, bit me; but he didn't cut off my air supply again as he spent an eternity using my body in ways I tried to forget.

Rob's voice reached my ears, the sound distant. But I knew it was my imagination because he wasn't there that night.

"Goddamn it! Annie! Come back to me! You're safe!"

My vision focused slowly. I hadn't imagined Rob's voice. His tear-stained face was inches from mine where I sat on the ground, hugging my knees to my chest.

I wasn't at the cross-country course. Charlie wasn't hurting me again.

I wanted to say Rob's name, to tell him that I was okay, but instead a sob escaped my lips, and then I was in his arms. He crushed me so tightly against his chest that it was difficult to breathe, but it was almost not enough.

"Oh, thank fuck," Rob's voice rushed out with a shuddering breath.

It started with trembling, quickly progressing until my entire body shook uncontrollably, driven by remnants of the fear and every other emotion I hadn't even bothered to name that the event had permanently lodged into my soul. One of Rob's arms loosened as his hand began running from the crown of my head down the length of my hair as his emotion-thickened voice murmured into my ear.

"It's okay. You're safe now, love, I promise. I'm here now, and I'll protect you. I swear, he'll never touch you again."

The familiarity of his voice and scent instantly stirred all the feelings of comfort and safety I'd always had with him. The crying and shaking slowly abated, eventually dissolving into hiccups and shivers. Yet, neither of us moved. I could feel my muscles slowly unclenching, my body softening into his hold as he continued whispering reassurances into my ear. Little by little, I began to feel safe again.

A throat cleared loudly several feet away.

Oh, God.

Lucas.

My body returned to a state of tension as I opened my eyes and tried to extricate myself from Rob's embrace, but his arms only tightened around me.

"Annie, I'm not going anywhere unless you want me to." Rob's voice was soft but full of urgency and desperation. "Fuck everyone else—you're all I need. All I've ever wanted was you, and if you give me a chance, I swear I'll never let you down again, I'll never let anything happen to you again. Just give me that chance; let me show you."

How many times had I dreamed about hearing those words from him? He was all I'd ever wanted. But now I had a boyfriend, and I loved him, too. I never wanted to, I never thought I could, but I did. And I couldn't just throw that away.

As I turned my head around to look at Lucas, he turned his glare from Rob to me, then back to Rob. After a moment, with a gentleness that contrasted starkly with the angry planes of his face, Lucas spoke.

"Come on, Annie, let's go."

"Don't," Rob begged desperately as I pushed my way out of his arms. "Please, don't do this. Not again."

Every word felt like a sledgehammer to my heart as I walked away. I was following Lucas, but parts of me remained on the cold ground with Rob, and always would.

chapter twenty

annie

Lucas drove us back to my mom's house. The atmosphere in the car for those few minutes was reminiscent of heading to a funeral, becoming more oppressive with each passing second. Lucas didn't speak until we were parked, and even then, he wouldn't look at me.

"Go on in. I need a few minutes," he said, his voice hollow, as he pulled the key from the ignition.

I studied his profile, willing him to turn his head so I could see his eyes for a clue to what he may have been thinking, but he just stared straight ahead, unmoving.

The front door clicked loudly in the silence as it closed behind me and I stepped over to the window, peeking around the curtain. I could hear the seconds ticking by from the clock on the mantle in the living room as I waited, watching to see what would happen. After several minutes, Lucas started pounding the top of the steering wheel with his fists. The sudden burst of anger in Lucas, a man who was always the epitome of calm, startled me and I jumped, the edge of the curtain falling from my fingertips and fluttering back into place.

I tried, unsuccessfully, to force myself out the door, knowing I had to do whatever it took to fix the situation since it was my fault. Just as it was my fault that Rob had just lost his brother, the main reason I had left him all those years ago. And now I had walked away from him for another man, who, from the looks of it, was going to leave me anyway.

Even running, I barely made it to the bathroom before the sudden onset of nausea overwhelmed me.

"Annie?" Lucas's shouts startled me into consciousness, and I opened my eyes to find myself face-to-face with the base of the toilet.

"In here," I shouted.

"Where?"

"Bathroom."

As I sat up, the bathroom door flew open and slammed against the wall.

"Annie. I thought..." he shook his head as if to clear it instead of finishing his sentence. "What's going on?"

"I got sick to my stomach and threw up. I guess I passed out after. I don't remember."

He looked away as he nodded and swallowed. "Are you okay? Do you still feel sick?"

After I shook my head, he reached down to help me stand, but wouldn't make eye contact. As the queasiness resurfaced, threatening to take over again, I followed him to the living room. Once I was settled on the sofa, he disappeared, and I heard muted noises coming from the kitchen. He returned after several minutes and handed me a glass of water, sitting in the chair opposite me.

"Thank you."

A half-smile touched his lips as his eyes remained focused on some unseen point in the distance, but he still didn't say anything. The longer we sat, the louder the silence became until it was practically deafening. And as if it was controlled by his obviously escalating tension, my heartbeat became more erratic and breathing more difficult. I wanted to fix it, but how?

"Lucas?"

His eyes focused on me, finally, as they softened, and the tension left his face to be replaced by a contemplative sadness. "Yes?"

"I..." My voice dried up after that first word. I forced a swallow and tried again, managing to blurt out, "I'm sorry." Though I wasn't even sure what I was sorry for, I just knew that whatever was happening was because of me. It was always my fault.

Lucas closed his eyes and sighed. When he opened them, he moved to the edge of his seat and reached across the space between us to take my water from me and set it on the coffee table. With my hands gently clasped in his, he searched my eyes earnestly.

"Annie, I need you to be honest with me. Whatever you say, it's okay, but tell me the truth."

I nodded my head slightly in response.

"Do you love me?"

"What? Of course I do, Lucas, I—"

"Annie. Please. I want you to think about it for a minute. I know you care. I know you like being around me, spending time with me. But what I need to know is if you really *love* me. Just-you-and-me love me. I... I know that I love *you* like that, that I want to see where we go, but do you feel the same way?"

"What's going on?"

My vision tunneled as I began to panic. It sounded to me like he was giving himself an out, setting me up so he could leave me. I'd just walked away from Rob—I couldn't let that happen.

"Please don't leave, I'm sorry, I'll be less needy. I'll... I'll try harder to be happy, we can go out more, anything you want, just please... please, don't leave..."

I couldn't continue, hysteria preventing me from being able to catch my breath. But then, instead of leaving, he was there, gathering me into his arms.

"I love you, sweetheart," he said as he held me tightly against him. "I'm not going anywhere."

We sat like that for a long time, the steady, reliable thump-thump of Lucas's heart under my cheek gradually lulling me into a state of calm. Eventually, I swiped the remnants of the tears off my cheeks and pulled out of his embrace so we could start working on the food for Community Thanksgiving. There were a lot of people counting on the event to have a hot meal, regardless of what was happening in our personal lives.

chapter twenty-one

rob

The wreckage that Charlie and I had left all over my house now cleaned up, I stood in my front hall trying to figure out what the fuck to do with myself. Everything I'd ever felt for Annie, all the pain and fear and anger and love—*all* of it was back at once, magnified to an intensity I was shamefully unprepared to face. The only thing I wanted to do was hunt Charlie down and fucking kill him, finishing what I'd started earlier in the day, but the thought of Annie's face when I'd almost done so kept me from following through.

And, fuck, the guilt. I was drowning in it. If I'd never bothered her that day in class, never insisted on getting to know her, Charlie never would have met her, let alone... And even then, it was my job to protect her, the only thing I had to do, and I didn't fucking do it! Instead? I spent almost thirteen years furious with her. Blaming *her* for everything.

Jesus Christ, it was suddenly so clear. She'd always been wrong about me. I really was the horrible person everyone always told her I was.

I knew I should try to work, to try to keep at least some of the customers I was bound to lose after spending the last two months partying with Charlie instead of fulfilling contracts. But I didn't.

I couldn't.

Besides, what the fuck did any of it matter? All of it had really always been for her, in case she ever came back.

But she'd found someone else.

"I didn't know where else to go."

My head hung from my shoulders in shame as I stared at my feet. Without a word, Mrs. Renner turned and started walking away. I stepped through the open door and closed it behind me. Following her to the kitchen, I stood in the doorway and waited as she sat down.

"Make us some tea."

I nodded, relieved she had even let me in, and started making us each a cup of tea as had become our custom when I came to visit. The familiarity soothed my nerves and steadied my hands by the time I placed our mugs down on the table.

"I'm sor—"

"I know that already, or you wouldn't be here right now with remorse written all over your face," she interrupted, holding her hand up to stop me from continuing. "I also saw you with Annie after the boxing match in your front yard."

"I couldn't stop myself. I don't know what would have happened if I hadn't seen Annie standing there. I wanted to kill him. I was *going* to kill him. He shouldn't be allowed the privilege of living after what he did to her."

My voice cracked on the last word, and I turned away, trying to steady the tremble in my jaw.

"I know, honey, I know. Part of me actually hoped it would end that way after what he did to her. But if it had, then—"

"What?" I roared, shoving back from the table so violently my chair went flying into the cabinets behind me. "You fucking knew and never told me? How... How *could* you?!"

"Shut up and sit down!"

In the fifteen years since I'd met her, Mrs. Renner had never once raised her voice at me, and the shock gave me pause. I remained standing where I was, glaring at her as I bit my tongue and waited for her to continue.

"Sit. Down."

My jaw set as I glared at her for another moment, but I saw that hers was set as well, and I knew I was fighting a losing battle. There was no one as stubborn as that old lady. If I wanted to hear her explanation, I was gonna have to sit my ass in her chair first.

"I told you years ago when she just disappeared that *something* must have happened. I'd given up trying to figure it out, but when you told me she was talking about Charlie in her sleep, I was sure he was responsible. I suspected he'd raped her when Lucas mentioned that she panicked if they tried to be intimate. She didn't admit it to me until a few weeks ago, but, at that point, you were off reliving your glory days as a delinquent."

My fists were still clenched from the effort I'd had to exert not to punch something when she talked about Lucas trying to be intimate with Annie, though I had to admit to an enormous sense of relief knowing that their relationship had never become physical. Selfish, undoubtedly, but I was relieved all the same.

"You can't get angry about them being together, Rob. However it makes you feel, he loves her. Hell, he practically worships her, just like you. He's young, and he hasn't been through the same things you and Annie have, so he doesn't understand her the way you do, but he's trying."

"And Annie?"

She sighed, eyeing me critically for a moment before responding, almost as if she was trying to determine if she should answer me at all.

"She loves you both."

"So, I still have a chance?"

"If you love her, leave her be. She has a long road ahead of her to deal with everything she's been running from, and she really needs to learn how to be happy for herself. She needs to find that strength she had inside before Charlie stole it from her. She needs to find *Annie* again. And frankly, you need to do the same. I've been telling you for years that you should talk to someone, but it's even more important now."

The thought of moving on without Annie stole the air from my lungs. It had never been more apparent than right then that for all those years, I'd never moved on at all, no matter what lies I'd told myself and everyone else. I'd always clung to the possibility that she'd come back. Everything in my life was for her. It had been since the day I met her, really. I didn't give a fuck if it was right or wrong or what anyone thought; it's how it was.

How could I just turn that off?

chapter twenty-two

annie

BANG!

I shot upright with my heart in my throat.

"Sweetheart?" Lucas asked sleepily.

"Lucas," I started breathlessly, "Lucas, wake up. It was a gunshot."

"No, that definitely wasn't a gunshot."

He yawned before glancing at the clock, a hand smoothing up and down my back.

"It's seven," he muttered. "It must be your friends." Then, more urgently, "Shit! I'm not ready to meet them!"

I groaned as relief washed over me. He was right. I'd forgotten that Carol texted to let me know they were coming early to help. Despite the adrenaline still pumping through my body, I smiled as I realized how much I'd missed her and Haley. I'd barely talked to them since I'd returned to Stockwood; they were busy with their lives and didn't need to be burdened with my shit, too. Even so, I felt a pang of guilt. I hadn't been a model friend to them over the years, but I would make sure I did a better job once I was back in the city with them.

As my eyes landed on Lucas, I felt them widen as realization settled over me.

"Lucas," I breathed out, "I only had one nightmare last night. I can't believe it."

Our eyes locked and I teared up as I flung myself onto him.

"It's because of you. Thank you, thank you, thank you."

I punctuated each 'thank you' with a kiss to a different spot on his face. I wanted to kiss him until he understood the magnitude of what I'd said, understood the painfully wonderful relief it brought, understood just what it meant that he'd done that for me.

Lucas seemed bewildered at first, but after a moment, his eyes darkened as he cradled my face, his intensifying gaze magnetic. After a slow, lingering, gentle kiss, his kisses became more urgent, more insistent, like they had a few nights before, and I could feel his erection growing under me. Desire rocketed through me at the same time my heart sank—I would no longer be able to say no. And while I relished the closeness that came from having shared that intimacy with him, I wasn't ready to try again.

Luckily, before I had to decide between hurting him by denying him and swallowing my reservations and doing it anyway, there was shouting from outside, reminding us both that we had company to deal with.

"Annie, for fuck's sake, open the damn door and let us in already! I can't listen to Carol bitch for another minute!" Haley's voice filtered in from the porch.

"Shit, Annie, your friends!" Lucas exclaimed, his voice suddenly tinged with anxiety.

What could he possibly have to be nervous about?

I hadn't told my friends about him yet; it was going to be as big a surprise to them that there was a man in the house as it was going to be for him to see how different from me my friends were. I laughed at the thought, stifling the insecurity trying to convince me that he wouldn't want me after meeting them.

"It's going to be fine, Lucas. They're going to love you, trust me. Just put on some clothes. You'll be fine."

"What do you mean?" he asked.

I looked over his attire, which consisted of boxers and lounge pants, my eyes then taking in his exposed upper body.

"I mean real clothes. Haley is... well, I guess you could say blunt?"

I wasn't sure how to explain that she would audibly assess him like he was on display at a meat market.

He laughed as he pulled a t-shirt over his head. "I don't mind blunt. I'd rather that than someone who doesn't say what they mean."

The front door now sounded like it would come crashing down at any moment and I could hear Carol and Haley arguing. I jumped up, dragging Lucas with me.

On the way to the door, I had the fleeting thought that I should mention I'd never told my friends about him, but I didn't really have time to explain why I hadn't. Or even know how. He'd figure it out soon enough anyway. Besides, the more I thought about it, the more the idea of surprising them appealed to me; I'd always been the dull, predictable friend.

"Enough already!" I admonished as I swung the front door open. "You're going to break the damn door!"

Haley rolled her eyes at me as she retorted, "About fucking time, babe. I've been listening to Carol bitch the whole way here about—wait, who's *this*? Your sister's latest squeeze? Hi there, hottie."

I shrugged at Lucas's look of confusion and gave him a look that said, 'I warned you.'

"No, Lori isn't out here yet. Lucas, this is Haley, and this is Carol. Guys, this is Lucas. I'll fill you in later."

"Hmm. He can fill me in now. Wait! You said he's not here with Lori, but he's in pajamas. And you're wearing a t-shirt that obviously didn't come from *your* wardrobe. Holy shit! Did you finally get laid, babe?"

My face felt like it was hot enough for my skin to just melt off my skeleton, but I managed to shake my head at Lucas as he tensed behind me. The heat in my face shifted from embarrassment to jealousy in an instant as Haley took her time to check Lucas out from head to toe with obvious approval, but I couldn't make myself tell her to stop. The words were right there, resting on my tongue, but just wouldn't leave my mouth.

"I told you not to bring him," Carol said with obvious disapproval.

My stomach flipped and acid burned my esophagus.

"You didn't," I breathed out. "God no, please tell me you didn't. Why would you do that?"

But before Haley had a chance to reply, a new voice rang out from behind them.

"Annie fuckin' Turner. Well, without the fuckin', of course."

Though I didn't need to see to know who had spoken, my eyes followed the voice until I was looking into Linc's face. He winked, looking me up and down as he whistled.

Fisting the hem of Lucas's t-shirt that ended mid-thigh along with my sleep shorts, I pulled, stretching the material down until it was achingly taut where it broke over my shoulders and I couldn't coax any additional length from it.

"Hey, eyes up here and watch how you're talking to her," Lucas seethed, his arm wrapping around me, and pinning me into his side.

"Easy, man. We just have a little history... a little *unfinished business*, right, Annie?"

"Knock it off, Linc," Haley said.

"I'm just fuckin' around, no hard feelings. Other hard things, maybe," Linc said with a shrug.

"Look," Lucas interjected as he moved me behind him, "I don't know who the hell you think you are, but you're not going to talk to her like that."

"Calm down, no reason to get all pissed off. Unless she left you hanging, too?"

He barely got the last word out before Lucas was in his face.

"Get lost, asshole."

"Hottie, calm down, he's just messing around. And Linc? Seriously? Knock it off, it's fucking annoying, and it's *not* going to get you laid."

Haley stood there after she finished speaking, waiting for Lucas to back off, but he didn't move. Though Linc was much bulkier and could easily have taken Lucas, he didn't make a move either. But that meant someone still had to defuse the situation.

I placed my hand hesitantly on Lucas's arm but was too ashamed to look him in the eye, instead staring at my feet.

"Lucas, it's okay, really. He always does that. It's fine. It's not a big deal. Come on."

I felt Lucas's gaze land on me, and I chanced a peep at him. He was gaping at me, incredulous.

"*Fine*? No. Not even close."

"Please, I'll explain later. Just let it be, it's okay."

He took a deep breath like he was trying to gather strength and patience before he spoke, his voice heavy and deliberate once he did.

"Sweetheart. Go inside. Put some more clothes on."

Lucas wasn't yelling. In fact, he was speaking quietly, and his features had softened, almost as if he knew something I didn't. But there was an unmistakable granite undertone that, while it was new coming from him, I instinctively knew meant there was no point in doing other than as he'd directed.

What a disaster. I couldn't believe Haley had brought Linc.

A sigh escaped as I pulled on a pair of jeans. I knew Linc didn't actually mean any harm. I'd seen the side of him that was interested, compassionate, and considerate, the side of him that could be fun and caring. All the other stuff was simply a façade hiding a painful past, just like it was with Haley. So as much as I never wanted to see him again, I also couldn't let Lucas throw him out or get into a fight with him.

Carol was in the kitchen when I emerged from the bedroom minutes later, but Haley, Linc, and Lucas were all still out on the porch.

"Guys, come in, please."

Linc and Lucas continued to stare at each with open contempt while Haley looked back and forth between them with amused anticipation. As much as I loved her, because I *really* did, I wanted to throttle her for encouraging the combustible situation.

"Seriously, Haley?"

"Shh, it's about to get interesting."

"I can't handle any more drama right now! I mean it! Either help me, or you and Linc can both leave."

She tore her eyes from Linc and Lucas to study me for a moment, the exasperation in her features dissolving suddenly.

"Linc, come on, knock it off, okay?"

After a moment, Linc looked away, and Lucas miraculously let him follow Haley inside.

"We'll be in shortly," I called, looking up at Lucas. As I watched, he shifted his gaze from the front door to me, his eyes brimming with questions.

"Annie, who the hell is that asshole, and what is he talking about?" he asked.

"Can we talk about it later? It's freezing out here."

"No. Now. Please."

I sighed, wrapping my arms around myself in a futile attempt to stay warm against the bitter cold air as I studied the bricks under my feet.

"Linc and Haley are friends. A-and... fuck buddies. A while back, Haley made it her mission to get me to have sex."

"What kind of friend would do that to you?"

"She doesn't know about Charlie. No one knew until recently. She never would have done it if she'd known. This wasn't a great introduction, but she's a good friend."

"Okay. But what does that have to do with her fuck buddy?"

"H-he's the guy she thought I should have sex with."

"So, what, you had a fuck date? With *him*?"

"I mean..." I trailed off as I continued to stare at the bricks on the porch, Lucas's reaction driving home just how disgusting and demeaning I already knew it was. "Yes. I mean, I knew him, I knew who he was, they're friends..." I was keenly aware that I was rambling incoherently, but I felt the need to explain why I had consented, that I hadn't agreed to try with a total stranger, but self-loathing was choking me.

"I thought I was your first since you were raped. But what you're telling me right now is that you fucked that guy in there?"

"Oh god, no, I couldn't. I was trying to explain... I tried, but... I couldn't do it."

"Why would you even agree to something that asinine?"

My face leapt into flames. "I thought... get past... Ch-Ch..."

"Okay, but something doesn't add up. If it was just a failed attempt to have sex—why is he so pissed off at you?"

"We... um..." I cleared my throat. "We dated first. I thought it would help. He... he wanted to keep trying. Dating, that is. But I said no."

"Well, that's just great," Lucas sighed, using his hand to raise my chin until I was forced to look at him. "Look, I don't care what you let happen before I met you. I mean, I do, but I can't do anything about it. Point is, no one is going to talk to you that way now. I won't allow it, I'm drawing the line there. No one—not your friends, *especially* not that guy. Got it?"

He glared at me as he said the last two words as if he was daring me to argue. That kind of bossy possessiveness from Lucas was unexpected. Yet, there was something indisputably reassuring about it at the same time. I felt cared about in a way I hadn't since I'd dated Rob.

"I'm sure it will help once they know who you are. I've barely talked to them since I came out here, so you were a bit of a surprise."

His shirt and chest were cold under my cheek when he pulled me in for a hug and kissed the top of my head before releasing a deep sigh. "Come on, sweetheart, let's go in."

He held the door open, and I ducked under his arm to walk inside. In the living room, I opened my mouth to make a formal introduction to everyone, but before a sound escaped, Lucas wrapped an arm around my waist and began to speak.

"We all got off on the wrong foot because there's some confusion about who I am. Let me clear it up. I'm Lucas. Annie's boyfriend. And I was brought up to be polite, so maybe it makes me old-fashioned, but I'm a little sensitive about people being rude to her. As long as everyone can knock that shit off, we'll get along just fine, and you're welcome to stay. Otherwise, I'm happy to remind you where the front door is."

I looked around. Lucas and Linc, unsurprisingly, stared at each other with mutual dislike. Carol and Haley smiled at each other like they were sharing a private joke to which no one else was privy.

It was going to be an interesting few days.

chapter twenty-three

annie

"**So, what's the** story, babe? Why didn't we ever hear about the hottie?" Haley asked.

It was Thanksgiving morning and the guys had just left after being tasked with working on setup at the brewery while Haley, Carol, and I finished food prep. I shook my head slightly as I felt warmth creep up into my cheeks.

"You're blushing! I knew it! You guys are totally fucking."

"Haley, knock it off," Carol said, exasperated. "You know that bothers her, and you've done enough already by bringing Linc here."

"Yeah, whatever, enough harping on me about that already. You know Linc doesn't have any family around here, and he's my friend. I wasn't going to leave him alone for the holiday. Anyway, Annie, you're not off the hook yet, babe. Who *is* this guy?"

"He's the grandson of a friend of my mom's. I met him by accident."

"O-kay," Haley responded. "And how did you guys end up together?"

I shrugged as I replied, already uncomfortable with the conversation and ready for it to be over. "He was persistent."

"You seem different with him," Carol chimed in. "Happier. More relaxed. I mean, eight months ago before you came out here, the situation on the porch would have set off a full-blown panic attack."

"You're right," I said thoughtfully after I'd considered her words. "I think being out here is helping. Unfortunately, it won't last since I have to go back to work in the spring."

"You'll figure it out," Carol said with a confident smile.

"Guys, seriously, who cares about that right now? I want to hear about the hottie."

"Haley, that's her *boyfriend*. You know, the kind of guy you stay with? In a monogamous relationship?"

Haley rolled her eyes. "Calm your tits, Carol, I'm just saying he's hot. If there are more like him around here, I might have to extend my stay."

"Well, you'll meet plenty of guys tomorrow, and I'm sure half the town would be more than happy to have a roll in the hay with you."

Haley snorted with laughter as she shook her head. "Roll in the hay? Who the fuck talks like that? Just say 'fuck', babe. It won't kill you."

"Anyway, I met Lucas literally the day I got out here," I continued, ignoring her. "I wasn't even remotely interested, but, like I said, he was persistent. He'd come over and sit on the porch until I didn't have a choice but to let him in unless I wanted a frozen corpse to deal with."

Again, I shrugged as if it wasn't a big deal, but I couldn't help the feeling of warmth the memory brought with it. He'd thought I was worth it enough to sit outside in the cold until I let him in.

"We became friends, and then I guess things just progressed from there. As you found out yesterday, he owns the brewery in town. And that's it, there's nothing more to tell."

"Um, yeah, there is," Haley laughed. "We've known you for over a decade, and that is the first time we've ever seen you willingly even *talk* to a guy, let alone *date* one. Except for that creepy fucker from your job, and Linc, neither of whom count. And not only did we see you with him, but he's your boyfriend. And he obviously sleeps here, which means you finally lost that v-card you've been holding onto so tightly, right?"

I froze; there was so much they didn't know.

"Don't hold back, babe! I've been waiting for this day for years. I want all the dirty details. When? Where? Was he any good?"

"Haley! Drop it!" Carol snapped.

Haley glanced up from the beans she'd been cleaning.

"I'm sorry, I'm just messing around, I didn't mean to upset you, really. I'll knock it off."

A few errant tears escaped, racing down my cheeks as I shook my head, desperately trying to maintain some semblance of composure.

"It's okay," I said quietly.

"Is it Lucas? Did he hurt you? I swear to fucking god, babe, I'll hurt the motherfucker right now if he did."

I half-laughed at Haley's threat, though I knew if I said yes, she'd make good on it.

"No, he didn't hurt me. It's just..." I took a deep breath and used my palms to clear the tears off my face, sniffling loudly as I made eye contact with them one at a time. "There are some things I've never told you guys."

"Holy shit. I had no idea. I never would have given you such a hard time or—" Haley cut herself off with a dramatic groan. "Or tried to get you to have sex with Linc. Ugh, I'm such an idiot. I should have realized. I'm so sorry, babe."

"It's okay. There's no way you could have known."

"Why did you ever even agree to that shit?"

"I thought if I could do that, Charlie... what happened... would no longer have control over me. I didn't want to feel trapped anymore."

"I wish you'd told us so we could have been there for you," Carol said quietly.

"I didn't think I could. I felt responsible. And so ashamed. I was afraid of what people would think of me if they knew."

"Christ, babe. You never should have carried that around by yourself."

I shrugged. But I also felt noticeably lighter now that they knew, and I gave them a watery smile.

"I love you guys."

chapter twenty-four

rob

Against Mrs. Renner's advice, I decided to go to Community Thanksgiving to talk to Annie. I had to be sure she knew how I felt and that she really did want Lucas instead.

By the time I made it over, the place was positively overflowing with people: people in need, people who were there to help, people who were simply there in support. I looked around, feeling proud of my town and proud of Annie. She'd always had such a big heart, invariably aware that there were people less fortunate, others who'd been through worse than her, and driven to do whatever she could to help them. It seemed so natural that she would have planned an event like Community Thanksgiving.

I stood off to the side unnoticed, searching the crowd. When my eyes found her, the breath I hadn't realized was trapped in my chest escaped. I watched as she talked to some out-of-towners until I noticed someone staring at her.

I'd started moving through the crowd toward the stranger when Lucas approached Annie from behind as he glared at the same guy I was about to send packing. Annie turned, smiling and wrapping her arms around Lucas, and my heart constricted.

My steps faltered, bringing me to a halt in the middle of the large room as I watched them. Why was I the only one who could see how wrong it was? My hands fisted tightly at my sides, twitching with the urge to hit something when Lucas's hands moved to her face.

No, not some*thing*—some*one*. Lucas.

As if in slow motion, I watched Lucas's lips move as he spoke into Annie's ear, her posture relaxing as he did until she pulled back to smile softly at him.

She looked so happy.

My head spun as I watched them having an intimate moment together, utterly unaware they had an audience, remembering just what it was like to be in his shoes, knowing it would have been me if Charlie hadn't stolen mine and Annie's future together from us.

But he had.

So, I was stuck in the nightmarish version of reality where I had to watch someone else loving her.

But at least she was happy. She, more than anyone, deserved to be happy, and I couldn't fuck that up for her.

"Hey there, handsome," came an unfamiliar voice from over my left shoulder.

I turned and started walking away, brushing the woman out of my way without even glancing at her. "Excuse me," I said on autopilot, though I didn't actually give a shit.

"No problem, hot stuff. I'm sure we can come to some mutually satisfying agreement for you to make it up to me."

I snorted as I tried to keep pushing my way through the dense crowd. "Not interested, lady."

She grabbed my arm and stepped around in front of me.

"You may not know it yet, but I can assure you that you most certainly are. You'll see, and you'll be thanking me. I'm Haley. And you are...?"

Christ, she was persistent.

"Rob," I muttered, smirking with satisfaction when her eyes grew big. I figured her boyfriend must have been behind me or something.

Good. That'd make it easier for me to walk away without causing a scene.

"Wait—*Rob*? Like, you-grew-up-here Rob?"

"Yes, I fucking grew up here," I snapped.

"Like, Annie's Rob?"

My breath rushed out of my lungs as if I'd taken a hit to the gut. Everything faded into the background as my eyes searched frantically until they found Annie again.

Annie's Rob...

"Holy. Shit. You *are* Annie's Rob! I can't believe it. I certainly can't fuck you now. Damn! Why did I have to ask your name first? Oh well. Anyway, hi! Like I said, I'm Haley. I'm friends with Annie."

She held out her hand with what looked to be a genuinely friendly smile, but I didn't trust her. I didn't know her from a fucking hole in the ground.

"Hel-lo? I swear I don't bite. And you don't have to be fucking rude." She looked at me pointedly, then glanced down at her hand that was still held out in my direction, but I had no interest in touching this strange woman, even for a handshake.

"Sorry. Nice to meet you, Haley."

My voice trailed off at the end as my eyes were inevitably drawn back to Annie. What if I was wrong about her looking happy?

I dragged my uncooperative gaze back to Haley.

"Why did you call me 'Annie's Rob'?"

"Because..." She trailed off and her eyes got big as she started laughing. "Oh my god, this is fucking spectacular. No one for years and now three at once. This is too good."

"*Three*?"

"Oh, yeah, Linc. You should meet him, actually. I'm willing to bet that would be entertaining. Lucas seems more the quiet, boring, let's-all-live-in-peace-and-harmony type, and even *he* got a little threatening. You, though," she laughed as she looked me up and down before raising her eyebrows knowingly. "You strike me as a pissed-off-all-the-time sort, more a hit-first kind of guy, right?"

I was on the verge of giving in to my first instinct to go beat the shit out of the guy I'd seen staring at Annie when I glanced back at Haley and saw her smirking, her eyes dancing in amusement.

"What the fuck is your problem?" I spat out as I realized she'd intentionally baited me.

"I was just having some fun."

"It's not a fucking game. If that's the kind of friend you are to Annie, she's better off without you."

I turned and started walking toward the exit, but I couldn't shake the feeling that someone was watching me. As I neared the doors, I spun around to find Haley standing where I'd left her, studying me with a thoughtful expression.

After glaring at her for a breath, I decided to flip her off and watched as her countenance morphed into a smug, self-satisfied grin.

That woman was goddamn crazy. I needed to get away from her before she goaded me into something I'd regret.

chapter twenty-five

annie

"**Hey, Annie. This** is incredible."

"Thanks, Carol. I couldn't have done any of it without an enormous amount of help, though. It's not really me you should say that to."

"It was *your* idea, though."

"But an idea doesn't do anything. It's everyone else involved who made it happen—you, Haley, Linc, Lucas, the local businesses who donated supplies or food. Without you guys, it wouldn't have happened at all, let alone on this scale."

"For god's sake, Annie, take the credit you deserve. Really. I've always admired you, but after you told us about... well, *that*, and what happened the other day, and you *still* pulled this off?" Carol shook her head.

"Okay, that's enough," I laughed off her praise, more than a little uncomfortable. I knew that I didn't really deserve any of it, even though she didn't seem to realize that. The truly inspiring people were all around us, the families who worked day in and day out to put food on the table, dealing with one adversity after another, yet still going back to work the next day.

"Hey guys," Haley called as she sidled up to us. "Babe. Your Jar of Thanks idea? Huge hit. Everyone's using it. And it was overflowing, so I found a bag behind the counter over there and emptied it once already. I put the bag in Lucas's trunk—don't forget to grab it out later."

"Oh wow, really? That's wonderful!"

Every Thanksgiving since that first one with Mom, the whole extended family would get together for the entire day and right before dinner, we would take turns talking about what we were thankful for. Now that everyone had grown up and had families of their own, it only happened every few years, but it was a tradition that I'd always loved. I'd wanted to share it with the community, but with the number of people coming to the event, it just wasn't going to be feasible for everyone to speak. So instead, I had come up with what I'd uncreatively dubbed the Jar of Thanks, a large jar that I placed on a table near the food with pens and notecards, where people could write down what they were thankful for this year. I was touched that not only had a few people used it, but so many that the five-gallon jar had already filled up once.

"Annie, wasn't it?" Lucas whispered into my ear as he wrapped his arms around me from behind a little while later.

Turning and wrapping my arms around his waist, I waited patiently until Lucas dragged his gaze back to me from where he'd been glaring at Linc, his eyes softening as he cupped my face and touched our foreheads together. He inhaled slowly, releasing his breath as a deep sigh.

"I'm sorry, sweetheart. I overreacted. I don't want people to be disrespectful to you. You deserve so much better than that. But I overreacted. I guess I've been on edge because of everything that's happened over the last week, but that's no excuse. And I should have apologized sooner. But bottom line is, I'm sorry, and I really want us to enjoy the time we have left before I have to go back to work."

I smiled, a little teary as some of the tension I'd been carrying around melted away with his words.

"It's okay. I see how I probably shouldn't have allowed Linc to talk to me like that at all. I guess I just feel like I deserve it because he put time and effort into me and got nothing in return."

"No one deserves to be treated that way. And no one should ever expect sex in exchange for putting effort into a relationship."

I could understand Lucas's words, and I even knew them to be true, but when I pictured myself on the receiving end, my emotions got jumbled. I'd be upset and angry on Haley or Carol's behalf, but for myself? I felt like I just needed to suck it up and get over it. That's how things had always been, even back in high school. God, Rob used to get into so many fights because of it.

But I couldn't think about Rob.

Though, in his own way, Lucas had taken on that same role, the role of protector and defender. And I owed it to him to get better.

"You're helping me in ways I don't know how to explain. If you can be patient with me... not give up on me..."

"Are you kidding? Sweetheart, I'm not going anywhere. Unless you ask me to. And even then, I might just hang out on your porch until you change your mind."

Lucas winked, flashing his trademark cheesy grin before his features turned serious. When he spoke the next words into my ear, his voice was no longer playful and teasing, but instead thick with emotion.

"I love you."

"I love you, too."

My heart swelled painfully with a happiness and excitement for the future that I'd thought Charlie had stolen from me for good.

Lucas had insisted that we all go back, catch up, and relax while he supervised the cleanup efforts at SB. It was a crisp, clear night, perfect for studying the stars from the darkened porch as I waited for him. Haley, Carol, and Linc had already had a few glasses of wine, and were all in the living room playing a game, music booming in the background. I enjoyed listening to them from the porch, glad they were having a good time, but content to be removed from the activity and the noise after the chaotic energy of the event.

"Mind if I join you for a few minutes?" Linc asked hesitantly as he stepped onto the porch.

"Not at all," I replied, scooting down further on the bench to make space for him to sit. He seemed to have dropped his cocky façade, something I'd only seen happen when we'd been on a date.

"Thanks." After a moment of quiet, he continued. "I owe you an apology. I'm sorry."

Wait, what?

"I've been such a dick and... really? You don't deserve it. I never told you this... but I really like you. I've never been in a real relationship, something that was exclusive—sleeping around's the only thing I know."

He stopped as he swallowed loudly and shook his head as if to clear it.

"Anyway, the more I got to know you, the more I liked you. Yeah, obviously, I wanted to sleep with you, that's how the whole thing got started, but I liked taking you out and being around you, too."

Another pause as he took a deep breath and sighed.

"Look, I don't know why you freaked out the way you did, and you don't have to tell me. But you were the first person I'd ever felt I could just be *me* around, so when you rejected me, I just... I shouldn't have lashed out at you. I realized at the brewery today that I never really had any claim on you, and I was destroying any chance at friendship. And I really would like to be friends, though I understand and don't hold it against you if you don't."

He had looked straight ahead as he talked, glancing over quickly only once he'd finished.

"I'm sorry for hurting you, Linc. I didn't mean to. Really, I never should have agreed to Haley's ridiculous plan to begin with, but hindsight's twenty-twenty, right?" I paused, feeling I owed him an explanation for why I'd reacted the way I had, but the words stuck in my throat. Instead, I said, "I enjoyed your company, too. We can definitely be friends as long as you're being yourself."

There was another loud peal of laughter from inside as I finished speaking, immediately followed by Haley shouting for Linc to be a tie-breaker for something. Linc and I looked at each other and laughed at the same time.

"Well, I'm being summoned. Friends?"

"Friends."

Linc seemed relieved as he turned and walked inside, and a moment later, his laughter mixed with Haley's and Carol's. I couldn't keep from smiling as I listened to them enjoying themselves inside and thought how fortunate I was to have such great friends and to have found love again. In fact, I decided I should fill out my own note for the Jar of Thanks once Lucas got back from the brewery.

My head snapped instinctively to the left as rustling in the bushes by the porch cut off my thoughts and my heart started racing.

Calm down. It was probably a squirrel or some other small animal.

The deep breath I was taking stalled as someone spoke.

chapter twenty-six

annie

"**Waiting for me** again?"

I wanted to run, to... to scream, but something, an unseen force paralyzed me. I couldn't even breathe as I watched him approach, violence and ill-intent implicit in every step. He was less than an arm's length away when I was able to force out a few words, and even then, they were barely a whisper.

"Charlie... please... don't hurt me."

The laugh that came out of his mouth was hollow, empty, swirling around with my surroundings as I became dizzy.

"Don't hurt you? You turned my fucking brother against me."

And then his hand was squeezing my throat. I couldn't see very well in the dark, even with his face only a few inches from mine. But my sense of smell was intact, and I was drowned in his putrid, alcohol-laced breath as he spoke, transporting me back in time to when he'd last had his hands on me.

"If you thought you could pull that shit and get away with it, you're wrong. You're going to regret ever fucking talking to my brother."

The hand gripping my throat tightened like a vice as his other hand worked at his pants. I tore at his hand with my fingers, but it was futile. And he knew that as well, smiling derisively as he stroked himself. I panicked, fighting for consciousness as my vision tunneled. In a last-ditch attempt to free myself, I finally managed to make my leg cooperate and kick upwards between his legs hard enough to loosen his grip on my neck and send him doubling over. Gasping frantically for air that arrived much too slowly, I opened my mouth to scream for help, but only silence followed.

The front door swung open, and Linc walked onto the porch.

"Hey, Annie, I grabbed a blanket in case—" he stopped abruptly. "Who's there?"

I tried to speak, to scream, to make any sound at all, but still nothing. My attempt to move toward Linc ended abruptly as Charlie grabbed my hair, yanking me to the ground, my head bouncing on the bricks as I landed.

"What the hell?!" Linc shouted, rushing over.

"Mind your own business and get lost, fucker."

Linc punched Charlie in the face, knocking him down.

"Annie, are you okay?"

I scrambled backwards and sat frozen, unable to move further or speak. Linc kicked out as Charlie started pushing up to his knees, knocking him back down at the same time the porch light flipped on and Carol stepped out.

"Guys? What's—"

"Call the police, Carol!" Linc shouted. "Then take Annie to the hospital!"

"What!? What happened?"

"I said call the police!" Linc yelled back at her as he helped me get unsteadily to my feet, though my head throbbed to the point I thought I might pass out. "Annie, do you know who I am?"

"Linc," I replied, his name scratching out.

"And do you know what day it is?"

"Thanksgiving." I shook my head slightly in my confusion about why he was asking me bizarre questions.

"Your head is bleeding. A lot. You could have a concussion," he explained calmly.

I looked down and froze in horror at the large puddle of blood on the bricks where my head had been.

So much blood. But I was still standing. How much more before I'd have been unconscious? What would it look like? And why was it on the bricks? It should've been on my body, smeared on my legs, not on the ground. This wasn't how it happened.

"I called the police, they're coming," Carol shouted, panicked as she and Haley burst through the front door together.

Haley stood stock still for a moment as she glanced around at the scene on the porch, taking everything in as sirens began screaming in the distance. And then, in the blink of an eye, she was there, next to me.

"Annie? What in... Are you okay? Jesus fucking Christ, you're bleeding a lot!"

My hand shook as I gestured toward my neck.

"He choked you?!"

"Haley!" Linc shouted sharply, "Shut up and take her to the fucking hospital! Now!"

"Who is that?" Carol asked.

"Charlie," I whispered, still staring unblinkingly at the puddle of my blood.

"That's Charlie?" Haley shouted, already moving over to where Linc was struggling to keep Charlie pinned down.

"Did you think you could fucking rape her again, you motherfucker?" she asked, her unexpectedly calm voice drawing my gaze from the bloody bricks.

Without warning, Haley's foot flashed forward, kicking Charlie in the face. Over and over; his face, the back of his head, his neck. She left nothing untouched as she continued to kick out viciously. I watched in morbid fascination as he lost consciousness and she didn't even slow, his head snapping around at unnatural angles. The violence was too much, even from Haley, and everything inside worsened as stomach acid rose into my esophagus. But I couldn't tear my eyes away from it, either, and I was ashamed that I detected in myself a modicum of satisfaction at what I was witnessing.

"Haley!" Linc shouted sharply as he stood, placing his hands on Haley's shoulders and forcing her back a few steps. "That's enough! He's unconscious, okay? He can't do anything right now, just calm down."

For the first time since the night I'd met her, Haley broke down and cried. Sobs that wracked her whole body as she walked over to me. I moved my arms around to hold her in a tight hug and stroke a hand I hoped wasn't covered in blood down her hair.

"Shh, it's okay, Haley, it's okay," I soothed.

I could hear Linc urging me to go to the hospital, but I ignored him. The hospital could wait—Haley needed me in a way she hadn't in a long time. And it was more important for me to be there for her like she was always there for me. Especially since I was responsible; she wouldn't have gotten so upset in the first place if it hadn't been for me.

chapter twenty-seven

rob

Bile rose quickly, burning my esophagus as I listened to the words coming through my phone's speaker.

"I don't know everything that happened yet, just that he attacked her on the porch," Haley was saying. "The police arrested him, and she's at the hospital now. She's got a concussion, and they're running some tests to check for other things. I just... after this afternoon, I thought you should know. I'll update you once we have more information."

Speaking was impossible. I couldn't even make myself breathe. And what would I say anyway? That it was all my fault and that I was sorry? What good was an impotent apology?

"You still there?"

"Yeah."

"She'll be okay."

"I'm coming to see her."

There was a long pause before Haley replied.

"I know you care about her, that's why I called. But I don't know if it's a good idea for you to come. We're all here: me, Lucas and his grandmother, Carol, Linc—the guy who stopped your brother. We'll take care of her."

"I... I won't make a scene. I just need to see for myself that she's okay." I swallowed, tamping down the emotion that threatened to take over. "Thank you for calling me."

"Like I said, I just thought you should know."

I hung up and went directly to the town police station, wanting—*needing*—to find out if there was a chance Charlie could get out on bail. I'd do whatever it took to make sure it didn't happen. If I had to, I'd bribe someone. There wasn't anything I wouldn't give up to make sure there was no way he could walk free and get anywhere near her again.

"Annie Turner's room, please."

"Room 2634. Up two floors, left off the elevator."

My feet moved slowly despite my ever-growing need to see her, each step closer to her room taking longer to complete than the previous one until I'd reached her door and stopped altogether. Standing in the hallway, I listened to my heart thundering in my ears, too afraid to go in.

Afraid of what I might see. Afraid of being sent away.

What if she hated me for what happened to her?

Indecision rooted me to the spot until my need to see for myself that she was okay finally outweighed my reservations. With a shaky inhale, I wiped my sweaty palms over my jeans, pushed the door open, and moved a few steps into the room.

Annie was lying in the hospital bed, her eyes closed. Lucas was seated on one side of her and Mrs. Renner on the other. The man I'd seen at the brewery was sitting in a chair in the corner, his head resting in his hands. Haley and the other woman I'd seen with Annie earlier in the day were both sitting in chairs near the foot of the bed with their hands resting on the bed close to Annie's feet.

There was no place for me—I didn't belong.

"Hey, wait!" Haley's voice rang out as I turned to leave.

I looked back to find Annie's eyes fixed on me, her face a jumble of emotions.

"I'm sorry. I..."

There was so much to say, so much to apologize for, but the words dried up in my throat. What the fuck had I been thinking? She didn't want me there—of course she didn't. Why would she?

I turned, exiting the room as quickly as I could.

"Rob, wait! Don't go!" Haley shouted a few moments later as she jogged up next to where I waited for the elevator. "Annie wants to see you."

"She does?"

"Yes. She does. Come back."

I nodded once, then followed her back to Annie's room in silence. At the door, Haley turned to face me.

"Wait here for a minute. As you saw, the room's pretty small. We'll grab our shit and clear out so you guys can have some space."

I shoved my hands in my jeans pockets since I didn't know what the fuck else to do with them and nodded as I studied the wear on my work boots. Haley disappeared into the room, and I paced outside the door as the seconds ticked by.

Had she changed her mind?

"Guys, this is Rob," Haley said as they filed out. "Rob, this is Carol, and this is Linc."

I cleared my throat as I extended my hand toward Linc. "Thank you for saving her. I'm sorry about my brother."

"You're not your brother, man. And Haley did the real damage."

"Not fucking enough," Haley snapped vehemently.

"I think if you'd done any more, the police would have arrested you, too," Carol said to Haley before turning to me. "Haley kicked him in the head until he was unconscious."

I rushed forward and crushed Haley in my arms. "I'm sorry about what I said earlier."

She shifted uncomfortably as she fought against my hug. "Whatever, it's fine. I'm not a hugger, so get the fuck off already."

I watched Annie's friends move slowly down the hall together until they'd disappeared inside the elevator, trying to gather enough strength to face her, knowing I'd failed to protect her from my brother. *Again.* I drew a deep breath, holding it as I stepped inside. Without looking up to confirm it, I knew Annie was watching me.

When I did finally meet her gaze, her emotions shifted across her face too rapidly for me to identify, though I stood there and tried anyway. I needed to figure out how she felt, what she wanted, so I could give it to her.

Mrs. Renner turned toward me, her face drawn and sad. After patting Annie's leg, she stood, shuffling slowly around the foot of the bed and resting a hand on Lucas's shoulder.

"Come on, Lucas. You can come back later."

Lucas raised his head, glancing at his grandmother before he turned to me. "I'm staying."

"I'm not asking."

"All due respect, Grams, no."

Annie turned away from me for the first time since I'd walked into the room and the absence of her gaze allowed a coldness, an emptiness to settle around me. I couldn't make out her words, but as she spoke, Lucas's eyes turned glassy. Nodding, he stood and kissed the back of her hand and her forehead.

It was a tender moment between them, intended for no one else, and the honorable thing to do would have been to turn away, to look elsewhere. But I didn't do the honorable thing. Instead, I covetously took in every tiny detail of their exchange, from the way her eyes darted away when he kissed her forehead to the slight brush of his fingertips across her cheek.

"Are you sure?" Lucas asked, plaintive.

Annie nodded and he turned and left the room quickly. Mrs. Renner followed, patting my arm affectionately as she passed.

The soft click of the door as it closed was impossibly loud in the oppressive silence that filled the room. I realized that I had no idea what to say, what to do. I could only assume Annie felt the same as she steadfastly stared at her hands, meticulously clearing her hospital blanket of lint. My shoes felt as if they were filled with concrete as I forced my feet to carry me further into the room and closer to her.

As I approached, I saw a bandage on the back of her head, and I could make out the blue and purple bruises on her neck with ease. There were clumps of dried blood in her hair, more smeared across her forehead.

Suddenly, I was no longer in her hospital room, but rather a bystander as she struggled to breathe, watching as Charlie's hands closed around her neck and blood dripped down her face. My legs gave out unexpectedly and I collapsed onto my knees next to Annie's hospital bed. I barely heard her speak over the sob that tore up my throat as I conceded defeat to my emotions.

"I'm so sorry," she whispered hoarsely.

"No!" I bellowed.

Annie recoiled and I swallowed in shame.

"I didn't mean to... I just... I can't let you apologize to me. This is *his* fault. This is *my* fault. This is not *your* fault."

"But I should have told you what happened. Back then. I never should have kept it from you."

"Then why the fuck did you?"

"I wanted to protect you. You had no one except him. I couldn't take your only family away from you. I just couldn't do that to you."

"*You* were my family, goddamn it, Annie—my future." I swallowed, trying to bury the anger that teased the surface.

Tears spilled down Annie's cheeks as she spoke. "I was afraid... I couldn't bear the thought..." She trailed off, her eyes unseeing.

"Afraid of what?"

My voice was hard as all the possibilities filled my mind. Instead of responding, though, she continued to stare into nothingness.

"Please, no more hiding shit, it's too late for that. What?"

The way she swallowed so slowly without a change in her blank stare told me before she said a word that I wasn't going to like what I was about to hear.

"You were so... jealous, so overprotective back then, remember? You would go on a rampage when you thought someone wronged me. Or wanted me." She swallowed again. "I was afraid... that you would go off the deep end and... and... end up in prison for the rest of your life. I couldn't let that happen, no matter what it meant, I... I had to keep that from happening."

I'd been seething moments before, bracing myself for whatever betrayal was coming. But instead, Annie had given me a glimpse into how she'd loved me so much that she'd sacrificed everything for me, to save me from myself. And that glimpse, it brought into stark relief just how undeserving of her love I was. Fuck, she'd done that for me, and I'd never even tried to track her down after she left for college.

Her eyes refocused on me and she wiped her cheeks with her palms. "I'm sorry," she said softly. "I really am. I wish I could go back and do things differently. But... I can't."

I wanted to rant at her for not telling me, not giving me the chance to avenge her, to protect her. But I also knew she was right. There was nothing else to be said or done, so I cried into her side, mourning what we could have had, what we *should* have had. Once I'd regained my composure, I spoke.

"I'm so fucking sorry. I should have protected you, but I didn't. Not then, and not now. I've failed you."

I stopped again, the weight of my guilt robbing my lungs of oxygen and making speaking impossible.

"Please don't do that to yourself. You didn't know. You *couldn't* have known. There is nothing you could have done differently. The only person responsible for what Charlie did is Charlie."

Her voice was fading, her features drawn with fatigue and discomfort.

"Don't talk, love."

She cried but didn't try to speak again. I knew I should walk away, but that didn't stop me from reaching for her hand anyway, cradling it between my palms as I tried to gauge her reaction to the contact. After a moment, her fingers curled to clasp my hand back and my heart stuttered painfully in my chest.

"I wish things had been different."

Her skin was impossibly soft against my lips when I pressed a kiss to the back of her hand, and I couldn't help lingering, soaking in the simultaneously familiar yet foreign sensation.

Gritting my teeth, I moved to release her and leave, but she clung more tightly as her eyes grew wide.

"It's okay. You're safe. He's in jail, and there's no way he can get out and come anywhere near you. I made sure of it." I swallowed thickly and continued. "I can call L-Luc... Someone to come back to stay with you, just tell me who."

"Don't go."

I looked down and she had fat tears streaking down her pale, haggard face, her eyes pleading for me to stay.

Goddamn, she was so fucking beautiful, even then.

Before I could stop myself, I replied, "Of course, love."

Her eyes fell closed as a shuddering breath left her body visibly more relaxed.

"I'm just getting a chair," I whispered as I pulled my hand from hers and moved a chair over, seating myself on her left.

It was funny, really; it was the same side I'd gone to earlier. I hadn't even realized until that moment that I was doing it again. When we'd dated, I always wanted to be on Annie's left side, to hold her left hand because I could look down where our fingers were intertwined and imagine a wedding ring on her finger.

Sitting down in the chair, I held her left hand again, though I fought the urge to look down at our fingers laced together. Instead, I studied her features as I used my other hand to brush her hair back gently from her forehead, noting the small changes since the last time I'd had the leisure to study her face. The changes in her pores, the fine wrinkling around her eyes and mouth, the paleness of her skin.

"Are you comfortable? Can I get you anything?"

She shook her head from side-to-side as she sighed without opening her eyes. I ached to do something—*anything*—to help. I felt so damn helpless sitting there and doing nothing. But that seemed to be what she needed, so I continued to smooth my thumb across her forehead until she fell asleep.

chapter twenty-eight

annie

"**Shh, it's okay**, love. I'm here. You're safe."

The sterile white walls of the hospital room filled my vision as my chest heaved, trying to take in more oxygen. Rob gripped my hand as he pushed my sweat-dampened hair away from my face. But I could still see Charlie choking me, taste the terror of my own impending death, smell—

"Look at me, Annie!" Rob's sharp shout dragged my attention back to him. "You're safe, I fucking *promise* you're safe. He'll never hurt you again. Just calm down and breathe, love. You have to breathe."

Rob helped me as I struggled to sit up and wrapped his arms tightly around me. His frame engulfed me, and I finally started to feel safe and my hysteria began to subside. Even so, I clung to him when he tried to pull away.

"I'm right here," he said quietly. "I'm not going anywhere. I'll keep you safe."

"I'm afraid to sleep."

"You *have* to."

He was right, of course, and I knew that, but I was so afraid of seeing Charlie when I closed my eyes.

"Please, don't let me go."

I was so ashamed to beg him to hold me that I almost couldn't choke out the words, but I didn't know what else to do. I was desperate for the comfort and security he could provide.

"You can't sleep sitting up like this," he replied gently.

Embarrassed and incapable of making eye contact, I gestured to the miniscule area beside me on the hospital bed.

"Annie..." his voice trailed off.

A glance up at him revealed a torrent of emotions engaged in a tug of war; he was in agony.

"I'm sorry," I breathed out.

"Fuck sorry. Sorry for what? Move over," he barked out angrily.

He was pissed off, but even pissed, I wanted him there, so I scooted to the far edge, leaving as much of the narrow hospital bed for him as I could. Even so, he didn't fit well, barely squeezing behind me on his side. If he leaned back at all, he'd surely roll straight onto the floor.

But he settled in anyway, using his right arm as a pillow as his left arm wrapped around the front of my body and tucked underneath my side in a snug embrace. I had no idea what the future would bring—I just wanted to make it through the night first—but there was no denying that in that moment, everything felt right. So, I relaxed into Rob's embrace, content in the knowledge that while he was there, nothing could hurt me.

Not even his brother.

Rob's warm breath washed over my face, as his heart beat steadily under my cheek and the scent of his skin and cologne permeated my nasal passages. My conviction of the rightness of it all was as excruciating as it was sweet, and I clung desperately to the feeling, refusing to consider the circumstances or timing. But when I swallowed to ease the dryness in my mouth only to discover the cotton-ball-level dryness was pleasant compared to the cut-glass sensation in my throat, I was instantly assaulted by violent memories, both recent and more distant.

My eyes flew open to find Rob's face only inches away. As the unwelcome images faded, I studied him, the contours of his face that, in some ways, I knew better than my own, the mass of hair that now covered much of it, the smattering of gray hairs at his temples and in his beard. So much had changed. And, yet, some things hadn't.

I lifted my hand and rested it gently on the upturned side of his face. His beard scratched against the sensitive skin on my palm, sending shockwaves of electricity through my body and into my extremities.

Things should have been different.

I smoothed my thumb over the warm skin between his eye and the top of his beard. Rob's eyes flew open, fear and concern momentarily clouding his features. He placed a hand on top of mine, pressing it against his face and his eyes closed as his breath hitched. The rise and fall of his chest accelerated noticeably as I saw moisture gathering in the corners of his eyes. There were so many things I wanted to tell him, but I couldn't bring myself to utter any of the words. Instead, I focused on the feel, the sound, the smell, everything that tethered me to that moment, until the physical pain was no longer bearable.

"I need a nurse. My head..." I scratched out.

"I, uh... I'll get someone."

My heart slammed into my ribcage at the unexpected voice coming from behind me.

"Lucas?" I whispered as I tried to turn around without rolling off the bed as Rob extricated himself from our embrace and my hospital bed with impressive alacrity.

"It's okay." Lucas's voice was soft. Too soft. "I'll get a nurse and give you guys a moment."

My feelings, which moments before had been so unambiguous, were again a knotted, tangled mess. I didn't want Rob to go, I just wanted to return to the moment before Lucas had spoken, when everything between us, everything we once were seemed to be putting itself back together.

But Lucas... I loved Lucas, too, and the thought of a future without him in it twisted my insides, tightening the knot of confusion.

I looked up at Rob, hoping to find something to help me figure out what I should do, but his face was mostly devoid of emotion, his features hard and guarded, his eyes shining with an enigmatic intensity. I lowered my gaze and worked to smooth out the wrinkles in the hospital blanket.

A few minutes later, Rob cleared his throat in the awkward silence that had blanketed the room since Lucas's departure and spoke.

"Lucas is here now. I should go."

Glancing up, I found Rob watching me with an inscrutable expression. I got the distinct impression he was waiting for something, like his words were a test, but I had no idea what the right answer was. And that wasn't fair to anyone. I looked back to my lap and nodded once.

"Thank you for staying."

"Of course."

"And, um, I'm sorry."

The softness of Rob's reply did nothing to hide the pain behind his words.

"Me too, love. Me too."

chapter twenty-nine

annie

It'd been several hours since Rob had left, and I'd be on my way home as soon as I received my discharge papers. My windpipe and voice box were badly bruised but not permanently damaged, and the gash on my head had been stitched closed. I would be sore for a while, but otherwise fine. I would be heading home soon with a handful of medications and a directive to see a therapist who specialized in trauma.

Lucas sat next to me as we waited, and my hand rested in his, but there was no reassuring pressure from him as he stared at the wall. Except when the medical staff had been in the room speaking to us, that was how he'd been since Rob had left.

"Lucas?" I asked, my heart in my throat.

"Hm?" he responded absent-mindedly.

"Are you mad?"

"No."

"Are you okay?" I was terrified of the response and immediately wished I could take back my question.

"Sure. Fine."

He continued to stare at the wall as we spoke, and I felt sick deep in the pit of my stomach. I'd done that to him. All I did was hurt the people around me.

"I'm sorry."

"For what?"

I closed my eyes briefly against the sudden dizziness as my heart thumped painfully. "F-for Rob."

His eyes immediately shifted from the wall to focus on mine. He watched me intently. Silently. My discomfort grew, but just as I thought I would need to look away, his eyes became glassy, and he turned back to the wall.

"Lucas, please..." I stopped as my voice cracked.

"Please what, Annie?"

"Tell me what you're thinking."

"We can talk about it later. Right now, you have enough on your plate."

"Are you leaving me?"

I wasn't sure how I'd forced the words out, and I couldn't breathe as I waited for his response, the loud, excruciatingly slow ticking of the second hand on the wall clock making the silence seem to stretch even further.

Lucas finally turned back to look at me again, his words slow and deliberate when he spoke. "Do you want me to?"

"No."

"Then, no."

He squeezed my hand, then turned back to the wall.

There was a police car already in the driveway when Lucas and I arrived. The car and porch were both empty, however; everyone was inside. Releasing a shuddering sigh, I tried to accept the inevitable—I'd have to relive what had happened the night before.

"Are you ready to go inside?" Lucas asked, his face averted as he looked out his window.

"The sooner we go in, the sooner it'll be over," I replied quietly as my hands began to tremble.

"Okay. Wait for me, I'll help you."

The air inside the car as Lucas closed his door was stifling, as if there was no oxygen left, and the car felt like it was shrinking down on me. Unable to sit still a millisecond longer, I opened my door to climb out as Lucas rounded the front bumper. But the effort to exit his low car set off a dizzying stab of pain in my head. An involuntary groan escaped my lips as I stumbled a few steps, catching myself against the trunk of the old maple next to the driveway.

"I said to wait!" Lucas shouted.

"I know, bu—"

"Then why didn't you?" he snapped.

"Because I didn't need help..."

My voice trailed off near the end as I fought the overwhelming emotions at being in a place that was now simultaneously comforting and horrifying, at feeling so helpless and confused, at wanting to fix what I'd done to Lucas, who'd never yelled at me like that before.

"But you could have hurt yourself! You have a concussion, you're—"

"Why are you yelling at me?" I asked, my voice barely a whisper. My jaw trembled as I fought against more tears. I wanted my voice to be strong and steady when I continued, but it was feeble and wavering instead. "You already insisted I leave in a wheelchair. You buckled my seatbelt for me. I feel so helpless. I needed to do *something* on my own." My voice broke on the last word, hot tears spilling over and rolling down my cheeks.

For a moment, a brief but blessed moment of silence before Lucas responded, I was somewhere else. Somewhere alone. Somewhere no one could talk to me, or yell at me, or judge me. Somewhere no one could hurt me, and I didn't have to try to explain things about myself that even *I* couldn't begin to understand. Somewhere blissfully silent and free of any expectations. Somewhere I could escape the oppressive emotion that was already drowning me.

"Do something on your own? You mean like deciding to have your ex sleep in your bed?"

Lucas was breathing hard, staring at me with such lividity that I was struggling to remember my conviction that he would never hurt me. He stepped closer, the rancor growing as he did, each step chipping away at my sense of safety, and I fought hard against the instinctive urge to turn and run as adrenaline flooded my bloodstream. He stood still, mere inches from me, for long moments doing nothing but breathing hard, his chest rising and falling with violent, jerky movements.

"Hell, Annie!" he suddenly exploded. "I don't know what to think right now. You were attacked, and you chose *him* last night. I'm your boyfriend, that's *my* job to be there for you, not your ex!

"I-I'm s-s-sorry."

"Damn it, Annie! He already had his chance!"

Lucas was shouting in my face, his eyes wild and desperate. I'd never seen him like he was, never would have guessed he was capable of it. Then his anger subsided, laying bare his heartache and despair.

"Damn it!" he roared again.

Charlie was suddenly in front of me, the same crazed look in his eyes from the night before as he grabbed my throat, the same look of grim satisfaction as he cut off my air supply.

"Annie! Annie!"

Voices shouted persistently in the distance, and I prayed for them to hurry, to get to me before it was too late. Charlie faded, and as everything around me came into focus, I realized my friends were the ones calling my name from where they stood in front of me. Behind them, an officer was handcuffing Lucas.

My eyes roved sluggishly from person to person as I watched with an odd sense of detachment and slowing of time.

"What the fuck happened out here, Annie?" Haley demanded. "We heard Lucas yelling, and then you screaming. When we got out here, he was shaking you, and you were fighting to get away. What the fuck did he do to you?"

"We were just arguing," I replied, my voice faint and scratchy. "The officer should let him go."

"But you're shaking like a leaf, babe. What really happened? Don't you lie to me, either."

"I'm not, it's what happened. I had a flashback. Lucas didn't do anything."

Haley's overt disbelief was written across her face as she studied me for the span of a few breaths before relaying what I'd said.

"But Lucas, once you're out of those cuffs, you can fuck off," she added.

The police officer, who I now recognized as former classmate Shawn Atchinson, removed the handcuffs. I was trapped in Lucas's burning stare, time slowing until he was free. Without even the minutest pause, he took a hasty step in my direction, but Shawn stopped him as I felt myself instinctively step back.

"Sir, the lady's right. I think it would be better if you left for a while. I need to talk to Ms. Turner for a bit anyway. You can come back later after you've had time to cool off."

Lucas looked at him in bewilderment. "She's my girlfriend. I'm not going anywhere."

"No disrespect, sir, but yes, ya are. Willingly or not."

I knew I needed to defuse the situation I'd been the catalyst for before it escalated any further, though I wasn't sure how.

"Lucas," I started, but barely any sound came out. I swallowed and tried again, just as unsuccessfully. Fighting the helplessness that tore at every fiber of my being, I turned to Haley and whispered into her ear again.

"Tell him I said to please do what Shawn said. We can talk later."

Guilt that I didn't go to Lucas and try to talk to him myself clawed at my heart. But as much as I loved him, I couldn't make myself go near him right then. I was too confused. Too scared.

"Lucas," Haley called out, her voice belligerent, "Annie said to fuck off."

I glared at her, shaking my head from side to side.

"Fine!" she huffed, rolling her eyes. "She said to please do as you're told."

Lucas's anguished eyes bored into me, tearing through me and into my soul. I wanted to be what he wanted, to do what he needed for reassurance, but it was just more than I was capable of right then. Filled with shame, I looked away, searching for some respite from the crushing weight of his expectations.

chapter thirty

annie

Once inside the house, I didn't even slow until I'd reached the bedroom and ripped off every piece of clothing, the same clothing I'd been wearing when Charlie had attacked me the night before. I even considered carrying them out to the living room and chucking them into the fireplace so I could watch them burn.

After changing, scrubbing my face, and brushing my teeth, effectively shedding everything I possibly could from the night before, Carol made me a cup of tea, complete with a heaping spoonful of honey to soothe my throat. Though, frankly, I would have preferred not to regain my voice for a while. Maybe ever. I didn't particularly want to relive what had happened ever again, let alone out loud. Not to mention for an audience. Really, I just wanted everyone—every single person there—to leave me alone. To go away so I could simply breathe without worrying about anyone else's well-being or happiness.

"It sure has been a long time, Annie," Shawn said after I settled onto the sofa between Haley and Carol, carefully positioning myself to leave a few inches of space between them and myself. "I'm sorry about the circumstances, though it's good to see ya. I'll try and make this as quick as I can. Can ya talk at all?"

"I'll try."

"Great. Okay, please start from the beginnin'."

Against my will, my head turned, and my eyes sought out an old painting of a woman in a garden that had been on the wall since I'd met Mom. The woman looked so peaceful, so content.

I wondered what it would feel like to be her.

"Annie," Carol said softly, tearing my attention from my thoughts. "You need to tell him *everything*."

I nodded absently; she was right. But that knowledge did nothing to help the words come any easier.

My heart lurched to a stop as the front door suddenly slammed open on its hinges.

Shawn was standing, gun drawn, before the crash of the door slamming into the wall had faded, his clipboard still tumbling through the air as he shouted, "FREEZE!"

"Whoa, what the fuck?!"

I'd been so certain it was Charlie that it took a moment to process that the voice didn't belong to him.

Shawn moved carefully around the furniture until he was in full view of the front door. After a brief pause, he holstered his gun with a chuckle.

"Well, hi there, Lori. Maybe next time don't take a door off its hinges when ya come in."

"Wait... Shawn? Shawn Atchinson!? Oh my god! I almost didn't recognize you under that uniform and all that muscle. How the hell have you been?" Lori asked, throwing her arms around him. They'd dated in high school; he was one of her many conquests.

Shawn's cheeks pinked as he returned her hug.

"So, why are you here with my boring old sister?"

Shawn cleared his throat and looked away, his discomfort apparent in the silence that followed.

"Your sister was fucking attacked, that's why. Which you would have known if you'd been here like you were supposed to," Haley bit out.

"You were attacked?" Lori directed at me. "Attacked how? Why didn't you call me if something happened?"

I was still formulating a response when Haley spoke.

"As in someone came after her and put her in the fucking hospital. She shouldn't have *had* to call you—you should have fucking been here already. It's Thanksgiving, for Christ's sake."

"Stop it, please." I tried to speak loud enough to be heard, but no one noticed over Haley and Lori's rapidly escalating voices.

"Hey, woah. You don't know me, you don't know what's going on in my life. Don't fucking judge me!"

"That's enough!" Shawn boomed with authority, finally back in cop mode. "Not another word from either of you, or you'll both have to leave. Understood?"

Haley nodded grudgingly, but my sister threw up her hands and muttered loudly, "See, this is why I don't try. Instead of being happy to see me, glad that I showed up, appreciative of the time I'm giving up to be here, it's always 'where were you, where have you been, why didn't you come?'"

Haley glared at Lori but said nothing.

"Thank you," I whispered, having known Haley long enough to realize just how much effort was required for her to bite her tongue.

Everyone else ignored Lori's mini-rant and settled back into their seats. Shawn picked up his clipboard and his pen from the floor, seemingly satisfied that everyone would remain quiet. Lori stayed in the front room, rearranging all the décor to look how she thought it should, just like she always did, despite how many times she'd been asked not to do it. I'd have to put everything back later, but was thankful that she was occupied.

"Okay, Annie, you were going to tell me what happened," Shawn said gently from his seat opposite me.

Swallowing the last of my tea, I carefully placed my mug on the coffee table, turning it slowly until the handle was at a perfect ninety-degree angle to the long edge of the table.

I thought. But maybe not quite?

I cocked my head from one side to the other, trying to determine if the angle was slightly off or if it was just how I was looking at it. Deciding it was off, I adjusted the cup a hair to the right, and then back again as I realized I'd moved it too far.

"It's time," Carol said softly as she placed her hand over mine.

I jumped at the sudden unexpected contact, yanking my hand back and sending the mug clattering loudly to its side on the coffee table, spilling the last few drops of tea. Carol's hand darted out and grabbed the mug, and she padded to the kitchen as she murmured about getting a towel.

I needed to tell Shawn what happened, I *knew* that, but I couldn't make myself do anything but start picking yarn pills off my sweater as I listened to the sounds coming from the kitchen.

Carol was making another cup of tea.

My eyes darted up to find Shawn watching me expectantly, and I immediately looked back down at my sweater as my hands began to tremble violently.

What if I told him and he said it was my fault? That I should have fought harder? That I shouldn't have stopped fighting? What if he told someone? The whole town—everyone—would know within minutes.

I shook my head quickly from side to side, as if answering a question, but one that no one had asked. Something wet landed on my hand and I jumped even as I realized it was my own tears.

Great, I was crying again.

"You can do it, babe," Haley encouraged. "You have to."

"No, you—I can't. I just... can't."

My palms slid roughly down the insides of my forearms, the painful pulling and catching on my skin a welcome and comforting distraction.

"It's all right, Annie, you can tell me," Shawn said kindly. "I just want to help to make sure he can't hurt ya again, or anyone else, for that matter. But I can't do that if ya don't tell me everything."

My eyelids felt heavy, falling closed as I took a controlled, deep breath in—uncomfortably deep—and held it for several heartbeats before pushing the air out between my lips. No one would know it, but I was searching.

Searching for that place inside myself that I'd once found so easily. It was like a little tiny hole I could fold myself into. And while I was there, I didn't have to feel anything.

I was eight the first time I found it. I'd been forced to molest a teddy bear for a room full of strangers to demonstrate what one of my abusers had done to me. The sense of filth, the shame, the self-disgust had been incomprehensible, rivaling how I'd felt when the same things had been done to me. The only way I'd made it through was by discovering this little hole inside myself where I could have a brief reprieve from harsh reality.

But as I sat there with everyone's eyes on me, the air pregnant with heavy expectations, I was having trouble locating it. My chest caved in on itself as I searched, and I knew I was getting close. Just a few more uneven breaths, and then I finally felt myself beginning to detach, the blessed numbness spreading, releasing the pressure on my lungs and allowing me to breathe.

Opening my eyes, I began.

I ended up recounting in painstakingly graphic detail everything that had happened the day Charlie raped me, the day I saw him outside Rob's house earlier that week, and finally what happened the night before, with some input from the others about their roles and what they saw or heard. Once all of Shawn's questions had been answered to his satisfaction, he stood, tucking his clipboard under his arm. He had been very much so the emotionless professional while discussing what happened, but his eyes overflowed with sympathy once he was on his feet.

"I'm so sorry all this happened to ya, Annie." He half-smiled and then turned and quietly let himself through the door.

"You okay, babe?" Haley asked.

"Yup, fine." And I wasn't lying. In that moment, I felt... nothing.

Haley, Carol, and Linc all looked at me dubiously.

"Well, I'm glad you're fine, Annie, but what the hell?!" Lori shouted as she stomped into the room.

"What do you mean?"

"Why didn't I know any of this?"

"Well, no one knew about the rape until recently. And I was just attacked last night."

"Why didn't you tell me?"

"I just told you that no one knew."

"But *they* did!" she retorted as she pointed an accusing finger toward my friends.

"Carol and Haley found out a few days ago. Linc, last night."

"What the hell, Annie? I'm your *sister*! I should know before anyone else does! You should have told *me* before you told *them*!"

"Why? When would I have told you, anyway? You never answer your phone. You rarely return my calls. You refuse to commit to anything and when you do? You usually end up canceling last minute, or just not showing up at all. So, really, when should I have told you?"

"But I'm your sister! You should tell me before anyone else!"

"I should tell you just because you're my sister?"

"Yes!"

"Maybe you should *be* a sister to her first!" Haley shouted, jumping into the fray to defend me. "You're so fucking selfish. Even now, you just found out she was raped, that she was in the fucking hospital because that same psycho attacked her last night, and you're making it all about you. Get the fuck over yourself, Lori!"

"Stay out of it, Haley, this is none of your business!"

"Shut the fuck up, both of you!" Linc's voice boomed through the house, silencing both Haley and Lori.

I glanced up at Linc gratefully before speaking. "Haley, just let it go, it's just how she is. Lori, now you know."

As soon as the last word left my tongue, I stood and left the room. I needed solitude and silence.

"Jesus Christ, Annie, what happened to your head?" Lori shouted after me.

"Seriously?"

"What, you're not going to tell me that, either?"

I shook my head in exasperation only to discover how big a mistake that was—the motion instigated pain so acute I saw spots and my balance wavered.

Lori was shouting again, but I heard nothing, all the sound around me disappearing as if I'd activated a mute setting. I had no idea what she was saying. And for once, I was incapable of making myself care.

chapter thirty-one

rob

As I rounded the corner onto my street on foot after several hours of walking in a failed attempt to clear my mind of all thoughts of Annie, I saw one of the last people I would have expected to see sitting on my porch.

Lucas lifted his head, silently watching me as I climbed the stairs. Why the hell was he there? Unless...

"What happened to Annie?"

"Nothing happened to her. She's fine. She's talking with the police right now."

Relieved, I released the breath I'd been holding.

"Then why the fuck are you here?" I asked.

"I... I don't even know."

"Why aren't you with Annie?"

The words left a bilious taste on my tongue that threatened to gag me. The real question was why *I* wasn't.

"Her friends are there." He swallowed as he stared ahead unseeing, speaking slowly as if in a daze when he continued. "Annie and I got into an argument."

My fists balled at my sides as I listened.

"And it triggered a flashback, so she started screaming. Everyone came running out of the house and the cop who'd been waiting for her cuffed me, thinking I'd hurt her. So, she was having this horrible flashback, but I couldn't do a damn thing to help her. And worse? I was the cause of it." He paused for the span of a few breaths. "Anyway, the cop wouldn't let me stay after that."

Why the fuck was he telling me all that shit?

"I love her so much, but, god, she's a mess. I mean, I knew that and went after her anyway, so I can only blame myself, though I had no idea how… there was just something about her… I couldn't stay away. But now? I don't know. I don't know. I just… I was yelling because I wanted to hit *you* and you weren't there. You had your fucking chance with her! And whatever the reason, it didn't work out. But every time I turn around…"

He suddenly shifted to look directly at me.

"I know she loves you and it's killing me. How did you do it? I know you love her—how did you not lose your mind when we started dating? I'm not an angry or violent person, I've never been jealous, but when it comes to her, I can't control myself. But I'm not that person. And I don't want to be. But the thought of losing her… I can't do that, either. How the hell did you do it?"

As I stood there trying to figure out what the hell to do, what to say, everything he said sank in and my vision immediately clouded with rage.

"Fuck you! Is she perfect? No—*hell* no. She *is* a fucking mess, always has been. But she's the strongest, most compassionate, most loving and selfless person you'll ever fucking meet. She's better than anyone else on the planet. If you can't see how everything about her, all that mess, makes her the beautiful person she is, you don't fucking deserve her. Get the fuck off my property."

I was livid, my breath coming and going in short, tempestuous bursts as I utilized all the self-restraint I could summon to avoid giving in to my urge to use him as a punching bag.

How could she *possibly* have chosen him over me? He didn't understand her like I did, love her like I did. Why the fuck couldn't she see that?

chapter thirty-two

annie

"**What're you doing** out here? It's fucking cold," Haley said, holding out a steaming cup of tea.

I took the mug from her, using the other hand to lift the corner of my blanket so she could huddle under it with me.

"I always loved sitting on this porch. I can see the mountains over there, see trees and bushes and flowers everywhere, at least in the spring and summer, and I can hear *everything*. Insects, birds, squirrels, even the weather. Did you know that when most storms come through the valley, they come from that direction? And you can hear them. The wind, the rain, you can listen as it gets closer. Watch it, too, like a blanket being dragged across the sky."

It was true that I'd always enjoyed the beauty to be found in watching nature and the shifting weather. But more than that, I'd derived immeasurable comfort from observing the cyclical changing of the seasons, year after year, from the *same spot*. Each passing year had chipped away at my expectation that something as unforseen as it was unwelcome would happen. I was able to develop a sense of permanence and stability for the first time in my life up to that point.

"Well, that's nice for you. All *I* can think about is that crazy motherfucker I kicked the shit out of right over there.

I smiled weakly. "There's that. But I don't want to let him ruin something I've loved for so long. He's had too much control over my life already."

"I hear you, I really do, but I couldn't do it. Kudos to you, babe, seriously." She laid her head on my shoulder, and we sat in a comfortable silence for a few moments before she spoke again. "So, where the hell is Lucas? I figured he would have been back by now."

"He's not coming. He didn't want to intrude on my time with you guys."

"I'm calling bullshit."

I knew she was right, and *she* knew she was right, even if that *was* what Lucas had texted.

"So, what's the real reason he isn't coming?"

I sighed. "I'm guessing for the same reason we were fighting earlier."

"Which is?"

"Rob."

"Speaking of, I hope it was okay that I called him while you were in the hospital. I assumed it was by your reaction when he showed up, but I probably should've asked first."

"You're fine."

"So, what about Rob caused the argument? The fact that you two still have the hots for each other?"

"What?"

"Oh, don't try to bullshit me, babe. It's obvious. *Painfully* fucking obvious. You guys look at each other like you're the key to each other's survival—frankly, it's disgusting. But I like him. He was an asshole to me on Thanksgiving."

"What? I didn't know you met him before the hospital. Oh, jeez, Haley, please tell me you didn't—"

"I wish," she interrupted me before I finished what I never wanted to utter aloud. "He's hot. But when he told me his name, I made the connection, so of course I couldn't sleep with him. But even if he hadn't told me his name, it wouldn't have happened, babe. Any guy out there with a dick jumps at an offer for no-strings sex. But Rob? He not only turned me down, but he got all pissed off and told me I was a shitty friend. Your turn. How did he cause an argument with Lucas?"

Just the thought of Haley propositioning Rob, even if he rejected her, turned my stomach and my whole body shuddered.

"Well, after you guys left the hospital, Rob stayed the night. I couldn't stop seeing Charlie when I closed my eyes, so I asked Rob to... hold me." I had to pause to breathe, shame and embarrassment making it more difficult than it should have been. "And he did. Until we woke up in the morning to find Lucas watching us."

"Oh shit! Oh my god, babe...So, what happened?"

"Nothing. Rob leaped out of bed like his ass was on fire, and Lucas left the room to find a nurse. Rob bolted the second Lucas returned."

Haley's gaze burned into me, but this time I wasn't sure what she was waiting for.

"What?" I snapped, irritated.

"What the fuck are you doing?"

"What do you mean?"

"Come on, really?"

"It's not that simple."

"Actually, yeah, it is."

Well, maybe it should have been, but it wasn't.

"It doesn't even matter, Haley. They're both gone. Rob and I ended years ago, and he certainly doesn't want to deal with my shit anymore, that much is obvious. I had to beg him to stay last night, and then he disappeared the second he had the opportunity. And Lucas? He's gone, too. And I can't blame him, either. How can I when *I* can't even figure out what's going on in my head, what I want? But it's okay. Really. I expected it to happen sooner or later. And I'm used to being alone, you know that."

Haley wrapped her arms around me, pulling me into her and resting her chin on my shoulder and sighing.

"I say this with all the love in the world, babe. You're a fucking moron."

chapter thirty-three

annie

By Saturday morning, I was alone again. Lori had left within an hour of her screaming match with Haley, and Haley, Carol, and Linc had left early the next morning.

I'd heard nothing from Lucas, not even a lousy text message. And despite what I'd said to Haley about being alone, I itched to call and try to fix things with him.

But what was the point?

Besides, I'd been alone before—I could surely do it again. I simply needed to ignore the emptiness that rested heavily on my chest, making it so damn hard to breathe. I knew from experience that eventually I wouldn't notice it anymore. I just had to get to that point.

Exhaustion consumed me. My eyes burned, my heart beat irregularly, my movements were weak and unsteady, and my head was in a thick fog. But sleep was no more than a distant fantasy because Charlie was there, waiting for me, every time I closed my eyes.

With a genetic predisposition to addiction, I'd avoided the narcotics I'd been sent home with, sticking to over-the-counter painkillers. But maybe if I took a few doses, it would knock me out and I could have a dreamless sleep for once.

I reached for the unopened bottle of hydrocodone sitting on the windowsill in the kitchen, first knocking it over in my exhaustion-induced delirium. Once I'd managed to grab it, I held it a few inches from my face, peering at the label with my eyes wide. But the words refused to come into focus. I rubbed my eyes violently, attempting to clear the blurriness from my vision long enough to make out the dosage information.

"Wake up, Annie."

My eyelids felt like they weighed as much as a car. Each. But I forced them open to slits and saw Lucas kneeling in front of me.

"Lucas?"

"Thank god, I was getting worried," he rushed out, the relief in his voice palpable.

"What's going on?" The lamp next to me was on, but it was dark outside. "What time is it?"

"It's almost midnight. No one's been able to reach you all day."

My eyelids were impossibly heavy, and I stopped trying to keep them open, succumbing to the need to let them close.

"Annie! Look at me, sweetheart. I need you to tell me exactly what happened."

"Nothing. I'm just tired."

"Look at me."

I dragged my eyes open again, a few millimeters all I could manage. Somehow, I hadn't noticed before but was now aware that my heart felt like it was barely beating and I had trouble making my lungs expand for each breath.

"Annie! You're freaking me out. Sit up and talk to me."

Lucas's arm wrapped around my back and began lifting me to a more upright position, but a wave of nausea rolled over me as the room spun unpleasantly.

"Stop! I'm going to be sick!"

Lucas grabbed the small living room trash can Mom kept there for catching yarn scraps when she knit, shoving it in front of me just in time to catch my stomach contents as they violently exited my body.

"Something's wrong. Just tell me what happened so I can help."

"I don't... I don't know. I..." The heaviness in my chest made it increasingly difficult to get enough oxygen, and it was impossible to clear the worsening mental fog. "Meds. And tea. That's all."

"Which meds?"

"Pain."

"They gave you hydrocodone. Are you allergic? Have you taken it before?"

I shook my head as he jumped up and ran into the kitchen, shouting, "How much did you take?"

"I don't know..." I replied as he rounded the corner back into the living room, the bottle in his hand. "I just wanted some peace from the nightmares."

chapter thirty-four

rob

"**She's resting now**, sir. We'll continue to monitor her until her vitals have stabilized for at least twenty-four hours before we can talk about discharging her. We'll also be monitoring for signs of pneumonia, which she's at risk for after having her stomach pumped. And she'll need to be evaluated by our on-staff clinical psychologist to determine if she poses a continued threat to her own safety."

I listened and watched in detachment from where I stood near the entrance to the Emergency Room as Lucas scrubbed his hands over his face before folding his arms tightly in front of him as he stared at the ceiling.

After a moment, Lucas looked back toward the doctor and thanked him.

"Thank you for getting her here. You did the right thing; overdoses like this can be fatal."

I was rooted in place as I watched them shake hands, my chest laboring as I tried to catch my breath. But I needed answers. All I knew was what I'd just overheard the doctor telling Lucas as I rushed through the doors. Lucas had only texted me that Annie was in the hospital.

"What the fuck? What the fuck did you do to her?" I bellowed as I neared him.

He stared at me for a moment, like he was trying to remember who I was or how to speak.

"No one did anything to her. No one was even there."

"Where the fuck were you? She just got out of the hospital after being attacked, and you left her *alone*?"

His posture slumped further as he stared at the floor.

"I needed some space to think. I just... it doesn't matter. I can't do this. I love her, but I can't. I don't know how to help her. And I can't watch her do the same thing my mom did, I can't go through that again. I just can't do it. I thought... I thought I could help her, that I could fix—"

"*Fix* her? Like she's fucking broken?"

"That's not what I meant."

"This whole time I thought you actually cared about her, but you just saw her as something needing repair. And now that you think you can't do it, you're going to just quit on her? Bail? That's pathetic."

"I love her."

"You don't know what love is!"

It took every fiber of my being not to give in to the violence I could feel simmering below the surface and beat the shit out of him as I thought about the effect him giving up would have on Annie. But if I did that, they would never let me see her.

Lucas must have heard the brutal undercurrent in my voice because he finally turned around and started toward the exit. I watched until he was out of sight, needing to make sure he was actually gone. As soon as he was, I allowed the nearest wall to support me as I took a series of deep breaths to release some of the volatile tension choking me. When I was satisfied that I was as calm and in control as I was going to get, I made my way over to the check-in station.

"Hi, Hannah. Annie Turner's room, please."

"Hi, Rob." Her voice was hesitant, unsure and she glanced sideways before her eyes darted back to me. "I don't know if it's a good idea to let you back there."

"Why not?" I barked out without thinking.

I had to calm down. If I kept growling at her, she'd never let me through the fucking doors.

"Well, I just watched you and that other guy who brought her in gettin' into it, and I'm not sure it's a good idea."

"I promise I'm not going to cause any trouble. And, Hannah... I don't want her to wake up and be alone. Especially if... well, you heard the doctor. She really shouldn't be alone. And her family isn't around right now, it's just me."

If I hadn't already been going to hell, I was now for pulling that shit, but I didn't give a fuck if it got me into her room.

"And the guy who brought her in—her boyfriend, according to him."

"That's over," I managed to say through my clenched jaw. "Despite how it may have seemed, he was leaving because he wanted to."

"I don't know, Rob. I know her mama's out of the country and all, but what about her little sister?"

"Her sister's a fucking flake, same as always. And she doesn't live around here, anyway. I don't even have her number."

"What about old Mrs. Renner? Didn't they used to be close?"

"If she doesn't already know, I'll call her myself once I see that Annie's all right. I promise, Hannah. Please tell me where her room is and let me back there."

She sighed deeply, eying me with uncertainty. "Look, I know you and Annie dated in high school and I've always liked you, so I'm going to let you back there, but I better not get fired for this. She's in room 807. Down the hall here. I'll buzz you through those doors, then take your first right. Her room's down there on the left, near the end of the hall."

"Thank you, Hannah. You won't regret it."

I jogged down the hall once Hannah buzzed me through until I reached Annie's door. The room was dark as I slowly pushed the door open, in stark contrast to the too-bright fluorescent lights in the corridor.

My heart beat into my throat as I stepped through the doorway.

I tried to keep my footsteps as quiet as possible as I moved further into the room, closing the door behind me with a faint click. Annie was hooked up to several machines that softly beat in a steady rhythm as they monitored her vital signs, as well as an IV drip attached to her hand. She appeared to be sleeping peacefully.

But I knew Annie. There was no way in hell she was sleeping soundly on her own after everything she'd been through. She must have been sedated.

Leaving the door cracked to keep an eye on Annie, I dialed Mrs. Renner's number from the hall.

"Hello?"

"Hi, Mrs. Renner," I whispered. "It's about Annie."

"Rob? I can barely hear you."

"Yeah, it's me," I replied, elevating my voice a fraction. "Annie's in the hospital. She overdosed on painkillers. They don't know yet if it was intentional or not. She's stable right now, but she'll be here for another day or so for monitoring. I'm here with her."

After a brief pause, she asked, "Where's Lucas?"

A slow, deep breath took the edge off the instant rage his name triggered.

"I don't know. He said he couldn't handle it, that he'd thought he could fix her, but he was wrong. And said he couldn't watch the same thing happen that had happened to his mom. What does that mean? I thought she had cancer."

Mrs. Renner's sigh on the other end of the line was heavy. "She had terminal cancer, and she was dying—that's true. But she saw what it was doing to Lucas and his dad as she got sicker and wanted to spare them from more torment. She overdosed on painkillers. Lucas found her while she was still breathing."

"Jesus, I had no idea."

"He rushed her to the hospital, but it was too late. She died on the way."

"I'm so sorry, for all of you. He must have felt like he was reliving it, but—"

"It's okay—"

"—it doesn't change what he said, or that he just abandoned her."

When Mrs. Renner remained silent, I continued.

"Anyway, I thought you should know since her mom isn't around. And I would let her sister and friends know, but I don't know how to reach them. I didn't see Annie's phone anywhere."

"That's all right. Lucas has a key to her house and can get her phone and let everyone know."

"Okay."

"How is she?"

"Sleeping right now."

"When should I come?"

"Whenever you want."

"We can do shifts until she's discharged, so you tell me when you want to go home for a bit."

I snorted. "Not happening. You can just come whenever you want."

"I'll come in a few hours then."

"Okay."

"And, Rob?"

"I don't want to hear it, I'm already trying not to hit something."

"When will you ever learn to just shut up and listen? I only wanted you to know that she's lucky to have you."

"No, she's not. Lucky would be if she'd never even met me. Then none of this shit would have ever happened because Charlie never would have... he..." My voice faded as I heard Charlie's in my head, telling me what he'd done to her.

"Honey, none of that is your fault. Don't you go blaming yourself for what he's done, you understand?"

A few minutes later, I was standing next to Annie again, the rhythm of my heart disjointed as I studied the contours of her face, the way her hair fell across the pillow. Even in the sickly glow cast by the machines, days past needing a shower, circles under her eyes and bruises on her neck, she was the most beautiful, the most incredible creature I'd ever seen.

chapter thirty-five

annie

With every heartbeat, I felt like my head was being slammed against concrete and was on the verge of exploding. I was thirstier than I could recall ever having been in my life. My throat was on fire. Even my hand hurt.

I still hadn't opened my eyes, keenly aware of the new heights of agony that would accompany the light. As I listened to the steady beeping, I knew it was familiar, but I couldn't quite break through the fog in my head to place it. Square white ceiling tiles peeked through my eyelids when I slid them open a fraction. I knew what I was looking at was as familiar as the sound, but identifying it was just beyond my grasp. With considerable effort, I forced my head in the direction of the incessant beeping. Monitors and IV. The hospital.

I turned my head to the other side.

Rob? I must have been dreaming. If I was actually in the hospital, he wouldn't have been the one sitting there.

And yet... there he was. Sitting in a chair next to the bed, holding my hand in both of his as he slept with his head resting on the bed next to me. I closed my eyes again and then it hit me—that unmistakable Rob smell.

I wasn't dreaming.

A nurse bustled into the room unexpectedly and started talking in a loud, chipper tone. "Miss Turner? You awake, sweetie?"

Rob jerked up, and though I couldn't see him through my closed eyelids, I could feel him looking at me, the weight of his gaze as physical a sensation as the pressure from him squeezing my hand. I nodded slowly in response to the nurse's question.

"Great! I'm Nurse Mandy. I need you to open your eyes so I can get a look at your pupils, can you do that for me, sweetie?"

I wanted to do that about as much as I wanted to gouge them out with my fingertips. But I did as she asked, even as I felt my face twisting involuntarily from the fresh onslaught of blinding pain.

"Great, sweetie, good job. I know it's unpleasant but keep 'em open for me. I need to examine you and ask you a few questions now."

Keeping my eyes focused on her face, I nodded in assent. I hadn't yet looked over at Rob—I was steadfastly avoiding doing so—but I could feel his eyes boring into me and my heart sped up.

"Sweetie, you okay? What's goin' on? Your heart rate is jumpin' all of a sudden."

"I'm fine," I barely managed to eke out, sounding like a two-pack-a-day smoker.

"You sure, sweetie? Your heart rate shouldn't be climbin' when you're just layin' there like that. Can you take a couple of slow, deep breaths for me?"

I inhaled and exhaled as slowly and deeply as I could manage, but the only thing I accomplished was making the room spin. My lids slammed shut against the unwelcome sensation of movement.

"Sweetie, you still with us?"

I nodded. "Just dizzy."

The scratch of Rob's beard was immediately followed by the contrasting softness of his lips pressing into my forehead as he squeezed my hand. I'd come to terms with us being over, having said our goodbyes to one another, but now he was there, and he was kissing me.

The hot electricity where he touched me was accompanied by an intensifying of the throbbing in my head.

"Sir, you're making it worse. You'll need to leave."

"No," he replied flatly, as if responding to her was a distraction.

"Sir, you need to leave the room now or I'm gonna' have to call security. She's not well, and you're makin' it worse."

"Do what you feel you need to do, but I'm not leaving her."

I recognized his belligerent tone. He'd set his mind to staying and there was no use in arguing with him.

"He can stay," I said weakly as I forced my eyes open.

"No, Miss Turner, he can't. We need your vitals stabilized and your heart and blood pressure are not stable right now because of him bein' in here."

She pulled a walkie-talkie out of a pocket in her scrubs and called for security. Within minutes, two men in security uniforms entered my room.

"Todd, Randy, I appreciate you have a job to do, but I'm not fucking leaving."

"You got to leave. If they say you can't stay, you can't stay. Come on, don't give us trouble."

Rob didn't respond or move, but I could feel his muscles tensing as he poised for a fight.

I had to do something. But what? Really, I couldn't do anything. And even if I could, did I want him to stay or go?

Todd and Randy approached Rob, one on each side as they pled with him to cooperate, but they were met with silence. They each grasped an arm and forcibly lifted him, but he kept his hold on my hand until my arm was stretched tight, all the while releasing a string of expletives.

"Get the fuck off me! I'm not leaving, goddamn it!"

"Just come on, Rob, just come with us."

He was fighting to free himself when everything around me started to swirl and spin.

Beep... beep... beep.

A distinct feeling of déjà vu washed over me just before I remembered everything that had happened. As I struggled to unfreeze my lungs, my eyes shot open. A split second later, Rob's eyes were inches from mine, his hands cradling my face.

"Shh, it's okay, I'm right here, see? Right here. I'm not going anywhere, I promise. I'm right here, Annie, always."

The weight on my chest lifted slightly as he spoke, which didn't make any sense since his presence was also what was causing it. His lips pressed gently into my forehead and he whispered against my skin.

"I'm here, with you, always, love, always."

As he sat back down next to me, Nurse Mandy appeared at the foot of the bed, a disapproving glare trained on Rob before she turned to me.

"Miss Turner, I need to ask you a few questions, okay, sweetie?"

I nodded.

"Are you having any shortness of breath, aside from what *his* presence is causing?"

My head moved side-to-side.

"What about chest pain?"

I shook my head again.

"How about your throat? Can you speak and swallow for me, sweetie?"

"Yes," I croaked out in a hoarse whisper, followed by a dry, painful swallow. My mouth felt like it had cotton balls covered with thorns lodged in it. "But it hurts."

"Yeah, sweetie, it's gonna' hurt for a while, those tubes always do."

"Tubes?"

"From pumpin' your stomach."

I looked between Rob and Nurse Mandy, both of whom were watching me with an unnatural attentiveness.

"Do you remember at all what happened?" she asked.

I shook my head.

"That's normal. You overdosed on hydrocodone. We pumped your stomach when you got here, unsure how long it had been." She spoke slowly, watching me closely.

What the hell was going on? Why were they staring at me like that? It was as if they thought I... Realization hit me with the subtlety of a baseball bat to the face.

"No!" I shouted, all the other sounds in the room fading into the background as my heartbeat thundered in my ears.

"Shh, it's okay, Annie, calm down," Rob soothed, sounding far away and looking uncertain.

"No! I didn't. Please, believe me."

"Can you tell us what *did* happen, sweetie?"

I closed my eyes and fought to remember. "Everyone had left, gone home. I was so tired, but I couldn't sleep. My head hurt. Then..."

I remembered that I had taken some extra painkillers to help me sleep. But could just an extra dose or two have done this?

"I took the painkillers, but took some extra to help me sleep. Every time I closed my eyes... I was so tired. I thought it would help."

"How many pills?"

I closed my eyes and tried to remember what I saw on the bottle.

"Eight? Ten? I think I saw a four on the bottle and I didn't count exactly how many I poured out. I was having trouble seeing. A small handful."

"Sweetie, that four was the maximum number of pills to take in a 24-hour period, not your dosage," Nurse Mandy replied gently, as if she was talking to a confused child. "The prescription says that in bold letters on the bottle, it would be very hard to confuse."

"I swear, it's the truth."

"Sweetie, it's okay, you can tell us, we just want to help you."

They didn't believe me. Helplessness smothered me as I started to cry.

"She said it was a fucking accident. She'd just been attacked, she was tired, it's understandable that she was distracted. Leave her the fuck alone!" Rob shouted at Nurse Mandy.

"Sir, if you don't calm down, you will be removed from the premises, and this time, you won't be allowed to return."

They glared at each other in mutual dislike until Rob turned back to me.

"How did I get here?" I asked.

Rob watched me intently again before responding quietly. "Lucas."

I craned my neck, looking around the room to see if he was sitting in a corner somewhere I hadn't seen him.

"He's not here," Rob offered.

But something about his tone was off. And he was studying me with a guarded expression as he spoke. There was something he wasn't saying.

"What's going on? Where is he?"

If Lucas had brought me in, that meant he'd come back, that he had meant it when he said he would come back. I hadn't believed him, but he'd been telling the truth. He hadn't left me after all.

Rob turned away from me suddenly as if something had caught his attention, but I didn't see anything. I watched his throat move as he swallowed slowly.

"Get some rest," he said gruffly without looking at me. "We can talk more later."

"I hate to agree with *him* about anything, but he's right, sweetie, you should rest," Nurse Mandy agreed.

The room was dark when I next opened my eyes. A glance around revealed that I was alone, except for a shadow in the far corner.

The shadow started across the room, but I couldn't see well enough to make out who it was. It wasn't until he'd reached me that I could finally tell, and by then it was too late.

"Time to finish what I started," Charlie whispered as his hand closed in an iron grip around my throat. I wanted to fight, but I couldn't move. The only thing I was able to do was watch his expression shift to mirthful amusement as he squeezed.

As I faded, I thought I heard someone calling my name in the distance. The voice was becoming louder and more insistent, but Charlie simply laughed.

"No one can save you now."

My eyes fluttered open as I gasped and shuddered.

"Can you hear me, Annie? You're safe. He can't hurt you anymore. It's a dream, love."

I realized as they loosened their hold that Rob and two nurses had been pinning down my arms and legs. As the moments passed, the blaring of the machine alarms slowly trickled into my awareness. I looked around the room with an odd sense of detachment, of disembodiment, as if I was observing from above. I watched as Rob wrestled his emotions: anger, sadness, regret, fear, pain.

Every single one of them negative.

Every single one of them because of me.

chapter thirty-six

rob

Something in Annie changed after the nightmare. The hospital staff didn't seem to notice, but I *knew* her, and to me, it was clear as fucking day. It was as if she lost her fight, her will to continue. For the first time since I'd met her, she seemed truly, utterly, defeated. Just... completely hopeless. I'd never seen her like that, and unease settled over me like a dense, heavy fog.

When offered a sedative to help her sleep, she accepted. She avoided eye contact with me and tried repeatedly to pull her hand away, but I'd be damned if I was going to let her go. Even then, as she slept, I held onto her. I always would.

I'd tried to talk to her before the sedative knocked her out, but she'd been completely unresponsive. Something was undeniably *very* wrong. Fuck the staff if they couldn't see it.

There was no resistance as I gently turned her hand over while she slept, running my index finger softly up and down the underside of her forearm. Near the middle, I could just barely make out the faint ridges and looked down. It was too dark to see anything, but I didn't really need to, anyway. I'd known the scars were there before I even felt them. I knew how many, how large and small, exactly where they were relative to one another.

I'd never forgotten.

I studied the profile of the strange girl who'd just told me her name was Annie, noting the rapid rise and fall of her chest, the rosy splash of color spreading across her face and neck. Her eyes darted up to me before returning to her lap and her blush deepened—a blush I already felt I couldn't get enough of. But before the flash of embarrassment when she looked back down, I caught the curiosity and compassion in her gaze.

I sat next to her and talked to her that day. She barely uttered a word in response, but I kept going to class day after day, sitting next to her, and talking to her anyway. It was never about trying to get into her pants after that first day when I'd scared her; I just wanted to be near her. Even though she didn't really seem to want me there, simply being around her made me feel lighter. I could be myself around her, I could breathe.

Even though the life currency Charlie and I had always dealt in was ruling with fear, doing crazy shit and getting into fights all the time, I suddenly and desperately didn't want that anymore. I just wanted the feeling I had when I was around her, that novel happiness and ease. And I wanted her to stop being afraid of me. Fuck, I wanted that so bad I couldn't think about anything else. And I figured that would happen if she spent more time with me, so, much to her chagrin, before she had a chance to protest, I signed up to be her project partner for the semester.

By the end of the semester, we were friends and spent as much time together as we could manage. Which really wasn't nearly enough for me since her mom didn't approve of our friendship, courtesy of the reputation my brother and I had. Though I hadn't been doing any of that shit since I'd met Annie. I just didn't want to.

All I wanted was her—to spend time with her, to keep her to myself.

As our friendship grew, I learned that Annie wasn't the person everyone thought she was. The somewhat outgoing social girl was a persona that she wore to meet the expectations of everyone around her. Really, she preferred solitude, and we spent much of our time together just quietly being near each other.

Not that we never talked, because we did. At least *I* did. I couldn't help it, she was so damn easy to talk to. About anything. I told her the little I remembered of my parents before they were both killed in a car accident when I was six. I talked to her about how Charlie and I were bounced around from family member to family member, moving just about every year since our parents had died, no one really wanting us, until we'd landed in her town with foster parents who didn't really want us, either.

I even told her stuff I'd never voiced before, about how lonely I was, something I hadn't even realized until it just came out while I was talking to her. How Charlie and I had stopped even trying to make friends many years before because everyone just forgot us anyway when we were offloaded to the next family member in another town.

I'd never put feelings of any kind into words before, but it was just so natural with Annie because she *really* listened. With compassion and understanding, acknowledging my pain instead of minimizing it like other people would. She even heard the things I didn't realize I was saying, naming and sympathizing with emotions I'd been unaware existed until she spoke about them.

And then, after all that was the most amazing part. She helped me find silver linings, so it wasn't all for nothing. I didn't understand how the fuck she did that, but she did.

It wasn't long before I couldn't deny to myself anymore that I was hopelessly in love with her. I tried, on more than one occasion, to kiss her, but she always refused, begging me not to mess up our friendship. She looked at me the same way I looked at her, so I couldn't understand her refusal, but I tried to just accept it anyway, afraid of scaring her away if I pushed too hard.

I knew I wouldn't see her much over winter break after that first semester, and I was practically paralyzed with fear that the time apart would change things between us. I would do whatever it took to make sure that didn't happen. So, one day close to the start of the break, a cold day with the first snow of the year falling softly, I decided I had no choice but to tell her that I was in love with her.

Annie and I were walking on the cross-country course, as we so often did, and had stopped at Annie's favorite spot: a big old willow along the back side of the course, where you couldn't see anything but the mountains, pastures, and orchards. Everything that time of year was barren, varying shades of brown and death, but we always stopped there anyway, and I knew it was the perfect place to tell her.

We were both leaning with our backs against the massive trunk, Annie with her eyes closed. It was time. My heart in my throat, I stepped away from the trunk, pivoting so I was standing in front of her with my feet straddling hers. Christ, my breathing was erratic, bordering on panting.

"Annie." I was close enough that I could feel her warm breath bathing the cold skin on my face as she replied.

"Hm?"

I took a deep breath and pulled my hands out of my coat pockets. I was so nervous my hands were shaking—big, jerky movements—but I didn't have a choice. I couldn't risk losing her; I *had* to tell her.

So, I gently cradled her face and neck in my shaking hands. As soon as my fingers touched her skin, her eyes flew open.

"What're you doing?"

I leaned in as I struggled for air, touching my forehead to hers. After a dry swallow, I forced the words past my lips, praying they would be reciprocated.

"I love you."

After the words were out, I thought I might actually be sick, so acute was my terror that she didn't love me back. After a short pause, her breathing became ragged and under my hands, I could feel her heart beating a rapid, irregular rhythm. I allowed myself a glimmer of hope and pulled my head back a few inches so I could see her face. She held my gaze as I searched her eyes, trying to figure out what she was thinking since she hadn't yet spoken.

Her eyes were glassy with unshed tears as the seconds continued to tick by until she finally whispered a response.

"I love you, too."

She'd barely spoken the last word before I'd crushed my mouth to hers. The thought crossed my mind that it may have been her first kiss and I should be more considerate, but my heart, my emotions, had taken over my actions and there was nothing I could do about it. Relief and elation flooded my body.

I was happy, fucking ecstatically happy.

After a brief hesitation, she was kissing me back just as feverishly as I was kissing her, only pulling away occasionally to drag air into her lungs. In that moment, it was as if all the emotion that had been building for months finally had an outlet and we couldn't get enough of each other. And that feeling, that knowledge that she wanted me, too, that she couldn't get enough of me either… it was the best feeling in the world. I felt invincible.

I couldn't get close enough to her, the bulky coats we wore forcing too much space between us, so, despite the cold, I broke our kiss long enough to yank our coats off, dropping them somewhere near our feet before my lips found hers again. When our mouths touched again, the novel sensation was somehow also familiar already and I knew I'd never tire of kissing her.

Every muscle in my body was tensed with excitement as my fingertips increased pressure along the side of her neck, holding her close to me. When her hands, warm and trembling, began to lift my shirt, her fingertips brushing the bare skin on my abdomen, I lost any vestige of control or rational thought. Months of unspoken love, pent up desire—it all took over. I felt like I would die if I didn't touch her skin right then and I frantically began to pull her sweater off.

As her arms slid out of the sleeves of her sweater, something caught my eye. Breaking our kiss, I turned my head to look closer and froze.

Her eyes followed my gaze and when she saw what was holding my attention, she panicked and took off running. It took a moment to process what had just happened, and then I grabbed her coat and sweater and was off after her.

"Annie, wait! Please!"

She kept running as if she hadn't heard me, though I was sure she must have. I sprinted hard after her, catching up after a moment and wrapping my arms around her from behind to stop her. My chest heaved as I struggled to catch my breath enough to speak.

"What the fuck is that?"

The rise and fall of her chest didn't slow and I could feel her hot tears falling on my hands where they held her back against my chest.

"Talk to me. I just want to understand what I saw. Is it what I think it is?"

Her whole body shook as she started sobbing, but she still wouldn't answer me. It looked like... but there was no way she could have done that to herself.

"Annie, please. I don't even know what to think right now. Or... or... what to do? I swear, I'll make sure whoever did this never fucking touches you again, just tell me who."

"I... can't," she said between sobs.

"Why not? I thought we could tell each other anything. Fuck, I've told you *everything*."

"You'll leave."

I tried to be patient as I waited for her to tell me, but every sob that escaped her was tearing me in half and rage that someone had dared to touch her began to fester.

"Annie, goddamn it, you need to tell me!"

I wasn't expecting it when she violently shoved away from me, so she managed to free herself from my hold. She moved quickly, putting several feet between us, her back still towards me as she hung her head and shivered.

"I did it, okay? I did it to myself. Go ahead, go, I understand."

All those scabs, all those pale crisscrossing scar lines... she did that to herself?

I bent slowly, grabbing her clothing from where it had landed on the ground when I caught up to her and walked around to stand in front of her.

"Please, put these on, you're freezing."

Keeping her eyes averted, she quickly dressed. There were no longer tears falling, but her red-rimmed eyes were so sad they seemed almost lifeless and her voice when she spoke was resigned, devoid of emotion.

"It's okay, Rob, really. I know you want to go, and you can. I don't blame you."

"You keep fucking saying that. Go where?"

"Just... go. You don't need to deal with my problems."

"Are you fucking *kidding* me right now? You think what I feel for you is that fucking shallow? I'm not going anywhere, got it? I told you that I love you."

She finally lifted her head, her face full of doubt. "You'll change your mind."

"No, I fucking won't."

"Promise?"

"I promise." I grabbed both of her hands in mine and squeezed. "I couldn't stop loving you even if I tried. I have as much choice about it as I do about needing oxygen to breathe."

Slowly, haltingly, she started to talk. She finally told me what happened during her childhood. How her parents had bounced her back and forth, abandoning her, not once, not twice, but over and over and over again. Their absence and neglect, the rampant substance abuse. How she was molested repeatedly, by different people, starting when she was six years old. How her father had shamed her and called her a liar, swearing her to secrecy when she told him what happened.

The deep shame she still struggled with from having to demonstrate for a room full of strangers what had been done to her so they could prosecute. How she battled chronic nightmares about being chased and raped. How she was so uncomfortable around guys, afraid of them, sure they all wanted to touch her and how she felt guilty for not wanting them to, like she was supposed to do whatever they wanted.

How she fought intense feelings of worthlessness and self-disgust but hid it because everyone expected her to be happy and well-adjusted.

How crushingly lonely she was.

She explained that sometimes all of it was just too much and the only way she could manage, could continue with daily life, the only way she felt she could even breathe, was to create a distraction in the form of physical pain. And so, she cut herself for a temporary reprieve.

I hadn't been through the same things she had, but I understood the caliber of pain she described, the sadness, the loneliness, all of it. She cut herself to deal with it; I got into fights and destroyed shit with Charlie. Really, there was no difference, except there was no way I could sit by and let her continue. I'd do whatever it took to ensure it never happened again.

She had looked anywhere but at me while she was talking and I remained silent as I stood holding her hands, understanding that she needed to just get it all out.

"Annie," I said as gently as I could when she was done. When she didn't look up or make a sound, I said her name again, shaking her hands slightly for emphasis.

The pain in her beautiful, expressive brown eyes when she finally looked up rent my heart in two.

"I love you," I said over the lump in my throat. "I can't even tell you how fucking much I love you. I'm not going anywhere. Not now, not fucking ever. You understand? I'm always going to be here, no matter what; I can't help it. You can always come to me, talk to me. Please, you *have* to talk to me instead of hurting yourself. I don't know how yet, but I swear I'll figure out a way to help that doesn't involve you doing this to yourself."

"I'll try."

"No. Promise me."

"I promise."

She dropped my hands and crashed into my chest as she wound her arms tightly around my waist and buried her face into my neck. She fit perfectly, as if we'd been made to hold each other that way. I kept her there for a long time with my arms wrapped around her. Once she'd stopped crying, I kissed the top of her head.

"It's you and me, Annie. Always."

chapter thirty-seven

annie

There were voices close by, speaking in hushed tones; too hushed for me to identify at first. A wiggle of my fingers told me Rob was no longer holding my hand and I was conflicted. I knew it was better, and inevitable—I was a fucking mess, even by *his* standards—but it still hurt that he had left. Again.

Well, that was maybe unfair. I had left *him* back then. But he hadn't fought for me, either. He'd always promised he would never let me go, that he would always be there, would always fight for me. But then he hadn't. And that had possibly been worse than if he *had* left me.

But I knew better this time, I knew he wouldn't actually stay. Though knowing that didn't make it hurt any less.

The quiet talking had stopped, and I wondered idly if I'd imagined hearing the voices to begin with. But when I peeked under my eyelids, I saw Mrs. Renner and Lucas sitting on the far side of the room. Lucas was hunched over, his head in his hands while Mrs. Renner rubbed his back absent-mindedly with a faraway look in her eyes.

Mrs. Renner turned her head and her eyes softened as they connected with mine, a smile warming her face. But I'd seen the sadness there before she'd turned, a sadness I had caused.

I turned away.

"Annie?" Lucas's voice was timid.

I didn't turn or respond. Instead, I studied a light stain on the wall. What had caused it? Was it blood that had stained the paint? Or maybe—

"I'm so sorry," Lucas's voice broke as he spoke.

What was he sorry for?

Before I had a chance to stop myself, I'd turned my head. My heart skipped and I ached to hold him, to comfort him through whatever was wrong; the anguish and remorse written in his eyes was heartbreaking.

"I'm so, so sorry. I was overwhelmed by… the similarities to… to what happened to Mom. I told you she died of cancer, but…" He paused and took a shuddering breath. "She was *dying* of cancer and… and she thought it would be easier for dad and me if she ended things. So, she did. She… um… she overdosed on Vicodin. I tried… I tried to save her, but…" His voice broke again, and his shoulders shook as he cried into his hands. "When you… it all came rushing back… I'm so sorry."

"What the fuck are you doing here?" an enraged Rob boomed from just inside the doorway, loud enough to vibrate the walls. I jumped and my pulse skyrocketed as the air charged with imminent violence.

"Rob!" Mrs. Renner reprimanded sharply.

"I'm talking to my girlfriend," Lucas spat out, his voice filled with as much hatred as Rob's.

Rob snarled as I watched his hands ball into fists at his sides. His steps were slow and deliberate as he advanced further into the room. When he spoke, his voice was eerily, terrifyingly calm.

"You lost your privilege to call her that the second you bailed on her." His voice quivered slightly on the last word and the volume increased as he continued. "The second you decided she was too much goddamn work and you couldn't fix her like she's fucking broken!"

Rob and Lucas were both standing, in each other's faces. The air crackled with anger and violence and the only thing I knew was that it was my fault and I had to fix it, had to stop them before they hurt each other. I wanted to speak, to intervene, but I couldn't.

"It's Annie's decision," Lucas shouted at Rob, "Not yours. Let her choose!"

"Mommy, why does Daddy have to leave?"

"Because he does."

"I'm going to live with Daddy again?"

"No, you're staying with me this time."

"No, she's coming with me, Jess."

"Fuck you, Ted, she's staying with me this time."

"You already have her sister."

"Mommy, Daddy, please don't fight. I'm sorry, I promise I'll be good, just don't fight, please."

"Let her decide who to live with!"

"Annie, do you want to live with Mommy or Daddy?"

"Both of you!"

"No, Pick one."

"But Mommy—"

"Right now, Annie, pick one."

"I can't, Mommy. I want you both."

"You have to. You can't have us both. Pick which one of us you love more."

"Mommy, no—"

"NOW, Annie! Who do you love more?"

Sweat puddled around me, my hospital gown sticking to me like I'd just showered in it as I shook from the flashback and faced the very real possibility of throwing up all over myself. As awareness of my surroundings returned, I realized Rob was holding my hand and watching my face, his other hand gently caressing my forehead.

"It's okay, love. It's not happening again. You did nothing wrong. Not then, not now. Everything will be okay, I promise."

His gentle, concerned tone was in such stark contrast to the rage and hatred from only moments before that my head spun and I wondered for a moment if I'd imagined the whole altercation with Lucas.

But then Rob tensed, his body becoming rigid and poised for a fight as he turned his head toward Lucas. He spoke quietly and slowly, his voice laced with implicit threats.

"Leave. Now. I won't tell you again."

The only sound for several heartbeats came from the machines I was connected to, though the unbridled hatred between Rob and Lucas was deafening. Oppressive.

They had been friends, but because of me, they hated each other.

"Annie, I made a mistake. I'm so sorry. I—"

"Enough!" Rob cut him off sharply, startling me. "You apologized, now get the fuck out. And leave her key here—you don't need that anymore."

Rob held out his hand and Lucas glared at him. As I watched them, Lucas turned back to me, the hatred melting away.

"Sweetheart, please..."

His tone ripped my heart apart, but I didn't know what I was supposed to do. He'd left me, too, just as I'd always known he would.

But it wasn't his fault, not really. I understood what had happened and that he wasn't really to blame. But he would leave eventually anyway, and he'd be better off without me.

They all would.

I swallowed, not even bothering to stop the tears that fell as I turned my head. Away from Lucas, yes, but also away from Mrs. Renner, away from Rob, away from everyone.

Footsteps broke the silence and I knew without having to look that Lucas was leaving.

The results of the hospital's psych evaluation were inconclusive; they weren't sure if I had intentionally overdosed or not, but agreed that I posed a suicide risk. I insisted they were wrong, but I wasn't very convincing since I knew they weren't.

I didn't want to hurt anyone anymore.

And where was *my* break from it all? I spent years with everything locked up tight, focusing all my energy on my career and staying too busy to think about any of it, but I couldn't do it anymore. And it was stifling, like an elephant sitting on my chest. It would have been so much easier if I just hadn't woken back up from my accidental overdose.

Better for me.

Better for everyone.

As soon as they figured out whose care to release me into, I'd be discharged. Mrs. Renner had been willing, but she wasn't confident in her ability to keep a close eye on me. Rob insisted it be him, but I refused. Carol, Haley, Linc—I refused them all. Which meant I was leaving with my sister.

If she ever showed up.

She was supposed to arrive the day before to get me, but something had apparently come up, so she was running late. Then she ran out of gas on the highway only to realize she'd forgotten her purse. And on and on and on. It was always something because everything was always more important than family.

More important than me.

chapter thirty-eight

annie

It was only a matter of hours after discharge that I realized how befitting it was that Lori was the person on suicide watch. After locking all the doors as soon as we got inside, I'd told her that I didn't care who it was, I didn't want to see anyone. Period. She had paused the movie she had started within seconds of walking in, asked me to repeat what I had said, then agreed to turn away everyone who came to the door.

It wasn't long before we heard the first of the knocking. Well, banging would be a more accurate description. Lori glanced out the front window before turning back to me.

"What about Rob?" she asked, her voice dripping with disgust.

She had never cared enough to hide her dislike for him. Lori liked all guys, and all guys liked her back. Except when it came to Rob. The first time they met, Lori had done her typical flirty thing that she did with every guy. But instead of flirting back or even blushing, the customary responses she received, Rob had snorted derisively at her, and then followed it up by telling her he wouldn't be interested in her even if they were the last two people on the planet and to "save that shit for someone who cares".

"No," I replied.

"Hey, Rob, Annie doesn't want to talk to you, so why don't you fuck off?"

"Let me in. Now, Lori."

"No can do."

"I said open the fucking door."

"Sorry, but no," she replied in a sing-song voice that made it apparent how much she was enjoying pissing him off.

"I swear to god, Lori, I *will* break down this fucking door if you don't open it!"

"Mm, nah, I don't think so. Because if you do? I'll call the cops. And then you'll be in a jail cell instead of here, anyway. So, answer's still no." She turned to me, shaking her head. "Seriously, Annie, I'll never understand what you saw in him."

And she wouldn't. She could never understand that he'd always been the one too good for *me*.

The banging resumed for a few more minutes before it tapered off.

Rob returned every day, but Lori never let him in. Each day brought me closer to losing my resolve and telling Lori to open the door, but I clung tightly to the knowledge that he would eventually stop caring and would be better off when he did.

On the eighth day home, I got a phone call from Mom.

"Hi, honey, how are you feeling? Your sister emailed me that you got sick or something and were in the hospital for a few days? I called as soon as I saw her message. Your Aunt Jeanine and I are worried. What happened, honey?"

I breathed a sigh of relief that Lori hadn't elaborated on the reasons for my hospital stays, though I wished she hadn't sent the email at all; the last thing Mom needed was to worry about anything.

"Hi, Mom, I'm fine. Nothing to worry about, I promise. Lori shouldn't have bothered you at all. Where are you calling from?"

She launched into a story about everywhere they'd been so far that led to them being where they were, which was precisely what I had expected. She sounded like she was enjoying herself, and I was glad. She deserved to take a break and do what she wanted for a change. She had spent most of her life making sacrifices for everyone else, so doing something for herself was long overdue.

"So, how's Mom?" Lori asked after I'd hung up.

"She's good. Having a blast. You shouldn't have emailed her, though—she doesn't need to spend her trip worrying."

"I know. I thought emailing her would be the responsible thing to do, so I did. But I didn't really think I needed to. I mean, come on... you're moody, no offense—you always have been—but perfect Annie suicidal?" She laughed and shook her head. "Yeah, right. So, where's your boyfriend? I'm surprised he hasn't come by yet."

"We broke up." The words hurt to say more than I'd expected them to.

"Oh, really? That's too bad. What happened?"

I really didn't want to talk about it, especially with her. Luckily, I didn't have to; she got distracted by her phone before I'd come up with a response.

Looking up from her phone after several minutes of furious texting, smiling like she'd just had a breakthrough in cancer research, she asked, "Wait. So, if we agree you aren't *really* suicidal, you'd be okay if I left?"

"Yeah. I tried to tell you—"

"Awesome!" she cut me off. "I'm going to meet up with a guy—Randall, I think—at the new brewery in town. Oh oh oh, Annie, did you know Stockwood has a brewery now? It's close, too, right down the street. You can come if you want, though you should take a shower first. You look pretty gross and don't smell so great either."

"No, I'm good. You go. Have fun."

Lori left for the brewery, and I knew she'd be gone for hours. I pushed up from the sofa, setting aside the pile of blankets I'd been under. The heat was cranked up, but I'd still been cold for days, unable to get warm no matter how many blankets I piled on myself.

My legs struggled and wobbled as I made my way toward the kitchen, out of breath and dizzy from the effort it required.

Just a little longer.

For a moment, I was stuck in the doorway, shivering as I looked around the kitchen I'd grown up in, seeing Mom bounce around to oldies as she cooked for us. Outside the window, I could see ten-year-old Lori doing cartwheels, the pride on her face when she managed to do five in a row. Rob was there, too, coming over to study after the first time I'd taken him to the cross-country course, carrying with him a crown he'd just woven using fallen branches from the willow I loved.

Sighing, I shook my head to clear the nostalgia, searching the counter until I found the bottle I knew Lori had never bothered to throw away.

chapter thirty-nine

rob

I hadn't seen Annie or even heard her voice since she'd been discharged from the hospital. Eight long days. The unease that started in the pit of my stomach had grown to the extent that I could no longer eat or sleep. I had waited at the medical center earlier in the day, knowing she had an appointment to remove her stitches, but she never showed up. It was likely that Lori had forgotten about it.

But not Annie.

Pacing around my house only made things worse. Since the day I'd discovered that Charlie raped Annie, I couldn't even walk past the area where he'd told me without replaying the scene in my mind. I'd already destroyed the room in a fit of violence that day, breaking every piece of furniture and putting holes in the walls. But the urge to do it over and over and over again was a compulsion that tried to take over whenever I was in the house, and it was getting increasingly more difficult to deny.

I couldn't live there anymore.

I wanted to keep the house for Annie because she had dreamed about living in the old thing for as long as I'd known her, but… I simply couldn't. Living in the same place where I'd found out what happened to her was making me fucking crazy.

I'd have to fix the destruction in the living room first, but then I'd sell the house. I had the skills and experience to do the repair work myself, but spending time in that room was utterly out of the question. I'd have to hire someone to do it for me.

My mind made up, I tossed my toolbox into the bed of my truck and headed into town. I'd make a few stops to get things rolling to sell the house, then head over to Annie's.

And this time, I wasn't going to leave until she let me in. I'd take the door off the fucking hinges if I had to.

Turning as my hand was about to land on the door again for a third round of vigorous knocking, I noticed Lori stumbling up the front walk.

"Where the hell have you been? Are you fucking drunk?"

"No, I don't get drunk. Not that it's any of your business, asshole."

"If you're out getting shit-faced, where's Annie?"

Lori gave me a look like I'd just asked her what direction the sky was and pointed inside.

"You fucking left her alone?"

"Calm down, I was only gone for a few hours. Besides, I talked to her—she's fine. She doesn't need a babysitter."

I had never felt more violent toward a woman than I did at that precise moment. I could picture grabbing her and shaking her until—

Luckily, Lori reached the front door, and my hostile vision faded as I attempted to corral my impatience while she unlocked the door, my breath suddenly stalling in dread of what I might find on the other side. The second the knob turned, I shoved forward and ran in, ignoring Lori's protests from where she'd stumbled to the floor.

"Annie! Annie!"

I was met with silence and began to panic as I frantically searched for her. When I rounded the corner into the kitchen, my eyes immediately zeroed in on the empty pill bottle on its side by the sink. Everything slowed to a standstill as my brain resisted acceptance of what I saw. Of what it meant.

No... it couldn't be... she couldn't have...

As suddenly as it had stopped, everything started back up again.

"Lori! Call 9-1-1!"

I flew into the next room, not even feeling my feet touch the floor, and slammed open the door to her old bedroom.

Annie was lying on her old bed, her greasy, tangled hair spread around her head. Her eyes, ringed with deep black circles, were closed and she was pale, so fucking pale. She wore the clothes I'd loaned her the night she tripped over me on the cross-country course, her thin, frail body horrifyingly still.

"Jesus fucking Christ, no! Annie!"

I screamed out her name, willing her to wake up as I leaped to the side of the bed to check for a pulse. When my fingers landed across her neck, she startled, her eyes filled with terror as they flew open.

"Oh, Jesus, thank fuck. The ambulance is coming. I won't let you do this. I can't."

Her expression shifted to confusion. "Do what?" she whispered.

"How many did you take?"

"How many what?"

"I saw the fucking pill bottle, Annie! How many?!"

"I didn't take them."

"It was empty! Just fucking tell me, I can't lose you!"

"I didn't. I..." her voice trailed off, and her gaze lost focus. "I was going to, but I dumped them into the garbage disposal instead."

I studied her face as my heart pounded in my chest. I had to make a decision. And I couldn't fuck it up—choosing wrong would either kill her or destroy her ability to trust me, neither of which were options. Was she telling me the truth? I wanted to believe her, but if I was wrong...

No, I could do it. I'd always been able to tell when she was lying. And I was sure she was telling me the truth.

I scrubbed my hands over my face as relief washed over me and I fought the sob trying to break through. "Fucking hell, you scared the shit out of me."

As I spoke, she wrapped her arms around herself, curling into a ball. I grabbed her hands, yanking them toward me, distracted momentarily by the lack of resistance when I did so.

"Fuck that. If you need a hug, *I'll* hug you." I brought her hands up to my mouth to kiss them but was arrested by the blood I saw on her forearms. "Oh, God, Annie." The words had rushed out unexpectedly as I felt my heart splinter.

"Don't... please, just... don't. I don't want to die, but I don't know how..." Her shoulders moved in a tiny shrug. "It helps."

I kissed each of her hands gently, desperately wishing there was some way I could take away all her pain and carry it for her.

"I'll be right back, love."

As soon as I stepped out of the room, I ran into Lori, who was sitting on the floor as she cried softly.

"I uh..." Lori trailed off. "I don't actually... it's my fault."

"She's okay. She didn't do it."

"But she was going to?"

I sighed. "Yeah."

"How could I have been so wrong?"

"Pull yourself together. I can't do this right now. Annie needs me."

"I'll help her—please, let me help her."

"No, not right now. Just..." I paused as I wracked my brain to find something to give her to do. "Tell the ambulance they aren't needed anymore. And you can get a bowl of warm water for me."

I rushed past her to the bathroom, emptying drawers and opening cabinets until I found the supplies I needed. Lori was outside the bathroom when I emerged and wordlessly accepted the bowl of water from her.

"Wait, Rob, what's that for?"

There was no way in hell she could ever know.

"Just stay out of her room for now."

Locking the door behind me, I turned toward Annie. She hadn't moved since I'd walked out. In fact, she was unconscious again.

"Annie?"

When she didn't stir, I grabbed her shoulders and began to shake her, terrified I'd been wrong to believe her.

"Annie! Wake up!"

Her eyes opened slowly and she began to shiver.

"Rob?"

"If you didn't take those pills, what the hell is going on?"

"I'm just tired. So tired. And so cold."

Everything suddenly clicked into place.

"Annie, love, stay with me for a few more minutes, okay? When's the last time you ate?"

"I don't remember."

"Did you eat today? Or yesterday?"

"No."

"What about something to drink? Have you had any water today?"

"No."

"Okay," I sighed. "It's all right, you can rest now. I've got you. I'll always have you."

Her eyelids fluttered, and she was asleep again as soon as they were closed. As she slept, I slowly and methodically bathed her forearms until all the blood had been washed away. Once her skin had been thoroughly dried, I used the tips of my fingers to dab on antibiotic ointment and then taped gauze over the horizontal gashes.

The only thing that kept me from breaking down myself as I cared for Annie was the anger boiling under the surface that Lori had allowed things to get as bad as they were.

The bandaging complete, I pressed a lingering kiss to Annie's forehead and left to find Lori. When my search indoors ended fruitlessly, I headed out the front door and discovered her on the porch.

"What the fuck, Lori?" I shouted. "Do you give a shit about your sister at all?"

"Of course I do!"

"When's the last time she fucking ate something?"

"I don't know..."

"Are you fucking kidding me?"

That meant eight days. Eight fucking days since Annie had last eaten. Maybe longer, because of the attack.

"What? Every time I asked her if she wanted me to get her something, she said she wasn't hungry. I figured she would feed herself when she wanted to eat."

"Didn't you notice that she was losing weight? That she was weak? Pale? Depressed? Anything?"

"Stop yelling at me! I did, but I just thought she had a lot on her mind."

So help me, I wanted to strangle her. She hadn't grown up a bit.

"I can't deal with your shit right now. Why don't you just leave?"

I didn't wait for a response before I spun around and went back inside. My hold on my temper was too tenuous to risk any further provocation.

Annie's wan complexion was still a shock as I returned to her room and sat on the edge of the bed, watching her sleep. I couldn't keep myself from brushing my fingers along her cheek, needing to feel the slight warmth of her skin to convince myself that she really was okay.

I needed to get her to eat, but wasn't sure how to do that when she couldn't even stay awake. I knew what I *should* do but was damned if I wanted to do it. And I knew Annie wouldn't like it either. Another trip to the hospital wasn't an option; I'd have to find another way.

Returning to the porch after doing some research, I steeled myself in hopes I'd be able to keep a lid on my temper. I was surprised to find Lori in the same position in which I'd left her almost thirty minutes before, with tears running down her cheeks.

"Annie's so weak, she can't even stay awake. We need some supplies that we don't have here unless we want to take her back to the hospital."

"Okay."

Lori looked up at me, pain and shame etched into her face. But I couldn't muster any sympathy for her.

"I really didn't know," she continued. "She could have died because of me."

"I understand you're going through some sort of painful self-realization about what a shitty sister you are right now, but your sister needs help, and she's all I really give a shit about."

She nodded, wiping her face. "Of course. Tell me what to do."

chapter forty

rob

"**I... um... I** owe you an apology." Lori swallowed loudly as she shied away from making eye contact, choosing instead to stare at the floor in front of her. "I always thought you were just a callous asshole. But even if you are to everyone else, it's obvious you love my sister. Anyway, I'm sorry."

Her apology should have been directed toward her sister, the one she'd really wronged—not me. *I* didn't give a shit what she thought of me or why. But I knew Annie would say it was a step in the right direction and she'd want me to accept it, encourage it. So, I forced the words I didn't want to say past my lips.

"Thank you."

My research assured me that Annie would recover, that under the circumstances it was normal for her to have gone right back to sleep, but it meant nothing to me when she had yet to wake up hours after I'd managed to get her to drink some electrolyte fluids and nutritional supplements. I wouldn't believe it until I could look into her eyes and see it for myself.

"How's our girl doing?"

"Mrs. Renner! I thought you were coming tomorrow."

"Great thing about being my age—I can change my mind anytime I want," she chuckled. When she continued, though, her voice was more serious. "I was worried. I wanted to check on you."

"Me? Annie's the one who's unwell," I replied as Mrs. Renner inspected my face.

"Yes, you. I have no doubt Annie will be taken care of, but no one's taking care of *you*. And Rob, you need to go home. Rest. Come back tomorrow."

I snorted. "Hell no."

"I'll stay with her until you come back. I don't sleep much at night anymore anyway. Go on, get some sleep. You'll be no good tomorrow if you don't—you look like you're already running on empty. Go on, get out of here."

As she so annoyingly always was, Mrs. Renner was right. But I didn't want to be away from Annie. I didn't want to risk her waking up and thinking I'd left her or refusing to let me back in. But I knew, realistically, I needed to get everything ready for when she was awake and on the road to recovery.

"Fine. But I need to tell you something before I go."

Fuck, I hope I'm doing the right thing.

"Something Annie is going to be pissed I told you. I just... ah, fuck. I can't. I can't do that to her. Listen, you know more than anyone how much I love her, don't you?"

"Yes."

"So, you know I would never do anything to jeopardize her safety, right?"

"Of course."

"Good. I need you to trust me about something even though it may seem like I'm wrong. Can you do that?"

It was her turn to study me, her expression thoughtful, though slightly dubious.

"Okay, yes, I trust you."

The breath I hadn't even realized I'd been holding as I awaited her response rushed out with my words.

"Thank you."

With trepidation, I slowly rotated the hand I was holding to expose the bandages on the underside of Annie's arm. Mrs. Renner's eyes immediately darted back to mine, filled with questions.

"No, she wasn't trying to kill herself."

"But, Rob—"

"I just need you to trust me."

"How can you know for sure?"

"I swear to you there isn't even a possibility that I'm wrong."

"It would be easier if I knew the truth."

"I can't do that. You can ask Annie, she might even tell you. I don't know."

"I don't like it."

"Do you trust me or not?"

"Yes..."

"Good. I'll be back first thing in the morning at the latest, hopefully before she wakes up. If you have to leave for any reason, call me, and I'll come back right away."

"I have nowhere I need to be. Go on, honey, before you fall over."

chapter forty-one

annie

My eyes flitted around the room as I woke, searching for Rob, but finding only Mrs. Renner.

He was gone.

As much as I had told myself not to, as hard as I had fought against it, I'd started to believe that he really meant it when he said 'always.' A sob escaped before I realized it was there.

Mrs. Renner padded over to my bedside and pushed my hair back from my forehead as I shook from the force of my cries.

"Let it out, honey. Let it all out. You don't have to hold any of it in."

Hearing her familiar, patient tone, feeling her hand on my forehead, the skin crêpey and softened with age, it triggered an avalanche of emotions. I cried because I was alone and lonely. I cried because I felt out of control. I cried because I was filled with shame for what I'd almost done. Because I felt so weak when I was supposed to be strong.

At some point, Mrs. Renner helped me to sit up and wrapped me in her arms. She didn't ask any questions or tell me not to worry or that things would get better with time, or any of those things that were supposed to be comforting to people but just made you feel even worse. Instead, she just held me, rubbing my back gently and letting me cry until my tears had dried up.

"Is Lori here?"

"No, honey, it's just me right now."

"Has anyone seen her? I'm worried... she was meeting a guy."

"Yes, she's fine. And she'll be back to see you, I'm sure."

"She probably won't. It's okay." After a short pause, "Mrs. Renner? I know Rob must have thought that I... But I didn't."

"Oh, honey, he knows that."

Nodding, I looked down and instinctively rolled my arms to hide the bandages I saw on them.

"It's okay, honey, you don't need to hide them."

If anyone had asked me a few minutes earlier, I'd have sworn I couldn't possibly cry another tear. And yet, the sharp stab of betrayal I felt brought with it a fresh batch of them.

"He told you."

"No, honey. The only thing he'd say was that it's not what it looks like."

"Is he coming back?"

"Of course. He just went home for a bit to get some rest."

"He really didn't tell you?"

"No. I wish I knew what was actually going on, though. But, honey? Even if you don't want to tell *me*, I think you should tell a doctor. They'll be able to help you, even if—"

"It wasn't."

"Rob really knows?"

I nodded, turning away in embarrassment. "Only him."

When Mrs. Renner was quiet instead of responding, I glanced back to her. She gazed at me thoughtfully, and I knew she was figuring it out. I watched as the sudden realization in her expression just as quickly morphed into sadness. The thought of seeing in her eyes the judgment I knew would come next was too much, and I turned away again as I waited for the words I knew would inevitably follow. Words telling me things I already knew. Telling me I needed help, that I shouldn't hurt myself. Telling me I wasn't normal, that there were healthier ways to cope.

But the words never came. Instead, she reached out and began gently moving her hand in small, comforting circles on my back. When I realized she wasn't going to say anything, I peeked back up at her and could see concern etched into her face, but also, unexpectedly, there was understanding.

The relief that followed was bone-deep, weight that I'd been wearing like a bodysuit suddenly gone. Letting out a slow sigh, I leaned back against my pillow and closed my heavy, swollen eyelids.

As consciousness found me anew, I felt noticeably less despondent and kept my eyes closed, afraid that like the details of a pleasant dream quickly fade, the improvement in my outlook would dissipate once they were open.

"Is she still asleep?" Rob whispered from somewhere close by.

"She was awake earlier, but went back to sleep a while ago," Mrs. Renner responded just as softly.

"I should have come back sooner. I didn't want her to wake up while I was gone."

"I told her you were coming back."

"That doesn't matter. Damn it!"

"Hush, before you wake her! And you're here now. She also asked about Lori."

"Lori's back, she's here. I think this may have been the wake-up call she needed. She said she can't stay much longer without getting fired, though."

"Annie should have someone with her for a while."

"She will."

"Who?"

"Me. I'll be here."

"How? You can't move your workshop here."

"I know. I'll lose whatever customers I have left. I'll figure that out later, it doesn't matter right now. I'm selling the house, so I'll have enough money for as long as I need. Until then, I'll use the money I was saving to open a storefront."

"You're selling the house?"

"Yeah, I can't fucking live there. The memory of Charlie telling me what he did to her haunts me. I can't even walk in the front door without reliving it. I have to go somewhere else. Hammerly is going to fix some damage I did to the walls, and then Hunter at Stockwood Realty will get it listed right after."

"Where're you going to live once it sells?"

"Same place I'll be living until then. With Annie—where else? I'll find another house eventually. Somewhere out of town, with some land. I'll know when I've found the right place."

"You're not thinking clearly."

"Yes, I am."

"No, you're not, honey. You're letting your emotions make your decisions. Decisions that will affect you for the rest of your life, that will jeopardize what you've worked so hard for."

"I'm not changing my mind."

Rob's tone had become stony and arguing further would be pointless. He'd always been prone to making snap decisions, but once he'd made up his mind? There was no changing it.

"Don't be so stubborn! At least wait a few weeks or so to see what happens. Things can change."

His tone when he spoke next was tense and strained like he was exerting exceptional effort and control.

"The last time I waited to see what would happen, to see if things would change? I fucking lost her. I'll never make that mistake again. It already cost me almost thirteen years—years that should have been spent with *her*, years we can never get back. Don't you get it? It doesn't matter what the downside is, I choose Annie. I don't give a fuck if I end up broke and homeless for the rest of my life, I still choose her."

"Rob—"

"I'm done talking about it."

His warm, calloused hand came to rest on the side of my face, his thumb tenderly smoothing my hair back a moment before his beard scratched my forehead as he pressed a gentle kiss there.

"It's you and me always, love. I fucking promise you," he whispered.

My feelings swung back and forth like a pendulum, from a sense of hope and relief that he wasn't giving up on me on one side to crushing guilt for demolishing the happy life he was leading before I came back on the other. With each swing, it seemed as if the pendulum swung further to the extremes, the emotions becoming stronger, more intense. When I opened my eyes in an attempt to mitigate the severity of the pendulum swings, I found myself looking directly into Rob's, and my lungs froze.

"Hi."

"Hi," I breathed out in response.

"How're you feeling?"

"Okay." I paused and looked down. "I heard you guys talking. I can't let you—"

"It's not your choice—it's mine. And I choose you. Always you."

"But—"

"Always."

Looking back up, I searched his eyes for anything he wasn't saying. What I found was love, peace, even, but not even a hint of doubt. No uncertainty or fear. My next exhale drew out with it the tension that had crept into my body as I listened to them talking.

What was left at the bottom of that exhale was a glimmer of hope, faint though it was. I was broken, devoid of any semblance of control, but Rob seemed confident and optimistic. Maybe I could let him take the reins, lead the way, help me find my way. A tremendous sense of relief accompanied the decision to relinquish that burden to someone else for a while.

"Hey, sis," Lori said softly as she quietly shut my bedroom door behind her.

"Hi," I replied, blushing. It was the first time I'd seen her since she'd left for the brewery before I almost took my life, and I was embarrassed, unable to look her in the eye. I was the big sister; I was supposed to be strong, and take care of *her*, not the other way around. "I'm sorry for being such a burden."

"You're not a burden, Annie." Lori huffed out a breath, shaking her head. "You've always taken responsibility for me, even when you shouldn't. It made sense before we came here to live with Mom, but then you just kept doing it. And, for some reason, I felt like it was owed to me by *someone*, even though I know that's not really true. So, I've always just let you do it. But I can't anymore."

She stopped speaking and I wanted to comfort her, tell her not to worry about it, but I couldn't talk around the lump in my throat.

"I... I should have known. I'm your sister! I, of all people, should be able to tell when you need help. I've just... I've never had to, you know? *You* always see those things for everyone, *you* always take care of everything, *you've* always been the one who was so put together, so untouchable, it just never even occurred to me that it was a realistic possibility. But it should have. I really... I had no idea, you know? And you could have died because of that."

"Lori-" I started, my chest caving in at the pain I heard in her voice.

"And I'm sorry for that, so sorry, Annie. For all the shit I always give you, I really do love you. And I can't believe that I almost lost you, that I let you down that badly. God, I'm so fucking sorry, Annie."

We cried together for a long time, and when our tears had dried, I felt a novel closeness to her—a sisterly bond we'd never had before.

chapter forty-two

rob

For the first week after I started nursing Annie back to health, I was wrenched from sleep every few hours by her screams as she thrashed in her bed, trapped in an eternal loop of nightmares. Sometimes they were replays of Charlie raping or attacking her. Sometimes they were flashbacks to when she was molested as a child, or her parents abandoning her. Sometimes they were of faceless men chasing and assaulting her. And still other times, she couldn't even bring herself to tell me about them.

I'd already forced myself into her life, moving in without even asking for her opinion, let alone permission, and I didn't want her to feel smothered, like there was nothing under her control. So, every night, I forced myself to sleep in a different room. After that first week, though? I gave up and just went to bed with her. As I'd known it would, holding her through the night helped, and the frequency of her nightmares gradually tapered off.

Within a few weeks, the cuts on her arms had healed, only the small white scars left behind to serve as a reminder, and those would fade with time. Her color improved and she gained back some of her lost weight. Most of her time was spent reading books about trauma, our compromise when I couldn't convince her to leave the house to see her therapist. And when she wasn't reading, she was quiet, lost in her thoughts.

Annie was sitting in the corner of the sofa in the living room, her knees pulled up to her chest, a maroon and olive throw Miriam had knit for her in high school tucked around her knees. As had become her norm, her mug of tea sat forgotten in her hand, perched on top of a knee as she stared out the window.

Glancing up at the clock on the mantle, I noted she hadn't even moved in almost an hour. Sighing, I looked back at her profile. Maybe it was wishful thinking, but her face seemed to carry less tension. I reached out and tucked her hair behind her ear, causing her to jump slightly.

"Oops," she muttered, instantly raising her mug into the air. "I spilled some."

"I didn't mean to startle you, love."

She looked up from where she was using her sleeve to dry the blanket and smiled softly. "It's fine. I wasn't paying attention."

I studied her and felt more confident that I'd been right; there was a new softness in her features.

"Would you like to play a game?" I asked as the idea came to mind. I wasn't big on games, but I wanted something to keep her attention for a while.

She glanced back out the window. "Maybe later?"

"Come on, the window will still be there when we're done," I teased.

She snorted lightly and stared at me as her face turned pink.

I raised an eyebrow at her and shrugged. "It will."

She took and released a deep breath, the corners of her mouth slightly upturned. "Fine. What game?"

"You pick."

"Your idea, so you pick."

"Suit yourself," I responded as I stood and walked over to the game cabinet.

Opening the heavy wooden door, I started scanning the boxes, looking for something that sounded interesting.

Monopoly? Too long.

Sorry? Fuck no, I never wanted to hear that word come out of her mouth again.

I continued scanning until I came across the perfect game, the one that had been Annie's favorite when we were growing up. Carefully pulling it out of the middle of the tall stack of board games, I turned and held it up for Annie to see.

"Go to the Head of the Class?" she asked dubiously.

"Yup."

"I don't know about that one..."

"Why not?"

She didn't respond, just kept staring at the box.

"Come on—you always kicked everyone's ass. This'll be an easy win for you."

"Yeah, but it's been a long time since I've played it."

"Oh, so you're afraid of losing, is that it? Don't worry, I won't rub it in."

I smirked as I watched the color in her face deepen and her eyes begin to sparkle.

"Okay, we can play something else," I started, trying to suppress my laughter. "Something you have a better chance of winning. How about... Go Fish?"

Her eyes flashed as she stood and started clearing books off the coffee table.

"You're the one who's going to lose, you ass."

A smile tugged at the corners of my mouth as I carried the board game over and started setting it up on the coffee table. The Annie I knew was still inside; she just needed a little coaxing. The road ahead would be far from smooth, but that didn't make any difference to me.

That's the thing normal people didn't seem to understand about people who'd been through the fucked-up kinds of things we had—we were never really over it. We would always have setbacks. They seemed to think we could just flip a switch and be good from then on, but it didn't work that way.

And I hated the expression those same people were so fond of to describe our kind of progress: taking two steps forward and one step back. It didn't fit—wasn't even remotely accurate. The journey with Annie had always reminded me more of one of the steep mountain roads that surrounded our secluded little valley. You moved slowly back and forth along the switchbacks that might seem to be taking you back the way you came, and might seem to be endless, making no real progress toward the top of the mountain. But really, if you just backed up far enough to see the whole road, you'd realize you were always advancing incrementally with each pass. And the winding road itself, if you just took a moment to notice, was at least as beautiful as the view from the top.

"Rob?" Annie asked from where she rested on the sofa with her head in my lap as I read to her.

"Annie?" I replied playfully, setting the book aside so I could see her face and using my fingers to comb gently through her hair.

"Can we tell everyone not to come?"

I snorted. I'd have liked nothing better. But I knew she wanted to see her friends, or she wouldn't have invited them.

"Is that really what you want? Christmas alone?"

"I'm not alone. You're here. Besides—hey, look!" Her eyes widened as she pointed out the window. "See it?"

"The snow?"

"Yeah. It's the first of the season. Do you remember..." she trailed off.

I chuckled softly as a grin broke across my face at the memory. "Like I could ever forget the day I finally grew the balls to tell you I loved you. The first time you told me *you* loved *me*. Best fucking day of my life."

She was silent for a moment, her eyes trained on the snow falling on the other side of the glass.

"Can we go for a walk?"

"Of course, love."

It was the kind of cold that, if allowed, would sink its sharp teeth into you and not let you go, so we donned plenty of layers and headed out the door. I was almost certain I already knew where she wanted to go and hoped I was right. When she turned in the direction of the cross-country course, it was confirmed.

Her pace slowed as we approached the old garage, coming to a complete standstill once we reached it. She just stood there, her back rigid and arms wrapped around herself, staring at the dilapidated building with unfocused eyes. My instinct was to hold her and demand she tell me what was wrong so I could fix it, but I forced myself to wait, to let her control when she spoke. But when her jaw began to tremble, and tears tracked down her cheeks...

Fuck that.

I tore my gloves off and flung them to the ground as I stepped in front of her and grasped her arms.

"Annie, what's wrong? What is it?"

"This is it," she said, her voice detached, eyes still hazy and unfocused.

"This is what?"

She took a slow, deep breath and then released it.

"I left a note for you at the end of that lit class, the one outside, telling you to meet me here that night; I'd decided that I was ready to lose my virginity to you. I told my mom I was spending the night at Katie's and walked over here to meet you. But he'd found the note instead, so it was him I found here when I arrived. Right in here, this is where… where Charlie…"

Her voice broke, triggering a veritable flood of violent thoughts and murderous intent as I imagined in vivid detail what it would feel like to hit him over and over until he stopped moving, feeling the crunch of bones breaking under my knuckles. And then to keep hitting him until he stopped breathing, the life fading from his irreparably damaged body.

And even that would be too good for what he deserved.

"You don't have to tell me."

That was what I said, but there was a war inside me. I didn't want to know, never wanted to know any more detail than I already did, wasn't sure how I could live knowing more of what he'd done to her. But I also felt a harrowing need to hear everything; to experience in some way the pain she'd lived through and shoulder some of that burden for her.

And because I knew that I deserved it. I'd failed to prevent it from happening, and I deserved to live with the intimate knowledge of every detail that had transpired because of that failure.

"I need to tell you." She wiped her eyes and then began. "He was standing right there, his back to me when I walked up. It was cloudy, so it was too dark for me to realize it wasn't you until…"

She then told me, quietly, haltingly, what occurred that night, every tiny detail from how the cold breeze felt across her exposed skin to the sensation from her hair being trapped in the blood dripping down her neck to the acrid smell of his breath and the tumultuous pounding of her heartbeat in her ears. As she spoke, she used her hand to indicate exactly where in the garage each transgression had transpired. She held nothing back, sharing everything in heartbreakingly graphic detail. I wanted to cover my ears and rail at her to stop, that I couldn't take any more.

But before the words escaped, I clenched my jaw to keep from speaking, reminding myself how exponentially worse it was for her to have experienced it, and then talk about it, than it was for me to listen.

"He started to walk away. Just four steps, though, before he turned and laughed as he told me he would make sure you knew what a slut I was. OW!"

Her shout brought my attention back from the vivid imagery I'd been stuck in, watching Charlie raping her right there in front of me, picturing every godforsaken detail. As it faded, I realized I'd clenched my hands around her arms hard enough to hurt her.

"Fuck!"

"R-Rob?" she stammered hesitantly, her voice small and filled with fear.

I wanted to, but I couldn't respond—all my attention was focused on trying to tamp down the visceral rage that was near to blinding me. I wanted—no, I *had* to demolish every evidence of what had happened to her. And then... then I would kill him for what he'd done.

"I'm sorry," she whispered.

The desperation in her voice as she apologized, the one who was wronged, who was violated, beaten, mentally eviscerated...it was too much. Deep inside me, a switch flipped.

I obliterated everything in sight, surrendering to the paroxysm of rage that controlled me. As if destroying the scene of the offense would somehow undo or negate the violence that had been perpetrated against her. Time was meaningless as I hit and threw and smashed things in a trance until nothing remained save grief for what she'd endured, and shame for what I'd just done in front of her.

Shaking and breath heaving, I turned toward her but was too ashamed to lift my head. "*You* have nothing to be sorry for. Nothing. Not now. Not. Fucking. Ever. *I'm* the one who should be sorry. It's just... when I think about what he's done to you... I promise I'll do better. I don't want you to ever feel afraid of anything again, *especially* not of me. I would never, *could* never hurt you. Ever." I swallowed painfully. "I should have protected you. I am so fucking sorry, Annie."

"There's no way you could have known. You couldn't have stopped it. I've never blamed you."

She would never understand that I *should* have known, *should* have stopped it. Now that I knew, it was so painfully fucking obvious that the signs had always been right there for me to see if only I had acknowledged them as such. If it hadn't been for my desperation to feel a part of something, to have some sort of family of my own, I would have seen Charlie for what he really was and never would have let him near her.

"I promise you I'll protect you from now on. I swear that Charlie will never hurt you again. Or, so help me, I'll fucking kill him."

Annie nodded absently, obviously not registering my words, as she gazed at something in the distance.

"Annie," I said gently, trembling as I held my hand out to her. I had never deserved her, just as I knew I never would, but fuck if I could ever live without her again.

She turned, looking down at my hand for a moment before she pulled off a glove and placed her bare hand in mine. Immediately, my heart calmed, the blood in my veins slowed, the buzzing in my ears faded. The touch of her skin was a balm.

"What can I do? I'll make up everything I've missed, I'll do extra assignments, anything."

It was halfway through the semester, and I knew I needed to bring up my grade if I was going to pass the class. I had never cared, but since meeting Annie, I wanted to do better, turn my life around. So, I'd swallowed my pride and was now begging my biology teacher to let me do something, *anything*, to bring up my grade so I wouldn't fail.

"Why are you suddenly bothering? You're already failing most of your classes."

"Please, Mrs. Miller, I—"

"You're wasting my time. Even if I gave you extra work, you won't be able to get through it all in time anyway."

Clenching my fists and my jaw, I struggled to keep my temper and find a different way of asking, knowing that Annie would be so disappointed in me if I blew up on a teacher. But before I succeeded in doing that, I heard her voice. I hadn't even known she was there—not until she spoke—but I didn't have to see her behind me to know it was Annie. I'd only known her for a matter of weeks, but I'd know her voice anywhere.

"How can you say that to someone? He's smarter than most of the kids in your class. And you're a teacher! You're supposed to help us learn, not tell some of us we can't!"

Mrs. Miller and I both stood in stunned silence for a moment before she began to chastise Annie for her rudeness.

"Screw you!" Annie interrupted, her eyes blazing.

"Annie!" I shouted before she went any further, trying to overcome my shock at her behavior and stop her from getting herself into trouble, especially for someone like me. "Don't. She's right."

"No, she's not! She's wrong, don't you dare listen to her. Come on, let's go."

I hesitated for only a moment before following her. But the guilt I felt slowed my steps. I knew she would get in trouble because of what she'd just done, sticking up for me the way she had.

"Annie..." I stopped walking when I realized she was planning to leave and skip two of her classes. I instinctively knew she'd never done it before and didn't want her getting into even more trouble because of me.

I wasn't worth it.

"Come on, I want to show you something," she said.

I sighed and followed her. We walked across town in silence in the direction of her house, and I wondered if that was where she was taking me, but I was too afraid to ask. We passed her street and kept walking until I finally realized where we were going.

Bewildered, I asked, "The cross-country course?"

"Come on, follow me," she replied with a soft smile.

We crested a hill, and she stopped at the base of a big, old tree, closing her eyes as her hand rested on the trunk. After a breath, she opened her eyes and turned, smiling nervously.

"This is my special spot. I come here... well, a lot, really, but especially when I'm upset or just need a little... inspiration, I guess."

"Inspiration? From this old thing?" I asked, incredulous, as I eyed the ancient trunk, twisted and knotted with age, not a hint of symmetry in its form.

"Don't you see it?" she asked breathlessly, her eyes lit up and more alive than I'd seen them before.

Fuck, I wanted to make her eyes light up like that every day.

"She's beautiful. This is a weeping willow, and she really does look like she's weeping softly, some unspoken tragedy in her past, doesn't she? And yet, she grows bigger and stronger every year. She's on top of this hill, and I like to think that she's up here for a reason, to catch the sadness from everything she can see, taking on that burden, so others don't have to." She reached out impulsively and grabbed my hand, placing my palm on the trunk next to hers. "Can't you feel it? Her power, her compassion? How she's drawing out the hurt?"

I felt something, all right, though it wasn't the damn tree. It was that moment, as Annie gazed into my eyes so earnestly, her walls down, allowing me a glimpse into her heart, into her beautiful fucking soul, it was *that* exact instant that everything I'd ever been, everything that'd ever driven me just stopped. Even my heart refused to beat for a moment.

And when it started up again, it beat for her and her alone. I knew right then, with a clarity unfamiliar to me, that I was standing in front of the only girl I would ever love.

I swallowed and started walking, ready to be as far as possible from the old garage; the knowledge of what had transpired there, the destruction that remained.

By the time we got to the willow, Annie had replaced her glove and I'd stuffed my hands into my pockets since I'd walked off without mine.

"Fuck, my hands are frozen. I need to run back and grab my gloves real quick. I'll be right back."

I was careful to avoid looking into the garage as I grabbed my gloves, aware that doing so would likely set off another fit of anger. Hell, my hands were already covered in dried blood that I inspected as I pulled the gloves on, the pain setting in as the adrenaline dissipated. I didn't give a shit, though. I knew it was nothing compared to what Annie was going through.

As I neared the willow, the wind picked up, the iciness of it burning my exposed skin.

Fuck, it was getting cold. I needed to get Annie home.

Bowing my head to shield my face as much as possible, I picked up the pace along the path. When I was about thirty or forty feet away, my eyes darted up instinctively, and I was entranced; I'd never seen anything like it. Annie was framed by her beloved willow as she stood in front of its trunk. She was still, her arms relaxed by her sides, her rosy face lifted toward the darkening sky. There was a calm in the stillness of her posture and expression, which was in stark contrast to the winter gale surrounding us, whipping the naked willow branches and her long dark curls. It was as if she and the tree were one. I was indeed standing before a goddess at that moment—one more beautiful, more powerful than any we had read about in school. And I knew then, as surely as I knew I would take my next breath, that she was my *reason*.

My reason for wanting to be a better man. My reason to look forward to the future. Just... my reason.

chapter forty-three

annie

The wind picked up while Rob was retrieving his gloves, the cold now like thousands of needles stabbing into the skin on my face, but I embraced the sharp sensation—it was invigorating. The wind danced in harmony with the emotions that roiled inside me while the frigid air had a cleansing effect, methodically cooling and extracting the ever-present inferno of self-doubt and agony that hid beneath the surface, threatening to consume me. As the storm raged, it breathed new life into me.

Rob stood not far down the path, watching me with what I allowed myself to imagine for a moment was veneration. And for the first time in my life, I actually felt deserving. I felt powerful and whole. We stayed like that, just standing where we were, for several seconds or minutes—I couldn't say for sure—our eyes locked and electricity passing between us as everything else slowed and faded into the background.

Rob started up the path, moving with purpose, his eyes holding mine captive as he drew closer. With every step, my heart implored him to come closer still, racing with anxiety at the intensity of my feelings, but also with the thrill of our connection. Only yards away, his step faltered as his eyes clouded.

"What's wrong?" I shouted over the wind that howled around us, sounding brave despite the uncertainty I felt at his hesitation.

"I don't want to scare you away."

"You won't."

He could never do that. As terrified as I was, I craved the intimacy I'd only ever had with him, that was born of the all-consuming intensity with which he had once loved me. With which I hoped he still loved me. His eyes held mine and, like it or not, I knew he could see into my soul as I watched the rise and fall of his chest accelerate, the rapid puffs of air from his shallow breathing a mirror of my own.

My mouth opened to speak, to say something to convince him, but before I could utter a word, he was there. His gloves disappeared into the wind and his bare hands tangled into my hair where it escaped below my beanie. He held me firmly as he crushed his mouth to mine with such force that I was propelled backward until I was pinned between him and my willow. A live current coursed through my body as I tasted his love, his anguish, his passion, the frigid air around us accentuating the fiery heat of his tongue. My heart beat furiously against my chest like a bird caged as I kissed him back, attempting to convey what I was unable to articulate.

The innate desperation and possessiveness of Rob's actions awoke within me something I had thought long dead. I'd forgotten what it was like to be wanted, to be loved with such passion; what it was like to be *his*.

And I wanted more of it.

His bare hand splayed across the small of my back, the sudden shock of cold making my breath catch as he pulled me flush against him. I struggled to process the sensory overload, my breath stuttering and my body trembling. His kiss became voracious and his other hand, half cradling my head, half cupping the side of my neck, tightened.

The touch of pressure along my throat conjured unwelcome images; instead of Rob, it was Charlie in front of me. Instinctively, I shoved away with all my strength as a scream ripped from my throat.

Rob's confusion as he stumbled backward disappeared seconds later as realization dawned on him. He roared into the howling wind, the sound still swirling around us as he stepped forward and pulled me back into his arms.

"Fuck! That hurts!" Rob shouted as he held his hands under a stream of lukewarm water.

I winced. "I wish you had taken turns with my gloves like I asked."

"And let you be the one standing here in pain?" He snorted derisively. "Yeah, right. That was never gonna fucking happen. If you really believed it was, you don't know me as well as I thought you did."

"You're such a stubborn ass! And you almost got frostbite because of it."

"But, I didn't," he retorted smugly.

Huffing in frustration, I watched Rob's reflection in the bathroom mirror. He chuckled to himself as he held his hands under the water, the rich, warm sound penetrating into the deepest, emptiest recesses of my soul and filling them with light and hope. His eyes twinkled, and a rare, joyfully lighthearted smile suddenly stretched across his face as he started humming to himself. His usually unruly hair was flattened against his head from the hat he'd been wearing, and my fingers itched to muss it back to its normal state.

Instead, I studied his features, seeing the slight wrinkles that creased the skin by his eyes, the deep creases in his forehead. His thick, full beard that had grown on me already; I enjoyed the rough, scratchy contrast it provided to the smooth, warm skin of his lips when he kissed me. And it made him appear a bit wild and mysterious, rough around the edges, even a little dangerous, which all suited the person I knew he really was.

With his black Henley unbuttoned at the neck, and the sleeves pushed up his forearms, I was able to study the edges of the tattoos that adorned his arms to his wrists and peeked up from his chest. Really, I wanted to see the rest of them, to know what they were, what they represented. He'd been sleeping in my bed for almost a month, but I'd been too distracted by the demons in my head to stop and look at them, let alone ask him about them.

I glanced up to find Rob watching me in the mirror. His light, amused expression was gone; in its stead was something infinitely more heated and fervent, and I forgot how to breathe. It had always been that way with him—an all-consuming intensity.

It had been so long since I'd felt anything so profound and I wanted to hold onto it, to revel in it and return it the way he deserved. But it was overwhelming, too, the feeling that I could never breathe.

And I was afraid. I was far from the same person I'd been when he last knew me. I wasn't sure I could still be what he wanted, what he needed. I was getting better, but I was broken nonetheless, and there were parts of me that always would be.

"H-how do your hands feel now?" I stuttered, looking away as I reached to grab a hand towel for him.

"Don't do that shit. Not with me."

"Do what?"

"You know what—don't act like you don't. You may have everyone else fooled, but I know you. Don't try to hide from me."

Denial was on the tip of my tongue, but I didn't want to lie to him; he deserved my honesty. So, instead, I said nothing as I held out the towel for him.

"Talk to me, damn it."

Turning, I stepped out of the bathroom.

"Love, please. I just really got you back today, and now you're already fucking retreating again," Rob said, his voice frustrated, with an unmistakable undertone of desperation.

"I'm trying. Today has been... a lot. Good, but just... a lot."

Instead of responding right away, he moved around to stand in front of me, cupping my face as he kissed my forehead slowly.

"I know I can be intense, and I'll try my best not to push you. Just don't withdraw—that I can't deal with. If you haven't figured it out yet, I want *all* of you, love. The good, the bad, the beautiful, the ugly, the happiness, the pain. I want to share all of it with you, everything that's you. You never have to hide anything from me. Today was... Fuck, I never thought I would feel something like today again after you left me, but this is my second chance, my chance to fight for you and hold on to you the way I should have thirteen years ago. And I don't intend to waste it. Love, I'm never fucking letting you go again."

He kissed my forehead again before pulling me into his arms. My hands came to rest against his chest, my head against his sternum. Even the prospect of a future with Rob was thrilling, though equally terrifying, and my heart raced. But his beat a steady, reliable rhythm under my cheek, soon lulling my doubts and fears into a dull and manageable state.

chapter forty-four

rob

I **startled awake** at the sudden battering, on instant high alert courtesy of the adrenaline flooding my bloodstream. Annie's body shuddered and fear rolled off her in waves as my arm instinctively tightened around her.

"Stay here. Don't move. I'll be back," I spoke in a whisper directly into her ear before pressing a quick kiss to her temple in reassurance.

We'd dozed off while listening to one of her mom's audiobooks in the living room earlier in the afternoon. But the soft glow from the embers in the fireplace accounted for all the ambient light at that point. Annie was lying on top of me, and though I was unable to see much, I could feel her head nod in understanding. I slid out from under her, squeezed her hand, and cautiously made my way in the direction the sound had come from, my body poised for a fight.

"Damn it, it's cold out here. Annie, open up!"

The voice was muffled by the door but recognizable nonetheless. I flipped the porch light on as I shoved my feet into my shoes and swung the front door open, stepping outside as my irritation broke free.

"Christ, Haley, I was ready to take your ass out. What the hell is wrong with you?"

"Hello to you, too, hot stuff."

"What are you guys doing here, anyway? We weren't expecting you until tomorrow."

It took me a second to notice a guy standing behind Haley and Carol; the one who'd saved Annie from Charlie.

"Linc."

"Rob."

"We didn't know you were coming."

A scene from Thanksgiving flashed through my mind, of watching him follow Annie's every move, seeing the longing in his eyes. As the memory played, I was filled with that same primal urge I'd had then to pound him into the ground, but I managed to suppress it.

Shifting my gaze, I glared at Haley as I held the door open, grabbing my coat off the hook by the door as I shouted inside to Annie.

"It's okay, love. It's just your friends. Here early and unannounced."

Annie came rushing to the door a second later and peeked around me.

"I'm so glad you guys are here!" she said with genuine excitement as she flew into Haley for a hug.

Seeing Annie so animated, so *happy*, took the edge off my irritation with her friends. I wanted her happy like that all the time.

"But for the love of god, Haley, do you always have to pound on the door? You scared the shit out of me. Again."

Haley shrugged as she pulled out of Annie's embrace. "Just making sure we don't walk into something we don't need to see."

Carol rolled her eyes and hugged Annie before giving me a tight smile and moving around me to walk inside.

"Linc!"

Annie's voice drew me from my thoughts. She again sounded happy as she walked toward him. Linc's expression softened as he looked down at her, asking her how she was as he pulled her into his arms for a hug. My hands balled into fists as I watched her hesitate and hold herself rigid for a moment before returning his hug.

I cleared my throat loudly and held the door open. "Let's get inside, it's freezing out here."

The reluctance in Linc's eyes as he let her go quickly shifted to something else when he looked at me: protectiveness.

I snagged Annie as she passed with an arm around her waist, kissing her forehead. I felt some of the tension melt away as my lips touched her skin.

"We'll be in shortly, love. Linc—help me grab some wood?"

"Sure," he replied.

I looked back to Annie, who hadn't moved even though I'd released her. She was scrutinizing my face, so I did my best to eradicate anything that might make her uneasy.

"Go on. We'll be right in."

She didn't budge, eyeing me dubiously as she shivered. I rubbed my hands rapidly up and down her arms to ward off some of the chill and pecked her nose.

"Please, love, it's freezing out here."

"Okay," she replied uncertainly, finally walking back inside.

The raging storm from earlier in the day had been replaced by a tranquil snowfall and several inches of powdery snow blanketed the ground and tree branches. The sky had a soft pink glow just like it always did when it snowed after dark, making the night seem like a living, breathing creature. I stopped walking and looked up, my breath creating dense white clouds when I exhaled. I wished I'd brought Annie out with me instead of Linc; it was hauntingly, eerily beautiful, and she would have loved it. I closed my eyes for a moment and listened to the faint sound of the icy flakes landing and I could suddenly sense Annie's spirit around me. The longer my eyes were closed, the stronger her presence felt, and the turmoil inside me settled.

When I opened my eyes a few moments later, I cast a sidelong look in Linc's direction and found he was watching me with open curiosity.

"Yes, I was going to make sure you understood she's off limits to you, but..." I shrugged instead of finishing.

"So, we're good?"

"I wouldn't go that far. Look, I don't know who the fuck you are aside from the guy who saved her from my brother, and I'll owe you for the rest of my life for having done that. But I also see how you look at her, and that just rubs me the wrong fucking way. But as long as you keep that shit to yourself..."

It went against my instincts to leave things be; the old Rob never would have let it go without a fight to show I was serious and not afraid to prove it, but I was trying to be a better person.

For her.

After depositing most of the firewood on the porch, we found the women all lounging in the living room, each with a glass of wine; Carol in one chair, Haley on the floor in front of the other chair, and Annie on the sofa. Haley was talking about her latest hookup, eliciting peals of laughter from Carol and Annie. I rolled my eyes, but it was good to see Annie relaxed and enjoying herself.

"Linc—beer?"

"Sure."

When I returned, I handed Linc his beer and gave Annie a chaste kiss on her forehead before sitting down next to her on the sofa and draping an arm around her shoulders.

"So, hot stuff, we've heard from Annie how she's doing, but how're *you*?" Haley asked, a gleam in her eye that I'd already learned meant she was up to no good.

Annie's body stiffened beside me, and I barked out a laugh. She was still as jealous as I was, and that thought warmed me to my core. Not that she had any reason to be; there wasn't a soul on the planet who'd caught my interest since the day I met her. But I knew she struggled to believe that, and I didn't want her to have any doubts, so I tugged her into my chest and pressed my lips to her temple until I felt her body begin to relax.

"It's Rob, in case you forgot," I replied to Haley, aware that laughter spilled into my voice. But the laughter quickly faded when I tipped my chin down to look at Annie, holding her gaze as I continued. "And I'm actually great."

Annie's cheeks pinked as she smiled shyly at me.

"Ew!" Haley laughed as she made an obnoxious, juvenile gagging sound. "Okay, moving on. So, I heard you're selling your house?"

"Yeah, I am."

"Any interest in it yet?"

My eyes darted down to Annie nervously before they returned to Haley.

"Yes."

I hadn't told Annie that yet. We hadn't really talked about it at all. She'd heard me telling Mrs. Renner that I was selling it and the reason why, but we hadn't discussed it after that day. She loved that house; she didn't have the memories I did. I'd briefly entertained the idea of just giving it to her because I knew how much she liked it, but there was no way in hell we were going to live apart ever again, and I couldn't live there anymore. So, instead, I'd put it on the market and accepted the first offer I received so I could get rid of the damn thing.

"Where are you moving to?"

"I'm staying around here. Stockwood's my home. But I'm going to move out of town a bit this time. Get a place with some land."

"Well, if you don't find a place before Miriam gets back from gallivanting all over the globe in a few months, you can always stay with me for as long as you need." She wriggled her eyebrows at me and grinned.

What the fuck was she doing? She knew I had less than zero interest in her. And she'd proven that she cared about Annie. A quick scan around the room revealed Carol rolling her eyes and Linc looking confused. Annie stiffened and I decided I'd had enough.

"Knock that shit off. Or you can find somewhere else to stay."

Haley had that same cat-ate-the-canary look she'd had at Thanksgiving. And then it clicked: she was intentionally making Annie jealous.

But why?

"Too far, Haley," Annie bit out, though her posture had relaxed.

Haley stared at her for several minutes like she was waiting for her to get the punchline to a joke before she got up and headed to the kitchen for more wine.

I grasped Annie's chin and tipped her head up so she was looking at me.

"You're it for me," I said softly.

I could see the happiness creep back into her eyes and ran my fingers along the column of her neck as I held her gaze. Her lips twitched into an irrepressible smile as she leaned into me, her hands coming to rest on my chest. I reached up to gently push her hair back out of her face as I bent down to meet her. The innocent kiss transformed instantly into something more primal when her lips pressed into mine.

Reaching down, I grasped her hips and yanked her to straddle my lap, wanting to feel the weight of her on me. But that wasn't enough, so I cupped her neck and pulled her closer to me as desire consumed me. Her palms slid slowly up my chest until she had wrapped her arms around my neck in a possessive embrace. The significance of what she was doing annihilated any vestige of control I had left; even the fact that we had an audience faded into the background until it was just the two of us. I kept one hand wrapped around the back of her neck, holding her lips to mine, as the other wrapped around her back and crushed her body into mine until you couldn't tell where one of us ended and the other began. I knew without any doubt that she was as affected as I was when she whimpered softly into our kiss.

Oh, Jesus, that sound. I needed more of that.

"Seriously guys? We're sitting right here."

I couldn't have cared less about them sitting there, but Linc's voice had the same effect as a bucket of cold water on Annie. She immediately jumped off my lap and wrapped her arms around herself as her face and neck transformed to a deep scarlet color. I wanted to assure her there was no reason to be embarrassed, but she shrank away from my touch when I reached out to her, suddenly fleeing the room without a word.

chapter forty-five

annie

I heard the soft click of the latch bolt on the door when it opened, and again when it closed, followed by the even softer click of the lock. Which, in my rush for solitude, I'd forgotten to engage.

Shit.

"Hey." Rob's voice was soft and full of concern.

I was curled onto my side, facing the wall opposite the door and imagined for a moment I could just wish him away. I was too embarrassed to ever look at him again, or anyone else for that matter. But my little jog from reality ended when the bed dipped under his weight as he sat down behind me.

"I'm sorry," I whispered.

"For what?" he asked, clearly confused.

"For being jealous. And then getting carried away in front of everyone."

He snorted. "First, I never gave a shit about your jealousy. Still don't. I love it when you stake your claim on me—it's sexy as hell. Always was. Second, I loved every second of you 'getting carried away,' as you put it. I couldn't give a shit less that anyone else was there, except that it bothers *you*."

I couldn't respond, at war with myself. Everything Rob had just said was... beautiful—perfect, even—and I wanted to continue what we'd started in the living room and see where it went. I felt a passion and vitality when I was with Rob that I'd never felt with anyone else, stronger than it had ever been, and, God, did I ever want more of it.

On the other hand, I had my ever-present dark companion. The one who whispered into my ear that I was worthless and dirty, that there was something wrong with me. That no one worthwhile would ever want me once they realized it. That the very fact that I wanted to go further with Rob meant I'd actually liked all the things that had been done to me. What Charlie had done. I couldn't seem to reconcile hating those things and feeling sexual desire; it had always been a struggle and seemed to be worse than ever.

I hadn't moved for a while, lying in the exact same position he'd left me in. Mostly naked. Freezing. Bleeding. Crying into the dirt, Charlie's chilling laughter loud in my ears for long after he'd gone. At some point, maybe minutes later, maybe hours—I had no concept of time—I started to throw up. Once my stomach had been completely emptied, I dry-heaved, my body in denial that there was nothing else to give.

When I was able to move, I ran back home and climbed in my window. I would tell Mom in the morning that I had gotten sick and Katie's parents had brought me home, but that I hadn't wanted to wake her up. I would carefully apply a thick layer of Lori's makeup until all the marks on my face and neck were hidden, covering the bite with gauze and claiming a curling iron burn.

As soon as I was in my room and sure I hadn't woken Mom or Lori, I stripped off what clothing I hadn't left on the ground at the cross-country course and flung it into a corner of my room. I turned on my bedside lamp and immediately regretted looking down; Charlie's fluids, mixed with my blood, had dried onto my skin like a nightmarish Rorschach. Somehow, I threw up again, after which I snatched a washcloth and began to scrub.

I scrubbed and scrubbed and scrubbed, trying desperately to erase what had happened. I scrubbed until the skin was gone and my thighs were raw and bleeding.

I had a strong urge to cut my arms, needing more pain to distract my mind, but I had promised Rob that I wouldn't. And while I knew I could never talk to him again, I couldn't bring myself to break my promise to him. I didn't know what to do, but I had to stop the growing, indescribable emotional torture that far eclipsed the physical pain from what had happened.

I found myself in the kitchen, studying the knife block until I selected one and returned to my room. Sitting on the edge of my bed, I stared at the blade, turning it over in my hands, contemplating the best way to put a quick end to it all.

Before I had formulated a plan, however, I wondered if I could cut away any reminder of what I'd just experienced. Then, in my mind, it would be as if it had never happened. No longer crying, I spread my legs apart from where I was perched on the edge of my bed and watched in fascination, almost as if someone else were doing it, as I moved the knife blade closer to my skin until the cold, sharp metal sliced easily across my inner thigh. Relief flowed with the blood that came trickling out, but it wasn't enough.

I needed more.

I sliced again, deeper this time, and the pain was practically euphoric. The image of Charlie's dried semen was seared into my brain, and I used it as a map for where to move the knife next, continuing to cut until I was sure no defiled skin remained untouched.

"Annie. Talk to me. No more walls, no more hiding. Not with me."

I broke into a sob as my fingers clutched at my thighs, the memory of my self-mutilation still so vivid.

"I feel... so... dirty." It was the only word I could find, and I hoped that he would understand, the way he used to.

Rob remained silent, but he reached around in front of me, his hands pulling to turn me toward him. I was paralyzed with shame, with self-disgust, and my body ignored the signals from my brain telling it to move. I felt his deep sigh as much as I heard it, the weight of his obvious disappointment making it even more difficult to breathe. The bed shifted as his weight left the mattress and I knew the time had come; he'd finally realized just how messed up I really was and—

My thought was cut short when the bed suddenly jerked away from the wall, the movement so fierce and unexpected that I almost rolled off onto the floor. And then he was there, squatting down between the bed and the wall, eye-to-eye with me.

He wore his emotions openly, everything written across his face. I searched, carefully, but I couldn't detect anything I was afraid of finding. No disappointment like I'd thought, nor frustration. No disgust or resignation. Not even a trace of doubt. Just... love.

As he stood, he gestured for me to make room for him. After only a flicker of hesitation, I complied. The covers flew back, and Rob's eyes scanned my body as he started to climb in.

But then he froze. His eyes darted up to mine, clouded with questions, before they fell back down. I glanced down quickly to see what he was looking at and my stomach immediately bottomed out; small blood spots were seeping through my light grey pants.

Shit. I hadn't realized I'd been digging into my thighs hard enough to draw blood.

"What the hell is that?" Rob's voice was hard, his body rigid.

My heart raced, but I managed to whisper out a reply. "I didn't mean to."

He was clearly pissed off when he replied. "Bullshit, Annie, don't fucking lie to me. I've seen your arms, remember?"

"I'm not. It wasn't intentional this time."

Rob's body stilled as the air around us charged with tension.

"This time?" he repeated slowly, his voice deceptively soft, but his eyes giving away the storm raging inside him. "How long have you been doing this to yourself?"

I felt like an errant child who'd been caught misbehaving, and the last thing I wanted was to talk about any of it, but I knew that once Rob had set his mind on something, there was no escaping it. So, I told him about what I'd done the night Charlie raped me.

"It helped. So, I did it for a while until I found other ways to cope."

"This is the first time since then?"

I wanted to lie, but I couldn't, not when I could feel his intense gaze on me even as I stared at the wall.

"Answer me. Is this the first time since then?"

"No."

"Tell me. Everything."

I swallowed, my saliva drying up in my throat.

"Th-the next time was after L-Linc..."

"What did Linc do to you, Annie?"

Rob's question was quiet, but I wasn't fooled. His fists were clenched so tightly his knuckles were as white as the snow outside, the veins in his neck protruded, his jaw was clenched. I could taste the threat of violence flooding the air, the heaviness of it weighting down my chest.

"He didn't do anything to me, I swear."

I forced myself to tell him about Haley's plan to get me to have sex and how that had ended, emphasizing that no one knew then about what had happened with Charlie. And then I plead silently with the universe to keep him from asking what I knew he would.

"Jesus fucking Christ," he muttered. "Is there more?"

I knew I had to answer him, even though I wished more than I'd ever wished in my life that I could just lie to him. But even if I tried, he would know.

He always knew.

"The next time... it was aft... it was after L-Lucas..."

Try as I could, I couldn't get the words out, terrified of Rob's reaction; it was the ultimate betrayal. My breathing was so shallow that even lying down, the room began to spin.

Rob closed his eyes and swallowed.

"After Lucas what?" he asked, devoid of emotion.

"Lucas and I... we..."

I couldn't make myself say it out loud. Rob seemed as if he had reached his limit, like he was on the precipice, though I didn't know of what.

All I knew was that it was because of me.

"You had sex with him?!"

He was incredulous, angry, his voice booming into the small space.

"Yes," I breathed out, the word barely off my tongue before he'd turned and left the room.

His rapid, heavy steps pounded through the house, followed by a door slamming. Within seconds, I heard a roar, the sound raw, more like a wounded animal than the man I knew it came from.

chapter forty-six

rob

My hand, which was already messed up from tearing up the garage at the cross-country course earlier in the day, hurt like a motherfucker courtesy of punching a tree until I deemed myself calm enough to go back inside. And now that I had exhausted my anger, I was nervous about how Annie would react to my having succumbed to my violent, savage impulses twice in one day. Especially when I knew that violence was the last thing she should be exposed to, that it could send her into another tailspin.

I decided to forgo icing my hands in favor of getting back to Annie as quickly as possible. So, stopping only to wash the blood quickly off my hands, I shoved supplies into my pockets and filled a bowl with warm water.

When I walked into her bedroom, I knew immediately that she hadn't moved since I'd stormed out. As I elbowed the door closed, a heavy sigh made its way up and out of my chest. No doubt about it—I *had* to find a better way to manage my anger. And soon. I was no good for her if I couldn't do that.

"I'm sorry," I whispered.

No response.

Fuck.

I shuffled to the far side of the bed and set the supplies down on the floor. Annie faced the window, but with unseeing eyes, her whole body folded into itself as if she was in a trance.

"I'm going to clean you up."

I waited a moment for a response, but when none was forthcoming, I rolled her onto her back, though her body remained tucked into a ball.

"Annie, love, please. Just let me help. I want to take care of you. I *need* to take care of you."

Eyes screwed shut, and body visibly trembling, she slowly unfurled her legs onto the bed, though her arms remained wrapped tightly around herself. Tucking my fingers into the waistband of her pants, I tugged slightly and then waited, letting her know I intended to remove them. After a moment, her hips lifted a few inches from the bed, and I peeled her pants down her legs and over her feet, absently tossing them into a heap on the floor.

Up to that very moment, I'd kept my eyes on my hands, but now I allowed my gaze to rise, my eyes traveling slowly from her toes, past her ankles, over her shins, her knees. Despite the situation, my breath caught; it was the most naked I'd ever seen her. I swallowed, desperately trying to focus on what I needed to do, and reign in my emotion and blossoming desire.

Any amorous thoughts dissipated, however, as my eyes landed on smeared blood and tell-tale faint white lines of scar tissue peeking out from between her clenched thighs.

Jesus.

I wished I could experience her pain for her. So she wouldn't have to. I'd go through it every day all over again if it kept any of it from her.

"Love," I said, my voice thick enough that I needed to clear my throat before continuing. "I need you to let me open your legs so I can clean you up."

Her eyes flew open in apprehension.

"What's wrong? Tell me."

Averting her gaze, she replied softly, "You won't be able to *unsee…*"

"Why can't you see it, love? You are, you always have been, you always will be, absolutely fucking perfect to me. Every quirk, every scar, every flaw? Those are part of what makes you perfect."

While I wouldn't use the word relaxed to describe her state, she *did* finally allow me to part her legs. Her thighs, the fleshy part from just below her underwear and extending about halfway to her knees, were crisscrossed with faint scars, so faded as to be almost imperceptible. There were dozens on each side, some longer that would have been from the knife, others crescent-shaped that would have come from her nails. And then there were the new crescents, these red with fresh blood that was smeared all over her skin like gruesome finger paint.

Ignoring the wave of nausea that washed over me, I took a slow, deep breath. Then, dipping the washcloth in the warm water, I began tenderly wiping her skin clean.

I startled when there was a knock at the door as it cracked open.

"Annie, can I come in?" Carol asked softly as she started to step inside.

"No!" I shouted as I rushed over to stop her from advancing any further into the room.

I couldn't believe I'd forgotten to lock the fucking door!

"What's going on, Rob? You stormed out of here, sounded like a madman outside, and then it's been silent ever since."

"I'm fine."

"Annie? Are you okay?"

"I'm fine."

"Are you sure? Can I just come talk to you?"

"No," I replied. "You can talk to her later." I tried to push the door closed, but Carol didn't budge. "Your concern is noted, now fucking go."

"No."

There was a current of steel in her reply that surprised me. I would have expected it from Haley, but Carol had seemed too subdued in my exchanges with her. But I needed her to back down and leave. Trying to hold onto my temper, I gritted my teeth.

"Just. Fucking. Go. You can talk to her later."

"I heard you the first time," she said, her voice filled with open distaste. "Look, you may *seem* to care about her, but I don't know you, and I don't trust you."

"It's okay, Carol. I'm fine, I promise," Annie jumped in.

"Are you sure?"

"I'm sure. I just need some privacy with Rob right now."

Carol hesitated another moment, then walked away, barely clearing the threshold before I shoved the door closed, making sure to lock it this time. Turning, I found Annie watching me, but her expression was inscrutable. I didn't move, staring hard at her, willing her to let down her guard and show me what she was really thinking and feeling. I wasn't sure what to do next otherwise.

Annie dropped her gaze first, letting out a gasp when she did. "Rob! Your hands!"

"I'm fine," I replied, still watching her face closely.

"No, you're not—you're bleeding!"

I looked down and saw that my hands had, in fact, started bleeding again.

"I'm fine. They're just a little banged up."

"That is *not* just a little banged up. You might need stitches. You might have even broken something."

"I don't need stitches. And it's likely I fractured a few bones, but there's nothing a doctor can really do about it anyway—they'll heal on their own in time. Trust me," I said as my mouth tipped up in a half smile. "I used to hit shit all the time, remember? I'm practically an expert at hand injuries."

But I also understood it looked gruesome, so I rinsed my hands in the murky water I'd used to bathe Annie's thighs, only to be stuck with my hands dripping with bloody water.

Spotting my sweatpants that Annie had never given back in the corner, I carefully shook the excess water from my hands over the bowl and reached for them.

"No! Don't touch those! Use *my* pants—the ones that are already ruined."

Annie's face flushed as I slowly dropped my sweatpants and grabbed her pants instead. I was amused by her reaction, though I could see that *she* was mortified.

"Don't be embarrassed. I love that you want to wear my clothes." I couldn't stop the smirk before I continued. "Did you ever really intend to give those back like you said in your note the morning after you sprained your ankle?"

"You remember what I wrote in a note months ago?"

"Yup. I studied every single word you wrote, trying to figure out if there was some hidden meaning. If you still had feelings for me and were just trying to hide them, or... anyway, answer the question."

The blush already adorning her face and neck deepened and her eyes flitted away. "I told myself that, but... no."

I couldn't help smiling as I walked back over to finish attending to her legs. If I had known *then* what she'd just confessed, I would've found a way to talk to her, wouldn't have taken no for an answer. But even so, it filled up some empty place inside me to know for sure she had never actually lost her feelings for me. Not really.

"Does it hurt a lot?" she asked.

"What?"

"Your hands."

"I can assure you it's nothing compared to what you've been through."

"That's not what I asked."

I wasn't really keen on talking about my hands or what led to me destroying them. And I sure as fuck didn't want Annie feeling responsible. She'd never understand that it all came back to me, was all *my* fault for ever allowing her walk to out of my life to begin with. But at least she was willing to talk.

"Yes."

"As much as they look like they hurt?" she asked, her voice filled with sympathy.

I looked down and studied my hands for a moment as I thought about it. They looked like shit—like they'd been through a meat grinder and then smashed with a sledgehammer.

"Worse."

"What did you hit?"

"The oak out back."

"Why?"

I shrugged. "It was better that than doing something I'd regret in here."

"What do you mean 'something you'd regret in here'?"

She was attempting nonchalance, but I heard the undercurrent of fear she thought she was hiding and saw her pulse speeding up at the base of her neck; she'd never been able to hide herself from me.

The silence stretched between us as I finished with her legs and set the supplies aside. Even with the few pounds she'd put back on, her thighs were too small as I grasped them in my hands.

"Look at me, Annie." I waited for her to comply before I continued. "I would never hurt you. Ever. You understand? What I meant was something stupid like putting my hand through a wall or door or something."

Without thinking first about how it might make her feel, I bent and placed a soft kiss over each bandage before I got up and moved everything next to the door to deal with later.

"Why are you still here?"

Her question caught me off guard, and I could feel my nose wrinkle and my eyebrows draw together as I gaped at her.

Where the hell else would I have been?

"I mean, I'm even more messed up now than I was when you knew me before. It's pretty safe to say that I'm emotionally unstable. I'm a mess. And I came between you and your brother, the only family you have. Why would—"

"Don't you fucking dare *ever* blame yourself for Charlie! Do you understand me? You didn't come between me and him. He came between *you and me*."

I was breathing hard, trying desperately to calm down, *without* hitting something.

"And I'm here because I goddamn love you, Annie, mess and all. It's you and me, always. How many times do I need to tell you that?"

I stared unblinkingly into her eyes for a moment, furious with her, with myself, with the situation, just with fucking everything.

Why the fuck wouldn't she just believe me?

But at least I was there. Even if I had to keep reminding her that I wasn't going anywhere, at least she was letting me do that. As I thought about how lucky I was to even have the opportunity to sit there and argue with her, my anger faded. I felt a smirk break across my features out of nowhere.

"Besides, now I have leverage for when you find out how fucked up *I* am and *you* want to bail on *me*."

Completely taken off guard, she laughed. A genuine, full, throaty, sultry laugh. *Her* laugh.

God, I had missed that sound. Missed being the reason for it.

When we were teens, I'd say the craziest shit I could come up with just to make her laugh. The best was when she was pissed off, though it usually backfired in some way because she ended up even more pissed that I'd made her laugh when she didn't want to.

Not that I ever let that stop me.

As I watched her laugh, the sound filled the room and spilled into the empty places in my soul.

Anything.

I'd do anything to be able to spend the rest of our lives together.

chapter forty-seven

annie

I **woke stiflingly** hot and unable to move. Swallowing the panic that immediately set in due to the feeling of being trapped, I focused on my surroundings. The early winter morning was too dark to allow me to see much, but I could *feel* a body wrapped around mine.

Rob's. I could smell him.

And his skin was like a furnace. He always slept in his boxers, but this was the first time I'd slept less than fully clothed and his skin was scorching where it touched mine.

My stomach dropped and I winced as I thought back to the night before. It had been excruciating for me to see what he'd done to his hands, and it occurred to me for the first time that it was how he must feel every time he saw something I'd done to myself. I'd never thought of it that way before. And it was eye-opening. It meant he must have the same depth of feeling for me that I'd always had for him. Despite the circumstances, my spirit lightened.

Though I felt like I would pass out if I didn't extricate myself from Rob and cool off. I shifted as much as I could, which frankly wasn't all that much, as I attempted in vain to untangle myself.

He'd been sleeping in my bed for a month, always touching me in some way, but that was the first morning I'd woken to him wrapped around me like a vine. I tried to shift a bit more, but the movement just made him tighten his clasp on me, crushing our bodies closer.

His eyes opened lazily as I struggled to wriggle my way free. With a sleepy half-smile, he squeezed me impossibly closer.

"Good morning, love. Where are you going?"

"I'm hot, but I was trying not to wake you up."

Without loosening his hold on me, he reached down with one arm and flung the blankets back. "Better?"

I rolled my eyes dramatically, to which he barked out a gruff laugh.

"You're a furnace, and I'm on fire—you can let me go."

He responded by looking straight into my eyes with a burning intensity as he pulled me even closer. "Never."

I rolled my eyes again, but his response made my chest ache with wanting to believe in it.

"What's with all this, by the way? You've never tried to smother me in my sleep before. What were you dreaming about?"

"You," he replied on a contented a sigh, closing his eyes. "Always you."

"Did you hear the part where I'm on fire? You can still hold me, but not like this. Roll onto your back?"

Nothing, no reply at all.

"I swear to God, Rob, you'll regret it if you don't move right now."

It started as a chuckle deep in his chest, growing until he was full-out laughing.

"I'm serious!"

"Oh, I'm sure," he replied, still laughing as he finally released me and rolled onto his back.

"Why is that so funny?"

I shifted onto my side, slinging my right leg across his hips and resting my right arm on his chest as I tucked my head under his chin and rested my cheek on his sternum. Still warm, but much better; I could feel the cold winter air seeping in from the old, drafty windows.

"I was thinking about some of the crazy shit you used to do after saying those words. Remember how creative you'd get with fulfilling that threat?"

Even though I was distracted by his fingers combing through my hair, I blushed and couldn't suppress an embarrassed laugh.

"I had to do *something*, you were impossible! You loved to push my buttons, and I had to find a way to get back at you. It was only fair. Besides, you know you loved every minute of it."

"Christ, yes, I did." He laughed again, the deep sound vibrating my bones in the best way. "Do you remember the fall of our junior year? When I took you out for your sixteenth birthday?"

I groaned. I knew *exactly* what mortifying event Rob was referring to and had no desire to revisit that memory. But I let him continue anyway because I enjoyed listening to the sound of his voice as he reminisced.

"We'd gone to Red Lobster, and you were wearing the sexiest fucking little red dress."

"Maroon."

"Fucking red."

"Either way, it wasn't mine. I didn't own things like that. I'd borrowed it from Katie, so in addition to being *maroon*, it was about two sizes too small."

"Too small my ass, it was perfect. You looked so goddamn sexy I barely managed to carry on a conversation with you. All I could think about was getting closer to you, touching you. So, I moved to the chair next to you, remember?"

"You asshole! You said you moved because you couldn't hear me."

He laughed shamelessly, shrugging. "I would've said anything to get closer to you. And once I was there, I couldn't keep my hands off you. I thought I was so smooth and nonchalant about it when I put my hand on your thigh, but then you literally flung it back at me."

"Well, no shit, we were in public. You knew how I felt about PDA. And on top of that, I was afraid of seeing someone who knew my mom since she wasn't exactly singing your praises."

"Yeah, well, my teenage hormones didn't care about any of that shit. All they cared about was my hand feeling your skin under it. So, I tried, fuck I tried so many times to sneak a hand over to your leg, but I just couldn't get away with it. And you were getting so fucking pissed off." He paused, squeezing me tighter as he laughed. "But I could also tell you liked it as much as I did. So, I refused to give up, even after you told me if I kept it up, I'd regret it." He scooted away a bit and looked down at me with a vulnerable curiosity. "Was I right, by the way? About you liking it?"

My face felt like it was awash with flames, but I managed to hold his gaze as I replied, my heart thumping painfully against my chest. "Yes."

He moved so my head was tucked under his chin again, but I'd caught the flash of relief in his eyes before he did.

"That's what I thought. So, anyway, if you recall, that's when the fatal words escaped my mouth, though I had no idea at the time. I told you that I couldn't help myself, that it was *your* fault because you looked so good."

He laughed again, obviously enjoying himself.

"So, I drove you home like I was supposed to, and we shared a kiss that had me adjusting myself painfully before you said goodnight and got out of the truck. And I—" he cut himself off with a bark of amused laughter. "I, in my infinite teenage stupidity, thought I'd won, that you'd been so hot for me that you'd forgotten your threat. But I'd underestimated you, hadn't I?"

"I still can't believe I did that. I mean, it was such an idiotic thing to do, for so many reasons."

My voice was muffled when I spoke because I'd buried my face in Rob's chest, counting the seconds until the trip down memory lane was over; what I'd done was somehow even more disconcerting years later than when I'd actually done it.

"Idiotic? Are you kidding? It was fucking brilliant. If I hadn't already been head over heels for you, that would have sealed my fate. But I discovered it was, in fact, possible to love you even more than I already did. A few weeks later, when I showed up to get you for Homecoming and you called out that you were ready to go as you walked around the corner, your eyes alight with laughter and triumph, your hair in that sexy, wild, curly mane around your head, wearing sweats and fucking tennis shoes, I was speechless. I couldn't decide between worshipping at your feet or kissing you senseless."

"I had no idea! You just stared at me, expressionless. I thought at first that you were pissed, which was fine with me because the whole point was to get back at you. But then you shook your head and just held out your arm for me. And I was a little disappointed I didn't get more of a reaction."

"Christ, Annie, I was trying to keep myself in check! My hormones went fucking nuts. I was trying desperately not to get a hard-on in front of your mom."

"I didn't actually intend to go, by the way—I assumed we'd just skip, but when you seemed to expect us to go, I *had* to follow through." I sighed dreamily, remembering that night. "Regardless, you somehow managed to make me feel like a goddess. Despite the fact that I was sporting ratty sweats and looked like I'd just been released from a mental institution. Despite the fact that literally every other girl at Homecoming was all done up, hair styled to perfection to match their beautiful dresses. Despite all that, I was the only one you had eyes for. Unless you count all the guys you glared at."

"Well, they were fucking gawking. I really didn't want to get into a fight at Homecoming, but I was so pissed they were looking at you instead of their own fucking dates. You were *my* girlfriend, not theirs. They had no fucking right to check you out."

"They weren't!"

He yanked roughly, pulling me on top of him until my face was mere inches from his. He stared into my eyes, the playfulness from a moment before gone, replaced by a stormy jealousy and possessiveness.

"No one ever wanted us to be together. Everyone always tried to break us up, or thought they had some right to you. But, goddamn it, you were *mine*!"

I moved back down to snuggle into the space where his neck met his shoulder. "Yes, I was."

Rob would happily have kept me in bed all day, and, frankly, I'd have just as happily stayed there with him. Feeling his chest rise and fall rhythmically as he breathed. Hearing the steady thump-thump of his heartbeat. Smelling his intoxicating mix of leather and spice and skin. Listening to his deep, rumbly laughter as we continued to reminisce about dating in high school.

Every so often, we would talk about something that would set off a wave of jealous, possessive rage, which was somehow more intense than ever before. But I didn't really mind; it made me feel loved and not so alone. For the first time in over a decade, I felt a welcome sense of belonging.

"As much as I'd prefer to stay right here, we need to get up," I said some time later.

He squeezed me tighter. "We don't *need* to do anything we don't want to."

"Yes. We do."

"Well, we have something to discuss first."

"Oh?"

"Yeah. Something of the utmost importance."

I lifted my head to rest my chin on his chest so I could see his face, where his eyes danced with humor—a dead giveaway that I wasn't going to like whatever he had to say.

"Really?" I deadpanned.

"Absolutely vital."

"Hm."

I could see him struggling to drop his smirk and clear his countenance, though the mischief in his eyes betrayed him. Whatever was going on in his mind was guaranteed to be obnoxious.

"In fact, I'm not sure I can go on without it."

"Oh, for god's sake, out with it already!"

"Can I have Haley's number?"

He barely got the words out, his chest rumbling with laughter, before I had shoved him away so hard that he rolled off the bed.

"You'll regret that."

He just laughed even harder from where he'd landed on his back on the floor, the sound rich, and warming the chilly winter air. "I can't fucking wait."

Everyone else was still asleep when Rob and I eventually wandered out of the bedroom, which was actually convenient; no questions about the bloody towel and bowl of water Rob carried. Looking at the bowl and towel as we walked into the kitchen coaxed to the forefront of my thoughts the events of the night before, and the dark cloud that was never far away inched closer.

Rob turned sharply just before dumping the bowl in the sink.

"You okay?"

I nodded. "Yeah, fine."

"Bullshit," he responded immediately, his voice level. He studied me with a contemplative expression. "Come here. Take the bowl."

"Why?"

He gave me an exaggerated eye roll. "Just do it."

I walked over, more than a little skeptical, but allowed him to hand me the bowl of bloody water.

"This bowl contains your... let's just say darkness. Okay?"

"Um, sure."

"Well, and this towel, too."

He dropped the towel unceremoniously into the bowl, causing the red liquid to slosh over the sides. My fingers twitched as I stared at it. I needed to wipe it up.

"I'll clean that up in a minute. Focus on me right now. So, this towel and this bowl contain your darkness. You with me so far?"

My eyes darted back to the small bloody puddle on the floor, lingering until Rob cleared his throat loudly and I looked back up.

"I'm not sure where you're going with this, but sure, I can see the symbolism."

"Great. See? I always knew you were smart, no matter what people said about you."

I gave him a blank stare, which earned me a chuckle.

"So, anyway, we've agreed these objects hold your darkness. Annie—eyes up here. I'll clean that shit up in a minute. Just listen. Focus on *me*. These things hold your darkness. So, cast it out, get rid of it, toss it. Tell it what you think of it and throw it away."

"That's stupid."

"Maybe, but humor me anyway."

I just stared at him, the bloody water on the floor momentarily forgotten. He couldn't be serious.

"I'm not kidding, do it. I'll even walk into the other room to give you some privacy. Just do it."

"Ugh, fine. But go away. And not just the other room. Get more wood or something."

"Done."

He grabbed a paper towel, quickly cleaning up the bloody drops on the floor before pecking my nose and walking out of the kitchen. I waited until I heard the door close behind him, then took a deep breath.

"Okay, this is ridiculous, I can't believe I'm doing this. If anyone could hear me talking to myself, they'd think I've completely lost my mind. Which I guess I have, so I might as well just do it. Okay. Here goes. Fuck you, pain. Fuck you and all your insidious relations. Fuck you, Mom and Dad. Fuck you Trevor, Dwayne, and Charlie. There's a special place in hell for people like you. Fuck you to everyone who's ever used me, or taken advantage of me, and made me feel like I deserved it. You've all had control over me for way too long, and I refuse to waste any more of my life enslaved by the things you've done to me. I'm better than that. I'm *worth* more than that. I *deserve* more than that. So, yeah, fuck you all. I hope every one of you rots in hell."

As I poured the bloody water down the drain and threw the towel in the garbage can, I felt hot tears streaking down my face. I hadn't realized I'd started crying. But I didn't feel sad. What I felt was *angry*. And strangely empowered, like I actually had a chance to win the fight and not just find a way to hide from it for another decade.

"Who's rotting in hell?"

My heart skipped, and I spun around even as recognition of the voice sunk in.

"Fuck, Haley, you scared the shit out of me." My heart pounded wildly as I started shaking. "Jesus, you scared me."

She smirked, though I could see concern flickering in the recesses of her eyes.

"You just used the 'f' word."

"Very funny."

"So, back to my question. Who's rotting in hell?"

"Me first—what the hell was your problem last night?"

"Whoa. I didn't realize you were *that* pissed at me."

"Seriously!?"

"Come on, babe, you know I didn't mean any of it. I was just doing it to get under your skin."

"Why?"

"Because I felt like you needed a nudge! I knew at Thanksgiving that you two belonged together. Nothing against Lucas, I liked him well enough. Look, you know I'd give my life for you. I love you, babe. And I think Mr. Dark-and-brooding is your happy, even if he *is* a little bit of a gruff and angry asshole. But you are always so damn hesitant, and I wanted to make sure you got there!"

I let out a quick breath and looked away.

"I didn't realize you were *this* upset. Really, that wasn't what I meant to do. I'm sorry. But I'm not sorry for wanting to make you jealous, to give you that nudge to make sure you don't end up sabotaging yourself. Besides, I wasn't kidding—he *is* fucking hot. I'd do him in a heartbeat."

"And there it is. I was beginning to think for a minute you'd gone all sappy on me." I sighed as I looked at her. Haley and I had been through more together than anyone would ever guess, and I knew she spoke the truth. "Well, you're forgiven, but if you keep talking about him like that—"

"Like what? Oh, you mean talking about how fucking hot he is? How I'd love to see what he's got under those clothes?"

I was about to retort when Rob strode into the kitchen. He must have heard everything Haley had said, but he didn't spare her so much as a glance. He didn't even slow as he approached me, trapping me between him and the counter. A hand on each side of my head held me still as he crushed his mouth to mine. After I'd been kissed so thoroughly that I was out of breath and disoriented, he pulled back just enough to rest his forehead against mine.

Our panted breaths mingled as he growled, "I'm fucking taken."

chapter forty-eight

rob

There's nothing I wouldn't do to make her light up like that every day for the rest of our lives; that irrepressible smile, flushed cheeks, wild hair. She'd never looked more beautiful. My heart pounded in my chest and my stomach performed somersaults as I thought about the woman I was holding on to.

"Do you have any fucking idea how incredible you are?"

Her face angled down as her cheeks flamed red with embarrassment.

"My hair is—"

"Beautiful."

I tilted her head up until our eyes met again, our faces only inches apart. The doubt and disbelief in her eyes baffled me. How could she not realize what was so damn obvious to me? If it took the rest of my life, I'd never give up trying to show her what I saw when I looked at her. I wrapped one of her hands in mine and flattened her palm over my heart so she could feel how it was about to beat right out of my chest cavity. I needed her to understand how much she meant to me, how much she affected me.

"Okay, guys, enough," Haley said as she made an obnoxious gagging sound behind me. "As nice as your ass looks in those pants, Rob, I came to see Annie."

"No one's forcing you to stand there," I replied.

"You're fucking hilarious," she retorted sarcastically.

"All right! Enough!" Annie shouted at us as she laughed and broke away from me. "I'm coming, Haley. We need to figure out breakfast anyway."

"What did I hear about breakfast?" Linc asked on the tail end of a yawn as he walked into the kitchen, Carol immediately behind him.

My body tensed as I remembered what Annie had told me the night before, and I reached a possessive arm around her waist.

"That you're cookin' it," Haley replied to Linc.

"Yeah, right. You know I don't cook."

"That's not what I heard. I heard that you cooked dinner for Annie. *And* that it was good."

My arm tightened instinctively around Annie at the thought of another man cooking for her.

"That was a one-time exception for the only dish I know how to make. And I seriously doubt anyone wants lasagna for breakfast."

"Calm down, guys," Annie said, "*I'll* make breakfast for everyone. If someone would just make a fire, I'll get started."

"I'll do it, love. Go visit with your friends while I whip something up."

"Wait, he cooks?" Haley asked, incredulous.

"I do." One of the many things I'd learned from Mrs. Renner over the years.

Haley raised an eyebrow. "Are you any good at it?"

"Yep."

"Well, fuck me sideways, he's hot *and* he cooks," she muttered as she turned and walked out of the kitchen.

Annie seemed undecided, glancing quickly back and forth between me and the doorway her friends had disappeared through.

"Go on, get out of here. Let me do this for you."

With a shy smile, she planted a chaste kiss on my lips.

"Okay."

After watching Annie leave the kitchen, I rummaged around for what I needed, setting all the ingredients out on the counter before getting started. As bacon started crackling on the griddle, I popped the first batch of buttermilk biscuits into the oven. While all that was going, I set the dining room table, knowing Annie would like everyone sitting around and eating together like that.

Really, it all felt so natural and easy to cook for Annie and her friends as I listened to them talk and laugh in the other room. She sounded happy.

And that made *me* happy.

The last of the biscuits had just gone into the oven, and the eggs were about to go into a skillet when the house phone rang.

"I'll get it!" I shouted as I turned off the burner.

"Hello?" I said into the receiver once I'd located it.

"You don't sound like Annie."

I laughed, in too good a mood to be offended by the bizarre and, frankly, rude greeting.

"That's because I'm not. Can I tell her who's calling?"

"Her mom. Who are *you*?"

"Oh, hi, Miriam, it's Rob. I didn't recognize your voice. How's your trip?"

"Rob? Rob who? Not Rob Weller..."

"Yes, Rob Weller."

"Why are you in my house and answering my phone?"

"I'm staying here with Annie. You didn't know?"

"No, I certainly didn't. Can you put Annie on the phone?"

"Just a minute."

My mind raced as I tramped toward the living room to find Annie. I knew Miriam had never wanted Annie around me in high school, had never approved of us even being friends, let alone dating, but I'd thought that was in the past.

"Annie, sorry to interrupt, but it's for you."

"Who is it? What's wrong?"

"It's your mom."

I scrutinized her face for any sign of something she might be hiding, but she just looked up at me blankly from her seat on the sofa.

"She was... *unpleasantly* surprised that I answered her phone."

"Oh, shit!" she shouted, realization dawning in her eyes. "I'm sorry, really. I'll explain."

Handing her the phone with a short nod, I walked back to the kitchen. The old, familiar feeling of being judged and found lacking, of never being good enough, settled over me like a blanket made of lead as I replayed Miriam's words.

After finishing the food, I served breakfast, but Annie was still on the phone with Miriam. I wanted to give her privacy, so I stifled my urge to go sit in her bedroom with her and listen to her conversation.

As I brought the food out to the dining table, it dawned on me how little I really knew about the last thirteen years of Annie's life. I'd been living with her for a month, but she rarely talked about herself. But that would have to change. Whether she liked it or not, I wanted to know everything there was to know about her. And in return, I wanted her to know everything there was to know about me.

Well, almost everything. Some things were better left alone and forgotten.

"Dig in while it's hot, guys. I'm gonna get some more wood for the fire, and then I'll join you."

"Holy motherfucking hell, that was delicious! You can cook for me anytime," Haley said.

A short laugh escaped my throat at the compliment. It felt good to have done something Annie's friends appreciated. Besides, she was right—it *was* good. Though I'd expected it would be; I'd practiced making Annie's favorite homemade buttermilk biscuits with Mrs. Renner for damn near a year until I'd perfected it.

"That it was, thank you, Rob. Sit! I'll clean up—you cooked," Carol chimed in as she stood and began gathering dishes. Her demeanor toward me was still chilly, though not quite as severe as it had been the night before.

"You guys are guests. I'll clean up."

"No, really—let me. Does anyone want anything while I'm up? More food? More coffee? Tea?"

It was agreed that everyone could use a round of coffee and Carol started another pot. I allowed her to clear the table like she insisted but put my foot down about her cleaning up the kitchen; she was a guest, even if she didn't like me.

After Carol sat down, the silence stretched from seconds into long, uncomfortable minutes. It'd been silent during breakfast, too, but that was because we were all too busy stuffing food in our mouths to be bothered with conversation. But with the food gone, the silence was becoming more awkward by the second.

"So, how do you guys know Annie?"

"I'll go first," Haley replied. "Carol, Annie, and I met in college—we were all business majors. I was Finance, Carol was Finance and Econ double, and Annie was Accounting. Our friendship trio was solidified because we all liked asking questions—surprisingly unpopular amongst the college crowd. Lazy fuckers. Anyway, Annie kept everyone on track, my god she was so focused! I mean, *seriously* dedicated. I don't know how the fuck she did it, but it paid off. No one even came close to competing with her for the top of the class, undergrad or graduate."

I had absolutely zero right to feel proud, but I did anyway, and couldn't help the smile I felt pulling on my features. "Of course not," I said softly. "So, what do you do now?"

"Actually, I just accepted a position as director of finance at a young tech firm. Bunch of masochists, really. They heard I'd just torn apart and rebuilt the finance department at my previous firm and asked me to interview. I wasn't looking to change jobs, but agreed to the interview as a favor to a friend. Poor fuckers, they thought they were interviewing *me*! Anyway, they basically lost their shit when I gave them some advice on how to structure a business decision that they'd just paid about fifty grand to get from a consulting firm. They offered me exactly what I asked for."

Haley paused, laughing and shaking her head. "No one gives you what you ask for; everyone knows that. So, you inflate what you actually want so you end the negotiation where you really wanted to be anyway. Since they offered what I'd asked for, though, I decided to make some additional outrageous demands just to fuck with them and see what they'd do. What they did was agree to all of it, which was an offer I couldn't turn down. So, I'll be building their finance department from the ground up when I start in a few weeks."

Holy shit, I'd had no idea she was that fucking smart. I needed to be careful not to say anything stupid.

"Wow! Well, congratulations on the new job. That's exciting."

"Thanks! It'll be a good challenge and great for my career."

Haley talked some more about her job and her coworkers, keeping everyone pretty entertained for a while. Eventually, she wound down, and there was another lull in the conversation.

"And you?" I asked, turning to Carol.

"Eh, I'm basically a glorified internal accountant for a non-profit, though that's only temporary. As Haley said, I got my undergrad in Finance and Econ, and I'm just about done with my MBA. I want to do something that will help underprivileged kids."

Working full time while getting a Master's? Fucking hell, she was as smart as Haley. If those were the people Annie spent her time with... she was even more out of my league than I'd realized. Jesus Christ, no wonder Miriam didn't want me around her.

My entire college education consisted of some elementary-level business administration courses that Mrs. Renner talked me into taking in preparation for starting my furniture business.

"What about you, Rob? What do you do?" Carol asked.

"Nothing as exciting as you guys, that's for sure. I design and build custom wood furniture."

"Oh, that's neat. Did you do an apprenticeship or trade classes or something?"

"No, I'm self-taught, unless you count the shop class we all had to take in high school."

I'd always liked things that were built with wood and realized I enjoyed building them myself in that class. Thanks to Annie's encouragement, and her convincing me I was talented enough, I'd gotten into a specialized college trade program I'd planned to attend after high school.

Until she left me, and I threw that opportunity away.

But they didn't need to know that.

"But I didn't do anything to pursue it until a few years after high school. I guess I have a knack for it because people pay me to build furniture for them."

"I think that's cool. I always liked working with wood, too, but I was embarrassingly bad at it," Carol replied. "Where do you work?"

"I have my own business, which I run out of my garage."

"Do you have plans to open a shop or anything like that at some point?"

"Yes, eventually. I was going to this coming year, but... well, it'll have to wait."

"Why?"

I was embarrassed, knowing already that no one would understand, no one had ever understood the choices I made, except Annie. But I figured I might as well tell the truth.

"Well, I've lost some customers because of everything that's happened with Annie and, as you know already, I'm buying a new house. And the house I'm buying is more expensive, so..." I shrugged, not really wanting to talk about it any further with them.

"Why not just get a less expensive house, then?"

"Because it's perfect."

"What do you mean?"

"It's got everything I need to run my business and everything *she's* always dreamed about having in a home. That's way more important to me than any storefront."

As expected, no one responded. But the silence was deafening as it stretched out and soon, I couldn't take it anymore. I could hear them screaming in their heads that I was crazy, that I was obsessed, that I didn't deserve her.

"And you, Linc?"

"I got a degree in Kinesiology in college, and now I'm a personal trainer."

"Any particular focus?"

"General fitness."

"And how do you know Annie?"

Linc cleared his throat and had the decency to look embarrassed. "I met her through Haley."

Haley laughed. "Since when are you such a pussy?"

"Fuck you, Haley," he replied, though his voice was devoid of malice.

"Whatever, you know I'm right. You've been a pussy since you agreed to my idea. Which brings us to how Annie and Linc became friends."

"I met her before that, you remember."

"Yeah, yeah, but that's not how you became friends, now is it? Why don't you tell Rob how *that* happened?"

Linc shifted around in his chair before responding. "Fuck off, Haley. Why do you do this shit? Just leave it alone."

As much as the knowledge that he had done *anything* with my Annie made me practically twitchy in my eagerness to start throwing punches, I had to admit, albeit grudgingly, that he seemed sincere.

"It's okay, I already know about the arrangement. Annie told me last night."

"Is that why you got into a fight with a tree? By the way," Haley continued in a mocking tone as she winked at me. "The tree will always win."

"No, it's not," I replied.

Haley wore a smirk, but everyone else seemed as uncomfortable as I was. Luckily, the front door opened at that moment, and for the first time in my life, I was happy to see Lori walk in.

chapter forty-nine

annie

Somehow, the conversation with my mom lasted over an hour. While I didn't share everything, I did end up telling her that I'd been attacked by someone, that I'd been in the hospital a couple of times, and, most importantly, that Rob had taken care of me and was staying with me for the time being.

"I don't know, Annie. Rob's a nice enough man, but he's still not someone you should really be involved with."

"I disagree, Mom."

"Of course you do. You've always been bullheaded once you set your mind to something. *Especially* when it came to him. But be smart about this, Annie."

"I am, Mom. I'm happier than I have been in a long time. A really long time."

"Yeah, until you guys break up. Again. Then you'll shut everyone out and stop coming home. Again. He already drove you away once and—"

"Mom! Stop! It's not what you think. That wasn't Rob's fault."

"No, you're right, it was *your* fault you didn't come back, but it *was* because you had been involved with him."

"Mom, please, just trust me. It's not something I want to talk about on the phone—we can talk about it when you get home—but it wasn't because of Rob."

She continued as if I hadn't even spoken, going down the same rabbit hole she always had. I rolled my eyes, though she obviously couldn't see me.

"And then there's that brother of his. He's bad news, Annie, I'm telling you. And Rob may not be like his brother, but they're still family and always will be."

"What are you insinuating?"

"Honey, don't be dense. I've told you before. When you marry someone, you're also marrying their family. Do you really want that guy to be family to you?"

She was right; she *had* told me that before. At least once a week from the day I told her I'd met him until I left for college. I felt like a teenager all over again.

"Mom, no one is talking about marriage, stop getting carried away. And I hear your concerns, but you're wrong about Rob. Can we talk about it when you get home? In the meantime, Rob is staying with me. Please be nice if he answers the phone again. I understand you have some objections, but, please?"

"I'm not going to pretend to be happy about it when I'm not. You should know better than to think I would."

"I'm not asking you to pretend to do anything! I'm just asking you to remember that before he answered the phone today, you thought he was a nice man—your own words—and then treat him that way. He doesn't deserve to feel like he's done something wrong because he hasn't. Or like he isn't good enough because that's bullshit. It was never true before, and it isn't true now."

"I don't like it, honey. It worries me."

"Got it, noted, you don't approve. But you don't have to."

I sighed, trying to calm down. I hated that she'd never thought Rob was good enough, that she didn't understand that I was the one who didn't deserve *him*, but I felt guilty for snapping at her and being rude.

"Listen, I should go. Carol, Haley, and Linc are all visiting and I think Lori just got here."

"Just one more thing, honey."

"Sure," I sighed.

"What happens when you go back home?"

"Mom..."

"I'm just being practical. You can't keep supporting yourself on your savings because you won't have any. Besides, there's nothing in Stockwood for you. Just think about it. You know I'm right. You'll be going back to your job in the city. What then?"

Even though I didn't want to admit it, I knew she was right. I couldn't just up and move to Stockwood. That would be monumentally irresponsible, especially without any idea what to do for income. I could always keep renting my house out, but that didn't even cover the mortgage payment. There was a good chunk of money in my retirement funds, but I couldn't touch any of that until I retired without financial penalties of a magnitude I couldn't fathom incurring. I didn't have a choice about returning to my job.

I sighed heavily. Mom was right.

Even if I was able to quit my job, which I couldn't, I didn't know if I could ever make that choice. I didn't enjoy it, not really, and the stress and long hours were destroying my health, which was the whole reason I was taking a year off to begin with. But on the other hand, I was really good at it, and I'd never have to worry about making ends meet as long as I stayed there. And I'd promised myself since I could remember that I would *never* be poor like I was before meeting Mom, no matter what.

There was simply too much uncertainty, too much risk, if I quit my job.

But going back would mean leaving Rob. I'd never expected to see him when I came back. Mom had never even mentioned that he was still in the area. And until the night I tripped over him at the cross-country course, I'd convinced myself that I had moved on. But the moment I'd realized it was him trying to help me up, everything I'd ever felt for him came rushing back like a tidal wave. And he was keeping me from locking it up again. Helping me accept that it was okay to hurt. Showing me that I didn't have to face it all alone—not anymore. Reminding me what it was like to be loved fiercely, unconditionally. I couldn't imagine walking away from all that. Away from him.

But the reality was that I would have to.

chapter fifty

rob

Something was very wrong. When Annie came out to join the rest of us after we'd finished breakfast, the spark that had returned to her eyes had disappeared; instead, they were dull and lifeless again. Sure, she painted a smile on her face and assured me everything was fine, but she refused to make eye contact with me. Everyone else seemed to believe her, but I wasn't fooled.

I reached out to her, needing to touch her skin, feel her warmth in order to convince myself that whatever it was, we were okay. But she avoided my touch, shying away from any affection at all. After what she'd permitted me to do in the kitchen in front of Haley, I was utterly taken aback by her reaction.

I watched her interact with her friends—happy, relaxed, almost the same as she had been before the phone call. But the easygoing happiness left her whenever she glanced at me or heard my voice. Her whole body would stiffen, her jaw tightening, and the smile would disappear from her eyes.

What the fuck was going on?

By lunchtime, I was a goddamn wreck. My heartbeat was so irregular I was sure I'd have a heart attack at any minute. I couldn't take my eyes off Annie, couldn't even *think* about anything else. Her friends had long since given up trying to engage me in conversation. Bottom line? I needed to talk to her, but we were surrounded by people who were fucking oblivious that something was wrong, and Annie wouldn't even look at me. Lori was in the midst of discussing some problems she was having with her boyfriend of the day when I reached my limit. Standing abruptly, I strode quickly to Annie and leaned down to speak directly into her ear.

"We need to talk."

"What?"

"Now."

"No, we—"

"Now."

When Annie made no indication she intended to comply, I practically growled in frustration as my grip on the chair arms tightened.

"I'll pick your ass up and carry you if I have to."

"No, no, I'm coming," her words rushed out.

The second we rounded the corner into the kitchen, I yanked her into me, kissing her like my life depended on it. And it did—at least any life worth living. I held fast as she first tried to pull away, then kissed me back.

I kept right on kissing her until we'd gotten back to *our* kiss, the one that I'd never told her hypnotized me as much as I knew it did her. Then, and only then, did I separate our mouths to rest my forehead against hers.

"Annie, I can't fucking take it anymore. What the fuck is going on?"

"I don't know—"

"Don't," I barked out harshly, angered by her bullshit denial. "I know you're lying, and that hurts. Just don't. Something's going on and you can tell me, no matter what it is. I can't handle you hiding shit from me."

She swallowed slowly, her gaze averted. I waited, digging deep to find patience, but then she tried to step away from me. Tightening my hold on her, I shook my head once.

"No, goddamn it."

She swallowed again before taking a deep breath.

"I'm not keeping anything from you. I just wanted to talk about it after everyone's gone so we could have some privacy."

"I can't wait that fucking long. Tell me now."

She looked down toward her feet before responding. "I'm leaving. In March."

"Explain."

"I'm moving back to the city when Mom gets back."

"Why the hell would you do that?"

"Because that's where I work."

"But you left your job."

She sighed again. "Not exactly. I took an extended leave of absence."

"Extended leave of absence? What does that mean?"

"It means I didn't quit. I just took some time off."

"Okay. Just quit, then."

Silence.

"Are you listening to me? Just quit. It's not that complicated. Problem solved."

"But I can't."

"What you do mean you can't?"

"The leave program is paid. I signed a contract saying I'll be back at work for at least the same amount of time I was out."

"There's gotta be a way out of it."

"In theory, yes, but for me, no. I have to go back."

"In theory yes? But not for *you*? What... what the fuck does that mean?"

My forced calm had been slowly disintegrating and I'd officially escalated beyond annoyed, straight to pissed off and yelling. But I knew that yelling at her wasn't going to help me plead my case, so I took a deep breath and started over.

"Let me try again. Please explain."

"I could pay back the money I get while I'm on leave and then I could actually quit. But I don't have that kind of cash laying around, so it's not an option for me."

"Why the fuck didn't you tell me this before?" I shouted, furious.

If I'd known, I could have done things differently, I could have given her the money she needed to walk away from her job. But now I couldn't do a goddamn thing about it.

"I hadn't even thought about work in so long with everything else happening around here. Not until Mom brought it up today. I wish things were different, but they aren't."

"Annie, I need you to be completely honest with me, got it? Do you want to stay here with me?"

"It doesn't matter, I have—"

"Yes or no? If you could, would you stay? Is that what you want? It is, isn't it?"

She was quiet, and I couldn't breathe as I awaited her reply, the seconds ticking by. In such a short period, she'd already become my reason for living all over again. And I'd managed to pick up the pieces after losing her once, but I couldn't fucking go through that again.

She couldn't say no, she'd destroy me if she did. After an interminable moment, she nodded her head almost imperceptibly as a lone tear escaped and trailed down her cheek.

My arms crushed her body into mine as my head spun with relief, and I cradled her head against my chest as if she would slip away if I didn't hold on tightly enough.

"Then that's all that matters, love. We'll figure out the rest, I promise. It's you and me, always."

I kissed her hard, but even that didn't feel close enough. But my rational brain was in full swing, reminding me that there were people in the next room and I sure as fuck didn't want a repeat of the evening before, so I broke away.

"I love you so much it hurts," I said through the emotion that clogged my throat, grasping her face between my palms as I placed hard, chaste kisses on her lips.

chapter fifty-one

annie

By midday on Christmas Eve, Lori was the only remaining visitor. Haley had apologized again for upsetting me before she left, but I'd already forgiven her. We'd been friends for over a decade, and her shenanigans were no surprise, even if they *had* pissed me off.

Having been locked up in the house for weeks on end was finally getting to me; I was a little stir-crazy. I'd considered a run since I hadn't done any kind of exercise since Charlie's attack, but it was icy outside and I didn't want another sprained ankle, or worse.

"If you really want to run, which I'll never understand, we can see if Stockwood Fitness is open today," Rob suggested.

"No. I hate treadmills. And gyms."

"Then how the hell do you run in bad weather?" Rob asked, perplexed, his brow furrowing in confusion.

"Well," I laughed, "I hate treadmills less than gyms. So, I have a treadmill in my basement at home. Though the roads and sidewalks closer to the city tend to stay clear more than out here."

"Well, somehow, I doubt your mom has a treadmill hidden somewhere in the house."

Lori laughed loudly from where she was typing furiously into her phone across the room from us. "Yeah, that'd be a negative."

"It's okay. I'll just have to wait until the roads clear up."

Rob studied me with a thoughtful expression, which most people tended to mistake for scowling, as he rubbed his hand back and forth along his chin and beard.

"I've got an idea," he said abruptly. "Get dressed. Something comfortable that you can move around in."

"What's your idea?" I asked dubiously.

His faux scowl remained, though his eyebrows lifted playfully, and his eyes twinkled.

"It's a surprise."

I rolled my eyes at him. "It's exercise?"

"Most certainly," he replied with a bark of laughter.

"Ew, guys, get a room," Lori interjected.

Rob laughed even harder, but I could feel my face burning and knew I was turning scarlet.

"I'm not talking about sex. You can come, too, if you want, but you'd need to change. You wouldn't wanna wear those jeans."

"Nah, I'll pass. I'm gonna watch something on Netflix, then I've got a date this afternoon, anyway."

"Same guy as before?" I asked.

"No, that was Jeffrey? Justin? Something like that. This is... I wanna say Mike?" She moved her phone closer to her face and scrolled quickly for a moment. "No, Mickey."

"It's Christmas Eve...isn't pretty much everything closed? Where're you guys going?"

"Stockwood Brewery. They're open until eight or ten tonight, I can't remember which."

I could feel the ambient temperature drop a few degrees as Rob tensed at mention of the brewery. Even so, I couldn't stop myself from wondering how Lucas was doing, though the guilt at doing so made my chest tight.

"Really? I'm surprised. Okay. Well, I'm going to change. Be right back."

I exited the room as quickly as I could without running, needing to be alone so I could breathe again. As I dressed, I tried desperately to force Lucas out of my mind; he had no place in my life anymore.

Even if I missed him.

Maybe *especially* because I missed him.

When I emerged from the bedroom freshly changed a few minutes later, Rob stared at me, his eyes dark and intense, his expression hard. I waited patiently, hoping I'd been successful at erasing any trace of what I'd been thinking about only moments before. The jealousy would eat him alive if he knew I'd thought about Lucas at all. After a moment, his eyes still boring into mine, he sighed heavily.

"Your choice. Walk or drive?"

"How far away?"

"Less than a mile."

"Let's walk, then."

The air was viciously cold. We hadn't made it far when I started to doubt my decision to walk.

"Fuck, it's cold!" Rob grunted, apparently coming to the same conclusion I just had.

"I know. I'm sorry."

"What the hell are you sorry for?"

"I chose wrong."

"Wrong? No, you chose to walk. There was no right or wrong answer to that question. Besides, we won't be out in it long."

"What would you have chosen?"

"Walk. Of course. I love the fresh air. I walk everywhere I can."

"Where are we going?"

"You haven't figured it out yet?"

"Obviously not. Where?"

"You'll see."

"You're a pain in the ass."

"I know."

There was no real way to respond to that, so we were both quiet for a while before I spoke next.

"Rob?"

"Yeah?"

"Tell me about your tattoos?"

He was quiet for so long that I began to think he wasn't going to answer me at all. "Rob?"

"You know what some of them are already."

"Yeah, but you only had a few back then. Literally half your body is covered now. At least. I know you wouldn't put anything on yourself if it didn't have some meaning to you. And I'd like to know."

"Okay."

I waited, but he didn't say anything else. "Okay? Does that mean you'll tell me?"

"Yes. But not right now."

We walked in silence as I wondered why he was so hesitant to talk about his tattoos. I hadn't seen anything that appeared to represent evil. In fact, the tree on his chest reminded me of my favorite willow and was downright beautiful, so I wasn't sure what he was afraid of telling me. I glanced over several times as we walked, but Rob was lost in his thoughts.

When we got to South Street, where I'd expected to turn right toward town, Rob led us directly across the street instead.

"Where are we going? It looks like we're going to your house."

He smirked at me, his good humor making a sudden comeback. "Astute."

"Don't be an ass, how was I supposed to know?"

"Well, considering there is exactly one road between your mom's house and mine, and considering you know the exact distance between them, you should have figured it out as soon as we turned right onto Somerset. Maybe you're just not as smart as I thought you were after all."

"Whatever, you could have been leading us into town."

I used my gloved hands to half-heartedly shove him for being such a smart-ass, but he barely moved as his laughter filled the space around us, warming the chill that had descended between us.

"You'll have to do better than that, love."

Challenge accepted.

In a display of pride and competitiveness that only Rob had ever elicited from me, I launched myself at him with everything I had.

Evidently, he hadn't really expected me to try. As soon as I made contact with him, he lost his balance and toppled onto his back in the snow on the side of the road, my momentum carrying me forward to land on top of him.

"Oof!" His breath whooshed out. "That's one way to take my breath away," he laughed breathily a moment later.

I was suddenly mortified, filled with shame and embarrassment. What had I just done? There was ice everywhere, both of us could've gotten hurt. It was precisely the kind of thing I used to do, always trying to prove him wrong when he taunted me, while he was endlessly amused by his insanely annoying ability to provoke me. But we weren't teenagers anymore. And I, a grown-ass woman, had just intentionally pushed a grown man to the ground... in the snow.

"I'm sor—"

My apology was cut short when Rob yanked my head down to his, kissing me hard. When he released me, my breathing was uneven and my body warm despite the frigid air whipping around us.

"My god, Annie," he rasped out, his breathing a mirror of my own as he searched my eyes. "I've missed you so fucking much."

His lips pressed into mine again, soft and unhurried this time, before he pulled away to roll us over. Standing first, he reached down a hand to help me to my feet, his fiery gaze holding mine captive as I felt a blush creep up my neck.

"Are you guys okay?"

I hadn't realized anyone else was there and I jumped, my heart instantly racing.

Lucas.

The sound of his voice mere yards away made my heart skip. With what emotion? I wasn't sure. But any desire to figure it out was overridden by the more immediate discomfort of having Lucas and Rob within sight of each other, let alone less than fifty feet apart.

Rob's voice was forced and his tension palpable as he responded before I'd managed to find my voice. "We're fine."

"Annie, you okay?" Lucas's voice brimmed with concern and pain.

Before I could reply, Rob did, his voice now clipped and combative. "I said she's fine."

"I didn't ask you," Lucas practically snarled back at him. "Annie?"

Finally, my voice cooperated. "I'm fine, Lucas."

"You sure? It looked like quite a fall."

The blush flared up, setting my face on fire with embarrassment. "I promise, I'm fine. Thank you."

I'd been looking down as I spoke but could no longer fight against my traitorous urge to see him and raised my head as I turned. Lucas stood on his grandmother's porch watching me intently as myriad emotions creased his features. He looked like shit. Dark circles ringed his eyes, which carried a deep sadness within them that I'd never seen before except at the hospital. He seemed defeated—nothing like the boyish, carefree Lucas I'd been in a relationship with a few months before. I knew I was the reason and my stomach twisted in guilt.

Rob's arm was suddenly around my waist, his gloved hand holding my hip in an iron grip as he began turning us around.

"Well, we need to—"

"Annie!" Lucas interrupted Rob. "I just... I'm sorry. It's good to see you. You look good... great, actually."

Lucas rapidly shifted his weight from foot to foot, his hand ran through his hair and scratched behind his head, his eyes darted away and then back to me. I'd never seen him like that before and, as I watched, it dawned on me that he was nervous. Indecision crossed his face as he paused. In that span of time, Rob's arm and hand tightened to the point of almost being painful as I felt the rest of his body harden with tension.

"I, uh... I would like... can we... maybe..." Lucas swallowed. "Can we talk?"

I had no idea what I should think or feel, let alone say. I still harbored some anger toward Lucas for abandoning me in the hospital, but I *did* care about him and I believed he cared about me. And I'd shared something with him that I hadn't willingly shared with any other man, so I owed it to him to say yes, right? Though that thought made me even angrier about what he had done.

The only thing I was sure of was that my feelings toward Lucas were jumbled and confusing, and I hadn't a clue what I should do. I glanced up without thinking, realizing belatedly that it was a mistake. Lucas watched me, his eyes pleading with a painful desperation that constricted my heart. How could I possibly refuse him?

"Um... all right?"

He exhaled sharply, his relief visible. "Thank you. Is now okay?"

My eyes darted up to Rob, hoping to find... I didn't even know what, but something. But he wasn't looking at me; he was glaring at Lucas with something akin to loathing, though infinitely more violent. Meanwhile, Lucas was already holding the front door open, waiting expectantly.

"Um, sure. I think I can talk for a few minutes."

I started toward Lucas once the grasp on my hip was released, but Rob didn't follow.

"Rob?"

"You go. I'll be at my house. Just come find me when you're done."

His eyes didn't waver from Lucas until he finished speaking. And when he did look down at me, the fear in his expression stole my breath. Anxiety over the situation, at my inability to figure out the right thing to do, the right thing to feel, at my desire not to hurt either of them, had my heart racing and my palms sweating profusely. Even so, I forced a smile, hoping to provide at least a little comfort and reassurance to Rob.

"I won't be long."

Rob responded by closing the distance between us for a long, hard kiss. When he broke away, he glared at Lucas one last time, then turned and started toward his house without so much as a backward glance. A deep inhale failed to settle my nerves as I turned in the opposite direction, stepping away from him.

And toward Lucas.

I followed Lucas inside to the living room, where he stood as he waited for me to sit. Once I had, he chose the chair closest to me, positioning himself so our knees were a hair's breadth from touching.

Long minutes later, Lucas was still leaning forward, his arms resting on his thighs and his hands clasped tightly together in front of him, just... staring at me.

I shifted uncomfortably under his scrutiny.

"What do you want to talk about?" I asked after clearing my throat several minutes later when I could no longer take the uncomfortable silence.

He glanced away quickly and swallowed. "I know I apologized once, but I needed to tell you again that I'm sorry. I know now that I never dealt with Mom's death. So, when everything with you was so similar to..." He trailed off as his eyes got distant and I fought against the urge to reach out and touch him to provide some comfort. "I wasn't able to be there for you. And I'm sorry, so sorry. I wish more than you know that I could go back in time and fix things, but I can't."

After a slow, deep breath, he continued. "These past months, spending time with you, have been some of the best I've had in a very long time. Maybe ever. You're such an amazing woman and... I don't want to lose you. I *can't* lose you. I know that I screwed up, but I'm asking you to forgive me. I've been seeing a grief counselor about my mom, and I can promise you that what happened in the hospital would never happen again. I love you, Annie, and I'll do anything, whatever it takes, to keep you."

I had been pissed at him for leaving me, but how could I be now? I, of all people, understood how the past could take over without your consent. How could I possibly hold that against him? How many times had he overlooked the same thing happening to me? But now I was with Rob and had a responsibility to bury anything I felt for Lucas.

"Lucas, I... I'm not yours to lose anymore. I'm sorry."

"Don't say that," his words rushed out, full of desperation. "You can't mean it. I know you love me, and your feelings couldn't have disappeared in just a few weeks. Please, you can't just throw away everything we had."

I felt a shift in my psyche as something broke free. Anger in a way I had never experienced flooded me from the tips of my fingers and toes to the hair follicles in my scalp; a conflagration of rage consumed every atom in my body.

"I can't just throw away everything we had? How can you even say that? *You're* the one who threw it away when you left me in the hospital!"

"I know," he replied, his voice cracking. "I made a mistake—a horrible mistake. I know that I seriously screwed up. And I'll never be able to tell you how sorry I am for that. But, sweetheart, we have something special, something worth fighting for. I *know* it. And I know you *must* feel the same way—I'm the only one you've been with since Charlie."

Somewhere in the recesses of my rational mind that cowered away from the anger-ridden side that had broken free and was reigning unchecked, I knew what he meant. But that knowledge wasn't enough to quiet the rage and shame his choice of words instigated.

"I wasn't 'with' Charlie. I was fucking raped by him."

"That's not what I meant, I swear."

I stood to leave, and Lucas jumped to his feet.

"It's because of *him*, isn't it? Rob? He's the reason you don't love me anymore?"

I did still love him, but I could never say those words aloud. And at that moment, I was so pissed at him, I didn't even want to.

"How can you just forget about me like that? Like... like what we had was *nothing* to you? Just... move on so quickly to the next guy?"

"I'm not moving on so quickly. I loved Rob long before I ever met you, and I will long after I've forgotten you."

The first part of what I'd said was simple fact, but the second part was total bullshit; I knew I'd never forget Lucas. And I'd said all of it just to hurt him. But regret immediately followed my words, deepening as his posture faltered, as if my words had been a physical blow. Anger, remorse, and shame overwhelmed me, making it impossible to breathe. I turned, fleeing without a backward glance.

"Annie, sweetheart, please, wait, I didn't mean it the way it came out," Lucas begged as he followed me through the house. "I swear. I'm fucking this up all over the place, but I'm just trying to tell you that I'm sorry and I love you and I miss you. Please, don't go!"

I kept walking, feeling my knees wobble more with each step, wishing I could go back to the year before. Before I'd ever come back to Stockwood.

"Sweetheart, please," he begged, his voice breaking as he started to cry. "I love you. I've never felt about anyone the way I feel about you! Please. Please don't go. My life feels empty without you. You... you make everything brighter. Please, don't leave me."

I'd stopped. His words summoned to the surface everything I felt for him.

"Please," he said softly as his fingers circled my wrists, gently pulling me around to face him. He raised his other hand shakily to cup my cheek as he searched my eyes. "Please, sweetheart." His thumb smoothed rapidly back and forth across my cheek as his breath bathed my face. "We owe it to each other to give this thing between us another chance."

His words felt like lava and I was filled to bursting with molten rage. Rage at Lucas, at Charlie, at every man, at every *person* who'd ever thought I owed them something.

At Rob for not fighting for me thirteen years before when I really needed him to.

At my sister for always taking and never being there for me.

At every single person I'd ever met who thought it was okay to use me for one reason or another.

At every person who thought I wasn't worth the effort.

And, perhaps most of all, at myself, for never having stood up for myself.

"I don't owe you a thing!" I screamed as I flung his hand back at him. "Not a single fucking thing! Not you, or anyone else! The only person I owe *anything* to is myself, and right now? I owe it to myself to walk away from the man who walked away from me when I most needed him to stay."

From yelling, from being so angry, from the anxiety any sort of confrontation always left me with, I was shaking violently and gasping for air, but I didn't care. I felt that I had finally done what I should have done many years before.

And so, I turned my back on Lucas and walked away. Ignoring his pleading was easy this time—I could barely even hear his voice over the cacophony of adrenaline and blood rushing through my ears and my focus was directed at preventing my knees from buckling under me as I fled.

I thought about walking farther until I'd calmed down, but I was too unsteady from the encounter. So, instead, I went straight to Rob's house. Music rushed to my ears from somewhere in the house as soon as the front door swung open. I wasn't sure where it originated from, but it was loud, the floorboards and walls vibrating. The song wasn't one I recognized and didn't sound even remotely like something I would listen to, but it suited my mood. The person was screaming like they were losing-their-fucking-mind angry.

Perfect.

My legs were weak as I started down the steps to the basement and I crossed my fingers they wouldn't give out completely before I got to the bottom; the last thing I needed was yet another hospital visit. The music was so loud it rattled my bones. So loud it almost made it hard to see.

And then I saw him. Rob was viciously attacking a heavy bag, blood seeping through the tape on his hands, sweat forming rivulets down his face and pouring off his bare shoulders and chest. I could even see beads of wayward sweat trailing down his calves and shins. He looked savage, dangerous. Though there was also a mesmerizing precision to his movements. Everything about him was beautiful and I wondered what the hell he was doing with someone like me. He could have taken his pick of anyone, even with his grumpy disposition.

His feet moved quickly, carrying him closer and further from the heavy bag as his hands darted out lightning-fast to connect with the material.

I wanted to do that.

My need to hit the heavy bag grew quickly until I was anxious and restless. I wanted to be patient, I didn't want to interrupt him, but I had no control over the bouncing in my leg, the tapping of my fingers. All the while, I couldn't take my eyes off him, fascinated by his movements, watching the power of his muscles shifting under his tattooed skin.

Rob suddenly looked up with a jerk, his eyes colliding with mine as he faltered. Deciding to take his hesitation as permission for my turn, I whipped off my coat, snow pants, and sweater, flinging them around the room in a manner uncharacteristically careless for my organized nature. As I stripped, Rob strode into a dim corner. The silence that followed a moment later when he cut the power to the stereo was disconcerting after the near intolerable volume of the music.

"You okay?" he asked, panting as he scowled at me, an undercurrent of caution in his voice.

"Show me how," I said as I gestured to the heavy bag, ignoring his question.

His eyebrows lowered and he hesitated, his mouth parting slightly like he was going to speak. But then, his lips pressed together into a thin line instead, and he gave me a curt nod.

After forcing my hands into boxing gloves when I tried to refuse them, Rob demonstrated form and stance, explaining how to hit the heavy bag to minimize the likelihood of hurting myself. I tried to listen, nodding at appropriate intervals, but little of what he said actually registered in my brain; all I could think about was getting to the part where I could start hitting it myself.

"Music helps with getting into a rhythm. What would you like to listen to?"

"Whatever you had on before."

His expression shifted from concern to dubious amusement. "I know you have somewhat eclectic taste in music, but that was *Jekyll and Hyde* by Five Finger Death Punch. I've never known you to like metal of any kind."

What the hell was it with people thinking they knew what I wanted more than I did?

"Maybe you just don't know me as well as you think you do," I spat out, getting more pissed off with each breath.

Rob froze as he stared at me in shock. Not that I could blame him; snarky wasn't something I'd ever been before. But it was like someone else had taken up residence within me—someone angrier, someone violent, someone who wanted to lash out, striking first.

"You okay? I've never seen you—"

"Just turn it on!"

chapter fifty-two

rob

I had no idea how long Annie had been standing at the bottom of the stairs before I sensed she was there. My heart had skipped as her presence settled over me and I looked up. It was painfully evident from the relief that washed over me when I saw her, how afraid I'd been that she wouldn't come. When Lucas had said he wanted to talk to her, it took every bit of willpower I could summon to keep from succumbing to my instincts and pounding him into the ground for even asking. To keep from dragging her with me, hauling her ass over my shoulder if I had to, whether she wanted to fucking go with me or not. But I didn't want to be that person anymore; I wanted to be better than that.

For *her*.

But there must have been some sort of magic at work for me to then walk away, leaving her with a man I knew she cared about just as surely as I knew he was going to beg her to go back to him.

The instant I saw her standing at the foot of the stairs, I knew something was wrong. Though there wasn't a chance in hell I was dumb enough to ask her while she was that pissed off. So, I just swallowed the need to know everything that had happened.

She was like a feral cat as she moved. Angry—furious even—her whole body betraying the violence she felt as she hit and kicked the shit out of my heavy bag, grunting and screaming. Leaning back against the wall with my arms folded across my chest, I watched her move. Her hair in disarray and sticking to her skin in random places. Sweat dripping down the sides of her neck. Her temples. Her cleavage.

Christ, she was fucking perfect.

I stood watching, entranced as my emotions swelled with each beat of the music until I felt there was nothing left of me except for my love for her. That I only existed so that I could love her.

Unease settled in my gut as she worked herself into a near frenzy, but I held back, figuring it was best to let her get it out. That is, until she flung off the fucking gloves and started throwing punches with bare hands as tears streamed down her face.

I stepped quickly over to the corner with the stereo and cut the music.

"Annie—that's enough!"

She continued without so much as a pause, as if she hadn't even noticed me shouting at her or the sudden absence of music.

"Annie! I fucking said that's enough!"

She glanced at me this time, her eyes wild, but she didn't even slow.

"Goddamn it, Annie, last chance—stop, or I'll do it for you."

"Fuck you!"

She didn't mean it, I knew that, but her words still hurt, more than if she'd hit me, the weight of them immobilizing me for a moment.

She'd never said that to me before.

Swallowing and setting my jaw in preparation for catching an elbow or two to the face, I moved around behind her and lunged to wrap her in a bear hug that pinned her arms to her sides.

"Get off me, damn it!"

"Annie!" I shouted in her ear to get her attention and let her know I was serious. After a few breaths, I tempered my tone and continued. "Calm down, okay? Just... calm down."

She struggled against me for a moment before the fight deserted her. Cautiously, poised to capture her if she tried to dart away or hit me, I turned her around and tipped her chin up with my fingertips.

"Talk to me."

I searched her eyes, but the emotions were shifting too quickly for me to identify them. I slid one hand up to cradle the side of her head, still wary of her trying to escape me.

"You can tell me anything. I mean it." My other hand slid up to the other cheek, so her face was resting between my palms. "It's you and me, always."

Her eyes darted back and forth between mine for a moment, and I could feel the violent anger seeping away. My arms ached with the exertion required to keep from pulling her into them and holding her there so I could convince myself she wasn't going back to Lucas.

I had to let her navigate.

So, I waited.

Just when I thought she was getting there, almost ready for me to hold her, she did something unexpected: she jumped up, wrapping her legs around my waist and winding her arms around my neck as she smashed her lips to mine.

Concern for her wellbeing? Anxiety about her conversation with Lucas? They fled in the blink of an eye. All that remained was the realization that she wanted me, and fuck if I didn't want her back. I was frantic as my hands darted around, trying to touch all of her at once, hampered by the need to hold her up. Stumbling over the clothes she'd strewn all over the floor, I eventually got us to the opposite side of the room. Pinning her against me with one arm around her back, I used the other to sweep a table clear of boxes and clutter and set her down. As soon as her ass made contact with the wood, I yanked her hips to the very edge of the table until her pelvis smashed into mine. With both hands free, one explored her leg and the other wound under the back of her shirt.

I kissed her almost violently, unable to get close enough, and I knew I should slow down. Be gentler. But I'd wanted her for too long, had been too scared that I'd lost her yet again. My lips traveled hungrily across her jaw, behind her ear, down the side of her neck, across the top of her chest as it heaved and trembled with her uneven breaths, but it still wasn't enough.

Nowhere near enough.

"Rob..."

Her breathy plea was everything I'd always dreamed of and more, but that thought drove home that it would be our first time together and I couldn't do it.

Not there.

Not like that.

Growling with effort, I pulled away, putting a few inches of space between us. When I spoke, my voice was so low and gravelly I barely recognized it.

"Not here."

Her hands trailed from my chest to my sides and flexed lightly into my skin as she shifted ever so slightly against me. The feel of her hands on me, the warmth of her pressed against me, the knowledge that she wanted me like I'd wanted her for fifteen fucking years... it was too much, and my head spun, taking me dangerously close to losing my resolve. Grabbing her hands, I brought them to my lips and kissed them softly.

"Jesus fucking Christ, Annie. I can't."

She froze and flushed a deeper red than she already was as she yanked her hands from mine and started scooting backward away from me. In a flash, I grabbed her hips and jerked her back to where she'd been.

"Hell no."

"It's okay," she said, her voice trembling slightly, and her eyes averted. "I misjudged—I didn't mean—I can't believe I—I shouldn't have—"

"Fuck that—you didn't misjudge shit! I just can't do it here. I have bad memories in this house. And I want to be somewhere other than this fucking basement, somewhere I can take my time. For both of us. I've dreamed about this since the day I first saw your mess of curls from the doorway of Room 212. I'll be damned if I can't savor it. And make sure it's everything you deserve. And that's not *here*. But, goddamn, Annie, it's not because I don't *want* to."

"When did you start boxing?" Annie asked when we were almost back to her mom's house. It was the first either of us had spoken since I'd explained why we needed to wait, and I was grateful the silence had finally been broken.

"About a year or two after you left. Mrs. Renner suggested it, actually. I tried running, CrossFit, weight-training, you name it. Boxing is what worked for me. I also lift regularly, but mostly I box. You could say it's my therapy."

"Sorry I interrupted your therapy session, then," she said sincerely. "I didn't mean to, but I thought I would explode if I didn't get everything out right then."

Fuck, I understood that feeling; that's how I'd felt most of my life. I knew how powerless, how terrible a feeling it was. I fucking hated that Annie felt that way. I only wanted her to experience things that made her happy.

She'd had enough bad in her life already.

"Don't be. It's what I took you over there for. Though I hadn't expected you to come in literally swinging and then beat the shit out of my heavy bag the way you did." I couldn't stop a deep chuckle from escaping. "You're full of surprises today."

"I'm sorry," she muttered quietly, the color in her face deepening.

"Sorry? It might've been the sexiest fucking thing I've ever seen."

We reached the front door as I finished speaking, so I fished the key out of my pocket and fumbled a bit as I tried to fit it into the keyhole. Every passing second carved away at my ability to breathe, encouraged my fingers to tremble more, just the possibility of finishing what we'd started, what I'd dreamed about for years, kicking my heart into overdrive and flooding my body with anticipation. I just had to steady my hands long enough to open the fucking door.

Finally, the key slid in and I turned it. Pushing the door open, I kept my hand on it and waited for Annie to walk in before I followed. The instant I'd cleared the threshold, the door was closed, and I had her back pressed against it. As my lips found hers, I reached down and pulled her legs up to wrap around me like they had been less than an hour before and she whimpered softly.

My body moved as if it had a mind of its own, ignoring the signals my brain was desperately trying to send to slow things down. Finally, the message got through, and I started to pull back, keenly aware that I was flirting with the loss of all rational thought and control, at risk of forgetting that I wanted more for our first time together.

"Rob," she whispered, my name like a supplication.

That word, that one word, was like gasoline on the fire inside me. I wrapped a hand around the side of her head and held her in place as I ground my lips against hers, kissing her hard, trying to make up for years of not being able to kiss her.

"Annie, tell me right now," I muttered, hoarse. "Are you okay with this? Is this what you want?"

"Y-yes."

"Are you sure? You have to be fucking sure."

She nodded slowly in response, but I had to be certain, there couldn't be any doubt. I'd never forgive myself if she wasn't ready and I'd missed the signs. If she regretted what we were about to share. I'd rather be fucking celibate until I died than have her regret being with me.

Long seconds passed as I searched her eyes, looking for *anything* to indicate she wasn't ready, any *hint* of doubt or uncertainty, but I found none. So, when her warm palms cupped my face and gently pulled, I followed, gratified that her mouth seemed as ravenous for mine as mine for hers.

"Christ," I panted out, shaking with effort to maintain my composure. "Fuck."

I couldn't even form a coherent thought at that point, let alone voice anything. All I knew was that I needed to be closer to her, that there was too much separating us. Lowering her feet back to the ground, I began tearing off layers of clothing until we'd shed our outerwear.

Annie's eyes followed my movements, her chest heaving, as she supported herself against the door. Love and desire were etched into her features, her skin was flushed; she was positively stunning, so much so that my heart ached at the sight of her. But it was such a good ache, one that reminded me how lucky I was to have her back, the kind that I never wanted to end even if it meant my heart gave out. Though I knew it never would—not while I had her in my life—because she was the reason it beat at all.

I fell forward, my hands against the door on either side of her head. I bent slowly closer, our gazes locked, until my face was mere inches from hers, and I swore I could see my thoughts reflected in her eyes. Our breathing accelerated in tandem as if our lungs were codependent. We just stood there, not even touching, but it felt like we were melding into one.

That old familiar compulsion to feel her skin under my hands crept up on me, and I allowed it to take root. Slowly, so as not to break the connection, I lifted my right hand, feathering my thumb over her parted lips as it slid across her jaw to cradle the side of her head. Where my hand touched the soft skin on her neck, I could feel her pulse beating furiously, as if it was calling to me, trying to tell me something. Breaking eye contact, I shifted my hand out of the way as I bent my head to taste the patch of skin that visibly fluttered with her erratic heartbeat.

"Oh my god," she exhaled violently.

Driven by her response, the knowledge that she liked what I was doing, I continued to tease the skin there with my lips. When I felt her hands in my hair, I froze, unable to resume until I'd processed the sensation. But then she let out another soft whimper. My body responded on its own, pressing into her, my hips grinding into hers.

Until I was on the edge of losing all control over my actions, all control over my responses. The sensation of her body pressed against mine, of her hands in my hair, her warm, uneven breaths bathing my face, of the small sounds that kept escaping her... it was too much, but also left me desperately needing more.

But as much as my body wanted to right then, she deserved more than just being fucked up against a door. I wanted to worship her, make love to her, leave no doubt in her mind how I felt about her. And so, shaking violently from the effort it demanded, I shifted her weight higher onto my hips and, with a small grunt, turned and headed further into the house.

chapter fifty-three

annie

The closer Rob carried me to the bedroom, the more anxious I became, until fear threatened to eclipse the significance of what was transpiring between us. I was afraid of everything that was happening: the intensity of my feelings and desire that borderline consumed me, the struggle I could see in Rob as he approached a loss of control, the nearness of what was about to happen, the rapidity with which Rob had gone from a painful memory to everything to me again.

Come on, Annie, it's not like this is going to last. You've never been enough to keep someone you love. And he definitely won't stay once he realizes how you really are. What kind of person wants sex after what you've been through? The kind who secretly liked it, that's who.

"No! Stop it!"

Rob's footsteps faltered and slowed as he pulled his head back to look down at me, his eyes clouded with confusion and concern. Two more steps, and then he was placing me on the bed.

"It's okay, love, we don't need to—"

"No, please. Please don't. I didn't mean to say that, not out loud."

His confusion grew. "I don't understand."

Maintaining eye contact was impossible if I was going to explain and I turned to study the curtains at the window.

"I was... talking... to myself. I have this voice... it tells me that... that I'm dirty, that I wanted everything that... if I ever feel like this, if I want to... then it means..."

I could only hope that Rob was able to follow my disjointed attempts to explain. I'd never before tried to verbalize what had just happened to me and it was monumentally more difficult than I ever would have expected.

"Love, listen to me. There's nothing dirty about this. About *us*. And nothing could ever justify what's been done to you. Nothing." He paused as he used his hands to turn my head until I was looking at him. "What can I do to help? I'll do anything, just tell me."

"Just... don't let me ruin this?"

I was nervous as the words left my mouth, afraid that I'd already done just that, uncomfortable with being so open about wanting him, battling the feeling of filth for doing so.

Instead of replying, Rob cradled my face as he bent, slowly drawing our faces closer. His nose ran softly along the side of mine before he brought our lips together, his mouth hot and insistent, his tongue dancing slowly with mine. Each deliberate and unhurried stroke of his tongue stoked my desire to the point my lungs ceased to function, and the unwelcome voice in my head was quite drowned out by the pounding of blood through my veins. As if his body was reading mine, his mouth got somehow hotter, harder, more demanding, moving faster as his hands firmed, keeping me right where he wanted me.

Right where I wanted to be.

Much-needed air flooded into my lungs during the short beat of time between his mouth leaving mine and his lips connecting with the skin under my ear. The sensation of his lips and beard on the sensitive skin severed the connection between my brain and my body and Rob's arm was suddenly the only thing keeping me upright. My head fell back as Rob's mouth moved agonizingly slowly down my neck, the scratch of his beard contrasting wildly with the soft warmth of his lips and tongue. Some foreign strangled sound I'd never made before escaped me and Rob's arm tightened around my back. The palm of his free hand smoothed over my breast as he sucked the skin by my collarbone into his mouth and gently closed his teeth around it and my body shuddered involuntarily at the sensation.

"Rob," I whimpered, my lust-fogged brain struggling to figure out what I even wanted.

"Hmm?" he hummed in response, the vibrations from his voice reverberating throughout my body.

Holy hell.

An odd, unrecognizable sense of urgency spread through my veins like wildfire, turning my body into an inferno. It was reminiscent of a panic attack except I wasn't experiencing any kind of anxiety I was familiar with. And yet, the sensation intensified as his hand trailed slowly down from my breast.

Over my stomach.

Down to my inner thigh.

Suddenly, I couldn't breathe. What was happening to me?

"Rob," I managed to get out again on a breathy whisper, trying to convey urgency through my lack of oxygen.

"Hmm?" he hummed again.

Tears filled my eyes. I wasn't upset—not even close—but the tears were there none-the-less.

"I'm scared." I hadn't even realized that's what I wanted to say until the words were out.

"No, love," he breathed against the base of my neck.

"Rob, please," I panted out, my anxiety mounting.

"Do you want me to stop, love?" His lips brushed the skin along the front of my throat as he spoke, his voice husky.

Did I?

I was afraid of what was happening between us, but I realized I was even more afraid of it *not* happening, of severing our connection.

"N-no," I stammered out in reply.

His lips pressed against my throat as he began nipping his way up one side from the top of my sternum to my chin, one arm still wrapped around me and the other now gently massaging the junction of inner thigh and pelvis in slow, hypnotic movements. Rob's mouth continued its trek, moving slowly back down the other side of my neck and ending at my breast. By the time he rubbed his nose across my nipple, my entire body was trembling uncontrollably. And when he gently closed his mouth around the same nipple and moved his hand to caress between my legs, every muscle in my body seized and time came to a grinding halt.

I couldn't breathe.

I couldn't move.

I couldn't think.

I couldn't do *anything*. It was a total loss of control, as excruciating as it was extraordinary. As I shook and tried desperately to draw in air, to relax the rigidity in my body, Rob kissed slowly back up my throat.

"Are you okay, love?"

Unable to formulate words at that point, I just nodded my head in short, jerky movements, my body still on edge. Rob lowered me onto my back on the bed, and I watched, transfixed, as he reached over his shoulder to fist his shirt and yank it over his head. Without the material in the way, I could see how rapidly his chest rose and fell, giving away how affected he was by what had just happened.

He raised his eyebrows as his hands grasped the bottom of my shirt, his desire-darkened eyes burning into mine as they asked permission. I nodded quickly in assent before I had a chance to overthink and change my mind. His fingers trembled against my bare skin as he peeled my shirt up inch by inch, leaving a trail of fire in their wake. Except when the shirt went over my head, our eyes remained locked together.

My shirt hit the floor and Rob's breathing became noticeably harsher and faster as his eyes took in my exposed skin. I was so focused on his face that I jumped at the novel sensation when his fingers traced the top edge of my sports bra, his touch so faint it was barely more than a whisper of air moving across my skin, leaving goosebumps in their wake. Time slowed as I watched him raise his head, his eyes asking permission again. Without thinking, I nodded, and, with some difficulty, he tugged my sports bra over my head and tossed it absentmindedly behind him as he devoured me with his eyes.

The longer he looked down at me, the more exposed and insecure I felt, suddenly acutely aware of how bright the room was. I fought for as long as I could, but eventually succumbed to my embarrassment and crossed my arms over my chest.

But in the next breath, Rob's hands were grasping my wrists, his grip gentle but also firm and unyielding as he uncrossed my arms and pinned them to my sides. His eyes bored into mine for the span of a few heartbeats before he swallowed dryly.

"Don't," he said hoarsely. His chest already looked like he'd just finished a marathon, but somehow moved faster. "I just... I can't help it... you're so... god, Annie, you just have no fucking clue how goddamn beautiful you are. Even more beautiful than I ever dreamed."

A hand released my wrist and flattened along my belly, his palm smoothing between my breasts as it moved up my body. That hand was gentle when it came to rest against the base of my throat, fingers lightly covering my pulse, nothing violent or threatening about the action. And yet the memory of Charlie's hand squeezing to cause me pain, to take my life from me, immediately rose to the surface and I could feel the adrenaline hitting my bloodstream and poising my body for flight.

"Stay with me, love. Stay with me. You're here with me." Rob's raspy voice broke through my mounting panic and gave me a foothold back to the present. "It's just us, just you and me, love. Just you. And me."

He bent his head and kissed me, his tongue coaxing mine into a rhythm so familiar to us and so consuming that it drove away all thoughts of anything except what was happening in that moment.

As my panic subsided, Rob feathered his hand over my chest, and then my stomach. When he reached my pants, he pulled back to look at me, once more silently seeking permission.

"Yes," I whispered.

His fingers hooked into the waistband of my pants and underwear, and he pulled them down my legs, his eyes never once wavering from mine. Once my feet had cleared the material, his shorts and boxers joined them along with our other clothing on the floor.

My eyes flickered down Rob's face to his chest, over his stomach, coming to a stop on his erection. Anxiety broke over me like a tidal wave as I remembered what things had been like the last time... with Lucas. I was afraid of the pain, afraid of the memories that pain would trigger, and confused by my contradictory feelings as I thought of Lucas.

But I couldn't stop now. It was too late to say no.

"What is it, love?"

I shook my head from side to side unable to speak, silently cursing myself for the tears that filled my eyes.

"We're not doing this if you have doubts. So, tell me now what's wrong."

"I just... it'll hurt. W-what if... what if I can't stay here..."

He swallowed as his face softened with understanding. "I'll try to be gentle. And I'll do whatever I can to keep you here with me. But not until you're ready."

I thought about it. I was scared, but I really wanted to experience that type of intimacy with Rob, to explore our relationship along a different dimension.

"I'm ready."

His eyes raked over me, my words visibly affecting him as his pupils dilated further. When he spoke, his voice was deep and harsh.

"Once I touch you..." his voice trailed off, and he inhaled sharply. "Are you absolutely sure?"

I was anxious. Scared. Aroused. Nervous as all hell. But my desire for a deeper connection with Rob drowned out all the noise from those emotions.

It was time. The culmination of our past together, what was always meant to happen but had been interrupted that fateful night many years before.

"Yes."

Starting at my ankles, Rob's hands traveled up my legs as he climbed back onto the bed with me. The closer he moved, the more I trembled, the harsher I breathed. The anticipation was simultaneously exceedingly terrifying and excruciatingly wonderful. As I tried to calm myself, a strangled sound escaped my lips. Rob's hands faltered along their path as his eyes fell closed on a deep, shuddering breath.

"Fucking hell, Annie. Christ."

The depth of heat in his eyes when he opened them was startling, and my heart skipped a beat in fear. He looked barely contained, his desire a near-violent intensity that was chillingly similar to when he was about to fight. He looked… capable of anything.

Of things that petrified me.

Of not just doing those things, but of doing them to *me*.

The sense of safety I'd always had with him rapidly disintegrated, even as guilt blossomed in my chest. Rob had never done anything to make me think he would hurt me, nothing to make me fearful of him, and yet I was in that moment.

It was then, in the space of the same breath that I was beginning to panic, a half-second from escaping the situation that had devolved from liberating to oppressive in the blink of an eye, that I noticed Rob's hands. It wasn't the broken skin still healing on his knuckles that caught my attention, nor the scars that crisscrossed the backs of his hands, or even the callouses on his palms that lightly scratched my skin where he grasped my thighs. No…what I noticed was their unsteadiness.

They weren't just trembling a little bit—they were shaking. *A lot*. Big jerky movements.

But it wasn't just his hands, I suddenly noticed. It was his arms, his chest, his legs. His entire body shook as his breath shuddered in and out. And then it hit me.

He was nervous. *Really* nervous. Maybe as much as I was. What we were doing meant as much to him as it did to me. How could I ever think that man would hurt me?

His hands resumed their shaky exploration as my fear melted away, his fingers flexing into the flesh on my inner thighs and pulling my legs apart. He bent as his hands slid back down to my knees and pressed to hold my legs apart as he blanketed the faintly scarred skin with soft, open-mouthed kisses. At the very edge of my awareness, the memory of what had led to most of those scars, what Charlie had done, was stealthily trying to take over. But Rob's scratchy beard on the sensitive skin between my legs, his warm mouth on my thighs... the sensations were intoxicating, drowning out everything else as overwhelming desire was coaxed to the forefront.

"Rob... please... I can't... it's too much... I can't breathe..."

The rush of his breath as he paused brought on several full-body shudders I was powerless to stop. As the seconds ticked by, I became acutely aware of, and deeply uncomfortable with being on display the way I was, but I fought to remain still, desperate to keep from disappointing Rob with my bizarre insecurities. The battle was lost, however, when I recalled that I hadn't showered after the sweaty boxing session, and my legs instinctively snapped together.

Rob's hand shot up immediately, turning my face toward him and holding me there until I opened the eyes I'd closed in mortification.

"Tell me."

I swallowed, my tongue stuck to the roof of my mouth as my vision blackened at the edges.

"Tell me," Rob said again, more harshly.

"You're... right there." I whispered, looking away, too uncomfortable with our nudity and the situation to maintain eye contact.

"Do you want me to stop?"

I wanted to say no, for him, but I couldn't force the lie past my lips. Instead, I told him the truth as my tears spilled over.

"Yes," I breathed out, filled with embarrassment from where his face had been, embarrassment that I was naked and on display, embarrassment that as hard as I was trying, I just wasn't comfortable with it.

"Okay."

With that one word, he pushed himself up off the bed, quickly putting distance between us. But instead of making it easier to breathe, I felt as if my chest was in a vice that tightened more the further he went.

"W-what? W-why?" I stammered out incoherently.

When Rob didn't respond, I chanced a glance at him and found his eyes on me, but I was unable to read his expression; he was becoming nothing more than a blurry outline as more tears replaced the ones that were already falling.

He was giving up on me. Not that I could blame him. It should have been a bigger surprise that he lasted that long. But damned if the rejection didn't hurt, regardless of fault. I squeezed my eyes shut against the pain, but it did nothing but cause more tears to spill over.

"What's wrong, love? You can tell me." Rob spoke softly, his voice tortured as if he were in pain, and I felt the bed dip under his weight again a fraction of a second before he was pulling me into his chest. "You have to talk to me. I can't help if you don't."

I expected his voice to be laced with frustration, but it wasn't. I couldn't detect even a trace of it.

"I'm too much trouble," I mumbled against his chest.

"What do you mean?"

"You're leaving."

"What? No. You said you wanted to stop, so I stopped. I'm not going anywhere. I was just gonna put some clothes on so you'd be more comfortable."

"I didn't mean... not everything. Just to stop kissing me so close to... to..."

My face was buried in his chest as I spoke, my skin aflame. I may have been thirty years old, but I'd never learned to be comfortable talking about my body or talking about sex. I couldn't bring myself to even refer to where his face had been close to aloud, and that inability just heaped on more embarrassment.

After a beat, Rob shifted, using his hands to pull me away from him until we were eye-to-eye and I didn't have any choice but to look at him.

"Listen carefully, okay? I don't want to pressure you into doing anything you aren't comfortable with, anything you aren't ready for. That's the *only fucking reason* I stopped. Got it? I didn't realize that you just meant to get my face out from between your legs." He paused, searching my eyes as vulnerability crept into his. "I'm fucking terrified of pushing you too far. And I know it's hard for you, I understand why, and I don't judge you for it, but I need you to communicate your thoughts to me. Openly and clearly. Okay?"

I nodded. "I thought you didn't want to deal with my shit anymore."

He snorted. "I can tell you right now *that* will never fucking happen."

He paused long enough to kiss me until we were both breathless again. When he spoke next, his voice was so gravelly and thick that his words were hard to understand.

"Tell me what you want, love. Should I stop?"

"No."

He shifted me onto my back, clasping our hands together and pinning them to the bed on either side of my head as he settled between my legs, pressing our hands into the mattress for the leverage necessary to shift around. His lips nipped gently down to the base of my throat, where he growled softly against my skin.

"What about now?"

"No," I breathed out slowly, not even sure I was audible until he resumed his descent to my left breast.

"And now?"

My breaths barely provided sufficient oxygen for me to remain conscious; certainly not enough to speak, so I just shook my head quickly from side to side. Again, he resumed his descent, stopping this time at my belly button.

"How about now? Do you want me to stop?"

His voice was barely more than a soft rumble that vibrated across my skin. My body was awash with sensation and, in some way I couldn't begin to fathom, everything I felt intensified every time he checked in with me.

"No please don't," the words rushed out almost as one on a rapid, shaky exhale.

His nose circled my belly button, his beard scratching my skin as it followed. But instead of pain, it left a delicious, fiery wanting in its wake, coaxing another soft, unbidden whimper from my lungs.

That one small, seemingly insignificant sound flipped a switch in Rob, and after the most minute pause during which he was frozen, he was stretched over me with such rapidity that I hadn't yet processed that he'd moved at all when I felt his erection pressing between my legs. He started to push forward, then stopped, his body violently shaking.

Panting with equal parts fear and anticipation, I asked, "What's wrong?"

His voice was tight and strained when he replied. "I want this more than I want to take my next breath, but... Fuck! I don't want to hurt you."

"It's okay."

He kissed me, a hard, chaste kiss, and when he pulled his mouth away, he slowly began to push himself in. Just as the pressure approached discomfort, I tensed and he stopped again, indecision tearing at his features.

"It's okay," I breathed out, only half-believing the words myself, but not wanting him to stop.

My stomach flipped at the realization that after all those years, I was actually going to make love with Rob, and my body reacted with a full-body shiver. After a breath, with an involuntary growl, his hips rocked forward, only stopping when he couldn't possibly move any further. I cried out, tears stinging my eyes as the pain registered.

Rob's body went rigid, utterly still except for the tremble in his muscles and the heaving of his chest.

"I'm sorry, Annie, I'm sorry," he whispered frantically. "I'm so fucking sorry. I didn't mean to do that, I'm so sorry, we can stop, I didn't mean to, I swear, I-"

My voice cracked as I cut him off. "It's okay. Just, give me a minute, please?"

"Of course," he exhaled, his breath hot and moist as it slid across my face.

He released my hands to cup my cheeks as he showered my face with soft kisses, his breathing beyond erratic. With his hands no longer holding him up, his weight pinned me to the mattress; I could barely move. I felt trapped, and my eyes flew open as panic bubbled up within me. But when my eyes opened, I found Rob watching me intently, his eyes cloudy and filled with emotion.

"I love you so much. So fucking much it hurts, Annie. Like there's a goddamn rhino sitting on me. So much it's hard to breathe every time I look at you. I've always fucking loved you. I *will* always fucking love you. I can't help it. God knows I tried for years to stop. There aren't words to describe..." He paused, shaking his head briefly as if to clear it. "The best I can do is tell you that, as fucking cheesy as it sounds, you complete me. You bring light to my dark, fill up my empty, fix what's broken and make me whole. Fuck, I'm not *me* without *you*."

Swallowing over the lump in my throat, the pain between my legs eclipsed by the agonizing happiness swelling my heart, I replied with the only words I could formulate, though I was aware just how woefully inadequate they were.

"I love you, too. Always you."

His mouth melded to mine as his hips began to rock gently, slowly. Gradually, he moved a little further out, pushing back in a little faster, a little stronger. The feeling was unlike anything I'd ever experienced, and soon the pain was no more than a memory.

Rob's movements became more desperate, less controlled, and I suddenly found myself on the precipice again, about to fall, the same feeling of urgency as before invading my body. As if he knew, he kissed me hard just before grabbing my hands again and pinning them to the mattress above my head.

"I love you," his voice ground into my ear.

And then I was falling, my body tensing. It was like before, but also different, more intense. Within seconds, Rob stiffened as well as he shouted into my neck.

"Oh, fuck, Annie!"

As I floated back down to earth and reality, I felt overwhelmed in the best possible way by the enormity of what had just happened, by the entire incredible and healing experience.

chapter fifty-four

rob

"**Annie... are you...** are you okay?" I asked between bursts of breath as I moved a hand to cup her cheek, catching her tears as they fell.

"Yes," she said on yet another sob.

"But you're crying."

"Good tears."

I nodded. I understood. That was, without a doubt, the most intensely pleasurable and emotional experience of my life, and I felt connected to her in a beautiful new dimension. As my head rested back onto her chest, I sniffed and blinked my eyes rapidly, trying to hold back my own emotional response to what we'd just shared.

As soon as I was able to move again, I lifted my head so I could see into her eyes, see what she was thinking. She gazed back at me, her face open and eyes filled with love as tears dried on her temples.

I wanted to tell her again how I felt, how much she meant to me. Explain to her what that experience was to me, but I'd already proven that my vocabulary fell dreadfully short when it came to expressing my feelings for her. So, instead, I brought everything to the surface, hoping she'd be able to read in my eyes what I was unable to articulate. Yanking out her ponytail holder, I tangled my fingers into her hair and kissed her gently, reverently; I was kissing a goddess, after all. When her soft tongue touched my lips, I instantly wanted her again, knew that I could never get enough. But I didn't move—not yet—enjoying the experience of kissing her while her body was under mine, her fingers intertwined with mine. Savoring the feel of her naked skin against mine, her cheek under my hand, her walls around me where I was still inside her.

And at first, she was right there with me, her breathing ratcheting up in tandem with mine. But then something changed; her relaxed body suddenly tensed as she broke our kiss, turning her head sharply to one side with a sob.

"Annie," I said quietly, my voice deep and thick from the need for her that coursed through my veins. "Love. Get out of your head. What we just shared was incredible, something beautiful. Don't you fucking think otherwise."

She didn't reply, but I could see the internal struggle in the emotions shifting across her features. Each crease betraying the pain she'd endured. The beast inside me began to stir, a beast with an insatiable hunger for destroying anyone who dared to wrong her, a beast who lived for protecting her and exacting retribution against those who managed to hurt her.

"Annie, look at me," I demanded.

Reluctantly, she turned, her eyes averted, and shame written across her face. The beast within roared to life and my jaw ticked with effort to keep it at bay.

"Whatever that voice is saying right now is fucking wrong, you hear me? Tell it to fuck off and then ignore it."

I pressed my mouth to hers, and our tongues began to tangle, slowly at first, until we were sharing *our* kiss as I guided her out of her head and back to reality.

Back to our beautiful, shared intimacy.

Annie's fingers absent-mindedly traced over my tattoos from where she was draped across my chest, and I was committing the whole experience to memory. Everything. I never wanted to forget a single heartbeat, a single breath of what we'd just shared. I inhaled deeply and sighed as I released it; I was relaxed and content in a way that was novel to me. A way that involved body, mind, and soul.

"Maybe you should box more often," I couldn't resist teasing.

Her face moved into a smile against my chest in response, though she didn't reply.

"I'm kidding, though I do think you should consider boxing regularly. I told you earlier that I find it therapeutic."

"I can agree with you there. I was... overflowing with anger—no, rage. And I had no clue what to do with it or how to handle it. Which is why I went off on you, though you didn't deserve it. I'm really sorry for that. Anyway, boxing helped a lot."

At her mention of being angry, my stomach had flipped; as much as I didn't want to ask what put her into that state, I *had* to know. Though my nerves made my voice gruffer than I'd intended.

"Tell me what happened to piss you off."

Annie started to sit up, but I was faster, wrapping my arm around her shoulders and pulling her back down.

"No. Stay."

She stopped resisting and rested her palm in the middle of my chest. But she was shaking.

What the fuck had Lucas done to her?

"It was a lot of different things. Lucas said some things that set me off, bringing to the surface feelings I've been ignoring, pretending weren't even there since I was young. But it really wasn't just him."

Annie shifted against me, bringing to my attention that I'd tensed up and was squeezing her too tightly. I loosened my hold before responding.

"What did he say?"

My voice was intentionally calm, conversational, even, though I was anything but. My blood boiled, and the beast paced at the thought of him saying anything at all to upset her.

"It doesn't matter, really. He was lashing out because he was upset. He didn't mean it, and I know that."

"It matters to *me,* goddamn it. Tell me. Now."

She bolted upright with her back to me, her arms crossed over her chest. Without looking at me, she spoke, so quietly I struggled to make out her words over the tumultuous rush of blood in my ears.

"He used the fact that... that he and I... that we... Asked me how I could have moved on to someone else so quickly. T-told me that I owed it to us to give our relationship another chance."

Don't fucking hit anything. Don't fucking hit anything. Don't fucking hit anything.

I shook from the effort I exerted to at least appear composed, though that was ruined the instant I opened my mouth.

"Fuck him!"

"I'm so sorry," Annie said as her voice broke.

"Why the fuck are *you* sorry?" I hadn't meant to growl at her, but I had anyway.

"F-for being with him. I know it hurts you."

I swallowed thickly before replying, trying to get control over myself. I wanted to destroy something at the same time I wanted to cry. My heart felt like it was being pulled apart inside my chest at the thought of Annie with someone else. But I knew she shouldn't feel guilty for it, so I thought about denying it to her, to give her the peace of mind she deserved.

But I refused to lie. Never to her.

"Yeah, it does; it fucking kills me that another man saw you, another man touched you, another man shared this... this *intimacy* with you. But we weren't together, Annie, you didn't do anything you need to apologize for."

chapter fifty-five

rob

Best Christmas morning ever? Waking with Annie curled up asleep on my chest. Her face was relaxed as her soft, even breaths tickled my neck. I didn't want to wake her, to disturb the peace she so deserved, but I couldn't stop myself from touching her; my compulsion of old had returned in full force and was beyond my control. My fingertips trailed lightly along the bridge of her nose, the curve of her cheek, the silky soft skin on the back of her arm. Touching her was almost too much, a sensory overload, but also nowhere near enough. My hands trembled as I continued to feather my fingers over any exposed skin I could discover. They trembled from excitement, from the effort to control myself, from the need for more—*always* more when it came to Annie. I'd never be able to get enough of her.

I was an addict. A glutton. I had been since the first time she looked up into my eyes, allowing me that initial glimpse of her fragile, magnificent soul.

Annie stirred, the leg draped over me shifting slightly across my hips. And that was all it took; I was instantly aroused and wanted her again.

Well, shit.

I didn't want her to wake up and feel pressured to have sex again. I knew she likely wouldn't be ready for a while, physically or emotionally, but there wasn't a damn thing I could do about my body's reaction to her.

Her eyelids fluttered, a soft smile touching her lips as she blinked slowly, sleepily. Suddenly, her eyes shot open in realization and she tried to push away. But I'd been expecting that reaction, had known that our nakedness would freak her out, so I'd been prepared and kept her from moving more than a few inches.

"You have no idea how happy it makes me to be holding you in my arms like this, and I intend to keep you here for as long as I can. Don't be embarrassed."

Her cheeks and neck were a deep shade of crimson, but she stopped pushing away and rested her head back down where it had been.

"Good thing, I guess, because I'm not even sure I could sit all the way up without help. Every muscle in my body aches right now."

I tightened my arms around her, enjoying the feel of her body pressed into mine as I barked out a laugh. "I forgot to warn you. Boxing will do that the first few times."

She groaned. "Yeah, you did, jackass. And now I'm paying the price."

I laughed again, her good humor driving mine higher.

"Whatever, the way you came down there? I could have warned you all I wanted, and you would have beat the shit out of my heavy bag regardless. It's not like you were really listening to a damn thing I said anyway."

"Yeah, you're right," she smiled into my chest. "Even sore, though, I'm glad I did it. It was exactly what I needed."

There was nothing to say in response, though I was inclined to agree, and not just because of the role it played in us having sex. We laid there in a comfortable silence, my hands leisurely working through the tangles in Annie's curls as I enjoyed her weight pressing down on me, my body heavy with relaxed contentment. All was well and right in my world as long as we were together.

After a while, Annie asked me again to tell her about my tattoos. I knew it was time to confess what I'd done. I couldn't put it off any longer. But, fuck, I was nervous as hell about it. Telling her I loved her was one thing. And that was easy, really—always had been after that first time.

Explaining my tattoos, however, was something else entirely.

Annie lifted her chin, looking up at me with her eyebrows raised in question. Uncertainty crept into her eyes as I watched, revealing how my own nervousness affected her.

I sensed it before it happened, but didn't try to stop it this time, allowing her to sit up and scoot away from me. She settled on her knees facing me, a foot or so away with the bedding tucked around her and waited as her fingers fidgeted anxiously with a fold in the sheet.

My hand trembled as I dragged it over my face and sat up.

"So, here," I pointed to my right forearm," you remember that I had a skull here when I met you, right? And on my bicep, I had a pentagram?"

She nodded.

"Okay, so... the next one I got, the first one after you left, is here—by my elbow—and is the Norse symbol for 'brother'." My jaw clenched as I practically choked on the word. "Which I'll be having removed or transformed into something else. I want nothing left from him."

I'd fucking cut it out of my arm myself if I had to. I couldn't fucking believe I was related to that piece of shit.

"Anyway, I had that one done when I was going through some shit with Charlie after you left me. Before Mrs. Renner talked some sense into me. Luckily, I was too fucking broke at the time to have anything else done. I'd planned to cover myself with symbols of violence and death."

I studied my hands for a moment, remembering all the horrible things they'd done during that time, things I never wanted to admit to Annie that I'd done, and let out a shaky breath. Jesus, if what I was about to tell her didn't scare her off, the shit in my past would.

At least she hadn't asked me about that yet.

My gaze flickered to hers for an instant, but I was too nervous to hold it. I'd already reached the point where I might start scaring her. I'd never thought I'd have to explain what I'd done to anyone, let alone Annie. Not that it would have changed anything, but still.

"Anyway, once I finally got my shit together, I wanted to do something else with these old tattoos I had that represented what I wanted to leave in my past for good. So, I had the pentagram transformed into a Norse symbol for protection, and then I had the skull incorporated into a Hamsa. To tie those areas together, I had this one added, the symbol for fortune in love. I..."

I cleared my throat. "I chose that hoping it would one day bring you back to me." My throat was already clogging with emotion again, so I cleared it more violently so I could continue.

"I don't really know how to explain this in a way that won't sound fucking crazy... You were gone. But you were also still here, you'd become part of me in a way that could never be undone. Everything good in me was thanks to you, every bit of happiness in my life had come from you, every good memory had you in it. Everything I had to offer was... yours."

I paused, turning my hands over and studying the scars that crisscrossed my skin.

"I don't like the word shrine, but I don't really know what else to call it, so I guess you could say I turned my body into a shrine to you."

I wasn't sure I'd ever wished I could read her mind more than I did at that moment. I could at least get a clue from her eyes, always so expressive, but I was too chickenshit to look at her. If I did, I might lose my nerve and never finish. I just had to get it all out first, *then* deal with her reaction and figure out how to make her understand.

"You gave me life, Annie. I wasn't living before I knew you, not really. And this one here is to represent that."

I pointed to my chest.

"This tree is a rendering of your willow as a tree of life, but you are the source of that life—see how the roots twist to form your name across my waist? The branches wrap around my sides, over my shoulders, up my neck, clutching me in a life-giving embrace, much as you did. And in the back," I twisted my torso so she could see my back, "the branches come together to both create and hold my heart, which only came to life the day I met you. I had that done with a Celtic knot because it, like my love for you, has no beginning and no end."

I'd never realized until I said it aloud how obsessed I sounded.

"The bark on the trunk—if you look closely—the lines resemble the pattern of the scars on your forearms, those scars and the pain that created them as much a part of who you are as bark is part of a tree. And to symbolize that your pain is also my pain, that I wanted to shoulder that burden for you, so you wouldn't have to anymore."

I took another deep breath and cleared my throat again, fighting the tears stinging the backs of my eyes as I relived everything I was telling her.

"If you remember, you told me I was Ares, god of war, because of my reputation. And that had a profound impact on me because I realized I didn't want to create chaos and destruction everywhere I went—not really. And I told you that you were Achelois, the moon goddess who washes away pain, because of your ability to soothe my soul and quiet my demons just by being near me."

I swallowed thickly, my vision tunneling.

"So, I have Ares on the underside of my arm as a reminder of who I once was, who you showed me I didn't have to be, who I never wanted to be again, but who I know sits just below the surface, waiting to come out if I let him. And then on the other side, I have Achelois, to remind me there was once good in my life and to guide me along a more peaceful path."

I paused to try to breathe, forcibly expanding and contracting my diaphragm.

I wished she would say something.

But I had to finish. Then it would all be out, in the open. And if I had to, I'd fucking block the door to keep her there, to make her listen until I could find a way to get her to understand that I wasn't obsessed, that I just loved her so fucking much.

"Almost done. You see the wind currents in all the empty space around the tree on my chest and back? If you look closely—" I swallowed abruptly as my heart tried to beat out of my chest cavity when she leaned in close enough for me to feel her breath fanning across my skin.

"They're words," she whispered, her fingertips trailing whisper-soft along one of the lines, her warm breath following their path.

"Yes. They are. After we told each other that we loved each other the first time, I gave you one of my favorite love poems, remember? And then, the next day, you shared with me one of yours? And for the rest of the week, we passed love poetry back and forth. Remember? Well, I, uh... I had them tattooed. All of them. Every word."

I could feel her gaze burning my skin, but I still couldn't raise my head to look at her, not until I finished.

"The last tattoo I had done about a year ago, not long before you came back, actually. I came across this poem, *Wishing Stars* by Lang Leav, and it was as if it was written just to explain how I felt in my heart."

I flipped my right arm over so she could see the flowery script adorning the inside of my forearm. She was likely reading it herself, but I recited it to her anyway, closing my eyes in an attempt to tamp down the pain of missing her that the words brought with them, despite the fact that she was sitting right there next to me. It was the kind of pain that would never really go away, even if she never left my side again until the day we both died.

I still search
for you in crowds,
in empty fields
and soaring clouds.

In city lights
and passing cars,
on winding roads
and wishing stars.

I wonder where
you could be now,
for years I've not said
your name out loud.

And longer since
I called you mine—
time has passed
for you and I.

But I have learnt
to live without,
I do not mind—
I still love you anyhow.

Annie's fingertips were still gliding along the letters on my arm when I finally gathered enough courage to look at her, petrified of what I'd find, already scrambling to figure out how I'd make her understand because her leaving me wasn't an option. I knew that any even remotely normal person would bolt, would go straight to the police and get a restraining order, would report me as dangerously obsessed. And maybe 'obsessed' was the right word after all. I didn't really give a shit what you called it, but I could never be dangerous to her. She was inextricably woven into the tapestry of my life, an integral part of who I was no matter what, and I couldn't imagine covering my body with anything else.

I watched the crown of her head as I waited anxiously for her to look up, every second an eternity. Just when I thought I could take no more of the waiting, of the uncertainty, she tipped up her gorgeous, loving face, with a gleam in her eye, and snort-laughed.

"Well, I guess giving you Haley's number is out. I think she'd be a little jealous."

chapter fifty-six

annie

"**Where are we** going?"

"I told you, it's a surprise," Rob replied as he steered his truck around another curve in the winding back road heading to the base of one of the mountains surrounding Stockwood.

"You know how I feel about surprises."

"Yeah, yeah, you've always said that, but, despite all your damn whining, how often have you not liked one of *my* surprises?" he asked with a cocky smirk.

I rolled my eyes because he knew that answer already: never.

"Touché."

When I looked over, I caught the edges of his tattoos peeking out of the collar of his shirt. I'd thought they were beautiful before he even told me what they represented, what they documented. Now? I knew that each line, each mark, was a physical branding of his love for me; every time I thought about that, my stomach flipped, and I couldn't breathe. I had no idea what I'd done to deserve such a wonderful man in my life in any capacity, let alone one who seemed so utterly devoted to me.

Rob's eyes darted over to mine quickly before returning to the road, but not so quickly that I missed the apprehension in his expression.

Where was he taking me and why was it making him nervous?

"Are you okay?" I asked.

"Great. Why?"

"Something's off. You're nervous. Or something."

"I am?"

"Okay, definitely nervous. Why?"

He didn't respond.

"Where the hell are we going?"

He huffed out an irritated breath, though I could see his lips twitch as he fought a smile.

"I told you it's a surprise, so you might as well stop asking, you pain in the ass."

"For the love of god, quit saying that!" I laughed, comforted somewhat by his teasing. "If I hear you say the word 'surprise' one more time, I'll have it tattooed on my ass."

Rob barked out a short laugh, followed by another cocky smirk as he glanced sideways at me.

"Surprise."

"You're such an ass," I muttered. He'd called my bluff, and we both knew it.

Why the hell had I said that?

His deep laugh filled the cab of the truck as he took one hand off the wheel to reach over and lace our fingers together. Rob rubbed his thumb rhythmically back and forth along the top of my hand, visibly becoming more agitated with each mile passing under us.

I opened my mouth to ask yet again where we were going, but before the words came out, he slowed the truck near the base of the mountain and guided us onto a gravel drive almost hidden in the trees. The drive wound at least half a mile through the woods until there suddenly appeared around a curve a large clearing—an acre or two. And there, in the middle of that clearing, was a house.

No, not a house. A *home*.

A beautiful, stuff-dreams-are-made-of home. The siding was blue-gray with soft cream-colored trim and shutters, and a brick-red front door. The structure stood two stories tall, with a deep wrap-around porch on the ground level and smoke rose lazily out of several chimneys.

It was as if we'd driven into the set of a movie; one about a close-knit family, filled with love. The stuff of fiction.

Rob slowed to a stop in front of the house, the crunch of the gravel under the tires tapering off into silence before he spoke.

"So, what's your first impression?" he asked, the austerity of his voice betraying his anxiety.

"The house? It's breathtaking. I'm pretty sure that's a giant old weeping willow peeping over the top of the house right there, and I've never met a willow that wasn't beautiful."

"So, you like it?"

I snorted. "That's an understatement."

"Would you like to see the inside?"

"Of course, but whose house is this? And why are we here?" I asked tentatively.

Rob brought my hand up to his mouth and rubbed his lips back and forth across the back of it a few times before he pressed a gentle kiss to it. All the while, his eyes, bright and shining with intensity, never left my face.

"I'll explain inside. Come on, let's go in."

After reluctantly releasing my hand, Rob hopped out and came around the truck to help me down, intertwining our fingers again the instant my feet touched the ground. We walked up to the house, hand-in-hand, and I paused on the porch to look around. Even in the dead of winter, there was such a warmth and charm to the house that it just felt like home. I could clearly picture it in the summertime: brightly colored flowers of all varieties blanketing the ground, a soft breeze swishing through the leaves of the abundant trees, birds chirping happily. And me, lounging on the enormous porch swing to the left of the front door, my head in Rob's lap, reading a book while his fingers combed through my hair. The daydream was so real that I felt a painful sense of loss as I returned to reality.

"I really love this porch," I murmured through the lump forming in my throat as I clung more tightly to his hand.

His face lit up at my words, but he remained silent as he pushed open the front door, gesturing for me to walk in ahead of him.

If the house had been beautiful from the outside, it was spectacularly stunning on the inside. There were mint-condition russet-colored wide-plank wood floors—Rob would know what kind of wood, but I was clueless; I just knew it was gorgeous. Setting off the flooring was thick, traditional baseboard trim and crown molding throughout, and tall ceilings like those in my mom's house.

"Wow," I breathed out. If I'd dreamed of the perfect house, it would have been the one I was standing in.

"Do you like it?"

"Like it? No. Absolutely not. Not even close. I *love* it. It's... it's... incredible."

My feet eagerly carried me through one spacious room after another as we explored the first floor of the house. When I pushed open a set of French doors to find myself standing in a library, my heart practically gave out. It was lined with floor-to-ceiling bookshelves along every vertical surface, except where there was a break for a fireplace, complete with a happily crackling fire, and even a sliding ladder for reaching the uppermost shelves.

"Oh my god, just look at this!" I exclaimed, my voice faint with emotion. "This library, it's... I don't have words, it's... it's everything I ever dreamed of for my own library, it's just... perfect."

"I know," he replied softly, his eyes shining brightly and an enormous, uncharacteristic grin on his face.

"What *is* this place? Whose house is it?" I asked, turning to face him, grudgingly tearing my gaze from the exquisite bookshelves. "Why are we here, Rob?"

"Come on, there's more to see first."

We walked through the remaining rooms in the house, taking in everything it had to offer, which was not insignificant. Not all of the house was in the same condition as the library, certain areas in need of a little TLC, but the house was still perfect in my eyes, a real-life fairy tale of a home.

Our exploration ended on the back side of the house in a sunroom of sorts. The first thing I noticed as we entered, though, was that the unobscured view into the backyard through the rear wall of windows in the room was dominated by what must have been a truly ancient willow tree, based on its size, magnificent even in winter.

"Oh, just look! It's incredible. And the twisting and splitting of that section of the trunk there, it reminds me a bit of *our* willow, don't you think?"

"I do, love."

I was lost in my memories of all the time Rob and I had spent together at our willow when he moved around behind me and wrapped me in his arms, resting his chin on my shoulder as he released a deep, contented sigh.

"Why are we here? Let alone on Christmas? Wait—did you rent it for a few days?" I asked excitedly, already dreaming about spending a full day in the library.

"No."

Oh.

"I bought it."

"You what?"

"For us."

My heart stopped for a moment before resuming at a much-accelerated rate. Surely, I'd misheard.

"W-wait, what?"

"I bought this house. For us."

Suddenly, I was turning, his hands moving me until I was facing him. One arm wrapped around my back and held me pressed against him while the other tipped my chin up. Once our gazes met, he spoke. Slowly. Deliberately.

"We haven't talked about it much, but you know I sold my house and was looking for something else. My agent sent me the info and photos for this house a couple of weeks ago. I didn't see it in person until today because I didn't want to leave you for that long, but I had a hunch it would be perfect. For *us*. So, I went ahead and bought it before someone else had a chance to snatch it up. I close in a few weeks."

He swallowed as he stared into my eyes, searching my soul as I fought the urge to turn away to find some room to breathe and process what he'd just told me.

"There's even another building out back—over there on the left, see?—that's already set up as a woodshop where I can build my furniture. The house sits on twenty acres, so there's plenty of felled wood at my disposal as well as a stockpile in the woodshop that came with the house. There's privacy, plenty of it, but it isn't so far from town that its location is a real pain in the ass. Of course, there's the library, beautiful landscaping from what I can tell, the tree-lined drive, and this willow for you. So, yeah. It has everything for both of us. Merry Christmas, love."

I thought I might hyperventilate, or maybe throw up, or both, as I tried to formulate words to explain to him how batshit crazy everything he'd said was, my mouth opening and closing soundlessly a few times before I could speak.

"You... how can you... this is too much, you can't... Jesus, Rob, you can't just buy a fucking house for me!"

He looked at me with his brow furrowed in confusion, as if *I* was the crazy one.

"Of course I can. I just did."

"Twenty acres! This must have cost a fortune."

"I had enough equity in the other house and cash in savings to do it," he said defensively.

"But that was for your store, you can't just give that up!"

"I'm not giving it up, it's just going to wait a while longer. I want this more than any fucking storefront, Annie. We're going to build a life together, and this is the perfect place to do it. Annie, w—"

"Are you proposing?!" I interrupted him.

I'd always known he was intense, but this was more than I could handle.

He studied me for a moment, his expression guarded. Or maybe I was just freaking out too much to clearly interpret what I was seeing.

"Would you say yes?"

"What? This is too much, too fast, I can't... I still have to go back to the city! Remember? I mean, what if... I don't know..."

I felt smothered. I needed room to breathe, room to think, room to be out from under his spell and the weight of his intensity and his expectations. He smiled ruefully as he allowed me to step back and put some much-needed distance between us.

"It's okay, I'm not proposing. But that has nothing to do with me buying this house for us. Which I already did. I've been telling you that I'll never let you go again. Didn't you believe me? I mean, did you really expect me to not look for something for both of us?"

"It's just... it's so fast, Rob, we've only been together for a few weeks and—"

"A few weeks?!" he boomed, his face hardening in anger. "Bullshit, Annie! We've never been apart. Not really. Not since that first time you looked into my eyes, and we saw each other's souls. I've always been yours, and you've always fucking been mine. We've *owned* each other since that day. The years we were physically apart? It's meaningless when it comes to us belonging together. There's nothing in life that I'll ever do again without you a part of it."

He stopped to scrub a hand over his face and look out the window as his chest heaved. When he turned back to me, his voice had softened slightly.

"Look, I know you're scared. And that's okay—you can be scared. But it'll fucking be with *me*. I'll help you. I'll show you that you don't have to be, that you're not alone—not anymore. That you'll never be alone again. That we can do this, together."

In some inexplicable way, his eyes were both hard and soft, both angry and patient. Filled with love. And resolve.

That fucking resolve that I knew meant there wasn't a damn thing I could say or do to change his mind.

Really, I shouldn't have been surprised by anything Rob did after he told me about his tattoos, but I certainly hadn't expected that he'd bought a *house* with the expectation that I was going to live there with him. Underneath all his muscle and hair and bad temper was the same boy I'd fallen madly in love with all those years before;

impulsive, possessive, a tendency to be bossy and controlling, but also sweet, thoughtful, and caring, always willing to make sacrifices for me. I cocked my head as I studied him, trying to quell the disjointed rhythm of my heart.

But wait.

I'd been wrong about him all along. He wasn't impulsive, though it may have seemed as if he was. At least not in the way I and everyone else had always thought; intentionally making a decision requiring sacrifice did not mean it was impulsive. His priorities just were different. He'd always put us first. *Me* first.

How was I just now seeing that? Had I really been so wrapped up in my own head, even back then, that I hadn't been able to see his actions for what they really were? I could suddenly see so clearly how he had done nothing but show me over and over since the day I'd met him that he was going nowhere, that he would always put my happiness above anything and everything else, including his own.

"Oh, Rob," I said, my voice cracking as my heart thundered in my chest. I was terrified, really, but I more than owed it to him to have faith in him. "Yes."

"Yes?" he asked with a mix of confusion and concern, looking at me like I'd lost my mind and using his thumbs to gently swipe away the tears that spilled onto my cheeks.

I stepped into his arms as I wound mine around his waist.

"To everything you said. I want it, too. All of it. I'm petrified—it's all happening so fast my head is spinning, and I don't know how things are going to work when I go back to the city—but you meant it when you said we'd figure it out?"

He pressed our lips together before he replied, his kiss both gentle and demanding, both soft and possessive. "Yes, love, we can figure *anything* out as long as we're together."

acknowledgements

I want to first thank my family for their overwhelming support through the entire process; my sister, my mom, and especially my husband, Joe, for his immediate and unflagging support for me to return to writing. When I first brought up the idea, his immediate response was, "Do it. Tell me what you need me to do to make it possible." And that mindset never once wavered in the over two years it took to get this book to market. I can't thank him enough; without his supportive attitude, his willingness to give up some of his personal time to pick up the slack so I could "just get the rest of this scene down on paper," I would not be here now. Thank you, my love.

Thank you to everyone who read this story in its early stages and provided feedback to help me improve. I want to especially thank Melissa for her encouragement, support, and faith in the story I wanted to tell, as well as her willingness to re-read anything I sent her and her patience in rooting out every incorrect usage of the em dash; my book is better in ways that, thankfully, the reader will never know. I want to thank Susan for her thoughtful and utterly honest feedback on my manuscript; her unique perspective and willingness to dialog about her thoughts enabled me to improve areas of my story I hadn't realized needed attention. I also want to thank Liz for her commitment to not only read this story, but to read the very rough drafts of the remainder of this series to make sure all the dependencies for the full story arc were in place in this first book. Finally, I want to thank Chloé, who not only encouraged me from day one, but read my book and gave me feedback even though it was the last thing she had time for; it's just another reason she's the best friend a person can have.

Last, though certainly not least, I want to thank everyone who played a role in my publication process. Thank you to my editor, Maddie, for providing a fresh perspective on my story and helping me to trim the fat for an improved reading experience, and to Olivia for making thoughtful suggestions to improve my storytelling and catching my stubborn typos. Thank you to Murphy for translating the image in my mind into an even more beautiful cover. And, finally, a special thank you to Kathy for letting me include excerpts of her beautiful writing to introduce my story and to Lang Leav for allowing me to use her poem.

To everyone involved, thank you from the bottom of my heart for helping my dream come true.

resources

"Trauma is perhaps the most avoided, ignored, belittled, denied, misunderstood, and untreated cause of human suffering."
-Peter Levine

I have included here a few resources related to the topics of sexual assault, childhood trauma, and the associated mental health impacts and challenges. You can find a more comprehensive listing on my website at www.kturnerwrites.com/resources.

RAINN
RAINN (Rape, Abuse, & Incest National Network) is the nation's largest anti-sexual violence organization.
www.rainn.org
800-656-HOPE (800-656-4673)

National Suicide Prevention Lifeline
National Suicide Prevention Lifeline provides free and confidential support for people in distress, prevention and crisis resources, and best practices for professionals.
www.suicidepreventionlifeline.org
800-273-TALK (800-273-8255)

ACA
ACA (Adult Children of Alcoholics World Service Organization) provides information and a safe environment to foster healing from growing up in dysfunctional homes with abuse, neglect, and trauma.
www.adultchildren.org

ADAA
ADAA (Anxiety and Depression Association of America) works to prevent, treat, and cure anxiety disorders and depression.
www.adaa.org

NIMH
NIMH (National Institute of Mental Health) is the lead federal agency for research on mental disorders and aims to transform understanding and treatment of mental illnesses.
www.nimh.nih.gov

NSVRC
NSVRC (National Sexual Violence Resource Center) provides leadership in preventing and responding to sexual violence.
www.nsvrc.org

about the author

Katherine Turner is the author of *Finding Annie*, the first book in the Life Imperfect series, and a life-long reader and writer. She grew up in foster care from the age of eight and is passionate about improving the world through literature, empathy, and understanding. Katherine blogs about mental health, trauma, and the need for compassion on her website www.kturnerwrites.com. She lives in northern Virginia with her husband and two children.

By Katherine Turner

Fiction

Life Imperfect Series

Finding Annie

Willow Wishes (2021)

Non-Fiction

resilient: a memoir (2021)

Fantasies, volume I: through my eyes (2021)

Made in the USA
Middletown, DE
02 May 2021